NORTH BY STARLIGHT

North by Starlight

Diane/David Munson

NORTH BY STARLIGHT

Published by Micah House Media, LLC
Grand Rapids, Michigan 49525

ISBN-13: 978-1-7325823-0-9

Cover design by Dragan Nikolic.
Cover images from © Can Stock Photo / Artranq / ryanking999

**Visit Diane and David Munson's website at:
www.DianeAndDavidMunson.com**

DEDICATION

To those whose hope is in the Lord

And we have the word of the prophets made more certain, and you will do well to pay attention to it, as to a light shining in a dark place, until the day dawns and the morning star rises in your hearts.

2Peter 1:19

Jesus said, "I have come into the world as a light, so that no one who believes in me should stay in darkness."

John 12:46

ACKNOWLEDGMENT

Many thanks to Micah House Media and the many others who supported this effort to shed God's starlight on this novel meant for the entire family. You know who you are and we thank you for your encouragement.

We give special thanks to Pam Cangioli for her expertise in editing and great support for our endeavor.

Chapter 1

Attorney Madison Stone's spirits soared high as the judge announced the ruling in Maddie's favor. Though she wanted to shout, "Hooray!" she kept her lips sealed tight. The long hours she'd spent advocating for this family had finally paid off.

Judge Cawley tapped a stout gavel against the wooden judicial bench and with authority intoned, "Court is adjourned."

A winning smile crept across Maddie's face, and she jumped to her feet so quickly one of her high heels wobbled beneath her. She grabbed the table edge to steady herself.

Relief washed over her. Though this was her ninetieth case, a milestone in her six-year legal career, it wasn't the win making her feel giddy. Justice being accomplished for a family and their small foster child erased Maddie's frustration at having to battle nonstop against opposing counsel for the past few months.

She started gathering the hodgepodge of papers spread across the courtroom table, when the foster mother of Maddie's court-assigned infant client enveloped her in a bear hug.

"Thank you!" Mrs. Wolsey chirped. "I can keep LeSwana in my home."

Maddie was about to warn the foster mother about attempted visits from the imputed father when Judge Cawley interrupted, "Ms. Stone, I need a word with you."

Alarm sizzled through Maddie. She sped to the elevated desk unsure what she'd done wrong. Had she made a misstep? It was rare for Judge Cawley to engage in chitchat with attorneys in her courtroom.

"Your Honor," Maddie said, setting both hands lightly on the bench. "I'm sure Mrs. Wolsey won't let us down. She loves baby LeSwana."

The judge leaned over. As if including Maddie in a conspiracy, she lowered her voice to a bare whisper and said,

"When I assigned you to this case, I had no doubt you would pull another rabbit from your giant hat."

"Your Honor, I need to correct the record." Maddie's face grew warm at the judge's praise. "Harry Black is our private investigator. He is the one who found the imputed father's earlier arrest for child abuse, despite his using an alias."

"You were the one who asked him to search." Judge Cawley treated her to a friendly smile. "I knew you wouldn't quit digging." She patted Maddie's hand, telling her, "Good job."

As the judge disappeared through a side door, her black robe swirling behind her, Maddie returned to the attorney's table, resisting the urge to shout, "Yes!"

She wouldn't violate court etiquette to bolster a lack of confidence in her courtroom prowess. If only her biggest critic and former boyfriend, Attorney Stewart Dunham, could have been here to see her win. Looking around, Maddie noticed both Brenda Gaynor, attorney for the imputed father, and Mrs. Wolsey had left the courtroom.

The moment Maddie stuffed the thick file into her leather briefcase, the cutting critique once voiced by her law school professor seared through Maddie's mind like a bolt of electricity.

"Ms. Stone, you're much too naïve to succeed in law," Professor Rooney had growled while looking directly at her. "Look to the student on your left and then to the one on your right. By the end of this year, one of you three will be gone."

"You were so wrong about me, Professor Rooney." Maddie lifted her chin as she picked up her briefcase. "Once again, I've proved I'm made of sterner stuff."

Maddie left the quiet courtroom carrying her dignity on her tired shoulders. The doors swishing closed, she looked forward to the upcoming Thanksgiving weekend she'd be spending with Vanessa, her paralegal, and Vanessa's teenaged son, Cole. Vacation thoughts quickly evaporated at the sight of Attorney Gaynor standing by the door leading to the stairwell and glaring at Maddie.

"I wouldn't consider this a win, Ms. Stone. I fail to share your confidence in the foster mother. We could end up back here again."

"You should tell your client to expect to pay more child support," Maddie shot back.

Her adversary slipped into the stairwell with a shrug. Fresh concern peppered Maddie's mind. She stepped onto the elevator wondering what adverse knowledge Ms. Gaynor had about Mrs. Wolsey. No closer to an answer when she exited the elevator on the first floor, she passed by lawyers huddled with clients and talking in hushed tones. She decided Gaynor's comment was sour grapes.

Adjusting the briefcase over her shoulder, Maddie rounded the corner with her usual speed, nearly running into the back of a man dressed in a suit and talking on a cell phone.

"Oh!" she said.

Before Maddie could zigzag around him, she heard him say, "Tell your parents not to worry. We'll be there in time for Thanksgiving. My case is almost finished."

A painful shudder ripped through Maddie. There was no mistaking the guy's nasal tone. With only one way out of the courthouse, as if it was another trial she must win, Maddie sprung past him, cell phone plastered against his ear.

She'd made it about twenty feet when he yelled out, "Madison, stop."

Maddie kept walking, her heart racing and beating out an odd rhythm. Seconds later, he caught up to her.

"Hey, what gives? Didn't you hear me, Madison?"

It was too late to pretend she hadn't heard him. She turned to face her former fiancé, fortitude building in her heart. Stewart had broken off their engagement at summer's end, claiming he desired to travel instead of being tied down in a relationship with Maddie. Bitterness climbed up her throat. She grasped the leather strap resting on her shoulder.

"I'm in a hurry, Stewart," she huffed.

He reached for her sleeve, his face lighting with a smile as if he'd really missed her.

"I hoped this day would come. We can't both practice law in D.C. without bumping into each other."

"You're right about one thing." Maddie retreated a step. "Our meeting was bound to happen. Enjoying your world travels?"

"You look terrific, Madison," he said, a peculiar gleam in his eyes.

Maddie shrugged off accepting any compliment of his. She stepped back farther, her instincts warning her to flee before it was too late. During the time she'd dated him, Maddie had failed to recognize his smooth ways were merely an act. The goofy smile of his now irritated her to no end.

How could she have imagined herself in love with this egotist?

Skepticism lacing her voice, she blurted, "Stewart, I'm surprised you aren't soaking up the sun on some exotic Pacific island, crashing into waves on your own personal watercraft."

"I'd like to be, Madison." He laughed. "But other lawyers keep suing my clients."

Maddie feigned pulling a slot machine handle. "Ka-ching, ka-ching. More money for you. More travels for you."

"Absolutely." Stewart wore his plastered-on smile. "But I can't get excited about travel without you."

Maddie extended her open palm. "Stop. You lost your chance."

She whirled around thinking that by turning her back on Stewart, she could forever blot out her misplaced feelings for him. Maddie rushed down the steps on her black heels, desperate to avoid further chance meetings with her past failure.

Chapter 2

Maddie rode the Metro to her office, seething the entire way. She couldn't resist checking over her shoulder to make sure Stewart wasn't riding in the same car. On the third floor of the law building, she bolted from the elevator, her mind reeling from their distasteful encounter.

I can't let him get to me like this.

Maddie's mind surged with regret. As she hurried into her freshly painted office in the law firm of Barron and Rich, her cell phone rang.

"Hi, Mom," Maddie said, trying to concentrate. "How is Florida?"

"If you must know, it's like summer. Dad and I are excited to be here until we head back to Michigan the first of March."

"You deserve a respite. Here in D.C. it's cold and dreary. I'm almost sorry I asked."

Her mom was apologetic. "I hope I'm not interrupting. I thought it would be safe to call during your lunch hour."

"No problem," Maddie assured her. "I just returned to my office after winning a hearing for my court-appointed child client."

"Congratulations. Dad and I are proud of you. We knew you would be a successful lawyer."

Maddie could almost see Mom's smile across the miles.

"Thanks," she said softly. "Hugs to you and Dad."

"Don't hang up," her mom interjected. "Will we see you for Christmas? Clearwater beach along the Gulf is pristine. You can recharge your battery after the breakup with Stewart."

There was his name again, never giving her any peace. Maddie dropped into her swivel chair.

"Mom, I'd love to see you and Dad. I have such wonderful memories of Christmas on the farm last year. To be honest, work keeps me pretty busy. I'll see if I can manipulate my calendar to fly down there."

"Maddie, dear, that's wonderful," her mom said, sounding happy. "I won't tell your dad yet. I don't want to disappoint him. Let's see how it goes. You get back to work, and know we love you."

Vanessa stepped into the office the moment Maddie set down her phone.

"I assume from the frown on your face your case didn't go well," Vanessa said, wearing a perky navy-blue dress and wide smile.

"I'm not frowning," Maddie insisted. "I was talking with my mom."

Vanessa plunked down a stack of files on Maddie's desk. "Take it from me, you are scowling. Anyway, Cole is super thrilled you're taking us to Williamsburg."

"Me too. You're cooking turkey for Thanksgiving at your house, right?"

"Oh yes, a good old-fashioned dinner. I adore holiday traditions. We're all packed to leave with you early Friday morning. You don't mind driving?"

"Not at all." Maddie tugged the file from her briefcase. "Just so you know, I'm not unhappy. The judge ruled in our favor."

"Then why the long face?"

Maddie wiggled out of her suit jacket and hung it over her chair. "Whew, it was a tough case."

"You handle many difficult cases. Why is this one worse? You won."

"No reason." Maddie lifted her shoulders, debating whether to mention her collision with Stewart. "I'm so ready for our weekend getaway. The files you dumped here make me wonder if I can afford to take time off."

"You'd better not cancel. Cole is studying our nation's early history. All he talks about is seeing the blacksmith shop and cabinet makers."

Maddie flipped open a file, closing it just as quickly. "Guess who stopped me on the way out of court?"

"You know I'm no good at guessing."

Maddie rolled her brown eyes. "Stewart. Seeing him makes me want to leave D.C. for good, but I won't let him chase me away. I enjoy this firm and my new apartment."

"You're one essential leader around here, Maddie."

"So are you." Maddie gazed at Vanessa without really seeing her.

Maddie had healed her broken heart following Stewart's grand gesture in breaking things off by working nonstop, drinking mega-pots of coffee, and sleeping sporadically. The hectic pace had worn down her usually upbeat spirit. To have him flirt with her at court was beyond belief.

She tapped her short, unpainted fingernails on the file. "He and I shared a love for the law. His charms blinded me to his glaring faults. I should have realized sooner he wasn't for me. Stewart doesn't share my faith, which is vital to me."

"From what I remember, he went to church with you a time or two." Vanessa stood close by, straightening the files.

Maddie swept her hand through the air. "All an act."

"Your bumping into him explains your negative mood. Forget Stewart. He has no hold on you. My baby brother is always reminding me not to give power to anyone who means harm to me or Cole."

"How is Charlie?" Maddie asked, eager to put the morning behind her. "When is he coming home?"

"He's on his third deployment and may call us from his overseas base. Cole misses his favorite uncle."

"And his only uncle," Maddie replied thoughtfully.

Was it her imagination or did Vanessa wipe tears from her eyes? It hadn't been easy for Vanessa to raise her son as a single mom after her husband had left her and Cole. Maddie's heart went out to her and she tried cheering her up.

"Vanessa, remind me to leave by four o'clock. With your permission, I want to buy Cole a smart phone and add him to my family plan."

Vanessa looked aghast. "How can you have a family plan account? You don't have a family."

"Please stop reminding me. At the rate I'm going, Cole might be the only person on it. If you'd rather, I can save it for his birthday next month."

"Most of his fifteen-year-old friends have them. You really shouldn't, but the phone sounds perfect."

"It's the least I can …"

Her words trailed off when Bill Barron, the firm's lead partner, burst into Maddie's office. His face looked like a severe thunderstorm about to let loose. Vanessa edged out the door. Bill dropped a file on her desk, almost knocking over a photograph of Maddie and her parents.

"You need to handle this ASAP," Bill barked, flexing his fingers.

"Like after Thanksgiving? That's tomorrow, you know. Or have you forgotten?"

Maddie stared at her workaholic boss who eschewed family times over the holidays, preferring to work. If she wasn't careful, she was on a fast track to becoming his clone. The idea made her uneasy. She refused to even glance at the manila folder, let alone open it.

"Thanksgiving comes every year," he said, unsmiling. "Forget your plans and catch a flight to Starlight."

Maddie caught her breath. She loved Starlight. Or at least she had in the past. Her mind rewound to years gone by, and she pictured herself soaring down Star Mountain's slopes with her father, fresh powder flying behind her.

"Vanessa will book your flight," Bill said, puncturing Maddie's mental travels and bringing her mind sharply back to the present.

She pushed the file toward him. "Starlight must wait. I'm taking Vanessa and her son to Colonial Williamsburg over Thanksgiving weekend. I refuse to let you or any case spoil our plans."

Bill pulled up a chair and thumped down on it, his lips etched into a thin line.

"Maddie, didn't you once tell me of your wonderful childhood memories in Vermont, skiing at Star Mountain and all the fun festivities in Starlight?"

"I can't fault your memory on that score." Maddie suppressed a smile. "And I happily volunteer to fly there any day next week."

Bill was already shaking his head. "This simply cannot wait. Another high- powered D.C. law firm has tossed sand into our gears. They filed an emergency motion demanding the probate court stop us from distributing the property of the deceased owner of the mountain. The court hearing is in Vermont next Tuesday."

"So?" Maddie demanded, watching his eyes for future reasons of urgency.

He pulled his eyebrows together. "Jordan Star is the sole heir and grandson of Maynard Star, now deceased. Jordan, who has been running operations in Starlight, intends to keep the lodge and village as they are. The law firm claims while on a European trip, Maynard executed and recorded a new will. They demand a postponement until the will and rightful heir can be found. We need to stop their delaying tactics."

"Who is this new heir?" Maddie snatched up the file without opening it.

Bill shrugged. "They don't say. I did some checking. This firm represents mostly developers and real estate companies."

"Oh no!" Maddie leapt to her feet. She rattled the file. "You know what they intend to do."

"Then go and stop them." Bill stared at her over the top of his glasses as if daring her to refuse again.

"Wait a minute. You're pulling on my sympathetic heartstrings. I'm sure there is no danger of Jordan Star losing his mountain."

"That's where you are wrong. This same law firm drove one of my clients into bankruptcy last year."

Maddie loathed the idea of Starlight going bankrupt. It staggered her overcrowded brain to contemplate all the twists and turns of what Bill was forcing upon her at the last minute.

"Bill, have you forgotten? I promised Vanessa and Cole, and they have their hearts set on Williamsburg. It's important they are not alone this holiday. Their only other family is in the Army stationed overseas."

He waved off her concern just as Maddie figured he would. "Your heading out in the morning will save an entire town and the people who live there. Or have you forgotten? Mr. Star's estate owns a scenic mountain, which is ripe for development."

"You make a valid point, and I have an idea. I could convince Cole we're starting a new tradition, like I had as a child."

Her eyes wandered to the file, and then Maddie realized such a notion was being unfair to her paralegal.

"No," she said. "Vanessa hasn't the funds for travel to Starlight. Besides, it's very short notice. She's already bought the turkey and, for all I know, has baked the stuffing."

Bill's eyes sparked. "You are a fierce advocate, which is why I need you on this one. How's this for a compromise: Their trip to Williamsburg is on me. Perhaps our client will provide lodging for them gratis in Starlight for Christmas. I'll make it happen. You head up there pronto."

While working this case on magnificent Star Mountain sounded delightful and just what Maddie needed, a sudden reluctance ruined her dream vacation. Could a lawyer of her limited experience accomplish Bill's demands? She put on the brakes.

"Hold it. You want me to find a missing heir this D.C. law firm doesn't name but is using to challenge Mr. Star's will?"

"If you didn't want to work your magic, you shouldn't have aced your last case. Judge Cawley phoned me earlier, singing your praises. Your star is rising."

"Are you saying it's going to plunge if I don't hop on the next plane and save the town of Starlight?" Madison stared at the senior partner.

He refused to budge. The air was thick with the battle of their wills. Maddie held firmly to keeping her commitment to Vanessa.

"Surely you respect honor." Maddie folded her arms on her desk, giving him an icy glare.

"I'll tell you what," he finally conceded. "Harry Black will help in your search. He can start by looking for a will filed by Maynard in Europe. Now go home and pack your bags."

"How can one man own an entire town?" was Maddie's gritty reply.

Her question floated in the air like bubbles in Bill's wake as he hurried away. It looked like Star Mountain and Starlight were hers for the saving. Maddie finally opened the file, feeling nothing like a superhero. As she stapled Harry Black's business card to the inside file cover, she got a kick out of the huge binoculars filling one half and his logo "Global Security, Solutions for your problems" printed along the bottom.

"Ready for round two, Harry?" she asked aloud, certain his expert help on LeSwana's case made the difference between victory and defeat.

Gearing up for another swift win, Maddie yanked out the motion to delay distributing Maynard Star's estate, her eyes scanning the flimsy filing with little interest until she caught sight of the signature line.

Her eyes bulged. Her temples pounded.

No!

Maddie Stone, play-by-the-rules attorney-at-law would be fighting next week in the ring against her former fiancé, Stewart Dunham, bender-of-rules and bender-of-the-law. This couldn't be.

INTENSE IRRITATION OBSCURED Maddie's mind for several minutes. The sight of Harry's business card finally brought clarity. She picked up her cell phone and punched in his number. He answered in a huff, with Maddie briefing him on the paltry facts she knew of the case.

"Bill says it's urgent. I wish I had more to go on," Maddie admitted to their ace private eye.

"We start digging to unearth whoever is this rightful heir," Harry replied, emphasizing the words *rightful heir*. "Keep me informed and I'll have my shovel ready. Meanwhile, I'll go back to changing the oil in my classic car."

Maddie ended the call, her heart fluttering. More than anything, she longed to beat Stewart in court. Then again, she was getting ahead of herself. She had an equal chance of losing to him.

She hurried to Vanessa's desk. "Did Bill give you the bad news?"

"Yes." A shadow danced across Vanessa's brow. "I'm to book you on a Friday flight to Bennington, Vermont. Will you join us tomorrow for Thanksgiving?"

"Yes. I refused to fly today," Maddie admitted in hushed tones. "When I leave Friday, it's for a prolonged assignment at a charming ski resort. So keep my return open. Though I can't take you to Williamsburg, there is good news."

"Oh?" Vanessa continued searching airline websites.

"Bill is paying for you and Cole to visit Williamsburg."

Vanessa picked up her phone with a smile. "That is nice news."

"I also discovered some disturbing news." Maddie held the file high. "Stewart is the opposing attorney."

"Oh Maddie." Vanessa's lips drooped and she wilted in her chair.

Maddie clasped the edges of the file in both hands. "Don't worry. I'm up to this and will never let him defeat me."

Chapter 3

On Friday afternoon, Maddie eased her rented silver SUV to a stop, her eyes taking in the sweeping portico of the Bavarian-style rugged lodge made entirely of logs. It was like she had stepped into the charm of Austria here in the Green Mountains. She pulled out the keys, and after collecting her luggage from the backseat, she breathed in a lung full of the crisp, cold air. A shiver tore through her. She should have worn a heavier jacket.

A quick touch to the fob locked the doors. Maddie forced a sigh, wheeling her two suitcases crammed with clothes into the lobby. Extreme pressure to fly to Vermont and succeed kept Maddie from even enjoying Vanessa's Thanksgiving feast yesterday. At least her flight had come off without a hitch, so here she was in Starlight, ready to rumble.

Maddie strode toward the ornate front desk, her thoughts fixated on whether her mission here in Starlight would go as smoothly. A minute turned into five minutes as she waited for the desk clerk to check her in. Her blood started doing a slow boil at the unreasonable delay while the casually dressed man chatted on the desk phone in less than a confidential tone.

Though he seemed nice looking in spite of his apparent slight to Maddie, what he said next set her teeth on edge.

"You know how ruthless lawyers can be," he asserted, his back to her. "Next, we'll get a threatening letter from the law firm of Dewey, Cheatem and How. Don't concern yourself. I'll call back and let you know."

When the tall clerk banged down the desk phone, Maddie expected him to walk over and check her in. Instead, he began scrolling on his cell phone. To him, Maddie was invisible.

"Excuse me." She cleared her throat. "I'm Maddie Stone from the law firm you mentioned, Dewey, Cheatem, and How. I'd like to check in."

His indifferent air bordered on rudeness. He kept his eyes glued to his cell for a good long while. When he at last gazed up, Maddie fixed her most penetrating glare upon him.

"Would you now?" he replied, smirking. "I suggest you ring that little bell for the desk clerk. I just took a call here on the house phone."

"You might have told me," Maddie quipped, pressing a doorbell-like button.

A buzzer rang in a room behind the front counter, and a college-aged young woman, dressed in a traditional red dirndl and green apron over a white blouse with puffy sleeves, hustled out from the office.

Her grin seemed apologetic. "Sorry, I didn't see you arrive. I'm Gretchen. Do you have a reservation?"

"Yes, for Maddie Stone."

"Ms. Stone, welcome to Starlight where we give your dreams happy endings."

"That sounds wonderful," Maddie said, looking around for the faux desk clerk.

Gretchen consulted her computer screen. "Your departure is open, so you'll have time for skiing. We have fabulous power snow right now. Star Mountain is friendly for beginners and also has challenging terrain for the experienced skier."

"Thanks for the heads-up." Not wanting to divulge her plans quite yet, Maddie simply added, "I'll be mixing my visit with business."

Gretchen slid a form across the desk for Maddie to sign. She scrawled her name and nodded toward the house phone, hoping Gretchen would divulge something about the abrasive guest she'd just met.

"There was a surly man using the house phone when I arrived. He seems to have disappeared. Is he an attorney?"

Gretchen glanced beyond Maddie to peruse the lobby. "Yup, he's gone. Trevor Kirk received an outside call, which he took here. That's why I stepped away from the desk. He's been in and out of town for a month on business. He dines here but isn't staying here. I'm not sure if he's a lawyer."

"Is he always such a grouch?"

The star-shaped earrings dangling from Gretchen's ears glittered beneath the lights. "I've not heard anyone complain that Mr. Kirk is grumpy. In fact, several single women in town think he's quite nice. Too bad he keeps to himself. I find him dreamy."

Maddie blinked back surprise at such glowing accounts of the man with whom she'd had a dustup. Gretchen handed her a keycard, explaining the folder contained her room number and Wi-Fi password. Maddie gripped the handles of her bags and headed for the elevator, all the while scanning the busy lobby for the mysterious Trevor Kirk.

She found her room plush and cozy. When she pulled back heavy curtains, a gorgeous view of Star Mountain made her stop and stay silent.

"I don't remember the mountain being so stunning," she said under her breath. "Gretchen is right. I should try out the slopes."

Maddie watched as skiers zoomed down snowy ski runs descending toward the village. She'd had her own fun times here, flying down the same groomed runs in past years. The sight of the leather briefcase she'd plunked by the door ended her musings. Work loomed large. She wasn't here for vacation. The last thing she needed was to be distracted by powerful family memories on the mountain.

Maddie freshened up before phoning her boss. Bill was on his way to a meeting.

"I'm meeting Jordan tomorrow to discuss the so-called 'rightful heir,'" Maddie said, her eyes traveling to the mountain.

"Go easy. He seemed in shock when I explained about the motion. By now, he should have his thoughts together."

"I hope so. Also, Harry Black is on standby."

"Don't disappoint me," Bill replied with a grunt.

Maddie rolled her eyes. More pressure.

"I'll be in touch," she said, hanging up.

Jordan Star better have good insights for her because Maddie needed the right ammo to sink Stewart's claim on Tuesday. He deserved nothing less.

EARLY THE NEXT MORNING, Maddie walked through the lobby of the Edelweiss Lodge waving at Gretchen and heading straight for the Cinnamon Stix café. The scent of cinnamon tickled her nose. She stifled a sneeze. Her stomach rumbled from too little food in the past twenty-four hours. She couldn't eat breakfast soon enough.

Outside the café, a large painting of snowcapped mountains hung over the stone fireplace. Maddie didn't recall seeing this beautiful landscape with its cascading fields of white flowers during her previous visits to the lodge. Upon closer examination, she decided the flowers must be edelweiss. No wonder Maynard Star had named the Edelweiss Lodge after these rare alpine flowers.

"Isn't it beautiful?" a female voice called from behind Maddie.

Maddie spun around to find Gretchen walking toward her.

"The décor is superb," Maddie said. "I didn't know you had a piano. Is it possible for me to play sometime? I haven't touched any ivories recently."

"We'd love to hear you." Gretchen sounded enthused by the idea. "If you get to meet Mr. Star, you'll see he's musical. Can you believe this view? I see it every day, Ms. Stone."

Maddie took a moment to soak in the striking Star Mountain out in the distance. The sparkling white ski runs and the clear morning enticed her to forget work and go try slaloming down the slopes. Of course, she wouldn't. Duty called.

"This grandfather clock by the piano is unusual." Maddie stepped closer. "Wait. This clock has no clock."

"No, it's Mr. Jordan's special star. He owns the lodge."

"I will say hello to him after breakfast," Maddie replied, without revealing the reason for their meeting.

She stood admiring the brilliance of the stained-glass star mounted in the clock. Bright lights beamed through a large and luminous crystal star, which surrounded another stained-glass star. Maddie stooped down to better inspect the small inner star. It was truly stunning.

"It is gorgeous. I understand why the star is locked inside the case," she observed.

"What you don't know is how Maynard Star, Mr. Jordan's grandfather, created this dramatic star." Gretchen's voice held a note of pride. "Maynard was a renowned stained-glass artist who founded Starlight and developed Star Mountain."

Maddie's mind whirled. Her breath caught in her throat as she realized what she was seeing. "My grandfather gave me a star similar to this one before he passed away."

"Wow." Gretchen's green eyes grew huge. "Maybe old Mr. Star made your star. If Mr. Jordan finds out, he'll try buying it from you. He's been tracking down every one his grandfather made."

"I'll be sure to describe it to him," Maddie assured.

Her growling stomach reminded her it was past time for breakfast, so she headed back to the café. As she waited to be seated, a uniformed server bustled past carrying red poinsettia plants in each hand. It was beginning to feel like Christmas. Maddie pushed her festive spirit aside to better focus on the daunting task in front of her.

Just when she decided to grab coffee and a muffin instead of enjoying a full meal, another server swept by balancing a tray on his uplifted hand with a plate of pancakes dripping with chocolate and whipped cream. Maddie's mouth watered.

"Those pancakes look delicious," she muttered under her breath.

"Yes, they are," said the hostess. "I can seat you along the window."

Maddie followed her and in moments flicked open the menu, finding the French toast made with almonds, cream cheese, and a "secret ingredient" rather tempting.

She asked the server, "What is the secret ingredient?"

"I can't tell you."

"You don't know, or you're not permitted to tell me?"

"It says secret, doesn't it?"

"Oh never mind." Maddie snapped the menu shut. "I'm too hungry to quibble. Bring me that and a glass of orange juice please."

The server left, and Maddie hoped the secret wouldn't add too many calories. She noticed her jeans feeling a bit snug. She sipped the freshly squeezed orange juice while checking messages on her cell phone. The cell coverage was spotty in her room, but thankfully, she had better reception here in the café.

Several text messages popped up on her phone. One from Vanessa overflowed with happy-faced emojis and photos of her and Cole dressed in colonial garb. Her brother had called from overseas, and Cole had been happy to speak with his uncle. A male voice rising up from behind Maddie's back caused her to stop typing her reply.

His voice was so loud she couldn't help overhearing him blurt out, "You'd better believe it. I intend to make a substantial offer."

Maddie swiveled her head, her eyes locking onto a man wearing glasses, the cell phone plastered to his ear. Modern communications made life simpler yet more complex. If only he would be polite and lower his voice.

She abruptly changed her mind when she heard him boasting, "Yeah. I'm sweetening the deal with what you hinted at before I flew up here. I suspect Jordan has received other offers. You'd better be prepared to bid much higher."

What bid? Did he have his sights set on Star Mountain for a developer who might scar this beautiful mountain forever?

The server delivered Maddie's breakfast. She'd enjoyed a few bites of flavorful French toast when her phone alerted, making a buzzing sound on the table. Her fingers flew to open the text before it buzzed again. It was Bill. He insisted on knowing of her progress to save Star Mountain and Starlight village.

Maddie plunked down her fork. She had nothing to report. Well, except her boss had been right about one thing. Starlight village was crawling with potential buyers. She typed as much to him in a brief message.

Bill shot back faster than she could chew her French toast.

Who do these buyers work for?

I intend to find out, Maddie typed.

Then she shut off her phone to avoid Bill's constant pressure. He should have come up here himself instead of insisting she accomplish the impossible in one day. If only she had a magic wand. Maddie had none to wave.

Rather than give into defeat, she dug into her French toast with renewed vigor. She might even spot Trevor Kirk if she lingered long enough. She was curious to know if he practiced law in Stewart's firm. She put nothing past her nemesis to do everything underhanded to beat her.

Trevor never appeared. Maddie guzzled her large coffee, charging the meal to her room and adding a generous tip for the server. She'd waited tables in college and never forgot how she would add up each day's tips to see if she had scraped together enough money to pay the rent.

As she made her way out of the café, Maddie stopped to marvel at the radiant star, basking in its glow. She hurried onto the elevator realizing she'd failed to ascertain the secret ingredient in her breakfast. Oh well. One thing she knew. To find Jordan's secret heir, it was critical that Maddie received his full cooperation.

Chapter 4

Maddie took the long way from her room to Jordan's office to get a better feel for the place. She hurried down the steps to the mezzanine, giving her a bird's-eye view of the merry lobby and café below. Her ears tuned to Christmas music being piped overhead. A lump caught in her throat.

How far away she would be from her parents over the holiday.

She forged ahead toward Jordan's office, firmly resolved to handle missing them. Several families with giggling children rushed past her in the hall, their joyful sounds bringing a torrent of memories. These happy families could have been Maddie and her parents so many years ago, or even Maddie and her children today if she'd been a better judge of men. Instead, she was alone here in Vermont.

Such wayward thoughts she stopped in their tracks. So what if she was alone? She was here to accomplish an important mission. Dwelling on past mistakes was a recipe for disaster, or so her dad always taught her.

Hope for her future merged with Maddie's strong desire to help Jordan and the local people. She set her chin and steeled her mind, vowing to fight for him, vowing to save Starlight!

She approached Jordan's office on the mezzanine, and walking through an open door marked "Office," she was immediately taken aback. Dozens of stained-glass star ornaments were displayed on special hangers, sparkling and shining along the wall.

Maddie gulped. Fresh doubt peppered her mind.

Could she single-handedly preserve everything the Star family had built over the years? That answer seemed as distant as the North Star.

Beyond a stained-glass clock adorning the wall above an unoccupied desk, Maddie noticed a lady with salt-and-pepper hair standing by a window and facing the mountain. Not wanting to startle her, Maddie coughed lightly.

The erect African-American woman turned and gave Maddie a toothy smile. "Are you Madison Stone?"

"I am." Maddie handed over a business card. "Mr. Star is expecting me."

"That he is. I am Sylvia, assistant to the Star family since before Jordan was born. I won't say how many years that is."

"These stained-glass pieces are wonderful," Maddie told her.

With a thin finger, Sylvia pointed at the display of multicolored glass stars. "These beauties have lived here even longer than I have, which is saying something. Jordan's grandfather was a true artist, breathing life into each piece of glass. Each one tells its own special story. Maynard Star passed his love for glass, tin, and solder on to Jordan."

Maddie set her leather case on a side table beside a small book about the village. It might be something to peruse later. But now she wanted to tell Sylvia something she'd just remembered.

"I once met Maynard when my grandparents first brought me here. Back then, they served family-style dinners and afterward, Maynard thrilled us diners with stories of how he built this lodge with pine trees cut from his land."

"Mr. Star deeply cared for others," Sylvia replied, her tone melancholy. "My parents worked for him. Do you know he sent me to business school with the understanding I would return and work for him? I've been happy here ever since."

"Does the café still serve family dinners?"

Sylvia's black eyes glittered. "No. Maynard was a visionary. He started the Cinnamon Stix café some years back to highlight Vermont-style cooking with an Austrian flair. Our chef is my son Dexter. I don't mind saying he's received multiple five-star awards."

"I certainly enjoyed my breakfast," Maddie said. Sylvia's comment prompted her to ask, "Is the Star family connected to Austria?"

Sylvia simply checked her slim wristwatch. "Come. Jordan is expecting you."

Maddie picked up her briefcase and followed Sylvia across the short hall to a closed door. Sylvia knocked once before swinging it wide open. The office was empty.

"Jordan is missing," Maddie quipped.

"He must have slipped out without me seeing him. I know he's on the property."

Sylvia drew her brows together and pointed to an empty chair beside Jordan's desk. "Please get comfortable. I'll track him down, I promise."

Sylvia left Maddie seated alone to fume. Was her client the absentminded type who would be zero help in tracking down the mystery heir?

She gazed around, observing the exterior office wall fashioned with polished pine logs. The photo of an attractive man dressed in a business suit and receiving a civic award seemed the antithesis of a distracted person.

Other awards and photos of smartly dressed men and women with Jordan caused Maddie to wonder if he was a driven entrepreneur and as cutthroat in business as Stewart. Doubt seeped into her mind. It was possible he'd sell his inheritance to the highest bidder.

Wait a minute. Maddie recalled an earlier conversation with Bill. Her boss had insisted Jordan wanted nothing more than to keep the lodge and surrounding village just as they were. If true, he'd likely be the exact opposite of Stewart and appreciate the value of home. Maddie tried to gather a sense from his mementos if he, too, wanted to travel the world.

"Ms. Stone."

Maddie looked up to see who just said her name. A man of medium height, snapping hazel eyes, and hair a lighter brown than Maddie's extended his right hand. A perfect match to the man in the photos, she instantly approved of his engaging smile, something the photographs failed to capture.

"Yes, and I assume you are Jordan Star." She reached for his hand.

"Thank you for coming all the way to Starlight, Ms. Stone."

"Please, call me Maddie."

He held on to her hand, saying in a deep bass voice, "You arrive at a crucial time for me and the town's people. I won't forget it."

"Unfortunately, I've done nothing yet except become acquainted with your staff," Maddie said, abruptly dropping her hand. "Many questions need answering—and soon. Shall we get started?"

"Let's sit over here." Jordan ushered her to the small conference table. "Can Sylvia bring you coffee or tea?"

"I drank plenty of coffee with breakfast in your café, but I wouldn't turn down hot chocolate, if it isn't too much trouble."

Sylvia, who had magically reappeared, nodded before quietly closing the office door behind her. As Maddie placed her briefcase on an empty chair and sat down, she further assessed her client. Jordan took the seat by the head of the table nearest his desk.

Though dressed in jeans and a flannel shirt, he had a touch of the big city about him. At the same time, he seemed to fit right into the relaxed atmosphere of Star Mountain. If she spotted him walking down the street, Maddie would never guess he was the owner of the surrounding tourist destination. Jordan appeared to be the same age as Stewart, which would make him a few years older than Maddie's thirty-one years.

The sudden thought of her adversary irked her. At this precise moment Stewart might be concocting some scheme against her and her client.

"I pictured you being older," Maddie said, raising an eyebrow.

Jordan clasped his hands on the table and leaned in. "And when I was told Madison Stone was coming here, I envisioned an aging man with a midriff bulge."

"Touché." She didn't try hiding her smirk.

"While we laugh at each other's expense, I tell you, Bill shocked me with the possibility of an unknown relative filing a claim to all of this."

His eyes flashed. "I just can't believe there is a newer will to Grandfather's estate. I am still stunned."

"Whoa." Maddie raised her outstretched palm as if a traffic cop. "You hit on the operative word: *Unknown*."

"What? Do you mean you don't believe there is one?"

"We don't know, do we? There's been no court filing to identify anyone. All I've seen is the motion from D.C. lawyers seeking to postpone you getting the estate by claiming there is another heir. I flew up here to ascertain the truth. Have you combed through your grandfather's papers? Is there any possible reference to a new heir or will?"

Jordan rubbed his chin. "I was concerned this might happen."

"Why? Do you know of another family member?"

"No, Maddie, I do not. For years, developers have been scheming and conniving to buy the lodge and more importantly, the mountain. You won't believe how many renderings of home sites and golf courses I found stashed in Grandfather's desk."

Sylvia stepped into the office and slid an insulated cup of hot chocolate in front of Maddie, telling her, "Good choice. I asked Dexter to drop in tiny marshmallows."

"How did you know I love marshmallows?" Maddie wondered aloud.

Sylvia beamed a magnetic smile. "This is Starlight. We strive for happy beginnings to each day."

"And you have succeeded," Maddie replied softly.

She sipped the hot cocoa, relishing its creaminess on her tongue. Her momentary cloud nine vanished when Jordan shoved a bunch of papers at her.

"Okay, Mr. Star, let's get cracking." Maddie snatched a legal pad and pen from the satchel. "At breakfast, I overheard a boisterous man talking on the phone in the café. He might be such a developer."

"Could be. Sylvia doesn't even put their calls through to me anymore. She could have sold it all a dozen times by now."

"We have lots of ground to cover. Tell me everything about your family tree."

"My father and mother passed away years ago. They were my family, along with Grandfather."

"I am sorry." Maddie looked up from her notepad. "Bill should have told me. When was that, Jordan?"

"Fifteen years ago this past Thanksgiving."

"How difficult for you. Do you mind telling me what happened?"

"Their private plane crashed," he said. His words seemed to get lost in his throat.

"And you weren't with them?"

"No."

Maddie set down her pen. Jordan seemed reluctant to talk about his family. Why? Was he still grieving? She was curious if he knew something he wasn't willing to tell her.

"Jordan." She lowered her voice despite the closed door. "It must have been hard losing your parents in your teens. Did your grandparents look after you?"

"Ah ... Grandfather did. Grandmother, Aunt Rosalyn, and my parents all died in my dad's plane when they left here for New York."

"How terrible," she whispered.

Jordan dropped his eyes to examine his hands. "My aunt lived in Austria. They were all planning to fly commercially from New York to celebrate the orphanage's twenty-fifth year. I stayed behind with Grandfather to help him at the lodge."

Maddie waited, and when he fell silent, she asked him to explain about the orphanage in Austria, telling him, "This is the first I've heard of that."

"My folks took me there when I was sixteen, a few years before they died."

She requested the spelling of Rosalyn's name and the name of the orphanage, which he gave her. Maddie looked up from her notes to search his eyes with hers.

"Tell me about your aunt."

"I met her in Austria and again when she visited Starlight before the crash."

"When she came here, did she mention any family back in Austria?"

"Not that I recall. I kept pretty busy helping Grandfather. She spent most of the time with my folks."

"How about your earlier visit to Austria? Meet any special people?"

"Hmm." Jordan ran his hand through this thick hair. "Aunt Rosalyn took me to a giant castle near Salzburg."

"You have hit upon something I'm familiar with," Maddie said, hoping to lighten his somber mood. "I've seen the birthplace of the man who composed the Christmas hymn 'Silent Night,' which I love playing on the piano."

He fiddled with his pen. "Did you see the fortress-like castle?"

"No, it was closed. Did anyone else go along with you?"

"My recollection is of a sword fight between two guys in costume and medieval drums being played. That's it."

"This next question is important." For emphasis, Maddie spread her hands on the table. "Is the orphanage your family's *only* connection with Austria?"

"I believe so. My aunt dedicated her life to the orphanage and the kids."

"Was she single? Ever marry and divorce?"

"Yes, no, and no."

"Jordan, if you aren't more open, I can't help you. Your terse answers will keep us inside all day."

He began tapping his pen on the table. "Sorry if you think I'm brusque. It's difficult to tell you what you want to hear. Aunt Rosalyn never married. Maddie, I didn't know her."

"So she wasn't the kind of aunt who sent you letters or gifts?"

Jordan shook his head. Maddie tried another tactic.

"Your aunt's life may provide no leads," she admitted. "Is a developer behind contesting the will and attempting to seize possession of the properties?"

Jordan flexed his jaw, telegraphing his anxiety. "There's also a guy poking around who's a geologist. I suspect he's looking for coal, oil, or even gold. Who knows? There are abandoned gold mines in the area."

"What's his name? Have you talked with him?"

"I don't know who he is. He's not staying at the lodge. Gretchen, my assistant who works the front desk, talks to him. She's a pipeline of information in Starlight."

"We need to examine your family's papers and photo albums, if you have any."

Jordan nervously drummed his fingers on the table as if deep in thought. At length he said, "There are boxes and trunks up in my attic I've not opened. I never wanted to."

"The sooner we go attic hunting, the better." Maddie closed her folder.

"I have wall-to-wall meetings with vendors. This weekend starts our busy season."

"On Tuesday, I have to convince the judge to toss out their claim. With zero evidence, I will be swinging and not hitting the ball."

"Okay, your baseball metaphor I can understand."

He reached into his side drawer and handed Maddie a thick file.

"These are Maynard's personal papers, which I thumbed through. You are welcome to take a look. Give it back to Sylvia when you're finished. I have meetings all day."

"You'll find out soon enough I'm a baseball nut. Now when can we meet?"

They settled on Monday noon at the lodge. He offered to drive her over to the family farm where he lived.

Maddie typed the appointment into her phone, asking, "What time is church on Sunday?"

"Ten a.m. Pastor Fisher always gives a stirring message. Maybe I'll see you there."

"I could use a nugget of inspiration. Meanwhile, I'm pushing Harry Black, our private eye, to dig into the Austrian orphanage and a new will being filed there."

"Sorry I'm not more help," Jordan said, walking her out. "My wheels are spinning."

While Maddie understood his being stressed over the delay in receiving his inheritance, she had to wonder. Did he really know so little about his aunt Rosalyn?

Disappointment dogged Maddie as she retraced her steps to her room. She'd uncovered no solid leads. Of course, Stewart carried the legal burden to prove his case.

But Maddie didn't want him to blindside her in court.

Her instincts practically screamed Jordan was hiding a secret, and Maddie wouldn't rest until she put her finger on just what it was.

Chapter 5

Maddie hardly noticed storm clouds swirling in the sky as she pulled the SUV into a parking spot Tuesday morning. The snow, more like icy sleet, stung her face as she trekked to the county courthouse along the slippery sidewalk. Too bad she hadn't thought to wear sturdier boots.

Just then, the sun burst through a clearing in the clouds. The sight of the white-domed two-story building set among trees and bushes dappled with snow made Maddie stop walking. Did they really hold court in there? The brick building looked more like a picturesque calendar than a place where people's lives could be changed in a flash.

Icy bits began pelting her with a vengeance. Worried this winter storm heralded bad tidings, all inspiration she'd received at yesterday's church service evaporated. The idea of opposing Stewart in a strange court and before an unknown judge dampened her usual confidence. And besides, Jordan's thick file of his grandfather's papers had revealed nothing to help her arguments.

"Here goes everything," she muttered, climbing the stairs and making a hurried stop in the restroom to check her appearance.

She wriggled from her coat. The beige jacket she'd selected to go with the silky blouse and black skirt looked professional, and Maddie approved. She wanted to project the image of competent lawyer, in spite of being new to this court. If her legal arguments convinced the judge, she'd be on a plane tomorrow flying back to her life in D.C.

After a deep breath and silent prayer, she headed into the small courtroom, her fashion boots making clicking sounds on the wooden floor. The black-robed judge sitting behind his bench looked up at her. Disapproval spread across his stern face like a dark cloud. Two attorneys stopped whispering with the judge long enough to turn their heads toward Maddie.

She wanted to disappear in the crowd, only there were few people in the front row of the spectator section. Her eyes locked onto a familiar form. There sat Stewart, his topcoat draped over the wooden pew next to him. Maddie made a beeline to a seat on the opposite side of the courtroom.

The judge quit staring at her, announcing for all to hear, "Having reached an agreement for trial in two weeks, the Birdsong case is adjourned."

The two attorneys returned to their counsel tables, casting sideways glances at Maddie. She remained standing, still clutching her satchel, wondering if her case would be the next one called.

In tune with her thinking, the judge rapped his gavel lightly. A clerk wearing a dress resembling a giant Christmas sweater stood below the judge. She held up a file.

Her voice sounding like a computer, she said, "The case of Jane or John Doe versus the Estate of Maynard Star."

Okay. This was it, Maddie's turn to shine. At least that was her plan.

Without glancing Stewart's way, she mentally rehearsed her arguments, convincing herself victory for Jordan was within reach. Maddie removed a leather folder from her briefcase and approached the swinging gate, which separated spectators from the inner well of the courtroom.

Stewart arrived at the same instant. Maddie stopped. He bowed slightly, gesturing for her to enter first. Maddie swept past her opponent, keeping her eyes on Judge Marks. She spread her papers on the table. Rather than wait for Stewart to speak first, she beat him to the batter's box.

Maddie held her back erect and said in a calm, cool voice, "Good morning, Your Honor. I am attorney Madison Stone appearing for the Maynard Star Estate."

"Attorney Stone, have I seen you in my court before?" Judge Marks squinted at her over the top of his black-rimmed half-glasses.

"No, Your Honor. I am a lawyer in the Washington D.C. firm, Barron and Rich. Mr. Barron is licensed to practice law in Vermont. Your court granted me special permission to appear on his behalf."

"Oh yes, I recall Bill phoned me last week. He and I go way back to law school. Madison Stone, you may argue this motion on behalf of the Maynard Star Estate. And you, sir, have you been in my court before?"

The judge, who had just said he liked Maddie's boss, focused a scornful eye upon Stewart. Maddie wanted to cheer. Instead, she barely glanced at her ex-boyfriend and focused her mind on her upcoming argument.

"I'm Stewart Dunham here on behalf of the claimant. I, too, am here by permission and am with the Hunter, Lance, and Bling law firm. Perhaps you know Mr. Hunter. He practices here on a regular basis."

The judge cleared his throat and swiped off his glasses. "Attorney Stewart Dunham, I am sorry I cannot allow you to argue your motion. Your client Jane or John Doe doesn't have a first name beginning with a letter 'S' as you do."

"Your Honor, I protest." Stewart's neck veins bulged against his shirt collar. "The clerk accepted my admission. I have it in writing. Moreover, I cannot give you the name of my client in open court."

The judge stroked his jutting chin. "For the record, Attorney Madison Stone represents Maynard Star. So the court can only presume Attorney Stewart Dunham represents a client with his initials of SD."

Maddie hid a blossoming smile. This was way too funny seeing Judge Marks give Stewart the raspberries, especially since Stewart had misunderstood the judge. She gave thanks for her father who raised her to not only study hard, but to also retain a healthy sense of humor.

Stewart puffed out his cheeks, giving away how he was seething inside. The judge reset his glasses at the edge of his nose, and with a smile at Maddie, told both lawyers to take their seats. They wasted no time in complying.

"I discovered something unusual about this case," Judge Marks said. "Both lawyers are from firms in the District of Columbia. How convenient. You can save your clients' money by driving up here together from the nation's capital."

"No way, Your Honor," Maddie blurted before thinking.

The judge lifted his heavy eyebrows. He tapped the file with a finger rather than address her outburst.

"Attorney Dunham, enlighten me, sir. Though you seek the court's postponement in settling the Star estate, you fail to provide any supportive reason in your petition."

Maddie felt compelled to rise to her feet. "We totally agree, Your Honor."

"So noted." The judge jabbed a finger at Stewart. "Do you have additional facts for me to consider? Your filing contains both names Jane and John Doe. I wonder, do you even know who your client is?"

Stewart got to his feet. He cast a withering glance at Maddie before addressing the court. "Your Honor, we aren't exactly sure of our client's identity."

"I find that hard to believe," Judge Marks shot back. "You state in here a new will was prepared, which supersedes the will Attorney Stone seeks to probate. Correct?"

"Ah ... A person claiming to represent Maynard's relative contacted our firm and agreed to meet. So far, we haven't been able to do so. We filed the motion to ensure the court and estate have as much information as possible."

"Attorney Stone, how do you respond to this new heir and will?" The judge ripped off his glasses and looked at Maddie.

She quickly processed Stewart's astonishing admission as she rose to her feet. "We are confident that Maynard's grandson Jordan Star, who currently runs the Star enterprise, is the only surviving heir. With no supporting evidence, the Hunter firm's motion is premature. Your Honor should dismiss their claim at once."

"You have no knowledge of who approached the Hunter firm?" Judge Marx asked her, shoving his glasses back on the tip of his nose.

"Correct," Maddie assured. "It seems this alleged person would have contacted our firm since we are the estate's attorney of record."

She sat down. The judge's eyes darted to Stewart. "Mr. Dunham, I have a mind to dismiss your petition. How do you propose corralling your elusive client and how much time do you need?"

"Our firm is employing every resource." Stewart bounced back to his feet. "Sixty days should be sufficient."

The judge lifted his gavel. Maddie held her breath. Surely he would dismiss Stewart's half-baked motion to delay closing the Star estate for another sixty days. *Bang* went the gavel. Maddie prepared to leave as the victor. And oh how she would rub it in that Stewart lost.

But then Judge Marks carefully took off his glasses and folded them into a case. Bill had called Maddie over the weekend to caution her about the judge's reputation for being eccentric and pulling anything out of his hat. She blew out her breath, preparing herself for the unexpected.

Silence filled the courtroom. Both attorneys waited.

"Mr. Dunham." The judge said his name as if spitting out gravel. "Since you've provided no evidence there is such an heir, sixty days is unreasonable. We adjourn until January 12, which gives you nearly six weeks."

His gavel dropped onto the bench with another loud bang. "Both attorneys in my chambers, now."

The judge hurried out the side door. Maddie snatched up her coat and briefcase, apprehension searing her mind over why Marks demanded to confer with the lawyers.

Before long, both attorneys perched on upholstered chairs in the judge's private office. He took great care in removing and straightening his black judicial robe onto a hanger resting on a hook on the back of his door.

Marks edged behind his desk, and out came his glasses from the case. He plopped them on his nose. His eyes flashed piercing looks at Maddie and Stewart over the top of his glasses.

"Tell me, do the two of you have some kind of history with each other?"

Maddie's eyes widened in horror. How could Judge Marks possibly know?

Stewart wasted no time distancing himself from Maddie. "No, this is the first time we've opposed each other in court."

"I see. Since you both work in D. C., you have me perplexed about what's truly happening here. I want to know, are Washington bureaucrats vying to take over Star Mountain for a new Camp David retreat for politicians? Or worse yet, is the Air Force determined to put a communication tower atop the mountain like they tried years ago? Try that trick and we Vermonters will rise up again."

"Your Honor raises an insightful question." Maddie folded her arms. "I think Mr. Dunham owes us an answer. He filed the petition."

Stewart shifted his weight in the chair as if uncomfortable. Maddie was not surprised. She knew him as a man who demanded control.

His vague answer, "Star Mountain is a great retreat for everyone," said nothing. Nor did his, "I know nothing about a government conspiracy to seize it."

The judge rapidly leaned forward in his chair. "Enough jousting of conspiracies. What I want from you lawyers is an assurance. As soon as either of you identifies this heir, you will advise the other firm so we can wipe this matter off my calendar. Agreed?"

Both lawyers nodded in unison. The judge tore off his glasses and gestured toward his door. "Good. Meeting adjourned. Outta here."

Maddie hustled away from his chambers and practically ran out the front door of the courthouse. Stewart called to her from behind.

"Maddie, wait up. Let's have lunch together."

Maddie spun around, her eyebrows flexing and her heartbeat rapid. "I already told you, Stewart. Three strikes and you are out. I have a meeting with my client."

She stalked off to her car, her boots leaving footprints in the fresh snow. Though it was lunchtime, she wouldn't eat in town, fearing Stewart might show up in the same restaurant and continue his unwanted attentions.

MADDIE CALLED HARRY BLACK the instant she took cover in her car. His number rang a long time before he answered, sounding out of breath.

"Sorry, Ms. Stone, there's a snowstorm here in D.C.," he huffed. "I've been shoveling my drive and sidewalk."

Maddie gazed at the blackening Vermont sky. "Heavy snow is forecast here too. Harry, we need your help."

"I'm ready. Need me to ship you a snow shovel?"

"Hah." Maddie's lips turned up as she started the car. "Here's the deal. Judge Marks is delaying closing the estate. Opposing counsel has until January 12 to name the alleged heir, which gives them time to wreak havoc on Starlight and Jordan Star."

"Your text yesterday said I'm to check into Rosalyn Star and an Austrian orphanage. That's not much to go on."

Cold began seeping through her flimsy boots. Maddie turned up the heat, pointing it at her feet. "Check into Maynard executing a new will in Austria. Harry, pull out all the stops. Opposing counsel's firm is known for representing developers."

"Roger that, Ms. Stone."

"When I'm back in my room, I'll text a few more details."

A seed of doubt planted itself firmly into Maddie's mind as she ended the call. Before driving to the lodge, should she phone Bill about her and Stewart once dating? It bothered her to keep something like this from her boss. Before she could punch in his number, her cell rang.

"Maddie, I need to cancel our three o'clock." Jordan sounded tense. "There's a problem with a ski lift. I'm heading up the mountain now."

"Ouch. I am sorry to report more bad news." Maddie told him about the judge allowing the other side until January 12 to produce their heir.

"That's not what I wanted to hear. I'll call later to discuss where we go from here."

"Jordan, in what part of Austria did your aunt live?"

Click.

Jordan's hanging up on Maddie didn't sit well. Her client kept throwing her one curveball after another. Yesterday he had cancelled their noon meeting. Now a broken lift was his excuse. Difficult clients were nothing new.

So putting irritation aside, Maddie shut off the motor. She set about town talking with locals, trying the police chief first. He was out helping a stranded motorist. From there, she met with the florist, the baker, and the grocer, where she heard one reoccurring theme. Everyone loved and appreciated the Star family, especially Jordan, the heir apparent.

On the way back to the lodge, she drove to the church. Pastor Fisher graciously ushered her into his small office.

"It was nice meeting you Sunday, Ms. Stone. What do you need help with?"

"Starlight's such a wonderful place. My grandparents brought me here as a teen. I never knew how Maynard started it all. As the Star family lawyer, I'm trying to learn how the business evolved."

"Ah ... you have found my sweet spot." He offered her a seat next to his desk. "Maynard Star was a visionary. I can't say enough good about the man. He took what God created and built a community of people who love and care for each other. Jordan has taken all the responsibility upon himself and keeps everything together."

"Did you ever meet Jordan's aunt Rosalyn?"

"Once when she came to visit. It was the day before the crash. You see, I moved to Starlight after she'd gone to Austria. Ask our police chief, who grew up in the village. Here's a pamphlet the local librarian wrote about Starlight's beginnings. She was a classmate of Jordan's."

Maddie thanked the pastor, making a mental note to connect with the chief. She returned to the lodge frustrated. She elected to eat an early dinner in her room, all the while searching the Starlight booklet for clues to jog Jordan's fuzzy memory.

Finding none, the email she sent to Harry Black seemed exasperatingly thin of facts. Maddie shut down her laptop with one thought churning around in her mind. Tomorrow she'd press Jordan to the wall until he told her the truth.

Chapter 6

Maddie peered out the window early in the morning, amazed as dawn crowned the mountaintop with golden shafts of light. Tall pine trees bore great white tufts glittering like jewels in the sunlight. It was the most glorious sunrise she'd ever seen.

She snapped a picture with her phone to recapture the beauty when she returned to work in the hectic city. A message waited for her. Maddie swiped a finger across the screen, opening what Jordan had sent: *Lift all fixed. Meet me for breakfast in the café?*

Maddie texted back: *Will meet you in twenty minutes.*

After a quick shower, she dressed in a warm sweater and slacks before dashing down the steps. Jordan was already drinking coffee when she sat across from him at the small table.

"I already ordered for both of us so we can get started right away."

A server brought Maddie a mug of steaming coffee smelling like hazelnut. A small sip confirmed she was right.

"We need to comb through your attic," she said. "First, I'd like to check a website to search your family's heritage."

"Sorry, Maddie. I use the Internet for tourism and reservations, but don't do social media or genealogy."

"We'll learn together."

Another server set down two plates of toasted cinnamon bagels covered with pumpkin cream cheese and bowls of sliced fruit. They ate a hurried breakfast. Maddie wanted her client's attention before he was called off again. On the way to his office, Maddie gave a friendly wave to Gretchen, who was busy putting up a Christmas tree in the lobby.

Jordan went ahead of her up the steps, gabbing the entire time on his cell phone to settle various issues around town. She marveled at the breadth of his position. While her job at the law firm demanded much of her time, the line of people needing Jordan's expertise appeared never ending.

After stopping by Sylvia's office to say a warm, "Good morning," Maddie scurried behind Jordan into his office. Before long, she stood behind him at his desk, gazing over his shoulder while he typed on a large laptop.

"You got me onto the Family Finder website." He pointed to the screen. "Now they want my account name. I don't have one."

Maddie scrolled down the list of contacts on her phone. "We can use my account and password to search for your family."

Jordan spun around in his chair, his knees colliding with Maddie's legs.

"I'm so sorry," he mumbled, his eyes traveling to her face above him.

She glanced back at her phone. "No worries."

"It's too cramped behind my desk," he said. "Let's move to the conference table where we can work together."

"Okay, I just located my info. So you've never been on Family Finder?"

"Never."

Jordan brought his laptop to the table and arranged two chairs on the same side, pulling one out for Maddie. They sat beside one another. She typed Jordan's family name into the Family Finder search function.

"Ready to see how many Star families have researched their roots?" Maddie asked, her fingers poised above the keys.

"If you think it's important."

"We strike out here, we're off to the attic," Maddie proclaimed. "What's your great-grandfather's first name?"

"Alexander ... Alexander Star. But you knew his last name."

"It never hurts to double-check. Okay, here goes."

Her fingers flew along the keyboard. The wait for the search results kept them both quiet until a certain Alexander Star popped onto the screen.

"He was born in 1919," Maddie said, doing the math in her head.

Jordan beat her to it, exclaiming, "No. Grandfather Maynard's dad would have been born in the 1800s."

"It appears no one has researched your family."

"Are we are stymied already?"

"Maybe they researched your grandfather." The keys beneath Maddie's fingers clattered some more. "Bingo! Here's a Maynard born in Vermont. Let's take a closer look."

Jordan slid his chair closer to hers. This time his knees bumped into her knees.

"Sorry again." He instantly moved his chair. "This is like an Easter egg hunt."

She rubbed her knees, unfazed by Jordan's nearness. Maddie scrolled down a bit and stopped.

"Check this out. I found a Maynard married to Helen."

"Those are my grandparents!" Jordan cried, jumping to his feet.

Maddie reached for his hand to pull him back into his chair. "Steady on. Let me open this family tree and see if anyone else has been researched."

Jordan set his face close to Maddie's cheek as the screen came alive.

"Look! There's my folks and even my name," Jordan said eagerly.

He turned toward Maddie, their noses nearly touching. Maddie focused her eyes back on the screen. She quickly read, and what she saw disturbed her.

"Hey wait. Why is this even in here?" Jordan demanded. "I have not done any research, and I have never been on this site."

This was precisely what Maddie wondered. She kept mum about her misgivings. She'd learned the hard way in dozens of court cases not to give voice to speculation. Maddie found it better to let facts, however unwanted, determine her conclusions.

She gestured toward the screen. "Here's a listing for your parents, Robert and Patricia."

"You are amazing." Jordan leaned closer to the computer as if scrutinizing the tiny names on the screen. "I see my aunt, Rosalyn Star, is listed. Scroll down below my dad's name where it should show my name."

Maddie kept her tone cool, brushing aside his compliment. "Jordan, see? You are listed here. The field beside your name is blank because you are not married."

"Hmmph," he sputtered. "So much for privacy."

She nudged him with an elbow and a chortle escaped his lips.

"Right," Maddie declared. "If you tried hiding a marriage and divorce, this site would betray you."

"If I was, you'd already know it. Everyone knows my business in this small town."

"I take it you have never been married?"

"Correct. I have been too busy running this place with Grandfather to date much." He sighed before motioning at the screen. "What is below Rosalyn's name?"

"It will be blank, like yours. You say she never married."

Maddie raised the field on the screen, and her mouth hung open in astonishment.

"What is that?" Jordan shrieked, sounding as incredulous as Maddie felt.

She stared in unbelief. "It must be a cousin you failed to tell me about."

"I have no cousins, which is why I am the sole heir."

"It says here Rosalyn has a daughter Nora Star," Maddie managed, hardly believing her eyes.

Jordan leaned back as if dazed. "How can that be?"

She faced him, unease blanketing her mind like a snowstorm. It was her job as his lawyer to ask the difficult questions.

"Are you sure Rosalyn never married? Could this be some family secret?"

"No. No. She stayed single her entire life. I never heard of her having a daughter."

"Do you think she was incapable of falling in love?" Maddie probed. "You know her orphanage would have been full of babies surrendered by girls who thought their lovers would marry them."

"Exactly." Jordan got up to pace around his office. "You answered the question. Rosalyn founded an orphanage. She certainly would know the dangers of such relationships."

Maddie studied the screen, concern building by the second. She navigated around the listing and came up with a startling conclusion.

She tried keeping her voice free of emotion as she said, "Jordan, I believe this account was created by Nora Star."

"How can this be? Who is she?" Jordan grabbed a pen and began jamming its clicker button on the tabletop. Repeatedly he punched the button down as if extremely upset.

Maddie lightly touched his arm. "We should stay calm. My legal training says dig deeper, do more research, turn over every rock. I could try contacting Nora through the website and see if we learn more."

"I don't think that is wise."

When Jordan ran a hand through his hair, Maddie shifted gears. With her client this wound up, how would he react to what she was about say?

She pointed to the chair. "Please sit. We have another issue to tackle."

"Now what?"

Jordan dropped into the chair, his brows drawn together and pen clicking.

"First, would you forget about that pen so I can think?"

Jordan folded his hand around the pen.

"Thanks." Maddie logged out of Family Finder and shut the computer.

Jordan's brow was still furrowed. "Why doesn't she know about Alexander?'

"What are you talking about? Who is *she*?"

"The Nora Star who entered the information on Family Finder." Jordan aimed a finger at the closed computer. "Why didn't she know about our great-grandparents?"

Maddie fought against brain fog, reaching for a coherent thought. "Can you recall a time when your aunt Rosalyn visited Starlight with a daughter?"

"Of course not. I already told you. We never heard of Nora." Jordan's trembling voice betrayed his emotions.

"That's my point, Jordan. If there was a Nora, then Rosalyn must have kept her a secret from the rest of the Star family. Conversely, she might have kept the Star family, including your great-grandparents, a secret from Nora."

Jordan's hand again found its way into his thick hair. "Your point is valid. Still, I have to wonder how she found us now."

"Somehow she heard of your grandfather's death. That somehow is what I want to find out."

"Where do we even begin looking for Nora? And why isn't her birth date included? If I could only talk with her, reason with her about everything Grandfather built here, I might change her mind."

Jordan started pacing like a caged tiger. Maddie let him expend his nervous energy. It was impossible to reassure her client at this moment, because she, too, had more questions than answers. Out the window, sunshine burst across Star Mountain's peak. It looked like fresh snow was falling.

"Jordan, come see this." Maddie walked over to admire the towering mountain. "I think I see a rainbow up there."

He walked up beside her. "I don't want to give up this mountain."

"Yes, yes, but do you see the beauty, Jordan? You are so busy fixing ski lifts and people's lives I suspect you miss seeing the wonder of it. Last night, I looked up at the stars and a strange feeling happened inside of me. I felt small compared to the immensity of the heavens. At the same time, a powerful belief burned inside of me. A belief God has a purpose for my life."

Jordan shifted his gaze upward. He seemed transfixed as if soaking in the sun's rays cascading against the snowcapped mountain.

"Focus your mind and open it to the possible," Maddie whispered softly.

Jordan breathed in deep. So did Maddie.

"Listen," she said. "I just realized. We're facing a mountain, and together we can reach the summit."

"I like the sound of that, Maddie," he said, looking at her with hope in his eyes.

Maddie turned her gaze back to the vista out the window. "I admit finding Nora Star is a complete shock. I promise you, Jordan, I won't rest until I learn every one of Star Mountain's secrets."

Chapter 7

It was a few hours later, and Maddie was still huddled in her room doing research on her computer. Her fingers started to cramp from all the typing. She flexed them, staring out the window at Star Mountain. The irony wasn't lost on her. The mountainous mess before her and Jordan seemed as big as the mountain was massive.

She'd assured Jordan they were up to the task. Was she?

Her cell phone vibrated, startling her from her unwanted reverie. An unknown number appeared on the screen, which she usually let go to voicemail. Because the area code indicated Vermont, she hit "Answer" and then the speaker button.

"Hello?" she said cautiously.

"Madison, it's Jordan."

"You confused me. Your number indicated an unknown caller."

"I want you to have my cell phone number. Make me a new entry in your contacts."

"Good idea. What can I help you with?"

Maddie closed her laptop, interested to know what might be on his mind.

"I don't mean to intrude, but I am making a delivery to the ski lodge. You said you skied here before, if you want to ride along and escape your room. You'll thank me for the views."

"Won't it be dark soon?" she asked, trying to decide.

"We have hours yet. It just seems darker when the sun dips west of the mountain. You will see what our pursuers desire to purchase."

"Okay, you've convinced me. I can join you in the lobby in ten minutes."

Maddie hung up, realizing she had business to finish. She sent Harry Black a message: *Search for info on Nora*

Star, may have been adopted by Rosalyn Star in Austria. Birth date and/or adoption date unknown.

She had a call to make, one she did not relish. Taking a deep breath, Maddie punched in Bill's private number, which rang a few times.

He answered in a rush, "I'm going in the judge's chambers. Can it wait?"

"No. We found the heir. Her name is Nora Star."

"What do you mean you found her? Where does she live? Did you speak with her?"

"Let me clarify. Jordan and I discovered her name on the Family Finder search website under his family name. I asked Harry to locate her. That's it for now."

"Couldn't be worse news," Bill grumped into her ear. "Keep me posted."

Maddie lost her zest for any outing with Jordan. Still, she had promised and she kept her promises. After changing sweaters and zipping the puffy jacket, she tugged on an ear warmer. Several more inches of snow had fallen overnight, so the views should be spectacular. A steaming cup of hot chocolate sounded like just the ticket for a drive up the mountain. She just might have time to grab one from the café.

She rode the elevator to the second floor and from the mezzanine spotted Jordan standing by the case that showed off the dazzling glass double star. In his snug-fitting jeans and ski jacket, he looked like a Wall Street trader, especially with his cell phone up to his ear.

She took the steps to the lobby, with Gretchen calling, "Hi there," and holding out a cup to Maddie.

She jetted over. "You're amazing. I was craving this before heading out in the cold."

"Jordan said you two are driving up the mountain." Gretchen stifled a yawn. "I know you like hot cocoa. He also mentioned you're a lawyer. May I ask you something?"

Maddie tried the soothing drink. "Sure, as long as it doesn't involve your employment here because I represent your boss."

"It's personal," Gretchen admitted shyly.

"Let me guess. You have a legal question?"

"Yeah. I skidded on an icy road and crashed my car into a tree."

"Oh no! Are you okay? You look a bit under the weather."

Gretchen rubbed her upper arms. "I didn't sleep last night. But that's another story. My accident happened a few weeks ago. These mountain roads can be treacherous, so beware. I was shaken up but not hurt. Wish I could say the same for my car."

From the corner of her eye, Maddie glimpsed Jordan heading her way. She honed in on Gretchen's problem.

"Is your insurance company dragging its feet paying for the damage?"

"How did you know?" Gretchen cried, her voice sounding like screechy brakes. "I had to pay for a rental. My car is totaled."

Jordan walked over, asking, "Ready? We should make haste as I have a meeting back here later with suppliers. I want to show you my stained-glass studio and some other places."

Maddie promised to meet him outside in a minute, so he headed out the front door.

She leaned over, and keeping her voice low, told Gretchen, "I'm not licensed to practice law in Vermont, but my boss is. Write down the details. I'll need your policy too."

Hot cocoa in hand, Maddie dashed outside to join Jordan in his car and placed the hot drink in the cup holder. She buckled the seat belt, telling Jordan in cryptic tones, "There's something I've been meaning to tell you."

"Has your investigator found Nora Star already?"

Maddie turned the heater knob to blow warm air on her feet. "It's about another star altogether. I have one exactly like yours in the lobby case."

"You're kidding me, right? They are extremely rare." He sounded baffled.

"So Gretchen told me. My grandfather gave me an identical star."

"That's amazing." Jordan's hands gripped the wheel and they started down the drive. "I was thinking maybe yours is a copy, but if your grandfather gave it to you, possibly Grandfather did make your star."

"There is one difference." Maddie snugged the ear warmer down over her ears. "My inner star is green where yours is red."

Jordan gave her a pleasant smile. "I have one like yours. I've been trying to purchase every one I can find. Grandfather made few of these double stars. Though he taught me to make cut glass, I've not tried anything as complex as his creations."

"I would like to keep mine, Jordan, if you don't mind. I have such wonderful memories visiting Starlight with my grandparents."

He picked up speed as they left the drive. "Of course you must keep your star. On this clear afternoon, the vista from Star Mountain will be breathtaking. You will think twice about ever returning to the city."

JORDAN DROVE MADDIE UP STAR MOUNTAIN, winding past rugged pine trees, their green branches dripping with globes of white fluffy snow. The stuff dreams were made of. Just when she wondered how much farther they would climb in this high place, thick woods opened to reveal an enormous chalet. It wasn't just any skier's retreat.

This one was made entirely of logs, and nestled in between chairlifts at the confluence of several ski slopes. Styled like those Maddie had seen in photos of mountain getaways in Austria, Base Trail Chalet had a special charm all its own.

More Austrian connections gave her pause. Before she could ask him, Jordan swung his legs from the car and pulled a box out of the trunk.

"The Galaxy Grill serves delightful food for our skiers," Jordan said, carrying the box. "Inside we offer a place for skiers to get warm and be refreshed, along with equipment rentals and sales for skiing, snowboarding, and tubing."

"You have enormous responsibility here," Maddie said, pointing to the collection of skies and snowboards resting against racks. "I think some adventurers are already inside taking a break from the cold."

"If you are here come summer, you can park your mountain bike where the skis are now," Jordan told her with a smile. "Come follow me. We'll go inside and see."

She trailed behind him on the shoveled walk. If only Maddie could break free from the confines of work. Her heart rate galloped along even thinking about slicing down the runs. Of course, it was a pipe dream.

Maddie stepped onto the deck beside Jordan. Her eyes traveled to a group of warmly dressed moms and dads sitting on a deck holding coffees or hot chocolates, watching over a gaggle of brightly colored preschoolers decked out in helmets and skis.

She chuckled. "Look, those little tikes are copying their teacher move for move."

Jordan laughed along with her. After each snowplow maneuver, the instructor waited for nearly half of the tikes to get up and get their skis back on. All the while parents shouted encouragement, "You can do it, Davie!" "Go for it, Emma!"

Maddie hadn't felt so alive in months.

"Jordan, thanks for bringing me here," she said softly. "You were right. The walls of my room were pressing in on me."

"Let me show you around the chalet." Jordan's face lit up as if reflecting the sun. "You toast your feet by the fire while I handle a few things."

"You are fortunate to be surrounded by such beauty."

"I am trying to take your advice and not miss the wonder."

"A lawyer cheers when her client says he is taking her advice," Maddie said.

Thrilled by the lively winter activities, she followed Jordan into the comfortable chalet where a blazing fire roared in the fireplace. He carried the box of paper towels on his shoulder, receiving not-so-covert glances from several young ladies sipping hot beverages at high tables.

Maddie suppressed an amused smile. Why was such a good-looking guy unattached? Jordan seemed friendly and kind, and he possessed an air of humbleness that kept him oblivious to his many admirers. Perhaps he'd had a breakup like Maddie. She wouldn't judge him.

Taking a seat at a high table, Maddie watched two skiers race toward the chalet, spraying snow as they skidded up to the ski rack. For a few moments, she shut her eyes, envisioning the freedom she'd felt when planting her feet into skis and sliding downhill, cold air biting her cheeks.

Work prevailed even now. Realizing she'd have time after winning this case to fly free as a bird down the slopes, she was content to watch skiers stomp snow off their boots and hurry inside to get warm.

Jordan returned holding two foam cups. "Madison, here's your hot chocolate."

"I'm Maddie, don't forget," she said, grinning happily. "Hot cocoa with whipped cream is my favorite. Thanks."

As she sipped the creamy concoction, a sudden memory popped into her mind, which she couldn't wait to share with Jordan. "I just remembered. I drank hot cocoa on this very spot as a kid with my parents and later during college breaks."

"Hey, you've sprouted a white mustache."

His robust laugh was infectious. Maddie found herself laughing out loud as she reached for a napkin. Jordan pulled one out for her.

"Did you go to college around here?"

"No, in Michigan. My roommate was from Vermont."

"It's possible I saw you back then," he said wistfully. "I skied here occasionally. Most of the time, I worked various jobs here on the mountain."

Maddie dabbed her lip, sudden compassion for Jordan springing into her heart. "I can't even imagine the hurt you experienced losing your parents and your grandmother."

"I don't deny it was the worst day of my life." Jordan lowered his eyes as if reliving the pain. "Grandfather was heartbroken too. As time went on, he cared for me and I looked after him. Pastor Fisher and his family made sure we weren't alone much that first year."

"Your grandfather is your heritage and you are his heir. Jordan, you are really succeeding here," Maddie said with feeling.

He cradled the cup of chocolate in both hands. "Since Bill's phone call about the new heir, I stay awake nights doubting I can make the kind of difference I'd hoped."

"That remains to be seen." Maddie reached over to press his hand. "Right now, I need a better understanding of your family."

Jordan's eyes latched onto Maddie's. "It's not complicated. Mom and Dad ran Starlight and activities on the mountain. Grandfather oversaw Edelweiss Lodge."

"Did your parents have close friends who might know about another heir?"

"Good question. None come to mind."

"Have you recalled anything else about Rosalyn?"

"A few things. Because she never married or had kids, Dad called Rosalyn 'an unclaimed blessing,' which annoyed her and my mom. Rosalyn loved to cook. Grandfather had Chef Dexter create a dish of cheese dumplings in her honor. It's still on the menu."

"It seems your grandfather would have known if Rosalyn adopted a child," Maddie said evenly.

"I agree," Jordan replied, his eyes darting around. "You looked through the file. I've scoured other papers in the office. Seems like I can't put off exploring the attic any longer."

"I sensed it might be hard for you, which is why I'll help. You may be surprised and find wonderful memories hidden away."

His face suddenly looked years younger. "You are the best, Madison Stone. I have been trying to wrap my arms around the idea that finding the heir is my sole responsibility. I have other burdens I'm not free to share with anyone."

Ah ha. Maddie was getting closer to what Jordan might be hiding. This wasn't the right time to probe what it was, not with guests hovering around them in the Galaxy Grill.

She finished her cocoa and told him something she should have said before. "Lawyers have a special privilege with their clients. Whatever you decide to tell me stays between you and me. No one else can ever know."

"I will bear it in mind." A look of discouragement passing over his features aged him again. "We should head back."

She didn't argue. Their frank conversation could only lead to her client opening up more in the coming days. A kernel of hope began to sprout as Maddie threw her foam cup in the trash.

She zipped her jacket before heading out in the cold. "On the drive back, I'd like to hear about your favorite place in Starlight."

"Maybe I can take you there sometime," he said.

Chapter 8

During their winding drive back to town, Maddie didn't let Jordan off the hook, asking again what he found most special in Starlight.

"You might guess the sunrises, ski slopes, or Edelweiss Lodge, and you'd be right. There are so many beautiful sights. In truth, it's the people."

"They have become your family," Maddie offered gently.

To keep their conversation on the lighter side, she shared one of her more humorous cases. "A jury once acquitted my client who was charged with fraud because the investors couldn't tell the difference between him and his brother. They were twins."

That drew a stout chuckle from Jordan. As they gained speed down the mountain road, he asked Maddie why she became a lawyer.

She turned slightly in her seat. "As a kid, I found myself sticking up for some unfortunate classmate or kid in the neighborhood. Then, one day, we became the unfortunate ones. Dad lost his farm."

"Maddie, what happened?" Jordan asked, his tone conveying empathy.

She tented her hands, her mind replaying the emotionally charged day.

"I was in the eighth grade. It's seared in my mind how crushed I was coming home from school and ready to start the Christmas holiday, only to find Mom in tears and Dad trying to console her. There was a loophole in the land contract: if he missed one payment, the land reverted back to the seller."

"That sounds rough for you. So you had to move?"

"We stayed with my grandparents for a season," Maddie said, a measure of relief filling her by just telling Jordan about it. "The following Christmas, we five traveled to Starlight. Here on this rugged mountain, a whole new world opened up to me. Skiing down the slopes, conquering the snow and wind, along with my fear of heights, I forgot the pain of the previous year. My grandfather gave me your grandfather's beautiful star that Christmas."

"Wow. I didn't realize how our lives are intersecting in such a powerful way."

Maddie rubbed her hands together. "Jordan, I just realized, your family helped me and my family. Now I have this chance to help you."

"Well said," Jordan said, his eyes on the road and hands gripping the wheel.

"So, I became a lawyer to stop the kind of injustice my parents experienced. Dad went on to acquire a larger farm, which he and Mom operate to this day. Well, except they're in Florida for a few months while their fruit trees hibernate."

"Good for them. I would enjoy seeing you in action."

"Then come to the January hearing." She adjusted her seat for a better view out the side window. "As executor of Maynard's will, it's appropriate for you to attend."

Darkness crept up, throwing shadows across the road as they returned to the lodge from their excursion up the mountain. Maddie spotted a flashy Mercedes out front.

"Look who's here!" she cried, pointing at a sign on the car's door. "Essential Oils, LLC."

"Do you know whose car that is?" Jordan snugged his car in tightly next to the Mercedes.

"No." Maddie released her belt with a snap. "But I want to meet her. I especially enjoy rubbing peppermint oil on the back of my neck after a hard-fought trial."

Jordan looked puzzled. "I thought you saw someone you knew."

"Never mind. It's a girl thing." Maddie waved her hand dismissively.

"Oh? Now you have snagged my interest."

"I didn't bring my essential oils for my skin, you know, so I wouldn't be hassled boarding my flight."

"She must be doing well, because she's driving one expensive car."

Jordan hopped out and came around to hold the door open for Maddie.

"Thanks for our great escape," she told him. "Our time on the mountain opened my mind to new possibilities. I hope it did for you."

They sauntered into the lobby together. Maddie felt a burst of heat from the blazing fireplace. She unzipped her jacket.

"Jordan, we need to meet and decide when we can search your attic."

He checked his watch. "Give me fifteen minutes. I'll squeeze in my meeting first. Enjoy your shopping."

Jordan headed for the stairs, whistling. He must have enjoyed their time talking. Maddie practically ran to the front desk. Gretchen had the phone receiver tucked against her ear, her shoulder raised. Only she wasn't talking.

"Gretchen," Maddie whispered, nodding toward the front window. "Do you know where the owner of the Mercedes is?"

Gretchen giggled, then mouthed, "In the Stix."

Maddie sailed into the café. A uniformed server stopped her. "Table for one?"

Maddie scanned the dining room, dismayed to see a lone man drinking coffee and reading his iPad.

"I'm looking for the lady driving the Mercedes out front," Maddie replied. "Is there an essential oils seminar going on?"

"No, ma'am. No lady's been in here for a while."

The man looked up from his tablet. "Can I help?"

"Maybe." Maddie walked closer before realizing her mistake. "You're the guy I mistook for the desk clerk when I checked in."

"Oh. You're the lawyer from Dewey, Cheatem, and How." He stood, and towering over her, said, "I heard you ask about my car. I'm obviously not a woman."

"Do I assume you're no gentleman either? That you use the 'essential oils' sign as a way to meet young ladies?"

The smile he flashed caught her off guard. He didn't sound the least bit offended when he replied, "I think you've made another wrong assumption."

"I suppose it's your wife's car."

He stepped toward her. "Now we are getting too familiar for not even knowing each other."

Maddie retreated a step. He wasn't done.

He held out his hand. "I'm Trevor Kirk and unmarried. Pleased to meet you, Ms., uh, you didn't tell me your name."

"I didn't." Maddie grasped his hand. "Madison Stone. Friends call me Maddie."

"We're not friends yet, but I hope to remedy that soon." Trevor pulled out a chair. "Can I buy you a coffee or hot chocolate, and tell you about my essential oil?"

She didn't miss his emphasis on the singular version of oil.

Maddie demurred. "Thanks. I'm late for a meeting."

"Maybe another time." Trevor's smile never wavered. "And Maddie, I don't sell essential oils. I'm a geological consultant and search for oil, among other minerals."

"How nice for you. I thought most oil was found in Oklahoma and Texas. Maybe there is some around Star Mountain too."

Maddie turned on her heel and left the café, zipping up her jacket as she strode through the lobby, ignoring Gretchen's question, "Did you find who you were looking for?"

Instead, Maddie grabbed a pen from a wire canister of pens and slipped out the front door. She hiked across the street, barely avoiding an oncoming car, and reaching the sidewalk, she snatched a tourist flyer from a display rack. While pretending an interest in various winter activities listed in the ads, Maddie had another purpose in mind. She stopped in the middle of the street to quickly write on the flyer the license number to the Mercedes.

Safely back inside, she spotted Trevor Kirk striding out of the café. Maddie hurried to the elevator to avoid him. She texted the license number to Harry Black, adding, *Need registration for this Mercedes and the scoop on owner. Possible buyer?*

Instead of entering the elevator, Maddie ran up the steps to Jordan's office, passing a man with a notebook in his hand. She rapped on the doorjamb. Her client looked up from stacks of papers spread around him on the conference table.

"Perfect timing," he said. "You just passed Gretchen's dad, my cheese supplier. He has a corner on the market because his goat farm is huge."

"I'm surprised Gretchen doesn't work for her dad."

Jordan's hazel eyes twinkled, looking almost as green as his sweater. "That's why I run this whole town. I saw Gretchen had more people skills than goat skills."

"You won't believe who I just met." Maddie heard her voice rising.

Jordan gestured for her to sit at the table. "Your beautician?"

"Beautician? They're called stylists now. That's okay. My paralegal Vanessa still calls them beauticians. Listen, I didn't buy any beauty products."

"She charged too much, just as I thought."

Maddie stuffed her hands in her jacket pockets. "The Mercedes driver is a guy and claims he's a geologist. That explains the essential 'oil,' as in crude oil."

"Oh great." Jordan's eyes bulged. "Another potential buyer sneaking around. I fear he is possibly connected to Nora, my missing relative."

"I'm already at work tracking down his habits and plans. Meanwhile, I'll be in my office." She blinked. "That is, my room."

"Maddie, want to grab dinner downstairs around six? We can catch up on the case and make plans to comb my attic and see my workshop, which we didn't have time for today."

"Cinnamon Stix at six," Maddie replied, ignoring the rhyme. "Just so it's not too late. I have hours of research ahead of me."

MADDIE HURRIED TO HER ROOM to conduct more investigation on her laptop. She'd found an interesting item when her cell phone rang. It was Vanessa.

"Were you just talking to Bill?" her paralegal wanted to know.

"Not recently, but you know how controlling he is. Duty calls night and day. I have to shut off my phone at night to keep it from constantly alerting and waking me up."

"Sorry to set you off. I thought Bill was on a call with you, so I asked to speak with you before he hung up. Guess I was wrong. I wanted you to know Cole can't wait to go tubing. He's all packed, though we don't leave for a while yet."

"Jordan and I have been keeping pretty busy."

"Okay, so Jordan owns the lodge and is paying for our upcoming stay, right?"

"Yes. He's amazing. He runs this entire place, and creates gorgeous stained-glass stars just like one my grandpa bought here years ago. He's a great skier, or so I've heard."

"He sounds special," Vanessa said. "But Maddie, your breakup with Stewart wasn't that long ago. Please be careful."

Maddie burst out laughing. "Vanessa, Jordan is my client. It's unethical for me to become involved with him."

"So you say. Does your heart know the rules?"

"No worries. I'll tell you, opposing Stewart on this case gives me startling insights into his true personality. I had no business opening my heart to him. I am a wiser Maddie Stone."

"I never trusted him after he stood you up for the firm's dinner." Vanessa's reply was swift, her tone sharp.

"I'd better run. Jordan is taking me to dinner soon to discuss my research."

Vanessa's sigh from hundreds of miles away echoed in Maddie's ear. "Listen to yourself. That's what I mean."

"It's strictly business, I promise. Jordan is too preoccupied trying to save his town and mountain to notice me."

When the conversation ended, Maddie focused on the U.S. Geological website on her screen.

Uh oh.

She bolted upright in the chair, her eyes widening in concern. What she found vexed her deeply.

Chapter 9

In a far corner of the Cinnamon Stix café, Maddie sat across from Jordan at a table where a candle glowed between them and she had a gorgeous view outside the window. The glittering lights strung through the trees gave the evening a wonderful glow.

With Vanessa's admonition to avoid becoming entangled with Jordan burning in Maddie's memory, she made sure to ask for a separate check when ordering her chicken dinner. She would never mislead the client sitting across from her, no matter how many candles burned brightly.

She forced her mind from the festive atmosphere to the business at hand, putting up a hardened barrier to any emotional lapses.

"Jordan, I may have found a reason why the 'new' heir is trying to stop us from finalizing the estate distribution." Though she spoke in hushed tones, Maddie used her most professional-sounding voice.

Just then, the server brought glasses of water, setting down a plate of fresh lemon wedges. Jordan squeezed in some of the lemons and tore the top from a packet of sugar, which he stirred into his glass.

"Presto, instant lemonade." He took a sip and smacked his lips. "I am all ears."

A group of noisy diners walked in, causing Maddie to change course.

"Let's wait until after we enjoy dinner. I feel like I'm running on empty."

Jordan nodded in agreement. "I don't often take time to eat a complete meal. It's usually coffee on the run along with a slice of chef's homemade apple bread."

"You should try relaxing with all this splendor around you."

"Maddie, I wish I had someone to enjoy it with."

Their meals came. Maddie's roasted chicken and asparagus looked delicious. She picked up a fork, and glimpsing Jordan's plate, stared in amazement. "What did you order?" She crinkled her nose. "It looks like a fried egg atop fried meat. Are those anchovies?"

Jordan's eyes drifted away from hers toward the window. His tone sounded wistful as he explained, "This is Grandfather's favorite Austrian dish. Chef Dexter always serves it for me on his birthday, which happens to be today. Aunt Rosalyn was also known for making this dish, or so Grandfather told me."

"I saw his birth date in the file," Maddie said, patting his hand with her free one, "and failed to make the connection. Time has a way of escaping my grip up here on the mountain."

"To Grandfather." Jordan lifted his glass of lemonade.

Maddie did likewise with her water glass. Through dinner, lawyer and client seemed more like old friends as they engaged in small talk, with Maddie sharing how much Vanessa and her son looked forward to visiting Starlight after Maddie had regaled them with her fun times spent here with her family.

"As a single mom, Vanessa doesn't have much for extras for Cole," she added. "I appreciate your offer to have them come in time for Christmas, especially with her brother serving in the Army's Special Forces in some secret part of Africa."

"When I heard he's on his third deployment overseas, I told Bill I would pay their way. What better way to thank my beautiful attorney."

Maddie's throat constricted and she coughed. He was veering into dangerous waters.

She held up a hand. "Hold it. Your agreement is with Bill."

After that, her gaze never left her food until they finished eating. Meanwhile, Jordan asked the server for a dessert menu.

"Please forgive me," he said, sounding earnest. "My comments are meant to thank you for changing your plans and coming to the rescue. To me, that's important."

"Let's quit talking about Vanessa and Cole's trip for now." Maddie adjusted the napkin on her lap. "We have bigger problems."

"I don't suppose we're any closer to finding the unknown heir."

Maddie shook her head. "Our firm is ramping up the search to find Nora."

Jordan closed the dessert menu. He withdrew a photo from inside his jacket pocket, which he handed to Maddie. She studied the photo of a much older man standing with his arm around the shoulder of the younger one.

"Is this you standing atop the mountain with Maynard? I hadn't seen his picture before now."

"Grandfather took me up the lift after my parents died. Pastor Fisher went along and snapped the picture. That's when Grandfather confided that as his only heir, I would inherit everything as far as my eyes could see. I was overwhelmed."

"I can only imagine it was unbelievable," Maddie said, reminding herself to be sympathetic but to also keep a safe distance.

"He asked me to promise to always keep the village and mountain the way things were. I gave him my solemn word I would honor his wishes. You implied earlier I am old-fashioned. You are right. My ways are his ways. Grandfather's values are deeply ingrained in me and that's unlikely to change."

"Maynard put pressure on you."

"You don't know the half of it, Maddie. His demands increased after my folks died."

"Are you saying there's more?" Maddie leaned back, perplexed. "Does it affect the estate?"

Jordan studied her face a moment. "I haven't wanted to discuss it with anyone."

"As my client, it's essential you tell me every relevant fact to my representing you. Otherwise, it's like you asking me to ski over moguls wearing a blindfold."

His eyes held hers, but he remained silent as if weighing what to tell her.

"Jordan, how does what you're hiding impact what we are doing here?"

"Ah ... I'm not sure."

Maddie's nostrils flared and she leaned closer to him. "I insist you tell me."

Tension sizzled between them. Jordan tapped a finger against his water glass. He then waved off the server who was hurrying over with a pitcher to refill their water.

"All right. Here goes," he said, his voice taut. "After my folks died, Grandfather extracted another promise from me. I wrestled for days whether to agree ..."

His words fell away.

Maddie urged him to go on, promising, "I'll keep an open mind."

The flickering candle cast a shadow over his face. He pressed his hands together, telling her, "Five years after his death, if I was not married and was not the father of an heir, Grandfather wanted me to donate the entire estate to the State of Vermont to establish a park, along with a trust to keep it running."

Maddie sat back in shock. She blinked back mounting resentment at his grandfather. How best to respond? It was possible Jordan was avoiding telling her about other family secrets.

She settled on asking, "Is there more I should know?"

"Not that comes to my mind."

She touched her mouth with her napkin. "Jordan, you have revealed a different side to your grandfather. He's trying to force you to marry and have a child."

Jordan bowed his head as if suddenly interested in the lone anchovy on his plate.

"Did you agree to his demand?" Maddie asked.

"Ye-es. I loved Grandfather and wanted to please him."

Maddie pushed out her bottom lip. "You do realize your promise has no legal consequence. You don't have to turn Starlight and Star Mountain into a state park."

"Maddie, it was his wish and I made the promise. I am a man of my word. That's the end of it. I'd rather donate than see this gorgeous place I call home turned into condos."

"So you're trying to beat the deadline." She pushed her plate away. "Dare I ask if you have found any prospective wives?"

Jordan crushed the napkin between his hands. "This is a small town. I've considered the few available single women. Gretchen works for me and besides, she's too young. Tourists pass through quickly, so there is no opportunity for a relationship."

Maddie had trouble processing Jordan's confession. It was like her mental computer was connected to a slow public Wi-Fi. Her heart, stunned by his admission, competed with her brain, which kept trying to assert logic into the equation.

"First things first," she began. "Do you realize if Nora Star is for real and she has a child, it would actually satisfy Maynard's desires?"

"That's a lot of ifs, don't you agree?"

Jordan's shoulders actually seemed to relax as he leaned in toward Maddie. "I have felt alone. Since you've entered my life, I realize a quality woman is out there for me to get to know. I am going to have to work at it."

Was he hinting she was the one for him?

Maddie exhaled. Words failed her for the first time in his company.

Jordan filled the awkward silence with a chuckle. "I am finally enjoying a woman's company and hope we do not solve this mystery too quickly."

The server setting their bills on the table provided Maddie with an exit opportunity. After signing for her meal, she rose to her feet with fresh determination.

"Jordan, I'm convinced we need to eliminate this imposter heir. You have too much on your plate already. I'll double my efforts, starting tomorrow."

"I want to help. When should we begin the search in my attic?" he asked, coming around the table to join her.

"Very soon. Let's talk in the morning and compare our schedules."

Maddie headed upstairs, her cheeks flushed. Her client had not only shared his promises and his need to find a wife, but he'd also managed to heap upon Maddie a new level of stress.

Though she might not know the perfect solution for rescuing Starlight, she'd learned one important thing at tonight's dinner. Vanessa had been quite right to warn her. Maddie must guard her heart above all things.

MADDIE SHUT THE DOOR to the room, her mind in a muddle. She'd savored her chicken until Jordan's thunderbolt about making a promise to his bully grandfather sandwiched in between his admission of enjoying her company.

Whew! What an evening!

Her ringing phone rattled her anew. Could it be that Vanessa already sensed what happened? Maddie dropped her eyes to the tiny screen. It was Harry calling.

"Sorry to bother you so late," her investigator said. "I have news on the license tag."

"You're the greatest. One second."

She swiped a pen and pad off the desk. "Go ahead, Harry."

He talked so rapidly Maddie had to put the phone on speaker so she could write.

"So Trevor Kirk is renting the Mercedes he's driving," she repeated. "And he listed on the rental agreement an address in Washington D.C."

"Correct."

"How did you find this out?"

"From the security division at the car rental firm," Harry said. "My source told me something else I find interesting."

"You have me curious." Maddie held the pen poised in the air.

"Trevor rented the car in the name of his company, Essential Oil, LLC."

Maddie didn't need to write this down. "I spotted that sign on the side of his Mercedes. I find it weird he put it on a rental."

"It's probably one of those magnetic ones," Harry suggested. "Oh, and so far, I found zilch on Trevor Kirk. No credit history, arrest, or otherwise. He's a regular Boy Scout."

Sounds of tapping on her door surprised Maddie. "Harry, hold on. Someone's at my door."

She put her eye to the security lens, and then opened the door with her finger held to her lips.

Gretchen smiled knowingly and handed Maddie an envelope, whispering, "My insurance info," before turning and leaving.

Maddie resumed her place at the desk. "Harry, I discovered something disturbing that I've yet to share with Jordan. Star Mountain and the surrounding area contain a treasure trove of rare earth elements, which are used in military weapon systems and by cell phone manufacturers. With his geological maps, Mr. Trevor Kirk is surely aware such valuable minerals are beneath where I am sitting now."

Harry's sharp whistle resounded in her ear.

"My sentiments exactly," she said. "We ratchet up our game. I need your help ascertaining what he's up to."

"Roger that, Ms. Stone. Will you inform Bill or should I?"

"Leave Bill to me. What have you uncovered about Nora in Austria?"

"My American contact at an Austrian security firm is retired State Department from our embassy in Vienna. He's having trouble finding anything about her. Can you narrow the orphanage down to a city or town in Austria?"

"I'll get working on that. Bye for now."

Maddie went hard at her Internet research well into the night. The full moon shone brightly, but attorney Madison Stone was on an important mission and paid no attention.

Chapter 10

A cold blast of wind blew down Maddie's neck the next morning as she hustled along the icy sidewalk in the village. She tightened her blue scarf to no avail.

"Jordan, it's freezing out here. Where are you taking me?"

"It is colder than predicted." He stomped his feet on the snow-dotted sidewalk. "We do not have much further. I promise this will warm us up."

He hiked forward quickly. Maddie lagged behind, not wanting to slip in her new boots.

"Wait up," she cried as Jordan dashed along. "You and I need to talk!"

A blast of recorded music bombarding her ears compelled her to look up. She saw the quaint church painted white, and it's steeple reaching upward seemed like a beacon of light against the gray sky. Jordan ran up the steps and pulled open the door.

Maddie caught a quick breath, intrigued by sounds of children's lilting voices. She hurried into the nave of the church. Feeling a blast of heat, Maddie loosened her scarf to strains of "Silent Night," a Christmas hymn she especially enjoyed.

Down front a group of twenty or so teens were singing beside a piano. Only no one was playing the instrument. They were singing along to pre-recorded music.

"Who are these kids?" she asked Jordan in hushed tones.

"They're from the church youth group and are rehearsing for their performance at the Starlight Christmas Festival."

The music crackled harshly before stopping abruptly. One of the teens ran over to check a speaker plug while another tested the system controls. Nothing seemed to work.

"It's over," a lanky girl pronounced. "The system's crashed again."

"Sorry. I asked our tech guy to fix this." Jordan stepped forward.

"Wait." Maddie stopped him. "Why should you be responsible?"

"Grandfather built the church. My father was the pastor prior to Pastor Fisher. I have tried to keep things afloat. My efforts seem to be lacking."

Without a word, Maddie slipped onto the piano bench, and running her fingers over the keys, soon found the right notes. The teens raised their voices in song: "Silent night, holy night, all is calm, all is bright ..."

When they finished, Maddie said, "Your harmony is lovely. Does anyone know the origins to the song you just sang so beautifully?"

"Not me," the lanky girl confessed, her hair twisted into a long braid. "Can you tell us?"

Maddie smiled. Her love for music made her heart sing. "The composer Franz Gruber taught school near Salzburg, Austria and played the organ. Joseph Mohr wrote the lyrics and asked Gruber to compose the melody. He did and 'Silent Night' was born. It was first played on Christmas Eve in Oberndorf, Austria."

"Was it very long ago?" the young girl wondered aloud.

"Yes." Maddie played a few chords from the song. "Two hundred years ago, in the year 1818, villagers came to celebrate Christmas Eve in a small church like this one. They heard the Christmas carol for the first time and it became instantly popular. It's been played for kings and rulers around the world."

"And now we get to perform it for our parents and friends right here in Vermont," a freckled boy said, turning a page in his music book. "Do you know our next song?"

"Not without the musical score," Maddie apologized.

He stepped forward. "It's called, 'Do You Hear what I Hear?'"

"Yes, I know it." Maddie looked up at Jordan, who had joined them by the piano. "Do we have the time?"

"Absolutely." His wide smile suggested he was in no hurry to leave her company.

Maddie took the music offered by the boy and began playing the soaring notes. Majestic words filled her mind as the choir sang, "The child, the child, sleeping in the night. He will bring us goodness and light ..."

Jordan applauded at the end. Maddie envisioned a look of approval in his eyes.

Her moment of gladness was interrupted when the boy asked, "Miss, if I give you the music, will you play for us in the festival? You're far better than the crummy sound system."

She hesitated, unsure if she'd still be in Starlight then. Not wanting to disappoint the kids, she offered, "I'm in town for business so let me see. Hopefully, Mr. Star will repair the system in time."

As she headed for the exit, Jordan caught up to her.

"Maddie, can you see how well you fit in here in Starlight?" he asked.

She had to wonder if with this impromptu church concert, Jordan was trying to manipulate her feelings. She kept silent, her mind reflecting on why she was sent here to Starlight.

Of course, as Jordan's lawyer, she would do all she could to achieve victory for him in court. Her quandary ran much deeper. Was Maddie supposed to save Starlight? Or was Starlight supposed to save her?

AFTER JORDAN CLOSED THE CHURCH DOOR TIGHTLY, Maddie walked down the church steps, winter winds buffeting her.

Maddie nestled the scarf to her neck and wasted no time asking him, "Can we meet in your office? As I said yesterday, I have something important to tell you."

His countenance fell. "I've been fearing this moment. You found Nora Star."

Lacy snowflakes began swirling around them, drifting down as if from a giant shaker of powdered sugar. Maddie wanted to move the case forward, but not out here in the cold.

"Jordan, I haven't found her. We should discuss my concerns in private."

"Your concerns, what are they?" Jordan asked, tugging on her hand.

Maddie's feet skidded, and she nearly lost her footing. He steadied her with his strong arm. She snatched away her hand and began walking as fast as she could manage. The recent developments and worry for Jordan's future were creating strain behind her neck and eyes.

She needed to relax. Her thoughts drifted to her parents soaking up the forever sun in Florida, which is where she might fly the moment she wrapped up this case with a pretty Christmas bow.

They reached the Edelweiss Lodge. Maddie happily rushed into the warmth, with Jordan right behind her. Gretchen waved him over, so Maddie took time to clean off her boots on the large all-weather rug. She mulled over her strategy for their conference.

One thing would help.

"I'm ordering hot cocoa from the Stix," she told him as she headed for the café. "Meet you upstairs."

She also brought a coffee for Jordan, who was already behind his desk checking his phone for messages. He set his cell aside at her urging, and they both took their usual places at the conference table.

"To be frank, I find the lack of progress thus far frustrating," she said.

Jordan fidgeted with his cell phone, telling her, "Me too."

These two words unleashed Maddie, and she didn't hold back, peppering him with questions.

"Have you met with any mining representatives lately? How many offers have you received from mining companies to buy your land?" she lobbed from across the table.

"None and none," he promptly replied. "Why?"

"I learned something troubling last night before our dinner and didn't want to broach the subject in the café. When Mr. Kirk said he was a geological consultant, I figured he came here from Texas to ski. After dinner, I examined the

U.S. Geological Survey. There are valuable minerals beneath us, sitting inside of Star Mountain."

Jordan acted unconcerned. "I have heard such rumors for years. Don't I, as owner of the mountain, also own the minerals?"

"I should think so," Maddie snapped, and then admitted she hadn't checked the deed. "I'll rectify that immediately. From what I learned overnight, these minerals are not only rare, they're essential for many electronic devices, including for the military."

"A Colorado geological firm showed up snooping around a few months back. Do you think your Trevor Kirk is working for those Denver people?"

"For one thing, he isn't our Mr. Kirk. He isn't working for us. I doubt he's consulting for the Colorado firm because I found out the rental car he's driving is from Washington D.C."

"What else should we be doing to protect these properties?"

At this juncture, Maddie felt uneasy speculating.

"Jordan, I'm no mining expert. I spoke to my boss this morning to fill him in. We both realize these folks have grander ideas than developers who want to build condos. Mining for minerals is a huge undertaking, requiring masses of people and equipment to extract them. China leads the way in developing and, in fact, controls most of the world's rare earth elements."

He shook his head fiercely. "Ugh. My mind is conjuring up horrible pictures of strip mining from the past."

"This kind of mining can destroy the environment," Maddie agreed. "Leveling Star Mountain might be their goal. I don't know if this new heir is part of such a scheme, but I assure you, I intend to find out. First, scouring your family records is a priority."

Jordan dropped his phone on the table with a thud. "Seriously, I've been so concerned with fighting off developers who want to change the outside of the mountain, I never gave one thought to the inside. And I admit, I put you off looking through stacks of family stuff."

Maddie fixed a sincere gaze upon him. "Your going it alone ends now. You have me to help you."

"I can't express what your being here means to me," he said, meeting her gaze. "First, I'd like to clean a bit, you know, and check for furry creatures nesting up there for the winter. I promise to get back to you soon."

"All right. It's possible there's nothing of any consequence in your attic anyway. I need to start thinking outside the box."

Jordan drained his coffee and said with grit in his voice, "Maddie, I have no interest in extracting one pebble of gold or other rare minerals."

"Just as I thought," Maddie replied, deciding to propose another strategy. "You could defeat the new heir by drawing up a trust document now and see if the judge will permit you granting the land to Vermont for a state park."

Jordan pressed his lips into a tight line. "I agree with Grandfather. The mountain's value is its spectacular beauty, and how it enriches the people who spend time in the green forests, well, that aren't so green now. Maddie, you need to help me keep my promise to Grandfather."

Maddie blinked back unbelief. Did he mean what she thought?

"Jordan, enlighten me. Which promise do you mean? What are you saying?"

"Ah … I see your dilemma. I refer to my promise to retain the mountain as it has always been, without giving it to the state. Will you assist me in this?"

"You can count on me," she vowed, her fears allayed that he implied nothing more.

Their conversation helped Maddie to know beyond a sliver of doubt that Jordan could never be anything more to her than a client.

Chapter 11

Maddie spent a restless night, her mind churning over Starlight being razed to the ground to make way for progress. Purple shadows lurking beneath her eyes come morning gave witness to her lack of sleep. Stifling a yawn, she styled her hair, dabbed on concealer, and trudged down to the Stix for plenty of coffee before heading to the county courthouse to review newly recorded mineral leases.

Many yawns and two hours later, she spotted Jordan's text. *Attic search is at one. Meet me at the farmhouse.*

She entered the address into her phone, shoved her notepad into her briefcase, and drove back to the lodge hopeful that good news was about to come her way.

Gretchen immediately beckoned her with a cheery, "Good morning."

Her feet feeling heavy like she had on ankle weights, Maddie ambled over.

"Did you hear from your insurance company?" she asked, stifling another yawn.

"Yes!" Gretchen squealed, her long blond hair fluttering over her shoulder. "They phoned yesterday saying how you sent them a letter. Guess what? They aren't going to total my car but will be fixing it."

Maddie clapped her hands together. A burst of adrenaline coursed through her veins. "Justice triumphs and I am thrilled for you."

"How can I thank you? What do I owe you?" Gretchen gushed.

"Nothing," Maddie replied with certainty. "It didn't take me long to dictate the letter to Vanessa, my paralegal, who by the way is coming up here with her son before Christmas."

"I've entered a reservation for them in the system. But are you sure, Maddie? I mean, you have totally saved me. I won't forget it."

Maddie made a dismissive gesture with her hand. "I was glad to point out key provisions in your auto policy. Besides, we work for Mr. Star and you work for him."

"I did hear something you might be interested in." Gretchen dropped her voice to a whisper.

"Oh?"

Maddie wondered if Jordan might have mentioned Nora Star to Gretchen. That was his choice to make, but as his attorney, Maddie would never divulge client secrets. So she waited while Gretchen answered the phone, briefly putting the caller on hold.

"I have to make this new reservation," Gretchen told Maddie. "Quickly, I heard a rumor that some other family member wants to buy the resort."

Maddie shrugged off the unfounded gossip. "Rumors are often far different than facts."

"My friend's a realtor. She knows everybody's business around here." Gretchen spoke in hushed tones while cradling the receiver. "Her new client hinted she's related to the Star family and is looking to buy a farm with acreage near Star Mountain."

"I find that interesting. Please have your friend call me."

Maddie dug into her purse and withdrew a business card. She handed it to Gretchen, being careful not to reveal anything about Nora. Gretchen returned to the caller and Maddie went into the café for a much-needed breakfast. She'd just finished her orange juice and was awaiting coffee and an omelet when a middle-aged woman dressed in slacks and a burgundy blazer rushed toward her, holding something in her hand.

"Excuse me. Do I assume correctly you are Madison Stone?"

Maddie remained seated. "Yes, ma'am."

The lady gave Maddie her business card with great fanfare. "I'm Linda Logan, the realtor friend Gretchen told you about. She just phoned me. Since my office is a few doors down, I didn't mind running over to introduce myself."

Maddie glanced at her card. She pointed to the empty chair at her table. "I've just ordered breakfast. Please join me."

"I don't want to intrude. You can call me at a more opportune time."

"Now is convenient." Maddie pointed again.

Linda beamed at Maddie and scurried to her seat. "Starlight's a small town where it's hard to keep anything a secret."

Maddie's eyebrows lifted, yet her lips surrendered nothing.

Linda dropped a napkin into her lap and ordered coffee when the server brought Maddie's cup. "Gretchen informed you of my out-of-towner wanting to buy acreage near the mountain."

"Yes, she did. I don't understand its relevance to me." Maddie put both hands around her cup.

"While I often hear from big city folks looking to buy near here, this woman made it sound like she's part of the Star family."

"And do you believe she is?"

"I don't know because I have not met her. She phoned me late yesterday to ask about property near Starlight."

"Word sure travels fast around here," Maddie quipped, taking a long sip of the hot java before setting down her cup. "Do you have her name and contact info?"

Linda shoved on a pair of purple reading glasses and quickly scrolled through her phone. "At first I thought nothing of this. Then the lady said she'd just found out her grandfather built Starlight."

"Oh? And what is her name?" Maddie pointed at Linda's phone, not wanting to overreact to this remarkable news.

"Jeanette Carpenter. I also have her phone number."

"And she claims to be a member of the Star family?" Maddie probed.

"It's odd." Linda narrowed her eyes behind the purple glasses. "I asked if her grandfather was Maynard Star and she's not sure. She's adopted and is doing a family search.

Jeanette doesn't know her parents' names and relies on anecdotal information from deceased adoptive parents."

"Do you believe her?" Maddie asked, conjuring up a picture of Jeannette seeing the probate notice in the papers and desperate to wiggle into the Star family fortune.

As Linda removed her glasses, her brow creased. "I don't think Jordan has any living relatives. I sent Jeanette descriptions of several properties and haven't heard back."

"Has she been to Starlight?"

"No. She seemed uninformed. I was surprised she'd want to buy a farmhouse with acreage. Jeannette insisted on that. And she wants to live near Star Mountain."

Maddie smiled knowingly. "She sounds eager. Try sending her more listings."

"You think?" Linda answered. "Maybe I should let you know what I learn?"

Maddie nodded, holding up Linda's card. "You understand me perfectly. Let's stay in touch."

AN HOUR LATER, Maddie roared down the road in her SUV, heading full throttle for the Star homestead. News of Jeanette's imminent appearance to claim her share of the inheritance gave Maddie all the impetus she needed to search Jordan's family papers no matter how many mice might be scurrying around them in the attic.

Four tires crunched on the snow. Maddie hit the brakes hard and the pedal pulsated against her foot. She slid until coming to rest at the end of Jordan's drive. Maddie jammed the car into park and hopped out, notebook in hand and cell phone crammed in her back pocket. She'd use either one to photograph important evidence and email it to her boss.

The farmhouse, with its spacious front yard, was built at the end of a dead-end street. Jordan had no drive-by traffic. The rear yard, with its steep ascent up toward the high mountain, gave Maddie no doubts such a remote location added to his isolated life. He lived by himself in a huge home while longing for a wife and family.

She climbed the front steps ready to take command of this situation and find answers. For unknown reasons,

Maynard had built a supersized house for two children. Maddie stopped for the briefest moment, a sudden thought erupting.

Were there other children beside Rosalyn who left home at an early age? Could he or she be one of Jeanette's birth parents?

Questions swirling around her like heavy falling snow, Maddie lifted a hand to bang on the door when she noticed a sticky note on the door's window. She tugged it down and read Jordan's note: *Come in. I may be on the phone.*

"A cell phone is going to become attached to his ear," Maddie grumbled as she pushed open the door.

Her eyes swept over the bright front porch with its big windows and comfy-looking wicker furniture. All of her urgency came to a screeching halt at the sight of various framed photographs. Maddie leaned over, snapping a picture of each with her cell phone camera.

Hearing Jordan's voice in the distance, she hurried through the entry door and hallway, walking into a spacious living area. The old-fashioned upholstered chairs and sofas surprised Maddie, but not the enormous windows with a spectacular view. In this house, just as in the Edelweiss Lodge, Star Mountain was Jordan's constant companion.

Windows running the length of the formal dining room let in lots of light. It wasn't hard for her to picture her own grandparents sitting around the large mahogany dining room table, sipping tea and eating apple strudel with Maynard Star.

Jordan's voice drew her down the center hallway. She saw him talking on the phone in his home office. Books and papers were spread on the coffee table.

He covered the phone receiver with his hand, mouthing, "There's coffee and Danish in the kitchen."

Maddie strode into the kitchen and stopped in amazement.

"That hefty white mixer and silver toaster oven look just like my grandma's," she said, suddenly cheered.

Transported back in time to her grandparent's home in Michigan, the memories were sweet. Then glimpsing the cinnamon apple coffee cake, she realized how hungry she was thanks to Linda Logan. Her startling revelation of another Star family heir roaming around town had ruined Maddie's appetite.

With no qualms about giving into temptation, she poured herself a fresh cup of coffee and sliced a piece of coffee cake. She took her goodies into the library and had barely taken a seat when Jordan appeared, coffee mug in hand.

"Sorry, I just concluded a conference call with a hospitality committee and have a follow-up call at three this afternoon."

Maddie lifted her cup in the air. "You prepared nicely for my arrival. Your décor reminds me of my grandma's house."

"It does need a lady's touch. Can you tell I'm not here much?"

"I suspect you live most of your life at the lodge. Is it because there's no woman here to bring her flair to the house?" Maddie's cheeks flushed warm even asking this. "Now I'm sorry. I have no right to pry into your personal life."

Jordan made a sweeping motion with his arm. "It's as functional for me as it was for my folks. I am comfortable here and do not shun ladies. I haven't met the one who has captured my heart."

He looked around the room, horror spreading across his face. "Based on your observation, my home is like your grandmother's, so if I do meet such a woman, I better not bring her here."

"Jordan, I didn't mean to make you apologize for your home. Like you, I'm single and if you came to my apartment, you might find it uninviting."

"So you find my house uninviting?" Jordan asked, sporting a crooked grin.

Maddie opened her mouth to speak, but Jordan interjected, "Let me warm up my coffee. We should head to the attic. Leave your coat on as there's no heat up there."

"Good thing I wore my heaviest coat," Maddie replied.

She followed him to the kitchen where he refilled their coffee, telling Maddie,

"I hope you have time to meet Trooper."

Looking around, Maddie replied, "I don't see his dog food or any evidence of Trooper in your house."

"Oh yeah." Jordan's eyes sparkled. "Trooper stays in the barn. He's not housebroken."

"Poor Trooper."

"He's fine out there, believe me."

Maddie could only sigh. Jordan swung open a door at the rear of the house that led upstairs. He snapped on the light and ducked his head going up the uncarpeted stairway to the attic. Maddie was hot on his heels, ready to bust this case wide open.

True to Jordan's prediction, she found the air much cooler as she reached the top floor. A lit ceiling bulb revealed antique furniture, boxes of all sizes, and several steamer trunks.

Maddie took it all in. "It's tidier than most attics I've seen. You don't have any cobwebs or squirrels rummaging around."

"I wielded a broom up here yesterday." Jordan pointed to a brown steamer trunk with decals on the side. "I saw my grandmother store her mementos in this one."

"Great. We start with the trunk you remember and will look for old letters or photo albums."

Maddie grunted as she lifted an old portable Victrola from atop his grandmother's trunk. She opened it and squealed.

"Eureka! This could be a bonanza."

Jordan peered inside, drawing his head near Maddie's. "You found something already?"

Maddie carefully lifted out a bundle of envelopes secured with a ribbon. She turned the packet over and spied an important clue.

"Jordan, look. The return address is Rumphrey, Austria. These are Rosalyn's letters to your grandparents and may help us discern if that's where she began the orphanage."

She handed these to Jordan before taking out three large photo albums. "Here's more of your family history."

Jordan set down the letters to clap his shoulders with his hands. "Brrr. I vote for taking these downstairs and reading them in the warmth of the living room."

Maddie's lowering of the trunk lid set off flecks of dust rising in the air. She sneezed.

"You have another conference call to make. I could take these back with me and peruse them in my room."

"Good idea." Jordan headed for the stairs.

It wasn't hard for her to recognize he wanted to escape the family memories. He'd voiced no objection to Maddie reviewing everything herself.

Downstairs, Jordan stowed the mementos inside a large canvas bag, telling her, "I need time to lock up. Thanks for your interest in me and my case."

"Let's hope I find the evidence we need in here," Maddie said, lifting up the bag.

She said good-bye and left the house. When she started the car and turned up the heat, she sneezed. Coming down with a cold was surely not on her to-do list.

Maddie revved the engine, the stockpile from Jordan's attic safely on the seat next to her. Before blasting off for the Edelweiss, she fired off a message to Harry:

Concentrate your search Rumphrey, Austria. Will advise if I find new info.

AFTER COMBING THROUGH the photo albums into late that evening, Maddie slid a few photos inside her purse to show Jordan tomorrow. She rubbed her tired eyes. A walk was what she needed to clear her head. She threw on her coat and slung her purse over her shoulder.

She picked her way along the shoveled sidewalk beneath a blanket of glittering stars. The village church bathed in bright lights beckoned her and surprisingly, the door wasn't locked. Perhaps unlocked doors were commonplace here on the mountain. She slipped inside.

A river of peace flowed through her spirit, unlike anything she'd known before in her life. Worries over the Star estate fell away. In subdued light from outside, the still piano drew her like a magnet and in moments, Maddie's fingers pranced over the keys as she played a musical score from Handel's *Messiah*.

Her fingers touched the last soaring notes, when the light coming in through the stained-glass window drew her closer. Maddie stopped before the image of shepherds rushing to worship the newborn baby king. Her coming here tonight stirred her soul to think of that first Christmas thousands of years ago. Thoughts of her future came unbidden, unwanted.

Was she becoming too caught up in her emotions to do a proper job on the case?

Her musings were interrupted by sounds of the door creaking open. She whirled around to see Jordan.

"I ... ah ... spotted your car out front," he said slowly. "Do you mind company?"

"I should head out. Work awaits, you know," she said with a nervous laugh.

"This won't take long."

"Oh? It can't wait until morning?"

"No, Maddie, it cannot."

He stepped toward her and clasped her hands into his.

"I feel so positive about your being in Starlight. It's as if you have brought a bright light all on your own."

Maddie sensed he was leaning in too close, like he wanted to kiss her. She drew her hands back abruptly and stood tall. This was the moment to put things in their proper place.

She looked up into his eyes. "Jordan, please. You are my client, and I have an ethical obligation to represent you. Your feelings for me can have no role in my assignment here in Starlight. I hope you understand and can accept my decision."

His face flinched and he ran a hand through his thick hair. "I'm sorry for overstepping the bounds. My case won't last forever, you know."

Jordan dropped his hands and turning to leave, he said, "I do want to win this and don't mean to distract you. But I remain convinced, Madison Stone, that you are a guardian angel sent from God to protect me, Starlight village, and Star Mountain."

She reached for Jordan's hand, sensing they needed to part on a lighter note.

"Join me a moment by the piano. I want to show you something."

Once they were seated on the piano bench, she snapped on the light and pulled a small photo with a gilded border from her shoulder purse.

"I've started going through the letters and photo album."

"Did you find anything to disprove Nora's claims?" he asked, sounding hopeful.

Maddie playfully tapped his shoulder. "I didn't find any relatives, but I did stumble across evidence of you and an early romantic interest."

Jordan snatched the photo from her hand and held it up near the light.

"What is this?"

She pointed with glee to a boy of about ten or twelve being kissed on the cheek by a girl of the same age. "To me, this looks like a birthday party, and a picture of you in younger years."

"That is me, and it's taken at the farmhouse. Who is this girl?"

"I thought you would know. She seems affectionate, at least toward you."

Jordan flipped the picture over. There was nothing written, so he flipped it back again under the light, squinting his eyes.

"She is cute," he said. "I wonder if this is Sandra Burton."

Maddie reached up and shut off the piano light. "Keep the picture and ask around town who she is. Maybe she's still available."

"Sandra is the librarian. And Maddie, you know what? She is single."

A smile leapt to her face. "This is a night filled with hope. Join me for dessert at the Stix."

As they stepped out into the frosty air, Maddie didn't have the heart to make her own confession. Jordan would be crushed to learn about Jeanette Carpenter, another possible heir.

Chapter 12

Saturday morning the phone ringing woke Maddie with a start. Her pulse racing, she fumbled for her cell phone and answered before thinking.

"I'm flying up to Vermont," a stern voice bellowed in her ear.

It took Maddie some seconds to realize it was her boss.

"Why?" she managed. "Has something happened I don't know about?"

"We need to wrap up this case. Last night, I happened to see Judge Marks at a D.C. holiday party—"

"You didn't talk about the Star case," Maddie interrupted breathlessly.

She shot straight up in bed.

"Of course not," Bill replied, his voice aggravated. "But I got the distinct impression he is unhappy."

Maddie set her feet on the floor, drawing the blanket around her pajamas. "Truth be told, I had the same impression in his courtroom. His bluster is who he is and shouldn't concern us."

"You may be right," Bill said as if climbing down from his high horse. "Why not fill me in and I'll decide what else we need to do."

Rapid-fire, she explained how she'd checked recorded mineral leases, reviewed Jordan's family papers, and about Harry's investigation into the Austrian orphanage. "We've narrowed it down to the city of Rumphrey. I'm sure Harry is hard at work while we speak."

"All right. Sorry to call so early. I couldn't sleep and got to thinking there is something I am missing. Probably too much eggnog and prime rib."

After promising to keep him informed, she ended the call and went to look out the window. The sun's rays were quietly peeking above the horizon. A short walk at dawn might help her to process Bill's harebrained notion to fly up and confer with her.

More like taking over, Maddie thought as she bundled up in her warmest clothes and slipped out of the lodge before she'd so much as sniffed a cup of coffee.

Tranquility she found, except for a few early birds twittering on bare branches laden with sparkling lights. Such eerie stillness intensified her worry.

Someone must have given Bill the wrong idea that she wasn't handling matters satisfactorily. Had Judge Marks criticized her appearance before him in court?

She strolled through the village, and reaching the street's end, Maddie gazed upward, reveling in the rising sun's rays burning off a blue mist that enshrouded Star Mountain. Her spirited conversation with her boss flitted through her mind. The more she thought about it, the more she realized Bill was just being Bill. He always wanted closure and wanted it yesterday.

The problem now was tracking down Nora Star. The court's clock was ticking, and in a few weeks Maddie would again oppose Stewart before Judge Marks. Nora was most likely Stewart's client, the heir he'd refused to identify in court.

Returning from her walk, Maddie entered the Edelweiss lobby to noisy sounds of a vacuum cleaner. She wandered toward the elevators and passed Gretchen, who was cleaning area rugs. Gretchen immediately shut off the vacuum and rushed over.

"Maddie, can we talk for a minute?"

She agreed, thinking Gretchen had more car trouble. They stepped into a small office behind the front desk with the desk clerk hovering in the doorway to keep an eye on the lobby.

"You helped with my insurance company," Gretchen said briskly. "I want to return the favor."

"There's no need," Maddie insisted.

After a glance over her shoulder at guests mingling in the lobby, Gretchen lowered her voice a notch. Maddie strained to hear above the rowdy conversations beyond the doorway.

Gretchen pocketed her hands, looking tense. "Since Trevor Kirk appeared in the village, several young women seem to be competing for his attention."

"Okay." Maddie waited to find out what was behind this clandestine meeting.

"I've seen him talking to you. He's friendlier toward you than any others, so I want to caution you."

Maddie's curiosity got the better of her growing impatience. "About what? Please tell me."

"I think he has a girlfriend, and I don't want him misleading you."

Maddie howled in laughter. "You think I'm at risk of being led astray by Trevor Kirk?"

Gretchen paused long enough for a guest to take a brochure off the front desk and saunter away. Despite Maddie not wanting to listen to gossip, she did anyway as Gretchen resumed her tale.

"Don't you find Trevor good-looking?" Gretchen's voice lightly trilled. "If you are available, Maddie, I'm not sure he is."

Maddie touched Gretchen's forearm. "Thanks for your concern. I assure you there's zero chance of anything besides business for me in this town."

Just saying so, Maddie reminded herself it was true. She turned to leave when a question penetrated her heart, which her mind promptly batted away like some annoying mosquito.

Gretchen wasn't about to let Maddie slip away so easily. "Maddie, you do have at least one man interested in you. Jordan Star."

"No, you have that wrong." Maddie waved off the suggestion. "Okay, you hooked me. Tell me how you know Trevor is involved elsewhere."

Gretchen stepped backward to check the lobby before confiding, "My sister is a flight attendant. Recently, when Iris was working a flight from Washington's Reagan airport to LA, Trevor boarded her flight."

"So?"

"So, he was with a pretty blond woman. They sat in adjoining seats."

"That could be a coincidence." Maddie had heard enough.

"He was chatting real friendly-like with her. Iris said the lady's hair was even lighter than my blond hair, something like winter wheat."

"And if the lady was his sister, then what?" Maddie asked, shifting into cross-examining mode.

"Aha, you have me there." Gretchen's hands flew to her cheeks. "On second thought, I don't think so. My sis is savvy from her world travels. Iris said Trevor looked very comfortable with this lady. He even bought a snack, which she shared. Iris put the bug in my ear to steer clear of him. I now share her warning with you."

"Did your sister recognize Trevor because he previously asked her out?"

Gretchen crinkled her nose. "No way. Iris was home when Trevor came to speak with my father about our farm."

"I see," Maddie replied calmly, not letting it slip how this new intelligence unsettled her. "Has your father helped Trevor in some way?"

"Trevor came over to see Grandma Parker."

"Who is Grandma Parker?" Maddie probed. "Why should Trevor talk with her?"

Maddie's questions evoked a winning smile from Gretchen.

"Why, she's my gramma, of course. She owns our house and all the land. Someday, my dad will inherit the farm. That's why she lives with us. Trevor talked about mineral rights."

"For your grandmother's property?"

"That was his intention, but Mayor Parker told him about every other property around the mountain."

Maddie's mind began to spin. What else didn't she know about this village and its people?

She held up her hands in bewilderment. "Help me sort this out. Is your grandmother also the Mayor of Starlight?"

"She's not, but everybody calls her Mayor Parker because she acts like she is. Gramma knew Jordan's grandfather, Maynard Star."

Maddie reached into her purse for her pad. She flipped it open and scanned through the list of properties from her courthouse research. "Your grandmother must be Opal Parker. She still controls her mineral rights."

"That's Gramma. But, Maddie, I know zip about her land rights."

Maddie snapped her notebook shut. "I'm trying to help the Star estate. Will your grandmother agree to meet with me?"

"Sure she will. Starlight is and has always been her home."

Gretchen wrote Gramma's number on a business card, which Maddie slid into her pocket. She would phone her upstairs.

"You've given me a warning and an update," Maddie said. "You and I are even."

As she headed for the elevator, she heard the phone ring.

"Hi, Mom," Gretchen said cheerily. "When can I bring a friend for dinner? It has to be a night when Gramma's home."

Maddie stepped onto the elevator to Gretchen promising her mom, "Nope, it's not a guy. You'll see."

As Maddie inserted the key card to her room, the phone inside rang. She hastened inside to grab the phone, and out of breath, she gushed, "This is Maddie."

"It's Gretchen. You won't believe it. Mom's invited you for dinner day after tomorrow. Gramma is fixing her special Vermont maple and apple cider chicken."

"I would love to meet your family. How about if I bring dessert from the café?"

"Gramma loves pumpkin pie."

"Pumpkin it is. Your grandmother sounds like quite a character."

"Wait until you meet her." Gretchen launched into fits of giggling.

Maddie put down the receiver, studying the towering mountain out her window. Gretchen's warning already served one key purpose. It had given Maddie new zest to unmask

Trevor Kirk and his nefarious search for mineral rights in Starlight village.

Chapter 13

Saturday and Sunday passed with no important developments. Maddie's sense of community was strengthened at church where she met some parents of the teens she had played for. The letters and albums from Jordan's steamer trunk provided her with no fruit. Worse, text messages back and forth with Harry yielded nothing of consequence in Austria.

The rhythm of working from the lodge and living among the mountain villagers began to waken Maddie's heart anew. Tonight she would meet Gretchen's family and wanted to look her best.

So on this bright and frosty Monday morn, she left to scope out the early-bird specials at Michele's Boutique. Gretchen knew all about Michele opening her doors after sunrise for tourists vacationing in Starlight before Christmas.

Maddie stepped into a wonderland of twinkle lights draped along the ceiling and among various banners, which carried uplifting messages. She admired one that read *Dream Big*, realizing her sterile law office needed some inspiring touches. Her eyes then glimpsed another sign urging her to *Dip the day in sparkle.*

Hope surged within Maddie. She quickly struck up a conversation with the friendly owner, an elegant lady with pretty, long blond hair and brown eyes shining with kindness. She greeted Maddie with a cup of warm apple cider.

"Welcome to Starlight, Ms. Stone. I am Michele and happy you are joining us this fine morning."

"How do you know my name?" Maddie held the cider and wondered.

"My niece told me all about you," Michele laughingly replied. "She is thrilled to sing in the teen choir at the festival, and says you'll be playing the piano for them."

Maddie pushed back gently. "If I remain in town that long. I don't want the kids getting their hopes dashed. I do need your help in finding new winter clothing."

"We Starlighters keep our hopes high, even when winter storms fly. It's in our nature," Michele said, her words and tone telegraphing strength.

"Please call me Maddie," she said, with an idea Michele might be alluding to the court case.

Talking about Jordan's private business to the villagers was something Maddie would sidestep. She decided to change the subject by pointing to a stenciled sign: A friend is a gift from God's heart.

"Is that for sale?" she asked.

Michele made a sweeping motion with both hands. "Everything you see in this shop is for sale."

"It's for my friend Vanessa who is coming to visit."

Michele set the gift aside at the checkout counter. "With your chestnut hair and brown eyes, colorful Austrian vests and sweaters will give you sparkle and shine. So will our star-shaped jewelry. Be sure to wear your vibrant selections and take your friend ice skating by the Starlight Christmas tree."

"I saw the tree going up in the square. I hadn't heard there's ice skating."

"Then you didn't see it this morning," Michele declared. "The lights are on and the ice is ready!"

With that, the two women hunkered down to doing some serious shopping and getting to know each other. Maddie left the boutique having made a new friend, and wearing a cerulean-blue knitted hat, mittens, and down vest. She carried her other purchases in a large shopping bag thankful she'd made a start buying Christmas gifts.

On her return trip to the lodge, Maddie stopped to admire Starlight's renowned Christmas attraction, the largest, highest, and most beautiful Christmas tree she had ever laid eyes on.

Its lush branches dazzled with brilliant glowing lights. Gold and silver ornaments, along with fabric red hearts, decorated the tree all the way to the top. Skaters whizzed by on smooth ice, which had been created along its north side.

Maddie couldn't wait to bring Vanessa and Cole here for an afternoon of skating and drinking hot chocolate.

Further on down the street, she walked by a different hotel. The Star family didn't own this one, so Maddie always buzzed right on by the Mountain View Inn. Not today.

The sight of a silver car was all it took for her to turn on her heels and dart inside. She felt like a traitor even swinging open the door. Still, it wasn't too late for breakfast and she was hungry after all the loading she'd done to her credit card.

Once before she'd spotted the Essential Oil Mercedes parked here at the inn, so it was logical for her to conclude this was where Trevor Kirk lodged. Thus far, not one of the mineral leases she'd examined at the courthouse mentioned his name. This might be a perfect opportunity to nose into whether minerals were his true reason for being in town.

Though she snagged a window seat in the Sugar Shack, Maddie angled her chair for a better view of the geologist's car. A server brought hot coffee within moments. The dark roast left a bitter taste on her tongue. When after thirty minutes Trevor failed to arrive, she considered leaving. He'd probably already eaten breakfast.

But then something Harry Black once said leapt into her mind. "Ms. Stone, there is nothing easy about surveillance. There is no such thing as the right technique, only patience."

After reminding herself to keep waiting, Maddie ordered a coffee refill. By the time she downed her third cup, her interest in monitoring Trevor's movements had escalated into a desire to confront him.

The server returned looking anxious. "Are you ever going to order breakfast? You've been here nearly an hour."

"Sorry, I lost track of time." Maddie passed on seeing the menu. "Bring me orange juice and a two-egg omelet with spinach and tomato. Have the chef make the toasted English muffin dry, okay?"

"Sure. I'll be back in a jiffy to warm your coffee."

She put a hand over her cup. "I'm done with coffee."

Just then, from behind the server, Maddie spotted Trevor walking into the restaurant. Dressed casually in khaki slacks, a sweater, and waist-length leather jacket, he exuded a sharp appearance. Maddie questioned what was beneath the duds, down deep where it counted.

She had a strong sense he roamed the country on the alert for ways to make money, caring not one iota for the people he encountered. Such were the thoughts rambling through Maddie's mind as he maneuvered through the tables toward her.

"So, the well-heeled lawyer, Maddie Stone, eats in restaurants with the grunts."

Maddie pushed away her coffee. "From your Mercedes outside, it appears other well-heeled folks eat here."

"I park out front to help promote the hotel," Trevor replied. "I'm here for breakfast. Are you expecting someone, or may I join you?"

"Sure." Maddie gestured to the chair across from her. "We can have that meal you mentioned the other day."

Trevor waved down the server. "Maddie, I haven't seen you dining in here before. I believe you are staying at the Edelweiss Lodge, the most expensive hotel in town."

"Well, you got one thing right."

Maddie waited to say more until the server brought her juice and left with Trevor's order for scrambled eggs, sausage, and a side of pancakes.

She tried her juice before telling Trevor, "I stopped here today hoping to bump into you. I think we're both in town for the same reason."

"Then I am fortunate." His blue eyes sparkled under the lights as he leaned forward expectantly.

"I assume you're doing geological consulting," she said, hoping to slowly draw him into telling the truth.

"Is it true then? We are working together?" His smile was broad like he was about to receive good news.

"What do you mean by that?" Maddie sat back, astonished.

"Let's not kid each other. We both know how this works. Your firm, I know it's really not Dewey, Cheatem, and How."

Maddie flashed an exaggerated smirk. "Right. I'm with the D.C. firm of Barron and Rich."

"Hah. Barron and Rich proves I am right. You are well-heeled."

"Okay, Mr. Mercedes, can we move off that topic? Or do you insist on always being right?"

Trevor removed his cell phone from his jacket and set it on the table. "If I've figured this correctly, your firm represents a client who wants to buy land for drilling. They don't want competitors knowing what they're up to, so they get a different law firm to hire a geologist to do the survey work."

Unfazed by his direct stare, Maddie said simply, "And?"

"It's obvious. I've been asked by another firm to conduct work here, yet I'm really doing it for Barron and Rich." His charming smile widened. "So, we are working together, right?"

"No." Maddie's scowl deepened the more she considered his ridiculous claim. "What are you talking about?"

"We're not on the same team? I hoped we had that in common at least."

"Which firm hired you?"

Trevor opened his mouth. "Uh ... No. I can't tell you. It would betray client confidence."

"I thought so."

"Maddie, I just assume Jordan Star is tired of operating a ski resort and hotel and is seeking to sell the mountain or the mineral rights."

"You think I'm working for the Star family?"

"If you're not, tell me this. Are you and Jordan Star an item?"

"Excuse me? What does that have to do with the price of eggs?"

Trevor turned over his cell phone and looked at the screen as if waiting on a call.

"You're seen together around town and on the mountain," he said. "You're either working for him or involved with him. You're both attractive and he's a single guy. So which is it?"

"Okay." Maddie felt her stomach burning from too much coffee. "My firm is working for him."

"And?" Trevor paused.

"And what?"

"Are you both single but not involved?"

Maddie was about to blast him when the server delivered their meals. Instead, Maddie waited, snapping her napkin onto her lap to show her irritation.

When they were alone again, she launched into him. "Trevor Kirk, you have nerve. You waltz in here, quizzing me about my personal life. You have no right asking me questions when you refuse to even admit what you're doing in town and who you're working for."

"Maddie," he said her name softly, his eyes sparking in apology. "I truly hoped I was working for you. I just told you that I think you are attractive. Now you tell me that you and Jordan aren't involved. This is what I call a 'good news' day."

Maddie's brain instantly recalled Gretchen's warning, and she leaned away from him. "Don't expect your dating prospects to improve here in town anytime soon."

"Why?"

"It's a small town. The word among the single ladies is you're romantically committed."

Trevor tossed down his napkin on the table. "Oh great. I defensively told one lady in town I'm committed elsewhere, now I'm stuck with that story? I am not seeing anyone, okay?"

"You admit you tell stories, but that's nothing to me."

Maddie tried her omelet. It tasted cold and slippery, something like the man sitting across from her. She picked at her food, and Trevor dug into his as if he hadn't eaten for days. Their forks clicking on the plates were the only sounds at their table.

After draining her juice, Maddie told him, "The mystery continues. I've almost enjoyed talking with you. We have nothing in common. I guess we'll see each other around town."

She placed the napkin on the table and wrestled her cell phone from its holder in her purse. "I'd love a selfie of us for old time's sake."

"Nothing doing, Ms. Stone. You've basically admitted you have no desire to see my face again."

Maddie laid enough money on the table to cover her bill and tip. She left Trevor sitting alone without saying another word or glancing back at him.

Chapter 14

Maddie vowed to spend the rest of the day more judiciously after her dustup with Trevor. And so it was a few hours later she scurried down the steps of the ornate county courthouse mulling over her discovery. Large snowflakes landed on the scarf wrapped around her neck.

She unlocked the rental, slid behind the wheel, and turned on both the car and heat. Maddie flipped open her leather folder to expose a legal pad full of notes. It was high time she checked in with her boss from her other office away from home—her car.

Vanessa's chirpy voice answered, "Barron and Rich."

"I'm surprised you're answering the main line," Maddie said, aiming the heat vent toward her feet.

"Flu is going around. I have two jobs today."

"You'd better stay well," Maddie cautioned. "I've arranged for you and Cole to be treated royally when you arrive."

"We can't wait to come up and explore. What can I do for you?"

"If Bill's not busy, connect me. I also may have an assignment for you."

"Okay, let me know. Meantime, I'll stay healthy and see you soon."

The line went dead and Maddie worried she'd been disconnected. To her surprise Bill clicked on.

"Have you found Nora Star?" he growled.

"Bill, I went back to the register of deeds and did more checking. Many property owners around Starlight, with the exception of our client, have already sold their mineral rights to a Denver company."

"Is this Denver company represented by Hunter, Lance, and Bling?"

"I'm not sure. I thought Vanessa could check D.C. court filings. These others are smaller parcels on the outskirts of

Starlight. Jordan owns the majority of the land, or he will when the estate finally closes. Rare earth elements will most certainly be found on Star family land."

She heard Bill's keyboard clicking before he said, "I assume you didn't find Nora, or you would have said so. What else have you learned about her or other possible relatives?"

Maddie updated him about Harry continuing to put out feelers in Austria, and how she was staying on Jordan to do more searching of family records in his attic.

"Meanwhile, a geologist named Trevor Kirk is in town doing research," Maddie said, a hard glint to her voice. "He implied a law firm hired him but ethically can't divulge the name. Did you hire him?"

"Whoa! No! That's weird. Be careful up there. Does his name appear on any of the registered mineral rights at the courthouse?"

"No, and I checked, believe me. Perhaps he's in league with Stewart and his firm seeking to delay closing the estate."

"It's interesting you suspect Stewart Dunham. He phoned me this morning, and wants to confer with you and me in Starlight. What are your thoughts?"

Maddie didn't trust Stewart or his motives. "I say we drag our feet in having a confab until I learn more. In my former dealings with him, I learned the hard way Stewart is not a man of his word."

"I trust your instincts. Resolve this case, Madison. I want to put your name forward on the fast track for partnership. Your time has come."

"Bill, thanks for that," Maddie replied, feeling both valued and doubtful at the same time.

She hadn't yet told Bill or Jordan about Jeanette Carpenter, who claimed her grandfather built Starlight. Rather than open that Pandora's box with her boss, Maddie simply begged off for an appointment. She didn't miss a beat phoning the realtor and asking Linda to return her call.

Her final call went to Harry Black. His voicemail answered for him, so Maddie told him about the list of properties she'd located at the courthouse. She'd just set down her phone and was about to drive off when she saw Trevor speed by in his expensive car.

Too bad she had no chance to follow or see where he was going. Dinner with Gretchen's family called, where Maddie intended to subtly ask about the elusive geologist and his quest to purchase mineral rights from Opal Parker.

MADDIE DROVE TO GRETCHEN'S family home at twilight. The shifting light and snowy conditions made it slow going. A hefty wooden door opened before she could even knock. An erect lady decked out in a plaid flannel shirt and blue jeans met Maddie with an inviting smile. Maddie quickly forgot all about being a few minutes late.

"Howdy," the lady said, greeting Maddie in the doorway.

Gretchen stepped forward, hugging Maddie and taking her boxed pumpkin pie. Then she introduced Gramma.

"Do I call you Opal, Mayor Parker, or just plain Gramma?" Maddie wondered aloud.

"I'm Opal to all my friends," she answered, acting nothing like a plain Gramma as she gripped Maddie's right hand with gusto.

Opal dropped her hand and sidled up close to Maddie.

"To be sure, Gretchen's friend is my pal too. You seem familiar, but then again, I don't know you. 'Course my eyesight isn't what it used to be."

Maddie drew her lips into her warmest smile. "I'm Maddie Stone. Your farmhouse is nice and cozy."

"Gretchen and her folks live here with me, I'm happy to say. Might you and Gretchen be school chums?"

"I'm a guest at the Edelweiss Lodge," Maddie replied, chuckling. "Your granddaughter told me of your close connection with Maynard Star. I'm fascinated to know how Starlight came to be. It's a step back in time and reminds me of my childhood."

"Well, dearie, your time don't reach as far back as mine, I'm guessin'. But come in and warm yourself by the fire. Old Mr. Winter is kickin' up a fuss tonight with the wind blowin' and snow fallin' in great big gobs."

Opal shut the door with a bang, but not before fingers of snow swirled into the foyer. After removing her coat, Maddie shivered, despite the house being toasty. She was glad she'd worn her new down vest under her coat, and zipped it to the scarf looped around her neck.

After cleaning snow off her boots, Maddie followed Opal into the farmhouse. The graying hair piled atop Opal's head gave "plain Gramma" a more dignified appearance than the homespun outfit she wore. Tempting aromas of cinnamon and spices surrounded Maddie, causing her mouth to water and her stomach to rumble. Truth be told, she hadn't eaten a home-cooked meal since visiting her parents last summer.

More introductions. Tom Parker, Gretchen's dad, handed Maddie a cup of steaming apple cider. Shannon, Gretchen's mom, took Maddie to her seat in the informal dining room. The sight of the festive table, decked with candles and a cloth covered with fall leaves, gave Maddie a taste of homesickness. Her mom always went all out for company just like this. Maddie rarely invited anyone over to her apartment—well, except for Vanessa and Cole.

She took her seat at the table, her eyes rounding in joy. "This is a feast. Everything looks delicious."

After the family took their seats, Tom offered a prayer of thanks to God for the meal and their new guest. Covered dishes were passed, and Maddie helped herself to the roasted chicken with tiny potatoes and creamed spinach. Mugs of apple cider were refilled. Lively conversation ensued as the family and Maddie became acquainted.

Gretchen passed a basket of freshly baked blueberry muffins, telling Maddie, "You and my mom have something in common."

"Besides loving these muffins?" Maddie said in jest.

"Yes, that and more. Mom earned her law degree right here in Vermont."

"How fascinating," Maddie said, hoping her interest showed. "Are you practicing law now?"

Her fork lifted above her plate, Shannon explained their interesting story. She'd been a lawyer with the U.S. Army when she met Gretchen's father, who was also in the Army.

When Tom left the military, they moved to Vermont, joining Opal.

"Gretchen's sister Iris lives here," Shannon added. "As a flight attendant, she's often gone. Gretchen attends college online. Tom and I run the farm, with Opal's help."

"Mom raises goats and her cheese wins a blue ribbon at the state fair every year. Cinnamon Stix features her organic produce and cheese," Gretchen proclaimed, snatching a muffin from the basket before Maddie could pass it along.

"I can relate," Maddie said. "My parents raise fruit trees in northern Michigan, mostly apples and sweet and tart cherries. I love our farm."

As Maddie said this, it was as if Opal, who seemed content to listen until now, found her voice and came alive.

"That's why you look familiar," she told Maddie. "You're a country girl like me. Working with your hands in the earth deepens your love of life. Makes you thankful for what you have. I don't knock those who live in the city, but all those tall buildings reachin' toward the stars mostly block your view."

"I haven't seen as many stars here as I'd like," Maddie confessed. "Too many late nights working."

Opal tugged on her earlobe. "That needs to change pronto. It's snowin' tonight, but on the first clear evening I'll take you up to the observatory. Once you look up at the night sky lookin' down at you, things will never be the same again. Millions of stars twinklin' in their places, always moving in sync each season. Christmas is my absolute favorite time of the whole year. It's when we remember how the Star of Bethlehem shone the way for baby Jesus."

"You are so right, Opal," Maddie said with feeling. "It's especially meaningful for me to be in Starlight leading up to Christmas."

Gretchen looked at her with wide eyes. "So you'll be here for Christmas? Come join us, right, Mom?"

"Yes, Maddie you are welcome to come here anytime," Shannon said, passing the plate of chicken around for second helpings.

"Thank you." Maddie felt truly blessed by her new friends. "I have a question. Did Starlight acquire its name from excellent views of the stars?"

Her question primed Opal to tell how Maynard Star began the observatory.

"Do you know Jordan is helpin' me raise money for a new telescope and special digital camera in the upcomin' Christmas pageant? Our church teens will be singin' and Shannon will be sellin' her cheese and bread."

Gretchen chimed in. "Jordan plans to auction one of his grandfather's star ornaments made from stained glass. Maddie, you know, the one you admire so much."

"That's astonishing." Maddie dropped her fork into the creamy spinach. "He adores that star."

"That's how much the kids mean to him," Opal interjected.

Maddie gulped. "Kids? I didn't know he had children. My, he is a man of mystery."

"Dearie, you've got the wrong side of the penny there. Jordan and each one of us sittin' around this table—well, except you for now—reach out to kids from the city to teach them about farmin' and the night sky."

"You've set me straight," Maddie said, wiping her fork on her napkin.

When would she stop jumping to conclusions about this case?

She ate another bite of the delicious chicken. A quiet hush filled the room until Maddie said, "That sounds like a worthy goal. I'd love to hear more."

Opal was unleashed. "Dearie, wait 'til you see the northern lights. We took a group of eighth-graders up here this fall. Their mouths hung open for a good ten minutes. Those kids were speechless. I'll get one of the letters."

She leapt from her chair, returning moments later with a typed sheet she unfolded with flair. She looked different, wearing a pair of thick antiquated glasses.

In a raspy voice that held great volume, Opal read aloud, "'Those green and purple lights in the sky were like a movie, only real. Gramma Parker, your night sky stayed in my mind for the whole bus ride back to New York City. I want you to know I'm going to college to become a scientist.'"

"That's just one letter we received," Tom explained. "Other students hope to move to Starlight from the city and learn farming with me. Others used our ice rink and want to become professional hockey players. They have many opportunities here."

Maddie learned much throughout the evening. As dinner wound to a close, she broached the one subject that really needed answering.

"Opal, your granddaughter told me," Maddie nodded at Gretchen, "that a geologist in town visited you recently."

The old lady studied Maddie's face with a penetrating gaze. "Yup. He drove up here in his showy car. That's why you're in town, right? Suddenly, everyone is aimin' to buy our mountain."

"Gramma, I already told you. Maddie isn't here to buy the mountain," Gretchen insisted.

Maddie realized Gretchen had already told her family about Maddie staying at the lodge and working for Jordan Star. She saw no problem in confirming her role.

"You all probably know I'm helping the Star family, and I am interested in knowing what this geologist wanted."

Tom interrupted, "There's actually been two of them."

"I nearly forgot." Opal gave a curt nod of her elegant head. "The first one burst in here a few months back from Denver. He boldly asked us to sell our mineral rights. No way we're doin' that. Next, he wanted permission to bore for samples on our land."

"Did you let him?" Maddie asked, her breath catching.

"We did not," Tom declared. "Others did, which is getting the entire town in an uproar because that guy claimed he'd found deposits of rare minerals."

Opal folded her arms across her middle. "Now everybody's hopin' to get rich. Losing their good sense. The Star family always refused to deal with 'em, so we don't think Jordan will let anything come of it for Starlight."

"This is important." Maddie pushed away her plate and clasped her hands on the table. "What about the geologist from Essential Oil? Trevor Kirk stopped here, right?"

Opal's lips formed into a thin line. "Trevor didn't offer to buy our mineral rights. You know what? He seemed more interested in knowin' if deposits were found on our farm. I think he was just checkin' on his competition."

"His being here is interesting," was all Maddie would say.

After enjoying pumpkin pie and more apple cider, she thanked the family for such a delicious home-cooked meal and the friendly conversation. She headed back to the Edelweiss Lodge in her cold car ready to unearth what Trevor was up to in Starlight and also if he was a cohort of Stewart's.

So preoccupied was Maddie's mind with solving the case that never once did she look up and see a single star.

Chapter 15

Though the morning dawned clear with no snow falling, Maddie didn't care about the weather. She was dismayed by the slow progress in finding the unknown heir. Back on her computer, she turned over every rock and stone for any Star person listed on the Family Finder website. This trail again ended in disappointment.

Maddie phoned Harry, and lawyer and private investigator had a heart-to-heart talk.

"Who is Nora Star?" Maddie asked with fervor. "And where is she?"

"Ms. Stone, I've located the orphanage she started in Rumphrey." Harry didn't sound enthused. "It merged with another one. I put in a call to my Austrian contact and should hear back before too long."

"You've searched all your Internet locater sites?"

"Oh, for sure. I found several Nora Stars living in America."

Maddie shot up in her chair. "When were you going to tell me?"

"Now's a good time."

"I'm ready." Maddie grabbed her pen.

Uncharacteristically, Harry never drew breath as he rattled on, "Strike one is ninety-nine-year-old Nora who lives with her great-grandson in Florida. I spoke with her on his cell phone and she never heard of Maynard. Strike two is a college-aged girl who is studying drama in college who I would call a 'Hollywood wannabe.' I am working on another Nora in Kansas, which I suspect is strike three."

Maddie tossed down her pen. "Good work. Let me know about your Kansas possibility and the orphanage, whatever you find. I'll advise Bill."

They hung up. Maddie texted Bill with everything she'd learned from Harry. Her empty stomach got her checking the time. After hours of drinking coffee and eating a box of crackers, she really could use a hearty dinner. She freshened up, and just before heading out the door, her cell phone buzzed in her hand.

Thinking it was either Bill or Harry, Maddie swiped her finger to answer the call.

"It's a perfect night to go explorin' with you," Opal chimed.

"Thanks for the offer." Trepidation lurked in Maddie's mind. "Work beckons and I'd be a delinquent running off to the mountain with you."

"You push hard. Anyone with eyes can see. I think it's wise to strike a balance."

"It is, but when your work is done. Mine isn't."

"Well, dearie, how about this? You should visit the other side of your client's life, to better represent him, don't ya know."

Maddie crinkled her brow. "What other side?"

"The mountain he loves. With everything he has, he could live anywhere. Why do you think he stays put?"

"You are a wise gramma. I was just going to eat something in the Stix, then I can be ready in about forty minutes."

"I'm leavin' now. We can eat the sandwiches I fixed. See you in ten."

Maddie heard a click and realized she'd better get changed. Darkness fell superfast in the mountains, she was learning. She turned the lamp to a higher setting as she dressed in jeans and sweater and her new winter garb.

With a few minutes to spare, she quickly checked emails on her phone, lingering over one from her mother who looked so happy in a photo with Dad under green palm trees. Mom renewed an invite for Maddie to join them at their winter retreat for a long weekend. The irony didn't escape Maddie. They had fled winter's snow for Florida, and here was Maddie, knee deep in thick Vermont snow.

The loud roar of a motorcycle out on the street interrupted her thoughts. Maddie closed down her computer knowing Opal would be here any minute. She'd just picked up the knit cap from the desk when she heard *tap tap* on her door.

Maddie looked through the peephole and saw Opal's distinctive twenty-year-old glasses staring back. What was that on her head?

She jerked opened the door. Opal stepped in, a different woman from whom Maddie saw last night. She wore a heavy jacket and antique military pilot's helmet, its earflaps dangling like pigtails. She held aloft some tall boots.

"I thought you might need these, dearie."

Maddie tried not to giggle at Opal's comical appearance. She pointed at her boots. "Why do I need those? I'm wearing my own."

"Maddie, where did I tell you that we're goin'?"

"To the observatory built by Maynard Star to see night stars from their best advantage."

Opal nodded, setting her earflaps quivering. "It's locked up, mind you. But we can drive to the lot up there. The snow's deep, so you need these high boots."

Maddie switched boots. She pulled on fur-lined ones, which stopped just short of her knees. After tucking her jeans into the tops, she hurried into her jacket.

A few seconds more, and she yanked a pretty knit cap over her head, flashing a lopsided smile. "There, do I look ready?"

Opal raised both thumbs. "Let's go."

As they walked through the Edelweiss lobby, Opal tossed Maddie the keys.

"What are these for?"

"You're drivin."

"No thanks. I don't know the way."

"If we're gonna make you into a local, you must learn your way around."

Maddie gripped the heavy keys, deciding it was best not to argue with Opal.

OUTSIDE OF THE LODGE, Maddie stood face-to-face with a monster pickup truck.

"This is what I'm supposed to drive?"

"Yup." Opal escorted her over to the driver's side.

Maddie kept shaking her head. "I can't drive this. It's too tall. I can't get into it."

Opal opened the door and presto, a step eased out from beneath the truck.

"There you are, dearie. Step up on the nerf bar and go on right into the truck."

Maddie held onto the door with a death grip and somehow managed to climb in. This was going to be worse than her inaugural ride on the D.C. Metro when she didn't know where to get off for her downtown law office. She'd ended up riding the circuit back to the correct stop and was late for her first day at Barron and Rich.

Opal slammed Maddie's door and ran around the front. After sliding into the passenger seat, she said, "Did you learn to drive in school?"

Maddie nodded, feeling around for the ignition.

"Thought so. Here in Starlight, we learn on tractors and snowmobiles."

Maddie's finger found the ignition at last. She inserted the key and jammed her foot on the brake. When she turned the key, she thought she heard the motorcycle roaring again. Maddie looked in the rearview mirror. She couldn't see anyone behind her.

The booming sounds were coming from the truck.

She turned to Opal with a serious question. "Whose truck is this?"

"Mine. When you live up here, you'll have one of these too."

Maddie ignored the jibe and pulled the gear selector. She backed out.

"Which way do I go?"

Opal informed her with a chuckle, "It's easy. You head straight up the road for seven miles, give or take an inch."

Maddie shoved the selector into drive and hit the gas. The tires threw snow beneath them. The engine thundered.

"Don't worry about your traction," Opal insisted. "We've got four hundred pounds of bagged cat litter in the backend. That adds plenty of weight to the rear axle."

Beads of sweat broke out on Maddie's forehead. She imagined slipping and sliding all the way to the observatory. Had she really signed up for such a dangerous outing? She needed to reexamine her judgment.

By the time she reached the village limits and turned onto the darkened road, the truck's heater was pumping out oodles of warmth. Maddie checked her rearview mirror. Her eyes flew forward just in time to see a blur pass across the road.

She slammed the brakes all the way to the floor. Both women lurched forward.

"Whew!" Maddie cried, her heart racing. "I almost hit something!"

"Yup, you missed a deer. Keep your eyes peeled. Where there's one, there's another sure to follow."

Maddie's foot found the accelerator, and they shot down the road about twenty feet when Opal yelled, "Sure enough, looky!"

Maddie pumped the brakes, slowing the truck as its lights illuminated two more deer charging across the road.

"Are there more?" Maddie feared she'd have to dodge dozens of deer.

Opal gazed out her side window. "Don't see any. We're good to go."

Maddie navigated the winding road with both hands gripping the wheel. Something Opal said a few minutes ago bothered her. This was as good a time as any for Maddie to ask.

"Opal, what makes you think I'll ever live in Starlight? I'm here on assignment."

"Oh, Gretchen and I think alike. We both see a changed Jordan since you came. We can tell you two are keen on each other."

"No, ma'am," Maddie objected. "I'll say again in case you missed it the first time. I'm here strictly on business."

Opal's low laugh rumbled in her throat. "You'll see things a mite differently in time."

Maddie did regret she'd so abruptly rejected Jordan at the church, but she was determined to ease her new friend into another topic. "Were you living here when the observatory was built?"

"Sure enough. I remember when Maynard did it. Helen loved astronomy and she had a small telescope. One day Maynard decided to build her a bigger one, and I'll say he did. Now, students from Green Mountain College and Dartmouth do research from here."

"I had no idea. This place is amazing."

"Sure is. Jordan has a good situation here. He owns the ski resort and Edelweiss Lodge. Students come here for astronomy class and mix their travel with skiin' and they stay at Jordan's lodge."

"Now you mention it, I've seen groups of students in the lobby. I figured they were here to ski on Christmas break."

"Slow down," Opal commanded. "Just over the hill, turn left. Be advised, that's where we find deeper snow."

Opal couldn't have been more spot-on. Only Maddie couldn't help doing a double take. The new road had no tire tracks. How did Opal know precisely where to turn with no markings?

Maddie leaned forward toward the wheel and gaped out the windshield as the tires crunched along, packing down the snow. She aimed the truck between tall reflectors staked along the roadside. Her eyes were ever on the lookout for more deer to erupt from the trees. She slowed down to a bare crawl.

"You're doin' fine. Now then," Opal said, pointing a finger out the windshield. "Slow down and watch for another drive on your left, just ahead."

Maddie spotted it first. "Here?"

"Good for you, dearie. You found it."

As Maddie pulled in, the snow got even deeper.

"Will we get stuck?" she asked, her pulse escalating at the idea of being stranded up on the mountain.

"Nope." Opal waved. "Pull ahead another hundred feet. We can walk from there."

Maddie stopped the truck and shoved the gear selector in park.

Opal tipped her head in the direction from where they'd turned. "If we continue up that road back there, we will come to Moonlight Trail. It goes back along a ridge for two miles and joins the Long Trail. You might be familiar with it."

"I know about the Long Trail, though I've never hiked it," Maddie said. "My college roommate did. Doesn't it run the entire length of the state?"

"Correct, and what a splendid place it is. Jordan constructed Moonlight Trail so hikers could connect up with the Long Trail."

Maddie killed the engine and turned off the lights.

"Good. Follow me." Before climbing out, Opal told Maddie, "We need it dark as possible for the star-scape we're about to witness."

Maddie slid from the truck, snow nearly covering the top of her boots. Opal shone a small flashlight ahead of them as they slowly trudged up the ridge toward the observatory. Their feet made drumming sounds in the snow as they walked along, and the snow spilled to the sides in heaps.

It was rough going. When Maddie reached the top, she fought for breath.

Opal cut the light with a whispered, "Look up, and be amazed."

Maddie quickly turned her eyes heavenward. Beneath such a bevy of starlight in the night sky above, Maddie suddenly felt small, puny even. A shudder tore through her, which had nothing to do with being cold. Awestruck, she dropped to her knees.

Words from her favorite Christmas song escaped her lips and softly, tenderly, she sang, "Silent night, holy night, all is calm, all is bright."

Opal joined her in singing the hymn. The strains from their tiny choir lifted up into the expansive Vermont sky, filling Maddie's spirit with pure joy. Moments later, she scrambled to her feet.

Opal punctured the beauty of the night by uttering, "Listen, Maddie, it would be a shame if Jordan loses this mountain and lodge. We villagers would be devastated."

"It is magnificent up here," Maddie said, trying to maintain her high spirits in spite of Opal's ominous warning.

"You can pretend to be cool, but I know you care. Your big heart is bursting out all over up here, just bein' away from the city and back high on the mountain."

Maddie smiled though she knew Opal couldn't see it in the dark. "You have a way with words, Opal. I mean that as a compliment. You don't speak empty phrases, and I don't intend to let Jordan's life become empty by losing this special place."

"All right then. We're countin' on you."

Opal swung the light around. They began hiking down the snow trail lit by Opal's skinny flashlight and millions of stars. A screech rent the air, startling Maddie down to her tall boots.

"Just an owl lettin' us know we're walkin' through his territory. Nothing to worry about," Opal promised.

When she opened the truck's massive door, the nerf bar slid out, and Maddie scrambled into the driver's seat once more.

"It's odd you call this step a nerf bar," Maddie observed. "I have a nerf football and it's made of sponge."

Opal laughed. "Ain't no sponge on this monster."

The truck coughed a time or two before the engine engaged. Maddie turned up the heat. "Are we going to be stuck?"

"Let's see. Put it in gear."

"Here we go."

Maddie pulled the selector into gear. She stepped on the gas. The tires did nothing but spin.

"Oh oh!" she cried.

"Get it in reverse," Opal ordered. "Try rocking it back and forth."

When Maddie put the truck in reverse, the tires spun some more.

"Dearie, listen to me. You need some help."

Maddie swallowed, her heart leaping in her chest. "Like calling a tow truck?"

"Not up here." Opal pointed to a shifter on the floor. "See where it says 4X4? You put us into four-wheel-drive and we'll make you into a real mountain girl."

Maddie obeyed her instructions. Like magic, the super-sized truck plowed through the heavy snow like a hot knife through butter.

"Whew."

Maddie forced out a ragged sigh, thankful she didn't have to haul out that cat litter on the dark mountain.

Chapter 16

At dawn's first light, Maddie awoke from a bad dream involving Stewart. She sat up in a lurch, feeling as if last evening on the mountain and the peace she had experienced never happened.

Maddie rubbed her eyes, too awake to fall back asleep. Her feet hit the cold floor. She quickly changed into jeans and a sweater. To the crackling sounds and pleasing aroma of the small pot brewing coffee, Maddie turned on her computer, wondering if Opal had taken her to the mountaintop last night simply to sing Jordan's praises.

That may have been Opal's motive, but the result for Maddie went far beyond human understanding. She stared out the window and breathed in deeply, craving to recapture the spiritual awakening she had received from standing beneath the vast starlit sky. Something had come and stolen it from Maddie in her dreams.

Then before her eyes, the rising sun illuminated Star Mountain in such shades of blue and silver, she found the beauty breathtaking. Opal had been right. Maddie's stargazing last night did inspire her to see life in a more expansive way. She refused to let one grim dream about her former life ruin her future life.

Her promise to be more positive hit a speed bump a few minutes later. Coffee cup in hand, the mountain seemed to grow higher before Maddie's very eyes. She became aware of every hurdle she must jump through to fulfill her promise to Opal, to do all she could to save Starlight.

The debate simmering in her head bubbled over, and she voiced her concerns aloud. "Should I send a letter to Stewart's firm and the court advising them there might be another heir?"

No one answered back.

Maddie sipped her coffee, feeling stuck in her dilemma. Then it hit her. She was getting ahead of herself just as Bill had the other morning. Tipping off Stewart or revealing any potential problems would be unwise.

To better focus, she began typing out her strategy. One thing became crystal clear and she put it at the top of her list: Connect with Jeanette Carpenter ASAP.

Second on the list was the question that had floated in her dream state: Was there really a Nora Star waiting to be found?

Maddie minimized her document to check for emails from Vanessa, finding instead a troubling development. Mere moments ago, Stewart had filed a new motion with the court. Her heart skipped in her chest. Dread consumed her.

What was he up to now?

Her eyes quickly scanning the document, she huffed, "You're playing more games, Stewart."

He wanted Judge Marks to extend the January hearing. During the time Maddie had been busy planning, he'd been hard at work lobbing another volley to sink her.

Battle stations ready.

Her eyes tore through the letter attached to his pleading. Maddie blinked, but even her dry eyes could not deceive her.

"Stewart's found out," she hissed.

She immediately phoned Bill, who hadn't yet seen Stewart's motion or letter. For a change, Maddie had one up on her boss.

"Bill, they've identified Nora Star as the daughter of Rosanne Star, the daughter of Maynard Star, as an heir to the Star estate."

"Will they be bringing Nora to court?" Bill interjected.

"Ah ... let me see." Her eyes darted down the screen like hungry bees. "Oh wait."

"What did you find?"

"Stewart admits something here that could buy us time," she told him, her finger going down the screen as she read. "He has not located Nora, and provides this information as he is sure the Star executor won't want to proceed with settlement knowing there is another heir."

"More games," Bill sputtered.

Maddie rubbed the back of her neck. "Exactly. Stewart is being clever. He found Nora on Family Finder as we did. So he advises the court, and effectively dumps the burden on us to either find her or prove she doesn't exist. He doesn't have to do a thing more."

"Vanessa is cuing me that opposing counsel is here for the Riley deposition." Bill sounded rushed. "Stewart's firm is up to something nefarious, I have no doubt. Madison, you and Harry continue exploring every avenue."

"Of course, but Bill, what do they gain by delaying us closing the estate while we search for a possible heir?"

A light went on for Maddie and she interjected, "I should file a counter motion and compel them to produce Nora Star for a deposition."

"Not until we investigate further," was Bill's advice.

Maddie sunk into her chair. "I can't argue with you, but I may have discovered another heir."

"What?" Bill yelled in her ear.

"That's right. Her name is Jeanette Carpenter. I met a real estate agent who's helping her look for property in the village. Jeanette claims her grandfather built much of Starlight. She is adopted and searching for her family."

Bill grunted into the phone. "When I drew up Maynard's will, I was convinced I had crossed every 't' and dotted every 'i.' I find this discouraging. What else did I miss?"

"Boss, don't travel down that road. You've always said we represent our clients only as well as the information they divulge. You did your due diligence. Now I am doing mine."

"Have you met with Jeanette or will that only confirm her claims?"

"I will meet with her soon and play it cool," Maddie assured him. "I'll call Harry and have him get the details of where and to whom we send a subpoena at Family Finder. That should compel their IT people to turn over the identity of the computer that created the account for Rosalyn Star and Nora Star."

"Excellent, Maddie. Stay on that. Do you think it's possible Nora married and Jeanette is her daughter?"

"If only it would be so easy," Maddie replied.

"Did Stewart indicate he located the new will?"

"No."

"In any event, Maddie, I trust you to resolve this case favorably."

Bill hung up, leaving Maddie free to phone Harry. He picked up on the first ring.

"Harry here. How can I help you, Ms. Stone?"

"Are you familiar with the Family Finder website?"

"Is it one of those heritage sites? I think my wife is searching their website to trace her great-grandfather."

Maddie quickly briefed Harry, adding, "We need to contact Family Finder and ascertain where to send a subpoena."

"Aye aye, captain."

A resounding *click* in her ear assured her of one thing. Harry Black was indeed on the case.

MADDIE RACED DOWNSTAIRS TO SEE JORDAN and confide in him about Stewart's motion and letter. He urged her to come in, and before she could say one word, there was a rap on his office doorjamb. Maddie looked up to see a twenty-something man in a red-and-black plaid flannel shirt tucked into his jeans, and carrying a spiral notebook. He smiled at Jordan. Maddie wondered how he managed to get past Sylvia.

"Excuse me, Mr. Star, I'm Barnaby Ross from *The Ledger*. Forgive me for interrupting your meeting. Do you have a moment?"

Jordan stood with an extended hand. "Mr. Ross, I've lived in Starlight a long time and we've never met."

"Call me Ross," the reporter said. "I'd like to verify some very disturbing info I picked up about the future of the town."

"Tell me what you've learned. I shall see if I can help," Jordan replied.

Detecting concern in her client's voice and watching his jaw muscles flex, Maddie thought it best to remain in the background. Jordan could handle this young reporter. She didn't want her identity as his lawyer being written up in *The Ledger*.

The young man dipped his head, looking down at his pad before asking, "Mr. Star, I'm in my senior year as a Northwestern journalism student. I'm doing my senior internship here at *The Ledger*."

"Okay."

Ross shifted his weight in the doorway. "You see, I've developed a source ..."

When he paused, Jordan prompted, "Okay."

"Right. I want to confirm what my source told me."

Maddie thought the young journalist acted uncomfortable with his assignment. She could relate. She'd lacked confidence working on her first legal internship.

"Um ... Mr. Star, most people in town say you have the biggest investment in the area so I appreciate your viewpoint about the rumor."

"You have me curious." Jordan adjusted his tie. "What is your question?"

Ross again consulted a page in his spiral notebook. "Are you negotiating to sell the ski resort and the mountain to an overseas buyer?"

"Who is your source for this rumor?" Jordan asked.

"I'd rather not say."

Jordan passed by Maddie, who sat at the opposite end of the conference table and pulled out a chair right by his desk. He pointed for Ross to sit before closing his office door.

Appalled by the question and Ross's digging around for a story, Maddie reminded herself to listen and not insert any opinion. She pulled out her cell phone. Though she scrolled through messages, her eyes and ears stayed on high alert.

Jordan sat behind his desk, and leaning forward, he flexed his brows. "I didn't close my office door because I'm giving you a scoop. Fact is, you do not have a story. I shut the door because if folks in this town heard you asking these things, it would have an adverse effect on the town's stability."

Ross barked out his next question as if trying out for a spot on TV news. "So you deny such a sale?"

"I'm not negotiating to sell anything," Jordan replied calmly. "No selling the mountain. No selling the ski runs. No Edelweiss Lodge. Did your source say I am?"

Maddie observed Ross scratch out a few notes before gazing up at Jordan.

"My source said overseas developers are jockeying to buy the mountain because it has extremely rare and valuable minerals. He also said geologists are in town trying to pressure local landowners to sell their mineral rights."

Maddie eyed Jordan spinning around in his wheeled chair and gesturing to a giant aerial photo that hung on the wall behind him. She made mental notes as he explained, "For generations, owners of these properties have bought and sold their mineral rights."

Jordan's manner and tone gave Maddie the idea her client would make an excellent teacher, and what he said next confirmed her opinion of his leadership qualities.

"Ross, it's like getting a bank loan. The owners keeps their property but can permit someone else to remove oil or minerals. After all these years, I still have not seen any oil wells or mines. I have not sold any rights or property, nor will I, and my family owns more property around here than anyone else."

"But he—"

Jordan wasn't finished. "Have you seen any mining trucks around?"

"No." Ross shook his head. "But my source seems to know everything going on around here."

"I see," Jordan said carefully. "You refer to your source as 'he.' Is he a local person?"

"I'm not sure. I think he may have been interested in buying property."

Jordan tented his hands. "Your boss relies on advertising revenue from local businesses, right?"

"Yeah, but how is that relevant?" Ross twirled his pen in the air as if it was a magic wand that would provide the answer.

"A false story that destabilizes the community can kill advertising and destroy the paper. Do you think your boss will risk your story from a questionable source? I'm telling you Starlight is not for sale."

The two men glared at each other. For her part, Maddie remained absolutely still and quiet. Finally Ross flinched. He stood up and opened the door.

"That might explain why I've been unable to get any other confirmation."

The intern trudged out, his shoulders hunched. Jordan's jaw was still ajar and he stared at Maddie. She darted to shut the door.

Maddie faced her client with a tight smile. "He isn't your problem. He'll go cover the upcoming festival and write a nice article about the caring people of this town. But we have a serious issue to discuss. Opposing counsel has found Nora Star."

Jordan's jaw dropped even further as she related Stewart's newly-filed motion and accompanying letter.

"They found her," he repeated, his voice hushed, his eyes flickering. "Will you be getting her answers under oath?"

"I should have said they found her name," Maddie corrected. "Presumably on Family Finder. They're leaving it up to us to find her, or prove she doesn't exist. That's because Judge Marks may not allow us to settle the estate and transfer properties to you until we prove other heirs are not legitimate."

"Other heirs?" Jordan stood up, his face a portrait of dread.

"A woman has surfaced who claims her grandfather built Starlight."

He took a swipe at his hair. "This is turning into a real nightmare. What else did Grandfather keep from me?"

"We're solving this together, remember? I plan on meeting this woman, but right now, your attic is shouting for us to get up there and scrutinize your family heirlooms to prove there's no such person as Nora Star or anyone else. Lead the way."

"Great idea. You still haven't met Trooper, my trusty sidekick," he added with a slight grin.

"Oh, yeah, Trooper your dog."

Jordan's grin widened. "Wait and see."

"Or maybe it's your cat. No, I don't picture you as a cat person."

Chapter 17

Maddie pulled into Jordan's drive unable to mask her disappointment. His family letters and albums she'd previously taken from his attic, and sitting on the seat next to her in a heap, had provided little more than a warm commentary of Star family vacations and holidays in Starlight. A few snippets gave her insight into Jordan's younger days, and while interesting, she still had no evidence to disprove Nora Star's damaging claims.

Maddie scooped up the items and brought them into his farmhouse with a mind to remain optimistic. Jordan had a tall cup of coffee ready for her.

"My freezing attic awaits. Good thing you remembered to dress warm."

"Today will be different," Maddie said, trying to sound upbeat. "Lead the way."

Up in the cold rafters, they drank coffee and exchanged a few pleasantries before resuming their search. In a steamer trunk covered with a small rug, Maddie spotted a box wound with twine.

"Jordan, look. This is addressed to your grandmother from Rosalyn in Austria."

He snugged a chair closer to Maddie and sat peering with her into the trunk. They worked as a team. He untied the string and pulled back the lid of the box. Maddie removed a towel folded around what appeared to be several objects. Between the folds, she spied something glittering in the light.

"What are these?"

She lifted the fabric to reveal two cast metal stars, each one connected to a steel rod with a wooden handle at the end.

"Oh my! These bring back so many lovely memories," Maddie gushed.

"You need to enlighten me," Jordan said, leaning closer to have a look. "I have no idea what those are."

She chuckled as she held the handle and pressed a star against her hand. "It's a rosette maker. At Christmastime, my grandmother let me help make rosettes. You know, Christmas cookies. I've never seen one shaped like a star."

"Duh! Would you expect anything else from the Star family?"

He took the device, also pressing it against his hand. "It looks like a branding iron."

Maddie turned her smile upon him, their noses nearly touching.

He quickly pulled his head away. "Sorry to crowd you."

"No problem," she shot back before examining the towel and removing a yellowed note. "Here's a hand-printed recipe."

Maddie slipped the recipe back into the towel. She didn't even need to read it. Her love of making rosette Christmas treats with her grandmother came flooding back, touching her heart with something she thought had been lost.

"Jordan, let me tell you how this works."

With that, Maddie proceeded to demonstrate as if she starred in her own cooking show and Jordan was one of her viewers.

"You mix the ingredients in a bowl forming a batter something like pancake batter. You dip the iron into the moist batter, and then dip the star iron into a pan of heated oil. The batter boils up to form a tasty treat, which separates away from the iron. When it cools, you dust the flaky pastry with powdered sugar. Yummy, they are so good. I remember getting powdered sugar down the front of my Christmas dress."

"You make it sound fun. Maybe you can show me sometime how it works."

"I'd love to. Cooking is my favorite thing, besides winning my legal cases."

"And playing the piano," he added with an amiable smile.

"Yes, but I can't wait to get started," Maddie said with enthusiasm. "We'll plan an evening of making rosettes. It will be different creating stars. I've only ever seen them in circular forms."

"I hope you mean a good kind of different," Jordan replied, rolling the irons back into the towel with the recipe.

Maddie ignored his remark as she tied the box shut.

"I guess we have to keep searching for my missing relative." He coughed out a sigh. "That's my least favorite thing to do."

"That was fun," she said, blowing out her breath in short bursts.

Jordan stood up and gazed around. "These stacks of Star family memorabilia are endless. It may take all day to sort through everything."

"You finish that trunk." Maddie set the rosette box aside. "I'll start this other one."

With that, he reached in the trunk for a photo album and began leafing through photographs. Maddie flipped open a lid to a separate trunk. She took out something light wrapped in crinkly newspaper. She peered closely at the newsprint. It was from *The Ledger*.

Maddie unwrapped a thin dinner plate dotted with roses, which bore no marks of the origin. Probably a bum lead.

The headline of the newspaper article grabbed her attention: "Lawsuit Threatens Edelweiss Lodge."

Maddie touched Jordan's arm. "Here's something interesting."

"Okay."

He quit digging in a trunk and sat on a chair to listen.

She cleared her throat and began reading: "'Construction of the nearly completed Edelweiss Lodge halted this week. Berndt Panzer, the contractor putting the finishing touches on the Star family hotel, demands payment for completed work. The centerpiece of this resort town had been expected to open in time for the ski season. That is now called into serious question. In court, Maynard Star's attorney represented the suit is based on Mr. Star's refusal to pay for shoddy workmanship.'"

"What happened to his suit?" Jordan interjected.

"Wait. The article goes on to say, 'Attempts to interview Maynard Star were referred to his attorney who assured *The*

Ledger a settlement will be reached in time to accommodate the arrival of skiers.'"

Maddie's eyes searched her client's. "Am I correct you didn't know about this lawsuit?"

"Right, as usual. Many things happened when I was younger I never learned of."

"Jordan, you've just hit upon what I've been fearing," she admitted. "We need to consider you were never advised of the birth of other possible heirs."

His shrug registered defeat. "I suppose that's the disadvantage of being an only child. The article does confirm one thing my grandfather taught me."

"What is that?"

"Always hold back payment until I am satisfied work has been done correctly.'"

"So, I can expect you won't pay for my legal services right away?"

"Not so," Jordan objected. "You're different than most of our vendors."

Maddie tore the newspaper page loose. "We'll keep this. It's part of the town's history."

"There's so much more to look at up here," she said, checking her watch. "I have a noon conference call with Vanessa before she and Cole fly up here tomorrow."

Jordan held her eyes with his. "I had hoped to have this resolved before they came so you could spend time with your guests. You head back, and I will stay here checking the various business papers at least."

"Are you sure?" Maddie asked.

"Who knows, Maddie? I might find a hidden birth certificate, which would answer all of our questions."

"Okay. Keep your phone handy. After my phone conference, I'll bring us lunch and help finish up the search."

TWILIGHT SPILLED ACROSS the sky in a rainbow of muted colors that evening. Maddie went outside the lodge and looked up in wonder at a white crown of glory shining on the mountain peak. The brisk night air should clear out the cobwebs from her mind after the confines of Jordan's attic.

The two of them had managed to haul down a pile of personal papers, which he was going through right now. Other than finding the fun rosettes and newspaper article about Maynard's old lawsuit, their search unearthed no real nuggets.

Light snow started falling softly all around her. In this surreal setting, Maddie faced a hard truth.

"I might lose Jordan's case," she said, her breath twirling away from her.

There, her secret was out.

She wandered into several inches of snow to draw near the trees where twinkle lights were strung and emitted a subdued glow. Playfully kicking at the snowdrift, Maddie gazed down at her boots, amazed to see tiny prints from red cardinals hopping near the trees. They swooped in and out of the bare branches, eating seeds from suet blocks hanging from the trees.

Her lips curved into a wistful smile. Maddie's inner light wasn't as dim as it had been up in her room. Small flakes began to turn into large fluffy snowflakes. Maddie caught a few on her mittens and bent her head to look more closely.

What? Could it be?

The gentle white flakes seemed to be shaped like tiny stars.

Maddie breathed in the crisp night air. This beautiful and magical display seemed to have come down from heaven above, just for her, stirring her soul to greater things.

Chapter 18

Maddie wheeled the SUV under the portico Thursday at noon, delivering her D.C. friends from the airport to the Edelweiss Lodge. She rolled to a stop announcing, "Welcome to your Vermont home for the next few days."

"This is beyond anything I imagined," Vanessa said, her light auburn hair peeking beneath her green knit cap. "It's more beautiful than I could see in the teeny Internet photos. No wonder you're in no rush to return to the office."

"I'm working night and day up here, Vanessa." Maddie felt better setting the record straight.

Her paralegal's smile fairly shimmered. "I know. Why would anyone leave this wonderland?"

"We're finally here, Mom." Cole's youthful face beamed as he shot out of the car. "Is it too late to try out the tubing runs?"

Maddie cracked open her door. "After you and your mom settle into your suite, change into something warmer. I'll go see about taking you up to the lifts."

Vanessa collected her purse. Maddie hustled to the rear where she was surprised to find Cole dragging out their suitcases. His brown hair showed from beneath his blue knit cap. In his winter outfit, he looked ready to enjoy his Christmas break with gusto.

As Cole turned and made for the entrance, he bumped into Jordan at the back of car.

Jordan stuck out his hand. "Hi. You must be Cole, am I right?"

Cole set down a suitcase and shook his hand. "Yes, sir."

"Call me Jordan, okay? How old are you, buddy?"

"I just turned fifteen."

"Do you like skiing?" Jordan asked.

"I never have," Cole said, yearning in his voice. "Someday I'd like to. Maddie says your tubing is great, though. Right, Maddie?"

Maddie, who had listened up to now, interjected, "That's what Jordan promised me. Going tubing is all Cole has talked of since we left the airport."

"Cole, I'm happy to show you the best runs," Jordan told him with a twinkle in his eye. "And when you're ready to ski, we can make that happen too."

Maddie reached for a lighter bag. "Jordan, it's nice of you to help Cole. Don't you have a business meeting?"

"I did." Jordan yanked the last suitcase out from the hatch. "It's canceled. Your friends have traveled a great distance, and greeting new visitors is my pleasure."

Vanessa joined them, adjusting her scarf around her neck. Maddie lightly patted her shoulder, introducing her to Jordan.

They shook hands, and Maddie sought to get them better acquainted by telling Vanessa, "Jordan and his family have owned the lodge and everything here on the mountain for generations."

Then, wearing a genial smile, she turned to Jordan. "Vanessa is my right hand at the law firm."

"I see you've already met my son, Cole," Vanessa said, dropping her hand.

Maddie noticed a faint smile gracing her friend's lips as her eyes looked up at Jordan.

"He reminds me of myself at his age," Jordan said, his manner friendly. "He and I are going tubing later. Vanessa, why not join us? It will be fun for you both. After all, that's what we specialize in here at Star Mountain."

"Oh, I would love to," she gushed. "Maddie, what about you?"

Maddie didn't think twice about bowing out. "Not this time. I have a date to keep with Jordan's attic, if you can believe it. Two trunks down and two to go. I admit your plan sounds more exciting. I suggest we all meet up for dinner."

"My house will be open. It's always unlocked," Jordan said, starting to wheel Vanessa's case. "Come, let me show you the best our hospitality has to offer."

The way Jordan catered to Vanessa, lugging in her bags, gave Maddie the slightest twinge of regret. She certainly would prefer to be his guest at the lodge instead of a mere "vendor," as he'd recently called her.

Moments later, Vanessa came running out breathless. "Maddie, I almost forgot Bill's message. He wants to know if you've met with Jeanette Carpenter. He didn't say who she is, but I was supposed to tell you right away."

"Thanks for the heads-up," Maddie said, her workload increasing by the second. "I'll connect with Bill. Now you and Cole go have a good time with Jordan."

MADDIE GUESSED FROM Cole's red cheeks and exuberant smile across the table that the tubing outing was a smashing success. If only Maddie could say the same about her investigation in Jordan's attic. His aunt Rosalyn had shown up in a scant three photos after moving to Austria. None were taken of her with any children.

In the Stix café, Maddie sat beside Jordan and across from her friends at the table for four. Tranquil Christmas music played in the background.

"Chef Dexter has truly upped his game," Maddie said. "You can tell by my empty plate, dinner was delicious."

Cole finished the last of his sweet potato fries and chimed, "I've had two firsts today. Sweet potato fries and tubing. Both are super cool!"

"I agree with my son. Jordan, you are being so kind." Vanessa flashed a radiant smile at Jordan.

"I've taken so little time off lately," he said, rubbing his hands together. "So I guess my ulterior motives are showing."

When Maddie set down her knife and fork on her plate, the clinking sound got everyone laughing.

"I have another fun project in mind." Maddie grinned. "Jordan and I recently found his grandmother's cookie irons in the attic. Want to help me make rosettes?"

"No thanks." A deep frown etched on Cole's boyish features.

"Don't you like cookies?" Maddie asked him, arching an eyebrow.

"Oh, do I!"

"I thought so." Maddie chuckled softly. "These are special cookies, and making them will give you another first, something like hitting a triple in baseball."

Cole laughed out loud. "Okay, Maddie, you saw me hit a triple last year. I'm in."

"Does that mean we'll have to skip apple strudel for dessert?" Maddie joked.

"I hope not." Cole shook his head from side to side. "Can't I have dessert too, Mom?"

"Of course you can," Jordan interjected. "What is Christmas break for, if not to have great family times?"

Maddie thought about Jordan losing most of his family at about Cole's age. Jordan's engaging smile at Vanessa prompted Maddie to do a double-take. And Vanessa's beaming smile to him in return revealed something more than cordiality. Maddie wondered. Did Jordan realize Vanessa's shining hazel eyes were practically the same color as his?

After eating their warmed apple dessert, the group arranged to meet in the lobby at ten o'clock. That way Chef Dexter and his staff would have gone home for the night. So precisely at ten, Jordan led the merry adventurers into the dimly lit kitchen. He snapped on the switch, and presto, their workspace was ready.

"I haven't made rosettes since my last year of high school," Maddie admitted, placing a rolled-up towel on the counter.

Vanessa gestured at her son. "Cole and I are okay watching, unless you give us something to do."

For his part, Cole hovered nearby as if eager to be in the center of the action. Jordan removed a pan from a rack hanging above the center island.

"Let's be careful to not mess up Dexter's kitchen," he said. "If he finds things out of order come morning, we'll be in trouble."

Maddie unfolded the rosette irons and removed the recipe, which she handed to Vanessa. "You and Cole can supervise. Read out what we need."

"Bill has kept me so busy," Vanessa complained. "Cole and I've been living on pizza and stir-fry takeout. This is going to be a real treat."

"Yeah, Mom."

"Let's see." Vanessa stepped closer to the lighting. "The recipe makes four dozen cookies. You need to find two eggs, a cup of milk, two tablespoons of sugar, a quarter teaspoon of salt, and one cup of flour."

Jordan retrieved two eggs from the fridge and carefully set them in a dish on the counter.

"Do we need cooking oil?" he asked, lifting the pan.

Vanessa scanned the paper. "Yes. Flavorless oil." She flipped the paper over.

"You also need, it says here ... a baby girl."

"What?" Maddie gasped, her jaw dropping open.

"It's not the recipe," Vanessa answered, sounding as perplexed as Maddie felt. "There's a note written back here."

Maddie snatched the note out of Vanessa's hand and squinted at it.

"Jordan, I can't imagine how we missed this," Maddie said to the beat of her pounding heart.

He rushed over. "Tell me quick. What's it say?"

"The note is handwritten and reads, 'Mom, I have come to love an orphan baby girl. She is so precious with huge brown eyes and curly hair. I would love to keep her.'"

"What's that got to do with cookies?" Cole inquired, leaning over Maddie's shoulder.

Jordan dropped the pan with a clatter. "Read it again, Maddie. Please."

This time, Maddie used her stern courtroom voice and read it aloud, "'Mom, I have come to love an orphan baby girl. She is so precious with huge brown eyes and curly hair. I would love to keep her.'"

"Do you understand what you just read?" Jordan gaped at Maddie, his forehead creased like he'd just aged five years before her eyes.

"Ye-es," Maddie answered cautiously. "Rosalyn had started an orphanage there in Austria."

"Right. And if she was tempted to adopt one of her own orphans, what might she have named her? Nora Star." Jordan answered his own question.

Maddie rubbed out a spasm in the back of her neck, the note clutched in her other hand. "That's certainly possible, because Rosalyn never married, as far as we know."

"Bill will want to know about this," Vanessa insisted.

Maddie waved the recipe in the air. "I still don't understand why I failed to see this note in the attic. I guess I was too excited over finding the cookie irons."

"Crying over spilled milk will not get the cookies made," Vanessa proclaimed, pouring oil into the pan. "I will heat the oil. Maddie, you and Jordan mix the batter."

"Yeah, let's get these cookies cooking." Cole sounded hungry again.

"Great idea." Maddie laughingly broke an egg into a mixing bowl. "Tomorrow morning is plenty soon for me to begin working again."

Cole deserved a fun time and didn't need to get drawn into legal issues. Maddie stirred the bowl, her mind raging in turmoil over Nora Star. After adding the other ingredients, she poured in milk.

"Vanessa, you might as well enjoy tomorrow on the slopes," she suggested. "Maybe Cole can learn to ski."

"No way. Cole, you are not skiing. I don't want you hurt. Jordan, how about snowshoeing?" Vanessa tossed a look at Jordan with concern written all over her face.

Cole leaned against the counter, his eyes bulging. "Come on, Mom. I'd love to learn to ski."

"I have an idea." Jordan slid the bowl under the mixer. "We can go tubing again tomorrow, buddy, if you want."

"Sweet." Cole stepped closer, his eyes glued on the batter whirling.

Vanessa widened her eyes, but stayed mum while Jordan operated the mixer. When he stopped it, he let Maddie wipe the bowl with a spatula. She stirred the batter a few times for good measure before restarting the mixer. Maddie stopped the machine the instant Vanessa pronounced the oil was the correct temperature.

"Drop in a bit of batter to see if I'm right," Vanessa said.

The dab of batter Maddie dropped into the oil bubbled and floated to the top. When it turned golden brown, she scooped it out hurriedly, declaring, "Oh yes, it's ready."

Vanessa pulled the bowl closer to the stovetop. Maddie showed her how to take a rosette iron by the handle and dip the metal star into the boiling oil.

"Now you try," Maddie told her. "Jordan, find a platter and cover it with loads of paper towel for blotting. Vanessa will need your help."

Vanessa took the hot oily iron, then blotted it on some paper towel before dipping it into the batter bowl. The batter adhered to the iron, and it was her turn to place the iron into the heated oil.

"Cole, come and watch the cookie form," she told her son. "See, it's turning golden. Now's the time to take it out, I think."

Vanessa slowly moved the iron over the platter, telling Jordan, "Take a fork and gently pry off the cookie. It's very flakey, so be careful."

They all watched as Jordan pried the cookie loose.

"Perfect!" Vanessa chimed. "Now, let the excess oil soak into the paper towel and we'll make another one."

Maddie shoved her hands against her hips. "Hey, this was my idea. Suddenly, I'm just a spectator."

"You promised me that if I came up here, you'd show me a nice time," Vanessa replied, heating both irons in the hot oil before dipping them both in batter. "Isn't that why you arranged this?"

Maddie chuckled good-naturedly. She and Vanessa were used to jousting with each other. It wasn't too long before the platter was filled with golden rosettes. Cole smacking his lips got everyone laughing.

Vanessa read from the recipe. "We're supposed to dust the cookies with powdered sugar."

"I'll see if I can find any." Jordan hastened to the cupboard, rummaging around until eventually holding up a box. "Success!"

He brought the powdered sugar over to Vanessa, who held a sifter above the cookies while he poured in the sugar. Once the cookies were nicely covered, she took Jordan's hand and held it high in the air like they were victors.

"Look what a nice job Jordan did. Let's enjoy his handiwork."

Old memories rekindled and new ones being made, Maddie was bursting with happiness as she bit into the light delicacy. "Yums," resounded through the kitchen with Cole exclaiming, "It tastes like funnel cake at the fair."

Vanessa began to chortle, pointing at Jordan. Maddie and Cole joined in the gigglefest.

"What's wrong?" Jordan asked, gazing around the kitchen.

This time it was Cole who did the pointing, prompting Jordan to look down. The entire front of his sweater was doused in white sugar. Vanessa rushed to find a towel and started brushing powder off his sweater.

She smiled up at him. "Hold still. Don't move your head."

Then wrapping the towel around her forefinger, Vanessa approached Jordan's face, commanding, "It's on your chin too."

She wiped it from his face, and he flashed a bright grin, joking, "Now I know how Cole must feel at times."

Maddie absorbed the family scene. She was moved in her spirit. To think something so special could come from Stewart's interfering with the Star estate seemed improbable. Yet Maddie knew nothing was impossible for God.

Conscious of the late hour, Maddie said, "Everybody take one more for the road. I suggest we wrap the remaining rosettes for Chef Dexter as a peace offering in case we've messed up his kitchen."

"I can take care of that," Vanessa volunteered.

"You and Cole need plenty of shut-eye for your day of tubing," Maddie directed. "I'll help Jordan tidy up."

Cole grabbed cookies in both hands and dashed away. Vanessa smiled and waved, leaving Maddie to wash out the bowl, pan, and spatula. Jordan dried.

As water drained from the sink, he turned to Maddie with anxious eyes. "Are you as stunned as I am about Rosalyn writing about a baby girl on the back of the recipe?"

"Absolutely." The weight of the discovery pressed down on her shoulders. "I hoped the rumor of another heir was just that. Rosalyn's note fuels our task in finding out if she did indeed adopt Nora."

"Where do we go from here?"

"I'll photograph the note and message it to Harry and Bill. Are there any other photo albums, family Bibles, or other papers we haven't investigated?"

Jordan shrugged. "I can rummage through Grandfather's desk again. Maybe he kept a safe deposit box at the bank. I haven't searched for a key."

"Do that first thing in the morning," Maddie said, gathering up the recipe.

Jordan's hand rested on the light switch, when he posed another question. "Do you know why Vanessa doesn't want Cole learning to ski?"

"I'm not sure. She might have safety concerns, or feels it's too costly for a single mother to encourage."

Jordan lifted his eyebrows. "It's not too expensive if her friend owns a ski resort."

"True, but she lives seven hours from here."

"So Cole's father isn't involved in his life?" Jordan probed.

"No. It seems Vanessa and I have that in common."

"How is that, Maddie? Was your dad missing too?"

She breathed out a tortured sigh. "No, my dad is a great father. What I mean is Vanessa and I both chose guys who wanted to be off seeing the world instead of settling down. Fortunately for me, I refused to marry him."

"You refer to Stewart, the attorney opposing us?"

"Yes," Maddie groaned, pushing out her bottom lip. "And unlike Cole's father, Stewart keeps reappearing."

Chapter 19

Maddie wound her way into the Stix the next morning to find Vanessa and her son. Cole faced the entrance eating a stack of pancakes like his stomach was hollow.

He looked up sporting a grin as she walked over. "I'm learning to ski today."

"You're not tubing?" Maddie wondered aloud.

Vanessa set down her teacup with a definite clink. "Our plans changed. Jordan phoned last night. He learned to ski when he was much younger than Cole."

"I see."

Maddie dropped onto the empty chair beside Cole. She had to admit these developments were taking her by surprise. Was Jordan's outreach to Vanessa and Cole something more than a client befriending the paralegal and her son?

Vanessa began to giggle and Maddie tuned her ears to listen to her explanation.

"He's even taking the day off to teach him to ski," Vanessa said, her cheeks growing rosy. "Maddie, I'm so glad you suggested we all make the rosettes. I can't thank you enough for inviting us here. Besides being away from work pressures, Starlight is a fairyland to me."

Maddie had no words. She silently opened her menu.

Vanessa leaned forward and whispered, "You don't think I'm encouraging Jordan, do you?"

Cole jumped up. "I see Jordan. I'll be back."

"I think it's nice for you both to be friends," Maddie said, trying to be discreet. She was still trying to absorb the news when she added, "After all, Jordan is my client. Our relationship is strictly business."

Vanessa's eyes shone. "So if something does happen, you're okay with it?"

Before Maddie could answer, the server arrived to take her order. Maddie's appetite suddenly shriveled to nothing at the sight of Jordan heading to their table dressed in bright ski apparel. She asked the server for coffee and a toasted bagel with cream cheese.

The server nodded. "Chef's special pumpkin cream cheese?"

"I guess so," was her tepid reply.

Cole and Jordan sauntered up, both guys grinning from ear to ear.

"Did you hear I'm teaching Cole to ski today?" Jordan asked.

"Yes. It looks like a sunny day on the slopes," Maddie answered, hiding her letdown. "I don't blame you for standing me up on a final tour of your attic."

"Touché, you caught me." His shining eyes said, *Can you blame me?*

He turned to Vanessa with his winsome face all smiles. "I hope you will join us. You admitted that you ski a little."

"I would love to." Vanessa put down her napkin, glancing at Maddie. "I hate the idea of you being stuck in a cramped attic. Perhaps I should help you."

"And spoil your vacation? Never."

Maddie's coffee arrived steaming hot, which gave her a chance to collect her thoughts. She cradled her hands around the mug.

"You all will go soaring over moguls. I will be digging for evidence of an adoption by Rosalyn or any other heirs. One trunk to go."

Vanessa and Cole strode away in high spirits.

Jordan leaned over, telling Maddie in low tones, "You know what? I found in the desk a most interesting key."

"For a safe deposit box?"

"Could be. I will take it to the bank on Monday."

He spun around. Maddie nibbled on her bagel, trying to figure out what had just happened. She wasn't left sitting alone for long. Chef Dexter approached her table, wiping his hands on a towel.

The African American chef looked elegant in his black buttoned-up chef's coat and red piping on the cuffs. His shiny black hair contained sporadic white hairs, so Maddie guessed his age to be in his forties. She loved his food and told him so, which evoked a smile.

"I'm glad I caught you before you left," he told Maddie.

She smiled in return. "Did you find the treat we left for you?"

"Ms. Stone, I came out to thank you for the rosettes." Dexter pulled out the chair where Vanessa had just been sitting.

"My friends call me Maddie," she urged.

"They are delicious and well made. Where did you find star-shaped irons?"

"Chef, I'm glad you enjoyed them."

He jumped in. "Enjoyed them? They are wonderful. I'm putting them on our dessert menu as our signature dessert."

"Jordan and I were looking through his attic when we found the rosette irons along with the recipe."

"Even better." Dexter smiled, his dark eyes sparkling. "We'll feature the new dessert as the 'Star Family Recipe.'"

"I love it." Maddie clapped her hands. "Jordan will as well, I think."

"I know you've met Sylvia in Jordan's office."

"Yes, and she is one friendly and competent lady."

He smiled a toothy smile just like Sylvia's. "That's my mama. My daddy, rest his soul, was the superintendent of the buildings and grounds for Maynard. I am older than Jordan and watched him grow up."

Maddie sipped her coffee, wondering where Dexter was heading with his homespun conversation. Then he flashed a wink so rapidly, Maddie wondered if she'd imagined it.

"We have few secrets around here," he said, nodding. "I know why you're here. We're all praying you save the estate for Jordan."

Maddie held her reply until after the server cleared the used plates. "The Stix has cleared out, so I am safe in saying I, too, hope all is settled in Jordan's favor. Please keep praying."

"Will do. And please, Ms. Maddie, don't you leave here too soon." Dexter leaned in closer. "It's easy for me to see Jordan is much happier with you here."

"What are you saying, Dexter?"

"Jordan put his life on hold by helping Maynard to run the lodge and village. Then he became Maynard's right hand. Jordan hasn't let himself find happiness and companionship."

Maddie could sympathize. "Never?"

A cloud passed over Dexter's face. "After college, he returned to run this place. There was a family who arrived every winter and summer for their vacations, and he fell in love with their daughter. I wasn't privy to everything, but there was talk of them marrying and her moving up here. But she left him for the draw of the big city. He was never the same again."

"I didn't know. He's a terrific guy and easy on the eyes too."

Dexter clasped his hands together. "That's good news, because I think he's getting sweet on you."

The essence of what he was saying sunk deep into Maddie's spirit. This was the moment to put to rest any idle talk about her and Jordan, and any fleeting idea she once had to be something other than his lawyer.

Mustering a gritty tone, Maddie set Dexter straight. "You know I am Jordan's lawyer. My relationship has to stay strictly professional."

"You won't always be his attorney," Dexter replied, sounding hopeful.

Maddie stopped him with a raised hand. "Do you know where Jordan is today?"

"Isn't he in his office?"

"No. He's up on the mountain teaching my legal assistant and her fifteen-year-old son to ski."

She pointed to the seats. "They were just here."

"Nice-looking kid."

"Yes, Cole is. And his mother, Vanessa, is single and the one who helped Jordan make the rosettes. Fact is, I think you should ask Jordan, along with Vanessa and Cole, to teach you how to make your new signature dessert. You watch for the same magical sparks I saw when they were creating together."

Once more, Dexter clasped his hands together. His eyes glistened.

"You think?"

"You might be creating more than star rosettes in the coming months."

"Our little chat pleases me no end." He gave her a high five. "And Ms. Maddie, thanks again for fixing the rosettes. I'm going to get busy finding more of those star-shaped irons. These delicacies will be a hit at our upcoming Christmas festival."

Dexter breezed away to his kitchen, whistling a happy tune. Maddie dug some cash from her pocket and threw it on the table. As she stood, she saw Gretchen stringing lights on a second Christmas tree, which had just gone up in the lobby this morning. An idea flooded her mind and before she left the café, Maddie swiftly made her decision.

DARKNESS HAD JUST SETTLED in for the night when Maddie found a comfy seat by the lobby fireplace where she sipped a large cup of hot cocoa. Chef Dexter made it for her "special," he'd said, piling it high with whipped cream.

Nailing down the details of her earlier idea kept her pretty busy, which suited her perfectly. The activity helped take her mind off finding nothing of any consequence in Jordan's attic. If only she'd gotten the key from him to take to the bank first thing Monday morning. He hadn't surfaced since he'd traipsed up the mountain with Vanessa and Cole.

Then again, without a court order, the banker might only allow Jordan to have access as the estate's executor. The possibility the Star case might be her first legal flop in years floated through her tired mind. She vowed not to let it happen and sought to lighten her mood.

She enjoyed watching folks laughing around the decorated Christmas tree, which captured all the family spirit of a Norman Rockwell painting. The home-like atmosphere had the opposite impact on Maddie. With no warning, she desired nothing more than to get on the next plane and fly home. She had lived out of a suitcase long enough.

Another thought went tumbling through her mind like a runaway dust bunny. No one waited for her at the apartment. Why hurry away from Starlight? Before the roaring fire, to the lively tune of "I'll Be Home for Christmas," she could see that for too long she'd elevated the law firm above her family, above her life.

Such an unrelenting focus on the law had led her to date Stewart. He shared none of Maddie's passions, and never really encouraged her to expand her horizons. She stirred her hot chocolate, wanting more for her future, when Vanessa and Cole burst in the lobby. Animated, they stomped snow from their shoes. Their hooting and laughter snapped Maddie out of her contemplative mood.

"It's snowing like crazy outside. Jordan said we might get six inches of fresh snow." Vanessa sounded out of breath. "How did things go today?"

Maddie lifted her cup. "This hot chocolate is the best. I'm warming up after hours in a cold attic."

"My toes are numb." Cole stomped his feet again. "I'm off to take a hot shower."

Vanessa removed her jacket, telling him to go ahead. "I'll bring you cocoa a bit later."

Cole dashed away. Maddie patted the empty seat next to her on the sofa, telling Vanessa, "I'm eager to hear about your thrills on the mountain."

Vanessa plunked beside her, bombarding Maddie with questions. "Did you find evidence to help Jordan save Star Mountain? Is he going to stay in Starlight?"

"Whoa, you are wired," Maddie said, leaning back to gaze at her.

Vanessa pulled off her thick mittens. "Sorry. After spending time with Jordan on the mountain, I so want things to work out for him."

"Me too," Maddie replied with gentleness. "I found photos of him with his parents, Rosalyn at her orphanage with groups of children, but nothing to suggest he has other unknown family members. None of the orphans in the photos were named Nora. That's good news at least."

"I know you, Madison Stone. You aren't hindered by the impossible." Vanessa hugged her jacket to her. "Is Harry doing enough to assist?"

"He actually flew to Austria last night. I await his call." Maddie looked into Vanessa's eyes keenly. "What was your day like?"

Vanessa rubbed her hands along her ski pants. "It's been ages since I've skied. I'll be sore tomorrow."

"And?" Maddie raised an eyebrow, waiting for the big reveal.

"I don't know what you mean."

"You said it yourself. You spent the whole day with Jordan. How was it?"

A dreamy glow swept across Vanessa's face. "He is attentive and spent tons of time helping Cole. By the end of our last run, Cole was skiing quite well."

"So you'll be buying him skis for Christmas?"

"It's worse than that. On our way back to the lodge, Cole asked if we could move to Starlight."

Maddie's hand flew to cover her mouth. "Did Jordan hear him say that?"

"Maddie, it was Jordan's idea."

"No way!" Maddie felt dazed by the speed of their relationship.

Vanessa raised her shoulders and let them fall dramatically. "I still can hardly believe it myself. We were riding up a lift together when Jordan suggested Cole spend summers working here at Starlight. He said there are plenty of grass-mowing and painting projects Cole could do to earn money for college."

"What did you say?"

Vanessa blushed. "I told my son that I would miss him too much during the summer. Ah ... then Jordan suggested I could visit on weekends."

"Visit Cole? Or possibly visit Jordan?"

Vanessa unwound the scarf from her neck. "He was so considerate to me today. It's been years since I went on a date. Not that this was a date ..."

Her words trailed away. Maddie pressed her friend and legal assistant to be careful. "Vanessa, please think this through. What signals are you giving him?"

"You read too much into Cole's ski lessons." Vanessa sounded defensive.

Maddie tapped her index finger against her temple as if she were the one doing the thinking. "Vanessa, consider this. Jordan grew up with no siblings. He spent his summer mowing and painting at Star Mountain. Thus far, our investigation reveals he will inherit the whole enchilada. He has no one to enjoy it with and no one to leave it to."

Vanessa fanned her face with her hand. "Yikes, you're moving way too fast."

"Vanessa, I think Jordan and you are at great risk from cupid's arrows. Worse yet, I think Bill Barron will rue the day he sent you up here."

Vanessa kept fanning her face.

Maddie drained her hot chocolate, saying not a word about Jordan's promise to his grandfather to find a wife within five years. She rose to her feet with another purpose in mind.

"I need to review my notes and prepare for an important meeting tomorrow. Are you and Cole free to join me tonight for dinner in the café?"

"That sounds great. I worked up quite an appetite keeping up with Jordan."

Maddie walked Vanessa to the elevators, saying, "I wouldn't be surprised if very soon Chef Dexter will be featuring Star Family Rosettes on the Cinnamon Stix menu."

"How lovely," Vanessa replied, hugging her jacket with a far-off look.

Maddie touched the up button and heard the whirring of the elevator on its way down. "Chef Dexter also sends his compliments on the cookies you had made. I suggested he have you and Jordan show him how."

Vanessa nodded and stepped into the elevator when the doors swished open, seemingly lost in her vacation. Maddie hopped on, punching their floor number. She chose not to reveal any details of her upcoming Monday meeting.

Better to wait and see just what she learned first. Moreover, she didn't want to risk Vanessa spilling it to Jordan before Maddie was ready to tell him.

Chapter 20

The four of them attended the church service on Sunday. Pastor Fisher's message on loving your neighbor at Christmas inspired Maddie to become more involved in her community back home. He asked her to play the closing hymn on the piano. When she'd played the last note, Maddie looked up, startled by who she saw in the back row.

Was that Trevor Kirk sitting there and smiling at her?

She jumped up and was instantly surrounded by the teens clamoring to know when she would practice with them before the festival. Maddie navigated past them, saying, "We'll see," and rushed to find Trevor.

He was gone.

Maybe her overworked mind had simply imagined his genuine smile. Jordan stopped her on the way out, surprising her with an invitation.

"We are going for lunch in the village. Then I'm taking Vanessa and Cole to go ice-skating by the Starlight Christmas tree. Put your job aside and have fun for a change."

"I have a few calls to make," Maddie said. "I'll catch at bite at the Stix and join you at the rink, say, at one?"

"Dress warm and wear thick socks."

That said, Jordan hurried outside to catch up with Vanessa and Cole. Maddie pulled out her phone to check the time. With Austria being six hours ahead, her call might interrupt Harry's dinner. She walked at a fast clip to the lodge and phoned him from her room.

"Ms. Stone, you caught me on my way to meet my contact. I'll touch base tomorrow."

Maddie sighed into the phone. "I feel like every lead is a false lead going nowhere. You stay on it, Harry. Be sure to make it home before Christmas."

She changed into her winter wear, ate a bowl of soup in the café, and soon found her place on the ice, skating smoothly and feeling carefree for the first time in many weeks.

Her meeting tomorrow might change things, but for now, Maddie felt content to enjoy her friends.

EARLY ON MONDAY, MADDIE SWUNG by Jordan's office before heading out. She found him sitting behind his desk, hands folded, and staring at his grandfather's stained-glass stars.

"I have just a moment, Jordan. You appear to have the weight of the world on your shoulders. Is there a new problem?"

His uncertain shrug gave away more than his exaggerated smile. Maddie instantly wanted to take back her negative-sounding words. She decided to take a seat and find out what disturbed him.

She fixed her eyes on his. "Okay, spill it. As your attorney, you can tell me anything. I keep it confidential, remember?"

"Vanessa and Cole are flying home tomorrow. I want to drive them to the airport."

"I was going to, but I know Vanessa appreciates your kindness," Maddie said, sensing there may be something more to his angst. "What else is on your mind?"

He tapped the side arms of his leather chair with both hands. "I wish we would solve this mysterious relative. Having Grandfather's estate open is a serious impediment to my future. Forgive the metaphor, but it's a huge mountain I can't move by myself."

"You're forgetting it's my job to deter an imposter and I've been trying. But if you really have an unknown relative, wouldn't you want to meet them? We could know something soon," Maddie said, trying to be encouraging.

"Really?" Jordan lifted his eyebrows. "Is there something I should know?"

"Now you've caught me. I am on my way to pursue a possibility."

He sat up straight. "What are you saying?"

"Remember the woman looking to buy property in Starlight? She's been told her grandfather built the town."

"Oh. I did my best to forget about her. If she's right, how is that a good thing?"

Maddie leaned forward, gesturing with her hands as if convincing a jury to find her client not guilty. "You start thinking about your life going forward, and making this the best Christmas festival Starlight has ever had. Meanwhile, let me learn if she's an imposter or family."

"Where are you meeting her?"

"Jordan, I refused to bring her here, but will see her up at the Galaxy Grill."

"Way up there?"

"Her choice. I should be off, but what about the key you found? Are you going to the bank?"

Jordan sprung to his feet, setting his chair to rocking. "Oops, I'm seeing the bank manager in ten minutes. You and I will compare notes later. And Maddie, please work your magic."

She fired off a mock salute and hurried away, hoping this chat would actually turn out in Jordan's favor. At least he hadn't pressed her to explain further. Maddie had learned from the school of hard knocks things went awry whenever she dropped her guard, Stewart being the prime example.

A kernel of doubt remained lodged in her mind on the windy and slippery drive up the mountain. As she hit a patch of deep snow, she wished for just a moment that she were in Opal's mammoth 4X4 truck with its giant wheels.

MADDIE ZIPPED THE JACKET TO HER CHIN. Her purse slung on her shoulder, she bent her head and battled the wind as she hiked from the parking lot to the Galaxy Grill. A sense of dread peppered Maddie. The woman she was about to meet could destroy Jordan's hopes and the very mountain she was standing on.

She burst inside out of the cold. A scraggly pine tree with strands of silver tinsel created a poor imitation of a Christmas tree. Jordan needed to switch out the Charlie Brown tree for something more festive.

Maddie scanned the café among the rosy-cheeked skiers for the realtor's potential buyer. There sat Jeanette

Carpenter huddled at a corner table, her appearance matching Linda's description with great heaps of blond hair atop her head.

Jeanette's face abruptly turned to smiles when Maddie walked over, and she stood gripping Maddie's hand with fervor. "Glad you wore the blue jacket Linda said you'd have on. It's been ages since my realtor explained you're the expert on Star family history."

"Thanks, Jeanette." Maddie removed her hand from the woman's clutches. "I understand Linda showed you several properties for sale in Starlight. Too bad she couldn't come today."

The instant Maddie snagged a chair, Jeanette erupted in laughter. Her excitement spilled forth like a gushing stream. "It's super how you're making time for me. This town is so lovely and friendly. The snowy mountain is wonderful and so different from the Arizona desert where I live now."

"You already have hot tea. I'll buy a coffee and be right back."

Maddie helped herself over at the beverage station, and then rejoined Jeanette with a steaming cup of hazelnut coffee.

"The view up here is spectacular." Jeanette pointed out the large window. "It's a great spot to talk about my connection to this fabulous mountain."

"It's too windy for skiing," Maddie said, calmly sipping the java.

While the two ladies drank their hot beverages, for a shining moment, Maddie imagined what it might be like if she lived around beautiful Starlight rather than in her confining condo back in D.C.

Jeanette interrupted Maddie's wayward thinking when she blurted, "I hope to buy a house that looks like it's set in Austria."

The little tidbit about Austria reminded Maddie what was at stake. She masked rising concern by drinking her coffee. Maddie regained her composure and decided to probe a bit further.

"Jeanette, are you from Austria? You sound American."

"I don't know much about my family," she admitted. "You see, I'm adopted, but based on everything I've learned, there is a strong Austrian influence. In fact, I now know my grandfather built much of Starlight."

"I've done a fair bit of local research and have yet to encounter the name Carpenter," Maddie said, furrowing her brow.

Jeanette waved a sheaf of papers in the air. "I've got my own research."

"May I see your papers?" Maddie reached out her hand.

"Certainly." Jeanette gave her the stapled pages with a fiery chuckle. "It's my grandfather who I'm the most optimistic about."

"Let's see what you have uncovered." Maddie skimmed the notes, trepidation building.

She flipped through a few more pages, telling Jeanette, "I can see why you're searching for family links in Starlight. You have compiled interesting facts about this special place."

"I'm a gal with an unknown past, so I'm determined to find my roots here and put down some of my own."

"A laudable goal," was Maddie's discreet reply.

Her eyes shifted to the top of the next page and her eyes rounded. Her heart skipped a beat. She hoped her face didn't divulge her complete surprise.

"Is this man your grandfather?" she asked Jeanette in a controlled voice.

"Yes ma'am. That's him."

"With your last name of Carpenter, I am shocked to see his name. He is obviously your mother's father."

"What a relief." Jeanette heaved a sigh and wiped her eyes. "My long search has paid off."

"I'm sure your grandfather had an important role in building this town. Jordan Star will be interested to learn about you. I will tell him about your discovery and encourage him to meet you."

Maddie's mouth grew incredibly dry, and she stopped talking long enough to finish her coffee. "Meanwhile, I suggest Linda bring you to the library. The village librarian has written a book filled with history of the founding people you should find enlightening."

"Wonderful!" Jeanette cried.

Maddie took a pad from her purse, which she slid to Jeanette to write down her phone number. "I'll call when I can arrange for you to meet Jordan Star."

MADDIE WASTED NO TIME roaring back to the lodge. She assumed Jordan had returned from the bank and hadn't yet gone up on the mountain with Vanessa and Cole, his new favorite pastime. Maddie knew he was anxious to learn about Jeanette Carpenter.

A question dogged her as she went straight to his office. Would Jordan make time for Jeanette or leave her to his lawyer?

Her client was eating a sandwich at his desk. When she scurried in, he gazed at her with an uptight look.

"Well?" He lurched to his feet. "Have we lost?"

"You'd better sit down, Jordan. I intend to."

"Your tone says it all." He resumed his seat with a ragged sigh.

Maddie took the seat across from his desk. "Jeanette Carpenter is adopted, and her roots go back to Austria. She's here looking for a farm to buy because she was told her grandfather built much of this town, including Edelweiss Lodge."

Jordan's shoulders slumped. "I don't understand. Her name isn't Nora Star."

"You know, Jordan, when ladies get married, they change their names. She let me look through her research notes where I saw her grandfather's name. I was so hoping she was mistaken until I read her notes."

"You have me gravely concerned. Maddie, what will happen to Starlight with another heir?"

"Listen," she said, reaching out and touching his hand. "I invited her to meet you because I think you owe it to her. You should show her around."

Jordan pushed his food tray away. "Can things get any worse?"

"I should be ashamed of myself for not telling you sooner," Maddie said, trying hard not to break out in a grin. "Things for you have gotten a lot better. Her grandfather is not Maynard Star."

"He's not? Who is he then?"

Maddie clasped her hands together on his desk. "Do you remember we found the name Berndt Panzer? He's the contractor that built this lodge, and who knows how many other buildings he might have built for Maynard."

"Help me to understand what you just said. My mind can't process it fast enough." Jordan's deepening frown betrayed his mounting frustration.

"In the attic, I read you the newspaper article where your grandfather refused to pay Berndt Panzer until he corrected the construction problems on this building."

Jordan stared at her blankly, and then burst out laughing. "He's her grandfather? I should fire you as my lawyer for that."

"It was terrible of me. I had myself so worked up, you can't imagine my pure relief when I saw Berndt Panzer was her grandfather."

"You really scared me."

A smile crept to Maddie's face. "I don't think you'll fire me because I just gave you good news. Now what about us celebrating at dinner?"

"We'll give Vanessa and Cole a great send-off. I have a Chamber of Commerce meeting in a few minutes, and then I'm taking them for one last run on the tubes. How about six o'clock?"

Maddie gathered her purse. "What did you learn at the bank?"

He withdrew a folded paper from the top drawer of his desk.

"This was inside Grandfather's safe deposit box along with a few other things."

Maddie took the letter, her eyes quickly glancing over the short missive. "This is incredible, Jordan. Listen to his reassuring words."

"Okay, I will."

"'Jordan, you are like a son to me. You show your love for me, the people here, and for the mountain. You rarely think of yourself, which is why I asked you to promise to find a wife and get married. Your grandmother and I were so happy on this earth. Knowing she is in heaven carried me through the worst of days.

"'So did you, and I thank you. I pray I did the same for you. Find happiness, my boy, in your faith, in your family. Don't try to run this place alone. Keep the gold pocket watch. It was your great-grandfather's. I hope one day you will give it to your own son. You make me proud and I love you.'"

Maddie wiped tears from her eyes. She set the letter down, and looking up at Jordan, she caught him dabbing his eyes. The silence that rose up between them was shattered when Sylvia knocked on the door.

"Your chamber folk are starting to arrive. Can I show them in?"

"Sylvia, it's great seeing you again. I'm leaving." Maddie rose to her feet, telling Jordan, "We will see each other at dinner downstairs."

"Thanks for everything, Maddie," Jordan said, his eyes gleaming. "I mean it."

She left Jordan to conduct his business. Maynard's words of praise and love for his grandson redeemed her opinion of him after forcing Jordan to promise to marry within five years or lose his inheritance. While his reasons were sound, she did not agree with his exacting such a promise.

She stopped in the café and placed a lunch order to go. While she waited for Chef Dexter to cook her medium cheeseburger and sweet potato fries, Maddie thought long and hard about her next priority to exclude Nora Star as an heir.

In the elevator, with smells of lunch in the bag tempting her, Maddie decided to call Bill for his blessing. She wanted to file a motion and ask Judge Marks to either compel Stewart to produce Nora for a deposition or throw their case out of court for good.

Chapter 21

Days later, moisture from Maddie's breath sparkled in the air as she bounded up the steps to the county courthouse while also talking on her phone with Harry.

"I'm due in Judge Marks' courtroom in five minutes," she said. "From everything I've heard, the locals call him 'Groucho.'"

"Okay." Harry grunted in her ear. "I don't want Groucho Marks holding you in contempt for being late."

"He wouldn't do that."

"Yup, Bill told me he did. Something about time in jail."

"What? Judge Marks threw my boss in jail for being late? I'd better hustle in there."

"Madison, it wasn't Bill," Harry shot back. "But a lawyer on the opposing side. Judge Marks fined her a grand. Anyway, I did a final sweep of all my sources and have come up with a big fat zero for Nora Star. No credit history, no birth records, no driver's license that I could find. Zip. Nada."

Maddie stopped short of entering the courthouse. She didn't want Stewart overhearing her conversation with the private investigator.

"Which you might not find if she lives in Austria," she countered, snugging the phone against her ear.

"True, which is why I'm still in Rumphrey. I found out after the orphanage merged with a local hospital some years back that there was a fire. No records have turned up proving Rosalyn adopted a child named Nora."

"Thanks, Harry. I hope this gives me a leg up before Groucho Marks. Bye for now. Don't want to risk my law license."

She hung up and rushed into the courtroom, her mind quickly reviewing the motion she'd filed. Bill had convinced her to hold off pressuring Stewart to produce Nora. He'd simply wanted her to persuade Judge Marks to change his mind and not make her wait until January 12th to distribute the assets.

Judge Marks pounding his gavel startled Maddie.

Was she in trouble?

Wait. The judge was actually dismissing an earlier matter. The clerk hadn't yet called her case. She was in the clear. Relieved, Maddie straightened her lapel and approached the well of the courtroom. She perched on a chair opposite from Stewart who sat flicking through the file as if he owned the world.

With narrowed eyes, Maddie was keenly aware of his presence. She refused, however, to glance his way. Because of him, everyone's life in Starlight seemed to be on edge, on hold. Including Jordan's. Including hers.

The clerk called the attorneys forward. Maddie placed her briefcase on the attorney's table and withdrew her file. She strode directly to the podium where she placed her research folder. Atop of this she rested her court file, which she opened with one swift move.

Judge Marks gazed down from his lofty perch. "Ms. Stone, you are here in advance of your scheduled court date. What have you to say in support of your motion?"

"Your Honor, Attorney Dunham recently notified my firm and this court that by researching an Internet website called Family Finder, he found a reference to one Nora Star, who he claims might be a cousin to the rightful heir, Jordan Star."

The judge interrupted, "Sounds like they've done some of your work for you."

"It may appear so, Your Honor." Maddie swallowed. "In fact, we have searched and searched to find Nora ever since being notified of her existence."

"I'd like to hear about your efforts," Judge Marks interrupted.

Maddie gripped the edge of the podium. "Our investigator just phoned me from Austria, where we have found no such person. We've subpoenaed the website owner. They can't find a record of who created the account, which they admit is highly unusual."

Judge Marks toyed with his gavel as if ready to bang it again. "Based on your failure to find the heir, you want the court to set a date to finalize? Is that what you're telling me?"

"Your Honor, that is exactly the relief we seek," Maddie assured him. "I might add, the website where we found the name Nora Star is unreliable. Any person with a computer and Internet connection can create a fake file, including Attorney Dunham's firm."

The judge scowled at Maddie. "Hold on. I don't approve of such unfounded claims in my courtroom."

"I agree, Your Honor," Stewart objected from his seat at the table.

Maddie tapped her file with her fingertips. "The entire claim by Attorney Dunham is based on unfounded assertions. It is time for the charade to end."

"Careful there, Ms. Stone. I decide when a case is ready to be closed," Judge Marks barked, thumbing through his file. "Please address Mr. Dunham's motion that you produce Nora Star for deposition."

Panic swept over Maddie. She fumbled through her court file and rifled through her research file. She had no such motion from Stewart.

Had he sabotaged her once again?

"Your Honor." She lifted her chin and dropped her voice an octave. "I have not received opposing counsel's filing."

Judge Marks ripped off his glasses and stared at his clerk. "Do we have a copy to give Ms. Stone?"

From her desk in the corner of the courtroom, the clerk waved a copy. Maddie picked up her file folder and walked to the desk where the clerk took time to write the date and time at the bottom of Maddie's copy.

While Maddie was waiting at the desk, and from the corner of her eye, she saw Stewart walk to the podium and plunk his court file on top of Maddie's research file.

He began addressing the judge. "Your Honor—"

"Excuse me." Maddie bustled back to the podium. "I am not finished. I'm still responding to the motion you never bothered to send to me."

The judge glared at both attorneys. Was it Maddie's imagination or did he sling a fiery eye dart at Stewart?

He finally intoned, "She is correct, Mr. Dunham. You will have your chance when Ms. Stone is finished."

In response, Stewart grabbed up his file and stalked back to the attorney's table.

Maddie's eyes quickly scanned the copy of Stewart's motion she'd just received from the clerk. "Your Honor, it is unbelievable for Attorney Dunham to demand we produce for deposition an heir of whom we have no knowledge. There is no credible evidence Nora Star exists. Since Mr. Dunham and his firm supposedly found this imposter, they should make her available for us to question her."

When Maddie attempted to slide the motion into her research file, she couldn't find it. She looked first at the clerk, then at Stewart. Maddie turned and sped to his table where without permission she rummaged through his files.

"Hey, what do you think you're doing?" he bellowed.

She ignored him and kept searching. There stuck inside his file she found her missing file folder. Stewart had swiped her research right off the podium! How dare he?

Her mind spinning, Maddie hastened back to the podium where she raised her file in the air. "Excuse me, Your Honor. As you see, Mr. Dunham stole my file while you were watching. We've been dealing with this type of skullduggery since he filed to delay the settlement. We renew our request to set an earlier date to finalize the Star estate."

Maddie turned and strode back to her table. Blood pounded in her veins and against her ears as she passed Stewart. Her eyes burned into his. He strolled to the podium as if confident he was winning. She would never forgive his shenanigans. Not in a thousand years.

Stewart began his argument before the judge. All the while, Maddie reorganized her files, her mind oblivious to what he was saying. She couldn't believe Stewart had the chutzpah to continue this charade before the court. Before she realized it, Judge Marks was speaking, his glasses resting on the edge of his nose, and his voice razor sharp.

"A name of a prospective relative entered on social media does not rise to the level of an official document such as a birth certificate. Based on representations by Ms. Stone, I find there is no further evidence of an additional heir. If Mr. Dunham doesn't produce Nora Star by the end of December, the court allows the estate to finalize."

Bang went the judge's gavel. His clerk called the next case.

Maddie took his ruling as a partial win. As she seized her briefcase, Stewart grabbed her arm. She twisted from his grip.

"I suggest you get out of my sight. You have sunk to a dangerous new low."

She whirled away. In the hallway, Maddie heard her former boyfriend and present nemesis calling her name. She could think of only one way to deal with her fury, and that was to take it out on the slopes. Maddie needed time to think before calling her boss.

Nagging questions tortured her mind all the way back to the lodge. She was missing something, but what? Was it possible Stewart's court filings were simply for revenge? That made little sense. After all, he was the one who had broken off their engagement.

BY THE TIME SHE REACHED THE LODGE, Maddie found a sense of calm. She wouldn't sink to Stewart's level, no matter what sneaky tricks he pulled. Soaring down a few ski runs would help her to know if she had a good reason to stay any longer in Starlight. She wanted to decide before calling Bill about Judge Marks' favorable ruling.

As Maddie waited for the elevator, it suddenly occurred to her, Stewart wasn't finished trying to damage her case. She must remain in the village to make sure he didn't actually produce Nora Star. Another thought leapt to the front of her mind. Maddie had never once asked Sylvia what she knew of a possible heir.

Maddie headed up the stairway slipping past Jordan who sat working behind his desk across the hall. Sylvia, his capable assistant, had just set a stack of files on her desk.

Maddie entered her office and quietly closed the door behind her.

Sylvia looked up in surprise. Maddie placed a finger to her lips before asking,

"Do you have time to answer a question?"

Sylvia's eyes shot toward Jordan's office, doubt spreading across her face.

Maddie knew of Sylvia's loyalty to the Star family and sought to reassure her. "I'm still trying to rule out possible heirs to the estate, but Jordan was a child most of the time when Rosalyn was living."

"Oh, I see what you mean." Sylvia nodded. "Yes, he was a youngster."

"Jordan says you know more about the Star family than anyone. I should have talked to you before now."

Sylvia's eyes lit up when she smiled at Maddie. "I worked for Maynard and later for Jordan's father when he was alive. I was a bit older than Robert."

"So you knew Rosalyn too?"

"Not very well." Sylvia leaned forward, adding in a gentle voice, "She was just different. I can't explain it. She was the one who ran off to Austria. She had no interest in living with the rest of the family or here in Starlight."

"Is it possible Rosalyn had a child, and Jordan wouldn't know?"

Sylvia tilted her head. "I don't know. Not here in Starlight. I suppose it's possible in Europe."

"Wouldn't her parents have known of it?"

"Most likely. And then, I believe I would have heard of it too."

Maddie gazed over her shoulder toward Jordan's office. "Is it possible Rosalyn adopted a child in Austria?"

"You mean like Nora Star?" Sylvia asked, tenting her hands.

Regret swept over Maddie for waiting to broach this matter with Sylvia. Well, it was too late now to undo any damage her delay might have caused.

She forged ahead. "You know about her? Did she adopt Nora in Austria then?"

"Jordan told me about the two of you finding Nora's name," Sylvia confided. "He asked me if it was true."

Maddie removed the attic recipe from her research file and handed the yellowed paper over to Sylvia. "On the back of this recipe, Rosalyn wrote to her mother about an infant girl. It appears she wanted to adopt her."

"Oh yes. I vividly recall that drama."

When Sylvia paused to read the note, her head began bobbing. "I told Jordan how her parents were against it. Maynard threatened to stop sending Rosalyn more funds for the orphanage if she went ahead with her plan. As much as I wanted to encourage Jordan, I have to admit she may have gone ahead and done it anyway."

"Really?" Disappointment dripped from Maddie's words.

"That child was a rescuer all right," Sylvia said with conviction. "She brought home dogs and cats that she tried convincing her parents were lost. Nobody's pets were safe in town. She'd find injured birds and try nursing them back to health."

"You think she did adopt a baby named Nora Star?"

Sylvia pressed her hands together as if considering how to answer. Maddie grew more anxious by the second.

"I've given your question thought as I should," Sylvia finally replied. "Jordan is good to me and I want to help him. I also want to tell the absolute truth. Rosalyn had the desire to adopt a child, but I don't think she ever did."

Sylvia winked as if confident she was right.

Maddie heaved out a deep sigh, pressure draining away from her neck and shoulders.

"You don't know how relieved I am to hear you say so." Maddie kept her voice low. "Tell me why you are convinced."

"Maynard was very wise and a caring daddy. You've seen how Jordan turned out. That's the influence of Maynard and Robert. Rosalyn was responsible like that too."

Maddie simply nodded, not wanting to interrupt.

"Rosie, that's what I called her, might have wanted to adopt every baby who came to her orphanage, but she knew she couldn't."

"Because her father wouldn't let her? She was old enough and far enough away to do what she wanted," Maddie said, testing every loophole in Sylvia's version.

"Rosie couldn't really own an orphanage." Sylvia shook her head. "She ran it with support from her daddy. Maynard always sent her money to keep the place running. I know, because I mailed her the checks."

Sylvia gave the recipe back to Maddie. "Maynard sent her a scolding letter about this baby. She knew where the money was coming from. That's what I told Jordan. There's no chance she adopted a baby."

"I see now you are an important part of the Star family," Maddie said. "Thank you for sharing what you know about Rosalyn."

Sylvia pursed her lips. "You are welcome, Maddie. As I said, Jordan means the world to me. I don't want to see him hurt."

"You and I are on the same wavelength. With the good news you've just provided, I am going to try out your splendid ski slopes."

Maddie tucked the recipe into her research folder, and giving Sylvia a friendly hug, she left with tremendous satisfaction that things were on the right track. She headed for the elevator determined to get changed and head for the slopes before any other brilliant ideas struck her fancy.

Chapter 22

Pure white snow glistened on trees and flashes of sunshine swept across Maddie's goggles as she slalomed down the ski run. Worry and doubt fell away from her shoulders like melting ice. Her spirit felt free for the first time in weeks as she soared downhill, ready for life's next chapter to begin.

Maddie reached the bottom with a flurry of snow spraying out from beneath her skis. She stomped her skis in triumph. She'd made it down the Epic Run without wiping out. In the past two hours, she'd regained not only her self-assurance, but also her technique and the confidence she'd had when skiing here many years ago.

Though her rumbling stomach signaled it must be lunchtime, she decided to enjoy a final run before eating. She skied up to her favorite quad lift as a chair approached. Another skier slid into position, as did Maddie. As the chair arrived beneath her, Maddie's skis lifted from the snow and swung below her seat.

Winds picked up. Blowing snow bombarded her. Maddie swiped a mitten across her goggles to clear her vision.

It was then the other skier said to her, "Good afternoon. Is that you, counselor?"

Maddie glanced sideways. It was Trevor Kirk lifting his goggles and smiling with his megawatt smile.

"What a coincidence," Maddie said, raising her goggles too.

The lift chair wobbled in the breeze. Maddie tapped her ski tips together to knock off some snow.

Trevor copied her move. "Are you taking the day off work?"

"Just a few hours." Maddie forced a chuckle. "It's been eons since I've skied. I decided to give it a try when there's no one here to see me fall."

The chair shook as the cable passed over a tower. Maddie steadied herself on the side bar. Trevor never lost his cheerful smile and seemed totally at ease bouncing around in the air.

"If it makes you feel any better, I've been skiing here awhile today and didn't see you crash anywhere."

Maddie clapped her big ski mittens together. "Flying down the powder came back to me pretty quickly. It's been a few years since I last skied, which happened right here at Star Mountain."

"You must have grown up here in the east," Trevor said, as if he knew all about her life.

"Nope," she snapped. "I actually grew up in Michigan and visited here with my family when I was younger. Plus, I came back with my college roommate who lived in Vermont. How about you?"

"You're probably a better skier than I am, Maddie. I grew up in California. I didn't learn to ski until after moving out east."

She found it intriguing that Trevor mentioned California. She couldn't resist probing his recent flight there with a blond woman, according to Gretchen's sister.

"California, huh? Trevor, you could probably teach me to surf."

"Hey, we should trade lessons. I saw you swoop down on your last run and you're more deft on this mountain than I am."

The lift swayed, and Maddie pulled in her arms.

"Sorry," she quipped. "For you to teach me surfing, I'd have to fly to California where I have no interest in going."

"I'd settle for lunch with you at the Galaxy Grill after this next run. It's time to eat, and I think I'd enjoy your company."

"You think so, but you aren't sure?"

Trevor turned his body slightly, setting the chairlift in motion. He put a hand on the side bar. "Now I'm sorry. Let me start over. I enjoy your company. Let's have lunch."

"I'm hungry too," Maddie replied, lowering her goggles.

As they neared the top, she added brightly, "I'll wait for you by the grill."

She eased off the lift and, pointing to the difficulty signs for the different runs, she asked him, "Are you doing blue, red, or black?"

"I've been sticking to easy blue runs," Trevor said, sounding apologetic.

Maddie started down a blue run, but then had a better idea. She abruptly pulled over and stopped. As she'd hoped, Trevor whizzed on by. Maddie smiled because as he'd predicted, she did ski better than he did. It was funny how just knowing she could outperform Trevor on the slopes made her interested in finding out more about him.

She enjoyed the rest of the run, happy to know she'd have a lunch partner. Clouds covered the sun and a chill swept through her. This was a perfect time for a break and to drink something hot. She lifted her goggles, and then removed and locked her skies. Trevor met her by the entrance before too long. They both took off their helmets.

With eyes shining from the exercise, he said, "Let's get refreshed. I'll meet you in the dining area."

"They have such different selections," Maddie said. "I can't decide if I'll order New England, Southwestern, or Austrian."

"Me either. I'm going to check out everything."

After washing her hands, Maddie went to a hot sandwich station, deciding on a Philly steak sandwich and sweet potato fries, along with a large hot chocolate. Snow swirled outside, and Maddie felt content to be indoors out of the harsh wind.

She found Trevor sitting at the same table along the window where she'd met with Jeanette Carpenter. Maddie said nothing of this strange coincidence as she slid onto the chair opposite him. When she saw his food tray, she burst out in laughter.

"Great minds think alike," she said, wanting Trevor to know she could be friendly. "I see you're also in the mood for hot chocolate."

He wiped his mouth with a napkin. "I don't know if it's because it's super cold up here, but their hot chocolate tastes pretty good."

When Maddie unwrapped her sandwich, Trevor pointed and grinned.

"Hey, we both like the same sandwiches," he said, unwrapping his Philly steak.

Maddie nodded toward his fries. "Regular, or sweet potato?"

"You were behind me in line." He revealed his sweet potato fries with that maddening smile of his. "Did you copy me on purpose?"

Her cheeks began to warm. She took a swig of her hot chocolate.

"We went to different food stations and to be honest, it's the first time I've seen a Philly on any menu in a while. I couldn't resist."

"My reasoning exactly." Trevor's blue eyes sparkled.

She dropped her eyes from his intense gaze before her cheeks blushed any further. Wondering how he happened to be skiing today, she asked, "Are you mixing your work with pleasure today?"

"My work often sends me down south and out west, so when I had this chance to visit Star Mountain, I decided to take vacation time while here."

"Do you often vacation alone?" Maddie probed, thinking of his blond girlfriend out west.

"At this point in life, that's my only option. As I told you before, I'm single."

Before Maddie formed a reply, Trevor added, "This work assignment has really been a bonanza."

"Really?" Skepticism crept into her tone.

"Yes, truly. I travel to Starlight far from my D.C. home where I find time to relax, and also meet a pretty, friendly, and single lady who is also from D.C. To me, that's a bonanza."

Rather than acknowledge his flattery, Maddie bit into her sandwich. A slice of onion dropped onto her plate. She felt increasingly warm, so she loosened the scarf from around her neck. The way Trevor looked at her with his gorgeous smile, she knew she had to shut him down for his good as well as her own.

"Slow down, Romeo. I told you the single ladies around town are convinced you are involved back in D.C."

Trevor's eyes locked onto hers. He exuded frustration. "Maddie, is it okay if I call you that?"

"Everyone else does."

"Maddie, here's the truth. I am *not* seeing anyone. I think it's great how we met here by chance and have things in common."

Confusion reigned. Maddie didn't know what to think about Trevor or seeing him today. She changed the subject.

"Are you staying for the Christmas festival? Everyone in the village is going all out to make this one the finest ever."

"You make it sound like I should."

Trevor's open gaze at her made Maddie think she could become lost in the blueness of his eyes. They were that magnetic. He leaned closer to her.

"Maddie, I just told you that I'm single. I'm not in a relationship. I'm curious to know about your situation."

She blinked back the unwanted question. Was he really interested in knowing? She wadded up her wrappers, which she stuffed into her empty drink cup.

"I'm not seeing anyone. I'm sad to say all I do is work."

Trevor raised his eyebrows. "It must be of your choosing. You are too lovely not to have dating opportunities."

"Don't get me wrong." Maddie could feel the tips of her ears burning. "Until recently, I was involved in a relationship, which didn't end as I would have expected."

Trevor's eyes turned sympathetic. "Oh, I'm sorry. I hope you didn't get hurt."

"I was dating another attorney but discovered how different his goals were from mine. Recently, I've been considering doing something with my life other than the law."

Trevor crumpled his wrappers between his hands. "Do you mean there's less chance you'll want to see me in D.C.?"

Maddie felt she'd already revealed too much for the short time she'd known him. She picked up her trash.

"Time to hit the slopes again," she said. "Are you going back out, or calling it a day?"

"If I can ski with you, count me in."

Maddie beckoned him over as they headed for the trashcan. "Okay, let's go."

She went to retrieve her skis, and Gretchen's warning to resist becoming involved with Trevor resounded in her mind. Yet here she was, enjoying his company. She reminded herself to go slowly.

For the next hour and a half, Maddie and Trevor rode the lifts, took a few selfies, and skied together on the intermediate red slopes where he kept up with her nicely.

Somewhere about the halfway point down the Epic, he began acting like a hotdogger.

"What are you doing?" Maddie called out.

Before her startled eyes, Trevor wiped out, his skis and poles flying in the air. Maddie was skiing right behind him. She fought the slippery snow beneath her. She tried to stop without crashing into him. Next thing she knew, she was rolling through fresh snow, her skis and poles going airborne.

Finally, she stopped skidding on her backend. Maddie caught her breath and looked around. Ski equipment strewn far and wide looked like some yard sale.

Trevor limped toward her. "Are you okay?"

"I think so."

Maddie rose to her knees, brushing snow from her face. "Nothing feels broken. How about you?"

"I'm okay. It looked like you were trying to stop and help me." Trevor extended a hand to help her up.

"That was the idea."

Maddie stood on wobbly legs, getting her bearings. She held onto his hand for a moment too long before letting her hand drop.

He began collecting her skis and poles. "Should we quit before we really get hurt?"

"Yeah, I'm beat." Maddie bent over to reattach her skis. "See you at the bottom."

Sliding down the run, she made a careful and deliberate descent while replaying the day's unusual events. Neither she nor Trevor had mentioned their reason for being in Starlight. It was if they had reached a silent agreement to avoid any possible damper on enjoying the day.

When she skied to the bottom, Trevor was already knocking snow from his skis and had them leaning on his shoulder. She despised gossip and rumor. Still, Maddie wondered. Was he a traveling kind of guy like Stewart?

"It doesn't matter," she said under her breath as she reached for her skis. It wasn't like she needed to connect with him ever again.

"What doesn't matter?" he walked up asking.

Maddie finished taking off her skis. "It's been fun exploring the slopes with you, Trevor."

"And with you."

His genuine smile piqued her interested side and completely overruled her cautious side.

When he added, "Let's do it again sometime," a giggle escaped her lips before she could stop it.

Maddie raised her goggles. "Maybe you could teach me to surf sometime. Do you ever get back to California?"

"Not if I can help it."

The grittiness she detected in his tone caused Maddie to do a double-take.

"Don't you still have family and friends there?" she asked.

"My brother lives in Chicago, but we don't see each other much. My folks are still in San Diego and I only go back for weddings and funerals. And I have no sisters."

"Me either, nor brothers."

Maddie remembered Gretchen's warning. No family in LA and no sisters, so she wondered, who was the blond lady he traveled with? Maddie brushed excess snow from her skis. Their conversation continued while they turned in their rental equipment.

Back outside, Maddie looked toward the parking lot. "I'm heading out. Maybe I'll see you around town."

"I look forward to bumping into you again sometime," Trevor said, throwing his hand in a wave.

Maddie walked toward her car, a lilt propelling every step. Possibly Gretchen's sister had mistaken another person for Trevor at the D.C. airport. But was that likely since he had been a passenger on her flight all the way to California?

Inwardly, she vowed to be warier of Trevor Kirk. While he acted cordial enough with his compliments, something hit her wrong. She sprinted to her car trying to fathom what it was.

Shoving the key in the door, the truth hit her with the power of a cascading flood. Trevor reminded her of several former clients who acted loose with the whole truth and nothing but the truth.

Chapter 23

Maddie intended to grab a hurried breakfast the following morning before phoning her boss for a brief conference. She was finishing her omelet and reading emails on her phone when a familiar-looking black chef's coat walked up to her table.

"Morning, Ms. Maddie."

"Dexter!" she exclaimed. "I see you've featured the Star Family Rosette on the dessert sign. Are people enjoying it?"

The chef, wearing his pillbox hat this time, pulled out a chair to join Maddie.

"Yes, ma'am. Everyone is raving about the delicate treat. And you were right. When Jordan and Vanessa helped me with the first batch, I observed their magic with my own eyes. I am very encouraged."

Though Maddie formed her lips upward, the smile didn't match her true feelings. Vanessa's involvement with Jordan had Maddie wondering if their budding relationship was for real or like foam on the ocean, which would disappear with the next oncoming wave.

"May I take a moment of your time?" Dexter asked, as if a problem gnawed at him.

"Something on your mind, chef?"

He nodded politely. "You know this is a small town. From my vantage point in the kitchen, I have a hard time keeping up with the goings-on. But I try not to miss much. It's my only entertainment."

"And that's why you're a matchmaker for Jordan?"

"Yeah, you see right through me. In fact, back when I was hoping you might be the one God sent to rescue him, I thought I was going to have to run interference."

"Why do you say that?"

"I spotted you talking with that Washington geologist here in the café. I noticed you both looked rather nice together. My spies in town told me at first you were both single, and you appeared to be enjoying your conversation."

Maddie patted Dexter's hand. "Why, chef, I've just discovered Starlight has its own Andy Landers. That doesn't explain your need to run interference."

"Oh, that's easy." Dexter waved his hand dismissively. "I was afraid you might fall for that jet-setting rock doctor and fail to see our Jordan."

"And now you believe Jordan is safe. What is your advice for me?"

"Ms. Maddie, I know quality when I see it and I'm concerned for you. My spies further report you were skiing with this guy and ate lunch with him up on the slopes."

Maddie patted his hand again. "My, my, chef. You can see a lot from your kitchen. His name is Trevor, in case you're interested."

"Yes, I found out his name. I don't want you getting hurt by a man who's mixed up with people trying to steal the mountain and lodge from Jordan. Think about it. He doesn't care about people."

Maddie opened her mouth to speak, but Dexter wasn't stopping. "Why is a good-looking guy not already married? I'll tell you why. I heard he's got at least one blond lady friend out on the west coast who's willing to have him."

"I know you mean well. Please, don't be worried about me."

"But I am." Dexter's dark eyes flickered with the concern he was showing. "You may not see it. I think you might be hurting because Jordan is paying attention to Vanessa. Just promise me, you'll proceed carefully and go light on the gas pedal. You can always call on me if you need to talk things through."

Maddie gazed at him thoughtfully, trying to make sense of his seeming interest in her life. Dexter wasn't spreading rumors needlessly. He actually wanted her to avoid making mistakes. Perhaps his own backstory fueled his caution. She wouldn't ask him now.

"Dexter, you are as thoughtful as your mother," Maddie told him. "You are both treating me like family and I am grateful. I have to admit, you folks are spoiling me. Back in D.C., I have only met one of my new neighbors and that was once in the elevator. I need to change that."

"I see my message is received. Good." He stood and bowed slightly. "I've overstayed my welcome and have hungry people to feed."

DEXTER'S DEPARTING SMILE lingered in Maddie's heart. She wasn't used to such kindness from strangers. A light dawned that Jordan and Sylvia and Dexter weren't strangers to her. They were becoming part of her and she needed to show them a similar depth of care.

Maddie signed the charge slip, adding a tip. She took her time walking through the lobby and out the front doors, the glistening snow drawing her outside to think. Her sweater wasn't heavy enough to keep out the cold for long, so she stood under the portico.

She swatted her hands up and down her arms, just like her dad taught her to do as a girl in Michigan when she'd be out ice skating or tubing. Her heart contracted. Maddie missed her parents. She stomped her feet in her boots, reflecting on what advice they would give her if they were here.

Well, since Dad and Mom were in Florida and not Vermont, Chef Dexter was a good substitute. She didn't fault him for putting up a stop sign when it came to Trevor. She'd already cautioned herself plenty after their captivating time together on the slopes.

Maddie stepped out into the falling snow. Tiny snowflakes drifting onto her cheeks revived her flagging spirits. The Trevor she'd enjoyed talking with seemed far different than the mercenary guy everyone else suspected. Still, was she wise to trust her instincts? They had failed her greatly with Stewart.

A shiver crept up from her toes and she bounded into the lobby, relishing its warmth. Her venture outside in the freezing temperatures served as a perfect visual to Dexter's cautionary tale. From here on, Maddie would give Trevor just a cold shoulder.

She glanced down at her phone while waiting for the elevator to arrive and was surprised to see she had a waiting voicemail. It was from Stewart's personal phone, no less. Maddie rolled her eyes. What did he want now?

Since their breakup, she'd deleted his photo from her address book. Too bad his personal number remained embedded in her mind like a barb, no matter how she tried to wipe it from her memory.

She stepped closer to the front windows to get better reception and listened to his message. He insisted, in that demanding voice of his, that Maddie call him pronto.

Maddie fumed. She never wanted to speak with him again. In reality, since he was opposing counsel, she had no choice. Before making the phone call and blasting him, she walked over to the coffee station and poured herself a small coffee, which she drank to steady her thoughts. She returned to the windows, and here, Maddie punched in his number, seriously doubting anything was so very urgent.

"Maddie, you won't believe my extraordinary news," he said, sounding almost giddy.

Just hearing him say her name grated on her frayed nerves. She steeled her emotions for whatever ploy Stewart might be about to pull against her next.

"I had hoped we were finished dealing with each other," Maddie replied, her voice dripping icicles.

"Mark my words, you'll be glad to see me again. I'm flying up to Starlight the day after tomorrow. Can you reserve time in the afternoon for me?"

"You must be kidding." Maddie clicked her tongue against her teeth. "I'm busy cleaning up the mess your firm has already caused my client. I have no time for you."

Her finger flew to press the red button to end call when Stewart blurted, "I'm bringing Nora Star with me. You need to arrange a court reporter to depose her. Make it around two o'clock in the afternoon."

Maddie's blood pressure skyrocketed. She couldn't discuss the case here in the lobby.

"Let me call you right back, Stewart. I'm about to get on the elevator and don't want to lose you."

"Okay, but I'm leaving the office in five minutes," he said brusquely.

"Wait for me," she insisted.

Maddie hung up and hustled to the elevator, jumping on when the doors opened. Thankfully, she was the only passenger and zoomed to her floor in no time. The ride gave her time to calculate her next move on the chessboard. Asking to call him back gave her a few extra minutes to think. By the time she inserted her key card, she knew just how she would accuse him. Maddie hit redial.

Stewart shouted in her ear, "I'm still here," before his phone even rang.

Her room door clanged shut, making her wince. Still, she went after Stewart with lightning speed. "Are you saying you just found Nora? Or have you been sandbagging and had her on ice all this time?"

"There you go again, Maddie. Must you always go negative? I'd rather you thanked me for finding our heir and arranged for the deposition."

Maddie's brain spun with more questions. She posed a single one to Stewart, hoping he'd let his guard down for a change so she could learn the truth.

"What else can you tell me about Nora, or are you going to make me learn everything through the deposition?"

"I thought I'd just wait and see how adept you are at pulling details from her with your questioning. Don't forget, you and I met on a case. I've seen you in action."

The last thing Maddie wanted or needed was a tortured walk down that highway with Stewart. She'd had enough.

"I'll set up the deposition and text you the date and time. There is no further need for us to talk."

"Wait, Maddie," he replied, his tone softening. "I am sorry for yanking your chain. Can you schedule it for the day after tomorrow at two?"

"It's short notice. I will try."

"Wait!" he practically yelled in Maddie's ear. "Nora is from Austria, of course. I assume you know all that. She was adopted by Rosalyn, Maynard Star's daughter. Nora grew up in Austria and has no interest in the estate. I mean none."

Maddie dropped onto the lone chair by the little desk. "Did you discover her, Stewart?"

"Ah ..." He paused. "I did not. We have a client who did."

"I know, and your client wants to bring nothing but lovely development and prosperity to the town of Starlight," Maddie said, unable to keep sarcasm from her voice.

Before he responded, Maddie felt compelled to interject, "Next, you'll tell me you don't know a thing about your client or how they found Nora Star."

"Maddie, I still have feelings for you and want to see you prosper. Truth is, I could care less about Starlight."

"Stewart, I believe you've finally said one true thing, that you care nothing for the people of Starlight. I will add to your confession that you don't care about me either, which your actions have shown me in so many ways."

His sigh in her ear was forceful. "Listen. Nora is willing to sell her half of the estate. Jordan doesn't have the reserves to buy her out so it's all going to be split up. Urge him to sell to our client, and you'll come out a winner. I don't want to see you getting hurt."

"Again with your lies. I know you've targeted landowners in the area by sending Trevor Kirk to their homes to lease their mineral rights."

"Whoa," Stewart bellowed in her ear. "I have no idea who he is."

"Your clients do. I believe they created a fictitious heir to pose as Nora Star. We've done our research and I think she may be an impostor. In any event, I'll notify the court about my deposing her here in the Edelweiss Lodge conference room. I'll try for the date and time you requested and text confirmation."

"Hold on, Maddie," Stewart said, as if unwilling to hang up. "Nora is eager to see the empire built by her successful grandfather. She'll spend a day or two in the village, so after the deposition, I suggest you introduce Nora to your client, her cousin Jordan."

"In your dreams, Stewart. Watch for my text."

Maddie terminated his call. His greasy voice set her stomach churning. She tapped her fingernails on the desktop, contemplating all she had heard.

Oh, how she wanted to save the Star estate. But, Maddie wondered, was it possible for her to protect Jordan and Star Mountain from Stewart's terrible schemes?

Chapter 24

Maddie flew from her room like a whirlwind to find Jordan. Her mind pulsed with shock from Stewart's disconcerting phone call. She skipped the elevator and scrambled down the stairs. Nora Star was coming to Starlight. Maddie could depose her. It was unbelievable.

Jordan's office was empty. Sylvia wasn't at her desk. Maddie hightailed it to the café. Maddie stopped short by what she saw.

The Cinnamon Stix had been transformed into a Christmas wonderland. Exquisite red and green glass ornaments dangled from the ceiling, hung on gold ribbons. Pots of white, pink, and red poinsettias dotted every inch of the perimeter. Each table boasted a small basket of fresh white mums and tiny silver ornaments placed in the center of vibrant red-and-green-checked tablecloths.

Among the many diners, Jordan was nowhere to be seen. Frustration propelled Maddie over to Gretchen, who was watering poinsettias in the lobby.

"Where is Jordan?"

"I haven't seen him for hours," Gretchen said, holding the watering can aloft.

"I texted him, but no answer. Please tell him to call me when you do," Maddie ordered, keeping the reason a secret.

Gretchen whirled a finger in the air and shook her head, fluttering her star earrings. "His mind is up somewhere in the stars, if you catch my meaning."

"No. I've been too busy to keep track of him. This is important."

"I'll be sure to tell Jordan, if and when I see him. Chef Dexter just brought out fresh apple cider and apple fritters. Help yourself. Oops, that's the phone."

Gretchen wasted no time running over and answering the desk phone.

Maddie liked her suggestion. A cup of warmed apple cider would help settle her, so she poured a cup and retreated to her room. She had the entire day to prepare for the deposition. Time passed as she drank her cider and analyzed various options.

Maddie typed on her computer with a vengeance, crafting questions designed to prove Nora Star to be a total fraud. She finally took a break from her legal prep and started pacing a circuit by the window.

Star Mountain's stark winter beauty led her to a most unwelcome possibility. Her failure to prove Nora had no valid claim to the estate could reduce the village to a mining town and the entire mountain to a desolate heap of rubble.

Maddie would be troubled informing Jordan of Nora's arrival no matter how many laps she completed by the window. She shouldn't delay any longer, and rehearsed the difficult news while riding the elevator to the mezzanine. To her surprise, she found Jordan sitting at his desk, his eyes glued to his computer.

"Are you busy?" she asked, lingering in the doorway.

Shadows rimmed his eyes. "Never too busy to visit with my resourceful lawyer. Is the gossip true? Rumor has it you're spending time on the mountain with the geologist."

"You surprise me." Maddie hurried in. "I thought you were going to ask me something else."

"What should I be asking?"

She perched on the chair across from his desk. "We'll get to that in a moment. Jordan, don't take my going skiing as anything amiss. It wasn't planned. I happened upon Mr. Kirk on the ski lift. I thought it made sense to find out what he's planning around here."

"See, you prove my point. You are resourceful."

Sylvia's voice interrupted from across the hall. "Jordan, that realtor from Washington D.C. is on the phone. Do you want to call her back?"

Jordan lifted an eyebrow, looking at Maddie. "Sylvia, put her through."

He nodded toward the door, asking Maddie to close it and remain for the call. "You might as well eavesdrop."

Maddie shut the door without a sound. He pushed the desk phone closer to her before punching the speaker button.

"Hello, this is Jordan."

"Mr. Star, this is Beth Tandy from Tandy and Associates Real Estate. I'm calling because I haven't heard back about the offer we sent you two weeks ago."

Jordan grimaced at Maddie and opened his desk drawer. "I still have a week, according to your offer agreement."

"Mr. Star, our generous offer is one you can't sit on too long," Beth replied testily. "You'll be a millionaire several times over."

Jordan pulled a document from his drawer and paged through it. "I appreciate the heads-up. I'm looking at your agreement now, which expires one week from today. I might as well tell you, I'm not inclined to accept your offer."

Gripped by concern over where this conversation was headed, Maddie frowned at Jordan and shook her head, hoping he'd terminate the call.

Beth went right for his jugular. "Mr. Star, look closely at the original offer. We retain the right to amend the timeline with written notice to you. I'm about to fax you an amendment. We demand an answer by close of business tomorrow evening."

"Why the sudden rush?" Jordan brushed his hand over the paper. "We are still considering your offer."

"Circumstances have changed."

"What do you mean they've changed?" Jordan's eyes flew to Maddie's.

"Haven't you heard? Nora Star is now in the country. Word is she has no interest in owning a ski resort or a mountain. She's ready to sell to our client."

Maddie flashed a timeout sign with her two hands. Jordan acknowledged her caution with a nod, telling Beth, "Let me get back to you in a moment. Hold on."

"Make it quick," she snapped.

Jordan put the call on hold. The urgency to protect her client rose within Maddie.

She leaned forward and in a rush told Jordan, "That's why I sped down here and hunted for you earlier. Stewart just notified me. They've located Nora and are bringing her to look around Starlight. I am to question her."

The haunted look in Jordan's eyes conveyed his anxiety. "What should I do about Beth's offer?"

"Listen to what she says," Maddie suggested. "Do not, I repeat, do not tell Beth Tandy a thing."

Jordan pushed the button to reconnect the call. "Sorry for the interruption, Ms. Tandy."

"The bottom line is this," Beth declared. "My client has offered you a generous price for the mountain and all the properties you own in town. We expect your answer by tomorrow evening. After that, you'll miss out."

"I'm not convinced there really is another valid heir," Jordan said, with newfound spunk in his voice. "I may be willing to wait and see."

Maddie flinched at her client doing the opposite of what she'd just advised. Of course, he owned Starlight. The village and mountain were his life and livelihood. He had the right to make his own decisions.

She tuned her ears to listen to the real estate agent's diatribe, "If the estate is forced to settle with Nora, you may not have the liquidity to buy her out. Then our client will have to buy property from Nora, you know, the mountain, ski resort, or whatever constitutes her share. After that, we'd have to deal with you for your half. Aren't you better off to sell before the estate is closed, and not have to risk the court splitting up the money? You get more going our way."

Jordan leaned back in his chair, and rolling his eyes, he looked totally defeated. "Go ahead and send your fax. I make no promises."

He ended the call with one swift click. Rubbing both of his temples, he asked Maddie, "My nightmare continues. Have they truly found Nora?"

"I'm sorry I couldn't speak with you sooner." Maddie's heart ached for Jordan. "You didn't answer my text. Gretchen had no idea where to find you. Sylvia wasn't in her office."

He snatched up his phone. "I see your text here. Sorry."

She waited for Jordan to explain where he'd been. When he didn't, Maddie told him about Stewart bringing Nora to Starlight in two days.

"And given Beth's call, I suspect she and Stewart are working in tandem to squeeze you. You heard her. This cabal is banking on your greed and desire to deny the other heir any inheritance. They're poised to buy you out for less."

Jordan pounded his fist on the table. He whirled around, pointing at the aerial picture of Starlight and Star Mountain behind his desk.

"No way! I won't see my hometown destroyed and this special mountain flattened."

Maddie reached over to the phone and started punching in numbers. "We need to bring Bill up-to-date. He might have an idea or two we've missed."

Jordan both grunted and nodded as if his mind was coming unglued. Maddie put the phone on speaker. Loud dialing tones filled the tense air between them. She didn't like being caught off guard by the realtor exerting sudden pressure on Jordan to sell, especially before Maddie had a chance to question Nora under oath.

Vanessa's chirpy voice answered, "Barron and Rich. How may I help you?"

"Vanessa, it's Maddie. How is everything with you?"

"I just had the longest talk with Jordan."

"That's nice," Maddie said, realizing Vanessa just revealed Jordan's mysterious absence. "I'm calling from his office and you're on speaker."

"Oh. Are you saying Jordan's there too?" Vanessa asked breathlessly.

"Hello, Vanessa." A momentary light spread across Jordan's face as he leaned across the desk. "It's me. We're hoping Bill is in."

"Oh yes, he's here. I'll put you right through."

The lilt in Vanessa's voice reminded Maddie of lightly falling snow. While they waited for Bill, Maddie told Jordan, "I won't give up. We may still prove Nora is a fake."

The speakerphone sprang to life when Bill snarled, "Give it to me straight."

For the next few minutes, Maddie recounted to Bill the shocking events. When she stopped long enough to draw breath, Bill jumped in.

"Based on what I know of the Hunter firm, nothing surprises me. Maddie, I have no doubt you'll depose this Nora woman and expose her phony claim. Give me an hour to draft up questions to supplement yours. Jordan, do not even consider meeting their demand to sell by tomorrow night."

Jordan edged his chair closer. "Bill, I will do anything to keep them from ripping apart this beautiful mountain for minerals."

"I have an idea," Bill shot back. "Another resort operator up north of you tried to buy your properties in Starlight before Maynard died. Why don't I contact them for you? Just in case. Even if Nora turns out to be a bona fide heir under a new will, we can still keep foreign investors from destroying the area. We will sell to a Vermonter, or perhaps work out a merger and joint venture."

Jordan's shoulders relaxed. A semblance of his earlier smile returned. "Bill, you're giving me a ray of hope. Do you think that's possible?"

"I do," Bill insisted. "I still have my file from negotiations for Maynard. I'll call the resort owner and connect back when I have news. Maddie, you prepare for D-Day, and don't let us down."

Maddie swallowed, searching for the right words. So much was riding on her skills. "I'll do everything in my legal power to protect Jordan. You both have my solemn pledge not to leave one stone unturned."

Bill answered with a vigorous, "Go get 'em. Now I've gotta run."

With a buzz, the phone went dead.

"I forgot about Grandfather's chance to sell to the other resort. I could live with a merger." Jordan's grin turned into a full-fledged smile.

Encouragement lifted Maddie spirits as well. "I knew Bill would have another trick up his sleeve, but it won't be necessary. I intend to decimate Nora Star."

Chapter 25

Maddie hunkered down in her room the next morning to prepare the deposition notice for Nora Star, a cup of coffee from the pot in her room by her elbow. Fingers flying across her tiny phone, she typed Stewart a terse message:

Will depose Nora tomorrow eleven a.m. Edelweiss conference room unavailable in the afternoon.

All the while, her mind replayed Bill's latest command. Maddie was to neutralize Stewart's client, proving she and the alleged new will were nothing but a scam, a flimflam, a swindle. To the drumming of her fingers on the keypad, Maddie vowed not to descend into using the same bottom-dweller tactics as Stewart in fulfilling her mission to unmask Nora.

Maddie kept working on questions to throw at Nora. Her mind in high gear, she ordered more coffee from the café. Gretchen delivered the cup to her room, a question mark written all over her face.

"Why are you holed up in here?" she asked, handing Maddie the insulated cup. "You reserved the conference room for tomorrow. Is everything okay?"

Maddie held up the foam cup. "Thanks. I needed more caffeine as I'm working diligently on a case. Welcome to the cloistered life of a busy attorney."

"When Dexter said you'd asked for coffee, I thought I'd bring it myself. I miss seeing you."

"You are special, Gretchen. The longer I stay in Starlight, the more I begin to feel a part of my new village family and hope my parents can meet you. When my case wraps up, maybe you and I can go Christmas shopping. I haven't had time to buy many gifts."

"Great!" Gretchen sounded thrilled. "I'm supposed to ask for Gramma, are you playing piano for the teen choir at the festival? It's coming up soon, you know."

"Will I miss Starlight's greatest festival ever?" Maddie swung her head to the side dramatically. "No way. Will I miss playing with such gung-ho young people? Not this girl."

Gretchen gave Maddie a thumbs-up. "Gramma will be so happy. Me too. She said if you balked, you're no mountain girl."

"Glad I answered right, because I wouldn't want to disappoint Opal or you."

Gretchen danced a happy jig on the way back to her post in the lobby. The hot java rejuvenated Maddie as she finalized her questions to zing Nora. She wanted to know why Rosalyn's daughter Nora had never reached out to her grandfather before his death. Nora might testify she had.

If so, Maddie would insist she produce letters, texts, and emails to support her claim. She also wanted a DNA sample to compare with Jordan's. Maddie hadn't ruled out that Nora could be Rosalyn's child presented as adopted. Possible questions eventually ran dry, and Maddie collected her legal papers, stuffing them in her briefcase. She made a final sweep of the room. Sure she had everything, Maddie hurried down to the Stix before venturing to court to file the deposition notice.

She'd just ordered Vermont Trailblazer Mac n' Cheese for lunch when a familiar young man strode right to her table wearing his signature red-and-black flannel shirt.

"Excuse me, Ms. Stone, I'm Barnaby Ross with *The Ledger*. Do you care to comment on a story I'm writing?"

Maddie vividly recalled the intern's earlier ambush of Jordan in his office. It seemed to be his standard tactic.

"I won't excuse you," she snapped. "You are interrupting my lunch."

Ross visibly stiffened. "My source suggests you are an obstacle to the rescue of the ski resort and the town by a wealthy buyer. I thought you might want to defend yourself."

Apparently Ross had learned something in journalism school because he wasn't easily discouraged. Maddie would have to up her game.

"I see." She glared intently at the young upstart. "You imply you are a reporter with *The Ledger* when I know you are a college intern."

The rookie stared back and held up his cell phone as if ready to record her.

Maddie lifted her chin. "You'd better not be videotaping me, Ross. You're poking your nose in a legal matter pending in the court."

"I'm not recording you, not yet anyway."

"I'll bet you haven't even read the court file, which would be Journalism 101," Maddie declared. "Further, you just slandered me, an attorney. If you print your allegation, you will be committing libel, an actionable offense. You should have learned about both in Journalism 102. Please leave me to eat my lunch."

"You don't have any lunch," he replied. "Are you trying to get rid of me?"

Maddie drank some coffee, which had become lukewarm. "My meal should be here any second."

The erstwhile reporter consulted a small spiral notebook that he pulled from his back pocket and tried again.

"I was talking to a source at breakfast this morning over at the Mountain View hotel restaurant. He said some other Vermont resort operator has been trying to buy the Edelweiss Lodge and the ski resort." He made a sweeping gesture out the window.

Maddie looked up from her own notepad. "And who is your source, which I am sure you will claim is reliable?"

"Can't say," Ross said flatly. "We at *The Ledger* carefully protect our sources."

"You'll have a hard time publishing an article without a quotable source, and it won't be me. Leave me alone, Barnaby Ross."

He shut his notebook with a sigh and started to leave when Maddie stopped him.

"One more thing. If you write something as libelous as you just mentioned, the new case filed at the courthouse will name you and *The Ledger* as defendants."

This time, Ross traipsed off in defeat. Maddie felt she'd accomplished her purpose. The server brought her lunch of pasta with melted Vermont cheddar cheese, baked hot and bubbly.

Maddie picked up her fork when the server refreshed her coffee cup, asking, "Chef Dexter wants to know if that young man was bothering you?"

"Not really." Maddie readied her fork to plunge into the spicy confection.

"If you say so. We heard you all the way in the kitchen."

She left Maddie to think she'd consumed way too much coffee today. It wasn't like her to get so riled up. She felt a pang of guilt for being caustic with Ross and causing Chef Dexter to worry.

Still, the reporter had seemed more than eager to peddle untruths. Maddie was right to squelch his overzealous nature before he published any articles that brought Jordan more trouble. She said a prayer of thanks for her meal, and before trying a single bite, she got to thinking just who Ross had met at the Mountain View café.

Who would have such knowledge, and who would tell such lies about her?

MADDIE'S DELICIOUS LUNCH did nothing to quell her agitation over Ross pouncing upon her. Her mental gears flamed into high gear as she slid into her cold rental and heaved her leather satchel onto the passenger seat. With a good inkling of his source's identity, Maddie would be careful to not falsely accuse anyone.

She let the engine and seats warm up before pulling away from the lodge. She drove past Trevor's hotel, and there in front of the Mountain View Inn was a white passenger van with the Essential Oil sign on the door.

Did Trevor need this enormous van besides his Mercedes?

With its side door open, it appeared someone was waiting for passengers to arrive. The courthouse wouldn't be closed for several hours yet, so Maddie decided to play sleuth and investigate this curious development.

She spun around the block. After parking a half-block away from the van, she kept watch over its open door as a mother eagle might over an egg waiting to hatch. Maddie couldn't see inside. Where they coming or going?

Then the driver's door swung open. Her heart beat erratically as she recognized the man easing out. Trevor looked stunning dressed in dark slacks and white shirt. With a striped tie knotted at his neck, beneath a black leather jacket, Maddie couldn't take her eyes off him.

Despite his handsome appearance, her distrust of Trevor had exploded ever since Ross so rudely bushwhacked her over the mac n' cheese. The wily intern had definitely said his source was from the Mountain View Inn. That was the same place Trevor stayed. Maddie didn't doubt Trevor was to blame for Realtor Beth Tandy harassing Jordan to sell Starlight on the spot. Besides, the geologist didn't need such an enormous van for one person.

Intent on discovering just what he was up to, Maddie stared out the window, watching him strut toward the front of the hotel. When he remained under the portico, standing like a doorman, her suspicions intensified.

Did he have high-powered clients in town? Were they Beth Tandy and her bunch?

Before long, her surveillance paid off. A businessman of medium height and wearing a suit and long dark overcoat meandered out of the hotel. He hopped into the front passenger seat before Maddie could observe his face. Trevor shut the passenger door, quickly resuming his pose as a doorman. His behavior seemed so peculiar.

Her eyes widened in surprise as two more men hurried toward the van, accompanied by two women, one blonde wearing dark slacks and a light blue puffy jacket. The other woman, a light brunette, wore a beige trench coat.

The party of four loaded into the back of the van. Trevor slid the door closed with a snap. Then he strode on his long legs to the driver's seat and climbed in. He acted so confident, so sure of himself, Maddie tried calculating just what he and his "Essential Oil" group were up to.

The van's backup lights flashed. Trevor must have put the van into gear. Maddie waited for him to drive away, but instead, he just sat there with the brake lights lit. Then she saw another man she recognized. Her pulse thundered loudly in her ears like a roaring lion.

This man hurried from the hotel, and in one swift movement, he slid open the passenger door before jumping into the van. He'd run so fast she failed to take note of what he was wearing. It didn't matter. Her concerns ran much deeper than clothing.

She sat back, reeling in shock. The man who had just rushed from the hotel into the van with Trevor was Stewart. This was the same lying attorney who had assured Maddie only yesterday he'd never heard of Trevor Kirk.

Stewart must be feeding false information to Barnaby Ross. Her emotions spiked, and Maddie became befuddled and angry at the same time. She wanted nothing more than to beat him at his game, to see him lose big-time.

But how could Maddie succeed when she had no clue about his strategy?

Trevor and his gang sped away. She jammed her car into gear, keeping her distance on the way to the courthouse so neither Trevor nor Stewart spotted her. A few minutes later, the van veered off onto the road ascending up the mountain.

Questions rocked her mind, questions for which she had no answers.

Where these well-dressed people developers? Prospective buyers? Might one of the women be Nora Star?

Maddie shot a glance over at her briefcase containing the notice of deposition. The brown-haired woman wearing the trench coat might be Nora. After all, Rosalyn had mentioned the baby girl had brown eyes. Trevor was probably parading her and the others past the ski area where they were all hatching a diabolical scheme to mine rare minerals from beneath Star Mountain.

Maddie devised her own plans as she snagged a parking spot in front of the courthouse. In a moment of clarity, she decided to phone Bill.

"I'll tell him everything," she said under her breath, ringing his number.

A recent memory gave her pause. Bill didn't need to know how she'd blistered the reporter at lunch. Better to leave that part out. The call went to his voicemail so no harm done. The tone beeped, and she left a message.

"Bill, I'm at court ready to file the notice. Did you reach the other Vermont resort owner? I've spotted suspicious characters in town. We should talk."

She ended the call with an odd sensation compelling her to glance over her shoulder. Maddie half expected Ross to be walking up to uncover what she was doing here at court. He was nowhere in sight, and no white van circled the block. Maddie tightly gripped the satchel's shoulder strap and stayed on high alert anyway.

After filing papers for Nora's deposition tomorrow, and seeing no one following her, Maddie realized she was being silly and overly anxious. Still, she wished she felt more confident about the outcome.

She couldn't help recalling today's vision of Nora tagging along with Stewart in Trevor's Essential Oil van. This got her steamed all over again. As a result, on the drive back to Starlight, question after question for the mystery heir flew into her mind like popping corn. The only problem was she couldn't pull off the narrow road and write them down.

She took another pass by the Mountain View Inn, where Maddie scanned the street for Trevor's white passenger van or his Mercedes. Seeing neither, she wished Harry Black, their private investigator, could fly up here and check these guys out.

But why couldn't she conduct her own stakeout?

Maddie backed in a parking place, which gave her a perfect angle to watch the Mountain View. She kept her eyes open for Stewart to return with his unscrupulous geologist, Trevor.

Her eyes looked up and down again while she scratched out more questions for Nora on her yellow legal pad:

Where were you born?

Where is your birth certificate recorded?
Have you ever legally changed your name?
Were you adopted?
Did you ever meet your maternal grandmother and/or grandfather?
If so, when and where for each?
Did they ever send you letters?
When was the last time you communicated with them?
Where is the new will?

A large object blazed by her driver's side window like a white blur. It was Trevor's van. He wheeled up in front of his hotel.

Maddie's heart started pounding. With laser-like focus, she sat forward, observing the same bevy of men and women scramble from the van. There went Nora Star in her trench coat behind the other woman into the Mountain View. Maddie tried to ascertain from that brief glimpse just what was her true motive for coming here.

The moment Nora slipped into the hotel, Stewart hopped from the van and fled inside behind her.

Maddie narrowed her eyes as Trevor rolled on down the road, maneuvering the big van into a tight parking spot. With his long strides, he sauntered toward the hotel, a wide grin plastered on his beguiling face. Maddie found his swagger annoying, maddening even.

She couldn't resist the urge and jumped out of the SUV. It was too late to turn back now. She shot toward Trevor before he reached the hotel entrance.

Maddie cut him off by walking directly into his path. He nearly slammed into her.

"Ah ... Ms. Stone," he said, backing up. "Seeing you here makes my day."

Maddie's hands flew to her hips. "Don't waste your charm on me, you vulture."

"Okay, I won't."

When he tried stepping around her, Maddie moved to block his escape.

"I saw you today with your swanky developers. You're trying to sell out the people of this village. You're driving around town with a Star family imposter and the lawyer who's trying to destroy one of the most spectacular places on earth."

"Hey, I'm just a consultant. Don't blame me. I've done nothing wrong." Trevor tried once again to steer around her. Maddie stood in his way. "These foreign mining developers will crush this mountain and strip it clean of its rare earth elements. If you were an honest geologist, you wouldn't deny it."

"Look." Trevor's icy glare was unwavering. "I have no doubt that you, being the strong attorney you are, will do whatever you need to do."

His dismissive attitude shocked Maddie. Had she really dared to begin admiring this man?

"Forgive me for standing in your way." She took a giant step to the side. "I mistook you for someone who cared."

Trevor flexed his cheek muscles. His nostrils flared as if he'd just bitten down a withering comeback. Then, without a further word, he disappeared into the hotel, leaving Maddie seething all the way back to the car.

Her drive to the Edelweiss, though short, was intense as she crafted the toughest set of questions to smoke out the murky and shadowy Nora Star.

Chapter 26

Maddie stewed in her room over confronting Trevor on the street. She was a peace-loving person. How had she let herself ratchet so out of control?

A few moments of quiet reflection was all it took for the answer to come bursting forth. Her fire to achieve justice for her Starlight friends had spilled over. She pledged to better command her emotions while at the same time working tirelessly to solve and win the case.

She was reminded of sage advice her father had offered her since high school. So Maddie put the unsavory row with Trevor where it belonged, in the rearview mirror.

That settled, she phoned Bill, hoping he was available to take her call. A brief chat with Vanessa helped her regain focus.

"Maddie, it's after five. Are you working late for Nora's deposition?"

"Is there any doubt?" Maddie replied. "Why are you still at the office?"

"Bill handed me the agenda to type for the partners' meeting tomorrow. How is everything in Vermont?"

"I take it you mean how is everyone, as in Jordan?"

Vanessa laughed softly in Maddie's ear. "Why, yes. Did Jordan tell you that Cole and I are returning for the Christmas festival? He invited us to fly up and he's picking us up at the airport. Maddie, he is the kindest man I have ever known."

"He's probably the nicest client I've ever had, a truly generous man." Maddie wanted happiness for Vanessa and Cole. She kept her apprehensions at bay, adding, "Let's pray we have good news by the time the festival begins."

"Are you calling with bad news?"

"No, nothing like that. Just trying to reach Bill. He didn't return my call."

"He's on another line. I'll interrupt him if you want."

Maddie flipped a page in her notebook. "Not necessary. Have him phone when it's convenient."

"Will do. And Maddie, Cole is bringing his guitar and hopes you'll perform a duet with him on the piano."

"What a wonderful idea. Please tell him I said so. I can email a song suggestion."

They hung up and Maddie went back to reviewing her questions with the TV on mute. An advertisement splashed across the screen of a family skiing downhill in Vermont. At the bottom of the run, the four of them smiled and hugged as if they were filled with joy just being in Vermont.

Maddie sat up straight on the bed. She looked up from her pad with a sudden idea. She fired up her laptop and was well into composing an email when her cell phone rang.

Bill was all apologies. "Maddie, I was on hold forever hoping to reach the other Vermont resort owner. His assistant finally came on and said he's in California until next week and will call me then. My plan is a bust for now. Can you hold off the vipers?"

"I won't sugarcoat it. I happened to spy Nora in town with a host of developers. The truth seems to be riding on my skillfully deposing her."

"You said it. You just might end up proving she's for real."

Maddie leaned back against the pillows with a sigh. "That could happen. I was about to send you an email. Perhaps we're missing a huge opportunity. If Nora is Jordan's cousin, I will try convincing her not to change Starlight, and suggest she act as Jordan's silent partner in running the lodge and the ski resort."

"It's an inspired idea, one I admire. But what gives you the impression Nora will play nice?"

"Call it a hunch. I believe all she wants is family. Nora was an orphan before she was adopted. Her mother Rosalyn lived alone in Austria running an orphanage. Nora wants a home, which is why she's here in Starlight."

"You've convinced me," Bill barked. "I'll attend the deposition myself."

Maddie pushed back. "You trust me to handle this right?"

"Absolutely. You conduct the questioning. I come alongside to help you shut this thing down."

"Bill, I have another hunch. Stewart, Nora's attorney, is spinning things for his own nefarious purposes. I don't see the need for you to come all the way up here."

"I want to be on hand, Madison, if Jordan decides to negotiate with her about a silent partnership. You let me draft up any contracts."

And so it was agreed. With Maddie unable to convince him otherwise, Bill promised to phone in the morning about his charter flight arrangements. Maddie ended the call knowing she was similar to Bill in one respect. Neither of them liked taking chances when it came to their cases.

After eating her supper, which she ordered from room service along with a carafe of hot coffee, she set the tray aside and took a peek at the deposition questions for the umpteenth time. Good thing she'd brought along her portable printer to print a backup copy in case her computer failed. Her fingers were banging along on the keyboard when the realization hit squarely in her heart.

The same safe motto Maddie adhered to in work was the rallying cry in her personal life. She'd considered Stewart a sound choice because he loved the law as she did. Or at least she once thought he did. He'd certainly proven to be the exact opposite. Well, so much for her hunches panning out. Her idea about Nora longing for family might be another flop.

A loud rapping on her door startled Maddie. Her finger typed a bunch of m's.

She hit delete before walking over to peer through the viewer, fully expecting to see Gretchen coming for the tray or even Jordan out in the hall. Her eye fixed on the distorted shape of a woman she almost recognized.

Maddie opened the door a crack, the security device still in place.

"May I help you?" she asked warily.

The lady smiled and drew near the opening. "Are you the attorney Madison Stone?"

The blue puffy jacket gave her away. She was one of the ladies Maddie observed this afternoon climbing into Trevor's van. Her mind tumbled. What should she do?

Maddie made a swift decision, hoping she wasn't making a mistake. Rather than banging the door shut, she would go along and try to discover Stewart's endgame.

"I am," Maddie told her. "Who are you and why are you coming to my room?"

"My name is Nora Star. Please, we need to talk."

A bolt of adrenaline spiked through Maddie's veins as she removed the security device. She opened the door, knowing she'd been right. Nora had come to Maddie because she did want to be part of Jordan's family.

She gazed from Nora's head to her feet when something unusual hit her. She pressed her lips together wondering if she really should let her in.

"Nora, you don't have any accent."

"It's better for me not to explain everything in the hallway," Nora said, glancing over her shoulder.

"Well … All right, come in."

Maddie lifted her ski jacket from the desk chair. Nora walked in tentatively, gripping the strap of a bag she carried over her shoulder.

"Sorry to arrive unannounced," she told Maddie, sounding apologetic. "There are things I need to tell you."

"Undoubtedly," Maddie snipped. "Earlier, I saw you in the company of real estate developers whose interests are contrary to those of my client. Before we go any further, I have to ask. Are you for real?"

Nora reached inside her purse, saying, "Your misgivings are no surprise. I have heard you are an excellent attorney."

"Which tells me nothing." Maddie glared at her visitor. "Besides your having no accent, your blue eyes look nothing like the brown ones I expected. The more I see you, the more I'm convinced you can't be Nora Star."

The woman pulled a leather folder from her purse. "You are correct. I am an imposter."

"I knew it!" Maddie raised both hands in the air.

With a flick of her wrist, the woman opened a leather folder, revealing a shiny gold badge. "I am Special Agent Eva Montanna with the Department of Homeland Security. In my undercover role, I've been posing as the fictitious Nora Star."

"Why would you do this?" Shock rippled through Maddie, down to her feet. "You must have more you can explain."

Agent Montanna flipped her leather holder and this time showed Maddie her credentials. The official document displayed her photo and "United States" prominently across the top.

"May I sit down?" she asked.

"I wish you would, Agent Montanna. I need you to tell me everything. My client has spent thousands upon thousands of dollars in attorney fees because of your charade."

Maddie pulled out the desk chair for the agent before she sat across from her on an accent chair.

"Can we use first names, Madison? I am sure you feel betrayed and have many questions."

Maddie tried to quiet her escalating frustration. Agent Montanna had one valid point. They should treat each other as equals who both fought for justice.

"Okay, Eva, and I'm Maddie to you."

"Fine." Eva set the large purse by her feet, still holding onto her credentials. "What I'm about to reveal is extremely confidential. You must promise not to repeat anything, at least not until I tell you it's okay. Agreed?"

Maddie's mind wrestled over the possibilities in a flash. She never would have predicted this outcome, not in a million years.

She folded her arms, and with a tilt of her chin, replied, "I have an ethical and legal obligation to represent my client and not to deceive him or the court. I agree only if you don't put me in any sort of conflict."

"That's my reason for coming to you this evening." Eva gazed at Maddie with unwavering blue eyes. "The government doesn't want to put you in a position to knowingly or unknowingly deceive anyone."

"Go on then. I agree to your demand."

Eva dropped the credential case into her shoulder bag. "As you are probably aware, certain laws protect our national interests. When we federal agents detect persons may be violating these laws, we often use undercover agents to infiltrate foreign and even domestic organizations."

"Like people trying to gain control of rare earth elements?"

"Oh my." Eva sounded surprised. "You have learned much. It's probably a good thing I came here tonight."

Maddie was determined to say nothing more. "Please continue, Agent Montanna."

"We agreed, I'm Eva," she said, a faint smile gracing her lips. "The purpose of my unannounced visit is to advise you there will be no deposition of Nora, and to ask you not to file any further motions to postpone or compel with the court. There is no need for any of that. We don't want to inconvenience the court with our undercover investigation."

Eva paused to seemingly study Maddie's eyes. "Does this make sense to you?"

"That's the problem," Maddie said. "I am trying to make sense of it all."

"I admit my coming here is a bit off the grid."

"Exactly." Maddie rubbed the sudden knot in the back of her neck.

Hadn't Eva already disrupted her probate case? Why be concerned now? Then in an instant she realized why Eva was pulling the plug on her little ruse.

She adjusted her chair and looked directly at the federal agent. "You are here, but are providing no real information to justify altering how I represent my client."

"I understand." Eva's curt nod exuded authority. "As we speak, FBI and Homeland Security agents from my task force are making arrests in D.C., Colorado, New York, and here in Vermont. We are arresting lawyers, realtors, financial brokers, and geologists."

Maddie's heart contracted with a thud. "Like Trevor Kirk, the geologist I saw you with yesterday? What about the D.C. attorney, Stewart Dunham?"

"As much as I want to ease your mind, I've told you all I am authorized to say. Tomorrow, the U.S. Attorney for the District of Vermont and the supervisory FBI agent will hold a press conference when they will release more details. I'm just the undercover agent."

Would both Trevor and Stewart be arrested? How awful!

Maddie shifted in her seat, unnerved, as if a rock had just landed in the pit of her stomach.

So what if they had been caught doing something criminal? She wasn't responsible for either of them choosing to plunge down the wrong path. Maddie waved a caution flag in front of her heart. She shouldn't let sympathy for their fate interfere with her representing Jordan.

Her thoughts whirling faster than a jet engine, Maddie sputtered, "My boss is flying up here tomorrow, expecting to meet you. Ah ... I mean Nora."

"Maddie, please phone him and tell him there's no need for him to come." Eva arched her light eyebrows.

"Bill Barron is no pushover. He'll insist I provide an explanation."

"Of course." Eva rested a hand on her chin. "Here's my dilemma. We don't know if we will arrest all the people in D.C. and elsewhere. So I can't let you divulge our undercover case just now. If it leaks, we risk the suspects fleeing. The press conference won't be held until we know it's safe for public disclosure."

"And Jordan Star, the owner of everything you see around here? What do I tell him?"

Eva yanked her shoulder bag up from the floor. "Well, I think his empire is secure once again."

"Wasn't it always safe?" Maddie countered, rising to her feet.

Eva stood, her tone taking on a sharper edge as she replied, "Had Jordan known of these attempts to corner the market of rare earth elements, and had he fraudulently tried to profit from it, he might be a defendant. But he's quite the straight shooter. Or he's just naïve. Or," Eva added with a wink, "maybe he has a super smart lawyer."

"That's it." Maddie smiled at the irony of the many nights she'd spent tossing and turning over a phantom. Could her life get any stranger?

"Eva, I could tell Bill and Jordan that I just found out Nora isn't showing up anytime soon. Bill stays in D.C. and that may give encouragement to them both."

"I'm okay with that." Eva handed Maddie a business card embossed with a gold badge. "Meanwhile, I will notify you in the morning if and when the press conference is scheduled."

Eva held out her slim hand and Maddie grasped it firmly. "Eva, I realize you, in your pretend role as Nora, would not have lied under oath at the deposition tomorrow. And you couldn't risk alerting the wrongdoers. Thanks for coming. You didn't have to. You could've just not shown up."

"To me, it's important to act justly and love mercy."

"And to walk humbly before God," Maddie added with a smile. "That's in the Bible."

Eva's own smile spread across her pretty face. "Yes, Maddie, it's from the book of Micah. It's my personal motto and life verse. Let's stay in touch."

Maddie walked the agent to the door. She stopped with one more question.

"What made you think it was safe to tell me about this secret?"

Eva leaned against the open doorjamb. "You were detained once by Ann Arbor police while breaking into your own locked car."

She winked once more at Maddie. "We know all about you. Goodnight."

As Eva walked down the hall, Maddie locked her door, fresh perspective flowing into her mind. It was as if cool night air had blown throughout her room. Maddie didn't know the precise steps to take next. She did understand that she'd just been in the presence of a rare breed.

Special Agent Eva Montanna believed and spoke the truth. She also acted in truth.

Maddie took a swig of cold coffee. As much as she wanted to grab the phone and call Jordan with news of the deposition being canceled, she decided it was too dangerous. After all, she'd promised Eva to disclose nothing about the undercover case, which was under way this very moment.

Nothing was stopping her from inviting him to attend the press conference with her tomorrow. Then again, he might ask more questions, ones she wasn't permitted to answer. Maddie decided to wait until morning after speaking with Eva.

Her obligation to Bill was more urgent. She must tell him something as he was planning an early flight to Vermont. Without wasting a second, she sent him a message: *Nora's deposition cancelled. No need to fly to Vermont. I'll phone in the morning.*

All the vitality during the disquieting meeting with Eva ebbed away. Maddie suddenly felt overcome by weariness and sorrow. Stewart had torn his legal career to shreds. He might already be locked up in jail.

The only thing she could do for him was pray. Someone else needed prayer too.

Maddie thumbed through pictures in her phone until reaching one of her and Trevor on the chairlift, smiling into the camera. She enlarged the photo with her fingertips. Their smiles as they soared up the mountaintop seemed frozen in time. The fleeting moments of happiness they had shared were gone. Special Agent Eva Montanna had just wiped them out with her giant erasure.

Maddie squeezed warm feelings for Trevor from her heart, from her mind, and from her spirit. She steeled herself for the blows that would surely come tomorrow when the extent of Stewart's criminal actions, and possibly Trevor's too, were unveiled.

The biggest question throbbing in her mind was how had she, Madison Stone, missed seeing the whole truth? She flopped down on the bed, tears stinging her eyes.

Would she never learn?

Chapter 27

Sleep didn't come for Maddie right away. When it did, a dreadful dream of Stewart laughing wildly and waving the deed to Star Mountain startled her awake. She climbed from the four-poster bed and pulled aside the curtain to peer out the corner window, which faced the village. The sun's yellow rays reached down from the sky, illuminating Starlight in a glimmering glow. If only her life could be so magical.

Stewart's gleeful dream-face haunted her as she hurried to brew the small pot of coffee. Comforting smells of hazelnut coffee began to drive away some of her gloom. She poured coffee into a ceramic cup, and cooling the brew with her breath, she wandered over to the window.

The more she awakened, the more Maddie realized how astonishing Agent Montanna's unexpected visit was last evening. Her jaw-dropping revelations had hit Maddie like a pop-up storm hurling hailstones. No wonder bad dreams had exploded in her mind during the night.

She drank her coffee, refusing to allow Stewart's shenanigans to steal her victory. After all, the fraudulent Nora Star had been unmasked. She was no longer a threat. Maddie could soon close and finalize the estate for Jordan, wrapping it in a bright silver package that he could open before Christmas.

A quick check of her cell phone revealed Eva had sent no texts or messages. Maddie selected a gray sweater and black slacks, an outfit she thought suitable for the press conference, if there was one. She wanted to be prepared just in case. Black boots, blue down vest, and matching scarf around her neck completed her look.

She declared herself ready for breakfast. So briefcase in hand, she hurried down to Cinnamon Stix, ordering a coffee to go and toasted bagel. She'd taken one bite when her phone rang in the case. Maddie managed to yank it out and answer before the voicemail clicked on.

"Good morning, Maddie," Eva quipped in her ear. "The press conference starts at nine. Sorry for the short notice. I just found out."

"You've given me enough time to make it, I think." Maddie signaled the server for her check. "Eva, will I see you there?"

"Yes. I'm on my way there now."

As they hung up, Maddie was well on the way to rounding up her client, corralling him at the front desk. They hit the road with Jordan riding shotgun in the passenger seat. On the drive to the U.S. District Court in Rutland, Jordan kept calling her attention to the scenery.

"That fir tree would make a perfect tree next Christmas," he said, pointing out the window.

Maddie barely glanced his way. "Oh really?"

"Hey, Maddie, the abominable snowman just ran into the woods."

She didn't notice. Her mind was navigating the twists and turns of her life here in Star Mountain at the same time she tore down the road, concerned she wouldn't reach the conference in time.

"I was testing to see if you were listening. You're not," Jordan snapped, bursting her concentration. "Tell me why you grabbed me and said I had to come with you pronto. Good thing I was still wearing my jacket."

"Thankfully, the roads are clear," was her reply. She still hadn't decided how much to tell him about Nora Star.

"Sure, it's great we're not in a snowstorm, yet here I am and here you are driving like crazy over to Rutland. What gives?"

"Before I get to that, when are Vanessa and Cole flying in?"

"The morning of the festival," Jordan said briskly. "You said Nora's deposition is cancelled. Did she change her mind? I can't bear the suspense."

Jordan sounded as edgy as Maddie felt.

"Okay, I've been waiting to call Bill. I may as well tell you both of the bizarre happenings."

She put her cell phone on speaker and using voice command, she called the office.

Vanessa answered in her upbeat voice, "Barron and Rich."

"Hi, Vanessa." Maddie couldn't help smiling as she told her, "Jordan and I are driving to Rutland. We need to speak to Bill."

"Hold on, I'll put you through," Vanessa said, the line falling silent.

Bill erupted over the phone, "What's going on, Maddie?"

Maddie held her cell to her mouth. "Jordan and I are driving to Rutland."

"Right. Vanessa said as much. You texted last night that Nora's deposition is cancelled. Are you holding it in Rutland instead? Should I be there?"

"Slow down. I'll explain." Maddie tried concentrating on the road ahead. "We're on speaker. There will be no deposition. Not today. Not ever."

"What are you saying?" Bill demanded. "Did the Hunter firm turn tail and run?"

"I met with Nora Star last night in my room."

Jordan turned in his seat. "What?"

"Now you tell me!" Bill shouted in his courtroom voice. "Did Stewart Dunham bring her to you?"

"No. I met her alone," Maddie answered quickly.

"Excellent," Bill replied. "Did you convince her to work with us as you planned?"

"Not exactly."

"You exposed her as an imposter, right?"

Maddie bobbed her head. "Yes, she admitted to being a phony heir. So there will be no deposition."

"Are you saying there is no other heir?" Jordan interjected.

"Good question," Bill exclaimed. "That's what I want to know."

"Gentlemen, hear me when I say there are no other heirs. End of story and end of their lawsuit."

"Maddie, I knew we could depend on you. Isn't that right, Jordan?" Bill crowed.

From the corner of her eye, Maddie spotted Jordan's pleasant grin as he proclaimed loudly, "My faith never wavered."

"That's right," Maddie chimed. "Mine shriveled a few times, but never left me. I can't take the credit, boss. Nora showed up at my room last night, insisting we had to talk. I didn't want to let her in, but I recognized her from seeing her yesterday in Starlight with Stewart, and Trevor the geologist."

"So you let her into your room?" Jordan asked.

Maddie paused long enough to round a tight curve. "I had to. She carried a badge and I presume a gun. Turns out she's an undercover federal agent."

"What?" Bill and Jordan hollered at once.

"You heard me. Her name is Eva Montanna. She's a special agent, sporting all the official credentials. Eva made me promise not to tell anyone and came to me as a professional courtesy. The FBI is arresting suspects who are involved in this attempted takeover of Starlight."

Jordan's mouth hung open as he turned to Maddie. "The police chief came in for breakfast this morning. He told me the FBI arrested several people at the Mountain View last night. Big secret."

Bill offered no response as if he was at a loss to decipher the situation.

So she spoke for both of them. "Jordan and I are racing to the federal courthouse for a press conference given by the U.S. Attorney. We expect to find out who's been arrested and what they're charged with."

"Okay, I have my marching orders," Bill replied in good humor. "Cancel my search for a new buyer."

"Righto." Maddie sought to further reassure him and her client. "To recap, no deposition is needed because there's no new will and no heir other than Jordan. Bill, let me phone you when the press conference is over."

"Madison," Bill whispered her name over the speaker. "Because the federal agent told you in advance, I take it our firm's in the clear. You can see how easy it is to become entangled into something unlawful. Did she say what the charges are?"

"Eva did not, which is what I hope to learn at the press conference."

"You've done another stellar job, Madison, just as I knew you would," her boss said. "You may be up for partner sooner than you thought. Keep me advised."

Maddie ended the call and put her cell into her coat pocket. Even though it was cool in the car, sweat started along her hairline. She loosened her scarf.

For his part, Jordan stared out the front window. To make it easier on him, she said, "Fire away. I can tell you're brimming with questions."

"So Nora does not exist. This federal agent made it all up. Why?" Jordan snatched his to-go coffee out of the cup holder.

"We may learn more when the U.S. Attorney unveils the charges. You should relax for a change and enjoy this worry-free morning. Prayers are being answered and your life is looking up."

"Letting go of worry has never come easy for me."

"Me either," Maddie agreed.

Jordan leaned his head back all the same and the duo rode in quiet except for the SUV's tires rumbling over ice chunks on the road. Maddie's thoughts rested on the good man sitting beside her, how he'd laughed and talked with Vanessa before she had returned home. They both seemed to thrive in each other's company.

Maddie marveled at what she might have arranged, yet a simmering question remained. Had she pulled the rug out from beneath herself?

Her thoughts took a turn at the same time she cranked a right turn toward Rutland. The answer must be a decided no.

She sipped her hazelnut coffee, its dark roast flavor tingling on her tongue. It seemed God arranged for her to meet Jordan, not to become romantically attached, but to discover the qualities of a genuine man. Jordan was true to the core, a shining light in his community.

Becoming involved with Stewart, a selfish man caught up in greed, had been a serious mistake. Yesterday, Eva had confirmed his dark and sneaky side. He had never been Maddie's hope for the future. If Vanessa and Jordan were meant for each other, Maddie was cheering for them.

Jordan breached her mind travels by blurting, "What will be revealed at the press conference?"

"Let's wait and see," was all she said.

Truth be told, his question had uncovered the far deeper concern vexing her spirit. She feared discovering that beyond all doubt Stewart and Trevor, two men to whom she'd been attracted, were under arrest and charged with crimes.

Disgust at being such a poor judge of character flared up within Maddie. Well, there was no way to remedy those poor choices now. She would see what chapter next unfolded in her life, and hopefully be a wiser woman going forward.

"Turn right on West Street," the British voice of her GPS ordered.

"That's it, the U.S. courthouse." Jordan threw up a hand. "Would you look at the swarm of media? It's a regular mob."

Maddie gulped. "Looks like we're not the only ones hearing about the press conference."

TV remote trucks with their hydraulic towers pointed skyward occupied every parking spot in front of the courthouse. Maddie zoomed around the block a few times, finally spotting a space at the rear of the building. She pulled in.

"Uh oh. It's for Law Enforcement Vehicles Only."

"You jump out here and I'll go park," Jordan offered.

"Nope. Maddie Stone never gives up."

Jordan beamed at her. "Don't I know it."

Going around the block paid off because Maddie nabbed a vacant spot.

"We can make it if we hurry." She cut the engine and snatched the keys. "Don't bring your coffee or Swiss Army knife on your keychain. We pass through security and magnetometers."

"Glad you mentioned my Swiss Army knife. I had to buy a new one after airport security confiscated my old one last time I flew."

He removed the knife while Maddie collected her satchel, and then locked the car. She dashed alongside Jordan, slipping once on the snow. He caught her elbow to steady her.

"Maddie, thanks for everything," he said, his voice catching. "And I mean everything. My life has changed in phenomenal ways since you arrived. I hope you find what I have found in Vanessa, someone to share your life with."

She squeezed Jordan's arm. "Thank you for that. Meanwhile, pay attention for the next hour because we should learn a lot. And I agree with you. Things are turning out far differently from what either of us ever imagined."

Chapter 28

Maddie and Jordan arrived at the courthouse as a sedan containing four people drove into the law enforcement parking spot Maddie had just passed. She was ready to walk in between it and an adjoining car when the driver jumped out, shoving his open palm at Maddie and Jordan like a traffic cop. They both stopped without argument.

"The driver looks like an FBI agent recruiting poster," Maddie told Jordan in hushed tones. "I suspect they're heading to the press conference."

A female agent, her gold badge showing on her belt, lunged out of the front passenger seat, and with the other agent, she opened the rear doors.

"These could be the prisoners," Maddie whispered, watching and holding her breath.

When a woman with brown hair and hands cuffed behind her back struggled to climb out, Jordan asked, "Maddie, do you know her?"

"I may have seen her in town yesterday. I'm unsure." Maddie kept her eyes glued to the other side of the car.

A man struggled to emerge, his hands also cuffed behind him. His face looked gristly with a day's growth of scraggly beard. His suit was disheveled. Maddie's hands flew to her face. It was Stewart.

A dark veil dropped before her eyes. The man she had once shared her life with was about to begin months or even years of agony. It made her sick to see him being hustled away in handcuffs.

"I think you may know him. Am I right?" Jordan asked between clenched teeth.

Maddie squeezed her hands together. "Unfortunately, ye-es. That's Stewart, the opposing lawyer who caused you and the people of Starlight such misery. What I don't understand is how an attorney who swears to uphold the law finds himself transported by FBI agents in handcuffs."

Her stomach lurched again at watching Stewart being escorted behind the woman into the rear of the federal building. She groaned aloud before realizing it.

"Why don't we go around to the front," Jordan said, taking her by the elbow.

Maddie was thankful for his warmhearted concern. "Good idea."

They cleared security, and she ushered Jordan inside the courtroom, where he said close to her ear, "This is my first time in court. I've never been called to sit on a jury."

"This is the first time I've been in this federal court," Maddie replied, looking around for Agent Eva Montanna with no success.

"So what am I seeing down front by the microphone?" he asked.

She squatted and pointed. "It's a poster board on an easel. That's where a judge would normally sit. Instead of a judge, we'll be hearing from the U.S. Attorney."

"Are those pictures?"

Maddie nodded. "I am sure they are photos of those arrested. They're too small for me to be sure."

"We just need a flying trapeze act to complete this circus," Jordan said, gazing around with wide eyes and mouth ajar.

Maddie straightened her back. "I agree. This many cameras in court are unusual."

The circus-like atmosphere gave her no concern. She instead scrutinized the gaggle of print reporters clinging to their little notepads as well as the photographers with press badges around their necks. They all stood in clusters talking to each other. Among them, Maddie didn't spot Eva anywhere.

Then a familiar red hunter plaid shirt walked in front of her. Sure enough, he was none other than Barnaby Ross. The intrepid intern wound his way through the group of reporters as if a pro.

Maddie had no intention of risking another ugly run-in with *The Ledger* wannabe reporter. She nudged Jordan past Ross. They paused in the aisle momentarily while Maddie scoped out empty seats. Spectators had already filled the first three rows. Men and women wearing dark suits crowded the inner courtroom tables, their backs to Maddie.

"You know, Jordan, this publicity could be a positive for Starlight," Maddie said, spotting a clerk over by the press releases. "You save me a spot here in the back, and I'll return shortly. Watch my briefcase."

Maddie pushed through the crowd, hustling over to a table where the clerk held a firm hand on a high stack of press releases.

"I'm Attorney Madison Stone and need a press release to find out who's been arrested," Maddie intoned, reaching for one.

The clerk kept her hand pressed upon the stack and shook her head vehemently. "Nothing doing. These are embargoed until after the news conference."

Maddie's hand hovered near the stack.

The clerk leaned closer. "If you persist, I will ask the U.S. Marshal to escort you from the courtroom."

"You can't blame a lawyer for trying," Maddie said wistfully.

"I won't, but my boss will," the clerk said in a cutting tone. "Find your seat."

Maddie drew her brows together and surrendered. Stymied for now, she intended to grab one of those press releases once the clerk walked away. She joined Jordan and snagged a perfect observation post.

"I see she wouldn't give you one of those sheets," Jordan said, wearing a sheepish smile. "Isn't that unusual?"

Maddie removed her scarf and stowed it in her leather case. Straightening, she told him, "Not really. The press release usually comes after the conference. That way everyone is forced to wait for the U.S. Attorney."

"That's not what I mean."

"Okay, I'll bite." Maddie folded her arms. "What's on your mind?"

Jordan's eyes were also smiling at her. "It's unusual for you not to get what you go after. Isn't it?"

"If you only knew."

His innocent question rocked Maddie. How could she admit she'd made such grave mistakes with Stewart and now Trevor?

Her phone vibrated, which she pulled from her pocket. Bill's number flashed across the screen. She answered with a hushed, "Bill, I'm in the courtroom."

"Tell me what's happening," he insisted. "All I see on the TV screen is a microphone on a stand and an easel."

She lowered her voice to a bare whisper, and said, "Media types are swarming the court. Mug shot photos are displayed down in the well of the courtroom, but the names are too small to read."

"How many photos?" Bill shot back.

Maddie squinted her eyes. "Unsure. I can't see them well enough to recognize anyone. It appears there may be a few women."

"Are they lawyers?"

She adjusted her phone closer to her ear. "Good question. I didn't consider that one of the women I saw yesterday might be a lawyer."

"Remember, the lawyer who first called me from Stewart's law firm was a woman. I don't recall her name. Oh, and one more thing. The partners' meeting is today at five. Your name is first on the agenda. Thought you'd like to know."

A sense of anticipation rushed over Maddie. Still, she wouldn't pin her hopes on being elevated to partner the first time.

"Bill, I'm grateful you respect my work. You give me many opportunities and I thank you."

The clerk walked down to the microphone, and Maddie fought the urge to hurry over and snag a press release. She wasn't ready to end the call with Bill.

"They're giving a two-minute warning," she told her boss. "On our way in, we saw FBI agents unloading several prisoners. Stewart Dunham was one, his hands in cuffs. None of the pictures appear to be him, so perhaps he hasn't been booked yet."

"Unbelievable. I wonder—"

"Conference is starting. Gotta go," Maddie interjected before he could grill her about Stewart's downfall.

She put away the phone and focused her eyes forward. A well-dressed man in a blue suit and starched shirt and wearing a striped bowtie adjusted the microphone.

He introduced himself, "I am Assistant U.S. Attorney Clayton Andrews. Our office has indicted and arrested eleven persons for conspiring to defraud investors in the mining and export of rare earth elements, which are essential in the manufacture of U.S. military weapons and systems."

Maddie nodded, and Jordan leaned over, asking her, "So they wanted the minerals beneath Star Mountain?"

"Yes. And their greed circled back and got them," she whispered.

The microphone squelched sharply. Maddie covered her ears as an aide sprinted forward to adjust the sound. When the squeals ended, Maddie lowered her hands.

The prosecutor returned to the microphone, continuing as if he hadn't been interrupted, "Federal agents arrested those persons working to cheat landowners in Colorado, as well as large resorts and adjacent mountain property owners here in Vermont," Andrews explained. "We arrested four New York investment brokers who used a falsified prospectus to cheat investors. Others include two attorneys from a D.C. law firm and five realtors and geologists who created false and fraudulent documents. They traveled via interstate commerce to aid and abet the conspiracy."

Maddie grabbed Jordan's arm. "Oh my! This is terrible. I think they've even arrested Trevor Kirk."

"The geologist who ate at the Stix? Gretchen told me about him."

Andrews's eyes swept over the audience and he pointed to the clerk. "On your way out, the clerk will provide a press release with further details. I will answer questions to the extent that I can."

Barnaby Ross's hand shot up. "How long has this investigation been going on? Where did it begin?"

The prosecutor paused and peered down at someone in the front row. "I think you've already stumped me. It actually started in Colorado, but I do not have the date. Let me ask the FBI case agent to join me up here."

From the back, all Maddie could see was a tall man in a gray business suit standing up and walking forward in one long stride. When he turned to face the audience, she gasped.

Andrews introduced him. "Special Agent Trevor Wagoner is the case agent from the FBI's Washington D.C. office."

Trevor took his place by the microphone, telling the audience, "This case originated in Colorado six months ago. I thank the team who helped me bring the case to such a swift conclusion."

Shock and surprise battered Maddie. She couldn't help blurting, "He's Trevor Kirk!" Her voice cracked as a tsunami of emotions bubbled over. "Jordan, I can't believe it!"

He put his hand over hers. "Trevor the geologist is really an FBI agent?"

"Sshh."

Maddie pressed a finger to her lips and strained her neck to see Trevor. Her mind was melting down. She had difficulty processing the words he was speaking. Her ears were ringing as she removed a tissue from her purse and dabbed her eyes.

Life was coming at her like an out-of-control fastball.

The deception! The outrage!

How could she have been duped again?

"I refuse to watch this, Jordan. I'm going outside."

Maddie snatched up her briefcase. She elbowed her way out of the courtroom, scooping up the press release by the exit before the clerk could object. She'd just reached the exit door when a hand grasped her shoulder.

"Madison."

Maddie whirled around to see Eva Montanna. The special agent gazed intently at her with big blue eyes. "I saw you leaving the press conference. Won't you stay?"

Maddie cleared her throat, not wanting Eva to sense how upset she was. Surely her red and blinking eyes were giving her away.

"I'm not sure my client needs to pay me to attend this conference when everything will be reported in the media. Besides, Jordan is in there."

Eva kept a grip on her sleeve. "Please, come back. Earlier, Trevor had asked me to make sure I found you. He wants to brief you personally."

Maddie's lip began to quiver and the dam holding back her tears released. She wiped her eyes with her free hand. "The indictment said a geologist was arrested. I'm so confused."

"I can explain," Eva said. "Let's sit here a moment."

She led Maddie to a wooden bench along the lobby windows.

"We arrested two geologists from Colorado who arranged sales for this group," Eva began. "Though I wanted to tell you last night, I couldn't."

"Trevor deceived me." Maddie blotted her eyes. "That's what has me upset. He played on my emotions. He pretended to be a single and carefree guy. He probably has a wife. In fact, I heard he was involved in a relationship."

Maddie didn't want to say aloud what she'd fully realized the moment Trevor strode to the microphone. He had entered her heart in such a huge way, even though she had put up every wall possible.

Eva clasped her hands in front of her. "Madison, if only you understood how difficult it is for Trevor working undercover. I've been in such a role myself. He feels terrible about the deceit. That's why he asked me to watch for you, so he could speak with you before the press conference. He commissioned me to find you, but I was delayed by a phone call from my supervisor in D.C."

"He didn't find me," Maddie replied.

"No, he was engaged with the AUSA. Trevor isn't married, but many undercover agents claim they are married or committed to avoid getting into compromising situations."

Maddie shrugged, willing herself to get over it. Eva leaned closer to hand Maddie another tissue.

"Besides, Trevor assured me there's nothing between you two. Is that right?"

"Not really." Maddie sniffed. "Eva, I'm just so relieved he wasn't arrested. I guess it's because I sensed Trevor did nothing wrong."

Eva pulled her hair up behind her head and let it fall to her shoulders. "I'm sorry I failed you both. Even though Trevor said he hadn't crossed the forbidden line of undercover work, I know he has real concern for you. That must be why he assigned me to seek you out."

"That's all very interesting." Maddie stood, shutting down further conversation. "I must be going."

"Won't you come back in and meet with Trevor?" Eva pleaded.

"No." She handed Eva her card. "This is my cell phone number. Tell Trevor he can call me."

"Where will you be?" Eva asked.

"In Starlight for a few days to take care of loose ends."

Maddie left, thinking Eva had some nerve to try and convince her to hear out Trevor. What could he say that would change anything?

She returned to the SUV where she turned up the heat, waiting for Jordan. With her name being on the partner's agenda, at least her legal career was going in an upward trajectory. Her personal life was a different matter altogether. Somewhere back in Starlight, Maddie seemed to have made a serious wrong turn.

THE COURTHOUSE WAS MOSTLY EMPTY when Trevor Wagoner left a follow-up briefing with AUSA Andrews. Eva Montanna hustled alongside him as he strode toward the front door deep in thought. He'd kept an eye out for Maddie but hadn't seen her anywhere. Perhaps she was outside. Then he realized it was too cold for her to be out there waiting for him.

Trevor stopped in midstride, asking Eva, "Did you have a chance to talk with Maddie Stone?"

"Yes, I spoke with her." Eva put her hands on her hips, and he felt the heat of her intense gaze. "When you stood up to answer questions, she left the press conference faster than you can blink your eye. Are you being square with me when you say you two aren't involved?"

Doubt coursed through Trevor. "Why do you ask?"

"Because of how upset she was when she left. She was in tears."

"Yikes. That's bad." Trevor swiped at his chin. "I should have handled things differently."

"So there is something brewing between you two. I thought so."

"Eva." Trevor paused, trying to find the words to counter her uncanny jabs. "You know how complex it is working undercover. When you're with mobsters and drug dealers, you don't let them see the real you. Because I wasn't facing physical danger, I grew at ease with Maddie. I enjoyed her company and was encouraged by the fact we both work in D.C. I was able to be more like my real self."

Eva whistled softly. "Well, buddy, it must have worked. I suspect she liked what she thought was the real you, but after my visit last night, she'd convinced herself that you were a criminal and part of the dark side."

"Oh, great," he grumbled, shoving his hands in his pockets. "First she thinks I'm a jerk ready to hurt her client, and then a criminal, and now who knows what."

Eva gave Trevor a side hug, telling him with a smile, "I saved the good news for last."

He instantly brightened. "I could use some right about now."

"Maddie is staying in Starlight for a few days. Go and talk with her. You shouldn't let this chance slip by."

"Eva, you spoke with Maddie," Trevor said, not wanting to be grasping at straws. "Do you think I have a chance?"

"Most certainly. Take it from me. Maddie wouldn't have left in tears otherwise. I think you are perfect for each other."

"Okay, then." Trevor hugged Eva in return. "And Eva, one more thing."

"Yes, I'll give our boss a heads-up that you need time to put finishing touches on the Vermont case before heading back to D.C."

They both laughed.

"Thanks for that, partner." Trevor opened the door for her with renewed assurance. "I'll see you back in the office ... well, sometime soon."

He climbed into the silver undercover Mercedes with one thought in mind. He needed to repair the damage with Maddie. If only Eva had been able to talk to her before he revealed his true identity. But she hadn't, so too bad for him.

Trevor hit the gas for Starlight, roaring away from court, a man on a mission to make things right.

Chapter 29

Maddie sipped lukewarm coffee the next morning at the Cinnamon Stix in low spirits. After getting back from court yesterday, she'd turned off her phone and put it on the charger. A few minutes ago, she powered it back on.

The phone in her hand, she found herself staring out the window, gazing at nothing in particular. Her mind stuck in reverse gear, Maddie kept rehearsing at lightning speed the bizarre moment when she'd witnessed the unmasking of Trevor Kirk.

He had caused untold angst for Maddie and extraordinary expenses for her client. But beyond all of that, Maddie despised how she felt being tricked by him.

Wait a minute. She leaned forward with narrowed eyes. A shiny Mercedes just wheeled into the front parking lot. Was it Trevor?

She couldn't be certain. The silver car displayed no Essential Oil sign. Maddie set down her cup, waiting and scarcely breathing. If it were Trevor, what would she say to him?

He stepped out wearing a brown leather jacket, jeans, and silver aviator-style sunglasses. When he set the sunglasses atop his head, she caught her breath at the sight of him. It was as if she was seeing a new Trevor.

Her heart pulsated with great feeling. Her mind shouted, "No! Don't get involved with him."

She understood the logic of her internal warning. All the while she'd known Trevor, he had been pretending to be one person and was really another. As Maddie watched him enter the lodge, she made a hasty decision to finish her coffee and leave the café to avoid seeing him.

Her cup was up to her lips for the last swallow when he walked up to her table. His usually jovial face looked clouded with apprehension.

"Good morning," Trevor said, his jaw muscles flexing. "Mind if I join you?"

Maddie suppressed the notion to jump up and run out. Escaping wasn't her style. She fixed her brown eyes upon his blue eyes and noticed a burning intensity in them that seemed to mirror what she felt inside.

"I'm still upset over what you've put me and the others through." She drummed her fingers on the table. "Jordan and Gretchen and folks around town are convinced you saved the mountain and village, so I guess you can sit down."

"You just named other people who feel that way," he said, taking the seat across from her. "What about you?"

She wrapped her hands around the nearly empty cup. "Honestly, my opinion vacillates. I mostly suspect your undercover scenario caused the town's people to have many fears when there was no real threat."

"But Maddie, there was a threat. That's the point of my going undercover to begin with. And we didn't know at first if your client was conspiring along with the others."

"Eventually you must have learned he wasn't."

"All of our cases have a suspect and a victim." Trevor lifted his square chin. "Jordan and the town are the victims. What more can I say?"

A strained silence stretched between them. At length, Maddie observed, "I see the sign's gone from your car."

Her lighthearted comment broke the tension. Trevor treated her to a sheepish grin.

"Yeah, the undercover operation is over, so I removed it and was heading back to D.C. Then I thought, why not take vacation time and check into the lodge here."

"Really?" Maddie turned that tidbit over in her mind. "For how long?"

His grin morphed into a broad smile. "That all depends. I really came here now to introduce you to Trevor Wagoner and convince you that he's not such a bad guy."

"You could be here forever if that's your goal, except I'm leaving tomorrow."

A server hustled over to their table, asking Trevor if he wanted anything.

He glanced at Maddie, telling the server, "I'm not sure how long I'll be welcomed here. Bring me coffee, black."

The server withdrew with a nod. Maddie continued fixing her eyes upon Trevor, trying to read his undeclared motives. She didn't want to be snookered again. Her phone vibrated on the table, interrupting her musings.

"Do you need to answer that?" Trevor asked. "I don't want to keep you from an important call."

Maddie ignored the phone. "No. If it's my boss, I can call him later."

"I was introducing you to Trevor Wagoner when we were interrupted. I want you to know I'm glad you are still in Starlight. Maybe we could go skiing again before we return to the city. That was a great time."

"You are bold, I give you that." She finished her coffee in one long sip. "The more I think about your conduct, the more I'm convinced you really caused injury to and inconvenienced Jordan Star, the community, and me."

"But Maddie, that wasn't me. That was Trevor Kirk, who doesn't exist."

"Your problem is, we only know Trevor Kirk and he's not well liked here."

Trevor reached across the table in an effort to touch her hand. She pulled back as if she'd received an electrical shock.

"This conversation is not going well," he said, sounding disappointed.

She gripped her phone. "How did you think it would go? We'd hold a parade in your honor?"

"Maddie, if you would just open your mind to me for one minute. Trevor Wagoner grew to know you. He admires and respects you. I feel you need to know him, to know me, the real me. So I asked for vacation time to stay and talk with you. There are things I need to tell you, but not here in public."

The server walked up with his coffee, and Trevor shrugged. "I need to check in. Could you pour my coffee in a to-go cup?"

Trevor rose and placed some cash on the table. "This should cover my coffee. If you are curious to know more, which I suspect you are, come to my room when you finish here. I'll tell you things that won't be revealed until trial, provided you agree to hold it in confidence."

He began walking away, and then stopped to look at her. Maddie saw in his deep blue eyes something she hadn't seen before, something akin to compassion. She relented, realizing he had, after all, been doing his job.

"Okay, I would like to talk with you, Trevor. What room number?"

"I don't know yet. I'm just checking in. I can text you in a few."

He strode away holding his shoulders erect. Maddie left the table and couldn't stop watching him. Curiosity to know more about Trevor magnified when she saw what he did next. He walked up to a small Christmas tree in the corner of the lobby, removed a paper ornament, and took it to the front desk.

He spoke to Gretchen animatedly for several minutes before making his way to the elevator, the paper star between his fingers. Maddie scurried over to the Christmas tree herself, which before now had escaped her notice. Gretchen must have added this one recently to the lodge's burgeoning Christmas display.

Maddie reached out a hand, touching one of the many star-shaped paper ornaments. Each one bore a child's name and age. She selected one for a ten-year-old girl, and taking it over to Gretchen, waved it under her nose.

"Who are these children?" Maddie asked.

"I'm so glad you asked." Gretchen's face lit up and she gestured toward the brightly lit tree. "Jordan puts up a tree each year for children whose parent is incarcerated in our county jail. Their name is written on a star. Guests choose a star and purchase an appropriate gift."

Maddie held onto the star, wondering about the little girl. "Do the children come here for their gifts?"

"After the guests wrap them and tape the star onto their gift, we keep them under the tree until we staffers deliver packages to their homes on Christmas Eve."

"Jordan truly is exceptional," Maddie said, infused with fresh Christmas spirit. "I am going to buy a gift for this child." She clutched the star close to her heart.

"You know what?" Gretchen asked as if drawing Maddie into a secret. "Trevor was holding a paper star in his hand when he checked in. He must feel sorry for the kids because he sends their parents to jail."

MADDIE RETURNED TO HER ROOM mystified by the dichotomy of the two Trevors. She ran a brush through her hair, staring at herself in the mirror. Serious eyes brimming with questions looked back at her.

"Should I ignore Trevor's text when it comes?" she asked her solemn reflection.

Did Maddie imagine it or did her eyes flicker with light as she said his name?

Her phone buzzed. She ran to snatch it, and true to his word, Trevor had sent his room number.

"I at least should hear him out," she said under her breath, trying to convince herself to let her guard down a fraction.

No one was entirely bad. Maddie scolded herself for one aspect of her harsh judgment of Trevor. She had to quit comparing him to Stewart, who would have relished his victory with no concern for her feelings. She grabbed her briefcase, determined to be more civil.

Apprehension soon crept into her mind as she headed to the floor below hers. She tapped lightly on Trevor's door with her fingertips. He swung it open in seconds, giving Maddie the impression he'd been expecting her.

She stepped in saying, "I don't like coming to your room, but I didn't want to talk about my client in the café."

"Take a seat by the window," he said. "Gretchen gave me a room with a fabulous view. I'll explain what I can, and hopefully take a load off your mind."

His voice has an edge, Maddie thought as she perched on the accent chair, identical to the one in her room. She drew out the legal pad from her satchel.

"Oh no!" Trevor objected. "We agreed this is off the record. You said you would hold it in strict confidence."

Maddie shoved the pad back into her briefcase and clasped her hands together. "Yes, I did. Writing everything down is my trademark."

"You're entitled to make a mistake every now and again," Trevor remarked, pulling his chair closer to her. "It was me who asked Agent Montanna to go see you in your room last night and ask you to attend the press conference today. I wanted you to have as much info as possible."

"She failed to tell me who you really were," Maddie countered, forgetting her vow to be open-minded.

"That's right, because we were still trying to locate and arrest people in Colorado, New York, and here in Vermont. We couldn't disclose the entire undercover operation. Still, I insisted she reveal her role to you as a courtesy, Maddie. We usually don't do that."

Trevor's eyes held hers with a steady gaze as if communicating something beyond his words. She chose to simply nod and wait for him to finish his rendition. Then she would decide how to respond, if at all.

"Now I'll tell you why it was necessary to deceive you, your firm, and Jordan Star," he said, his eyes again seeking hers.

Maddie didn't like the ensuing heat and dropped her eyes, inspecting her pale fingernails instead.

"Okay, here goes." Trevor picked up the tale where he'd left off. "You heard Clayton Andrews explain we made arrests in Colorado where our investigation began. Several property owners in the Rocky Mountains received purchase agreements for their land and mineral rights from a D.C. law firm, which was working with real estate agents and New York investment brokers."

"The press release said they were investors. I saw you showing people around Starlight with Eva Montanna—or I should say Nora Star."

"Hold on a sec." Trevor raised a hand, palm out. "You're way ahead of me."

Maddie cupped a hand over her mouth and uttered an exaggerated, "Excuse me!"

"As the case agent, I watched the scheme unfold as it moved forward," Trevor explained. "As it did, we were gathering enough evidence to convict the suspects. The Colorado part was winding down to a close. Let me backtrack to say rare earth elements are exactly what the term says. They are rare."

Maddie was beginning to see things from his viewpoint, telling him, "I know something about them. Foreign governments, including China, it seems, are trying to corner the market on the world's supply of rare elements. Our government has done little to protect the limited supply we have."

"You've done your homework, which doesn't surprise me."

His eyes locked onto hers and this time Maddie met his gaze.

Trevor's lips spread into a grin. "Back to the case. We discovered a syndicate of investment brokers working with real estate agents and geologists to locate deposits of the elements around the country, and arranging for investors to acquire ownership for eventual sale of the minerals overseas. Then we discovered they created false prospectuses—"

"That were being sent through the mail or by wire in violation of the U.S. criminal code," Maddie interjected.

"Exactly! And they were being assisted by D.C. attorneys who knew it was unlawful."

Maddie coughed out a sigh. "It is unbelievable how Stewart Dunham became a co-conspirator. I, ah, knew him before this case. How did your investigation bring you from Colorado to Vermont?"

"I confronted a geologist who was helping investors target the rare elements. When he learned of his pending indictment, he flipped, or better said, he agreed to introduce me into the plot to help the group further their aims."

"Voila!" Maddie gushed. "That's when the Colorado geologist started vouching for his new best friend, geologist Trevor Kirk."

"You're grasping things quickly," he said, sounding pleased. "We learned the group had already discovered a deposit of rare elements in and around Starlight, including Star Mountain."

Maddie jumped to her feet, heading to the window. "Had their scheme succeeded, they would have destroyed this splendid place. I saw a documentary of the mining process. It can be devastating."

"I couldn't agree more."

"So we can agree on something." Maddie gestured toward the majestic mountain. "You can imagine from Jordan's viewpoint what was at stake. He received so many contacts and demands from developers, it drove him to shut off his phone."

"I'm sure you could share a lot with me, but—"

"I'm getting ahead of you."

"Yeah, if you could wait."

Maddie returned to her seat, showing a smile. For his part, Trevor cupped his hand on his chin, telling how his team tried to determine the exact relationship between the Colorado group and others in Vermont.

"We learned investors were cooling to the Colorado land deals. Why, you ask? The New York investment firms couldn't get their hands on Jordan's property. Problem was, they'd claimed in their prospectus they already owned properties in Vermont. The investment house had even searched for heirs to Maynard Star's fortunes and determined Jordan would inherit it all and thereby control everything."

"Jordan told me many times he has no interest in selling mineral rights," she interjected. "He is true to his grandfather's calling."

Trevor's eyes sparked. "Maddie."

He stopped to stare at her. The way he said her name made her wonder what else he had on his mind.

"Go ahead, Trevor. I'm listening."

"Okay," he laughed. "I was going to say, I suspect his fantastic lawyer helped him. Anyway, Stewart had a final trick up his sleeve. So entering center stage …"

Trevor rose to his feet, stuck both thumbs into his chest, and took a theatric bow.

"What are you saying?" Maddie asked, perplexed.

"In D.C., I met the Colorado and New York contingents, along with Stewart. He decided to invent the other heir, believing Jordan would sell to investors rather than share his inheritance with Nora."

Maddie leapt once more to her feet, agitation rising. "So it became a matter of timing. He wanted to force Jordan to sell before Nora could claim her part, but a lawyer can't do that. We're sworn officers of the court. How dare he propose such a fraud?"

"Well, he did. I heard him."

Trevor walked over to Maddie. She thought for a moment he was going to take her hands into his, but he didn't.

He simply stated, "I think you or Jordan went on the website, Family Finder, and found Maynard Star's adopted granddaughter, Nora Star."

"How do you know that?" Maddie asked, incredulous at his superior knowledge.

"I have more insights. We may want to sit down."

They did, with Maddie wishing she had a cup of coffee to keep her mind more alert. She had a lot to absorb.

When Trevor sat across from her, the first name off his lips was Maddie's nemesis. "Stewart and his realtor friend wanted to create an heir, but were afraid they'd get their hands dirty. So I offered to go on Family Finder and create Nora's account."

"Whoa!" Maddie cried, confronted with Trevor's manipulative side. "You entrapped Stewart. I dated him. I knew he wasn't capable of a felony. If you hadn't given him the idea, he wouldn't be in trouble. Stewart is the victim here."

Trevor reared back his head, folding his arms across his chest. "No, Maddie. He had criminal intent. I wore a wire during the meeting. It was all recorded. It was Stewart's idea. I only agreed to help them accomplish their scheme."

She moaned. "If you were wired, he's a goner."

Her face grew warm realizing she'd confessed her past affection for Stewart. What would Trevor think of her now?

He studied her face, his eyes clouded. "You dated Dunham?"

"That was dead and gone long ago." Maddie waved her hand dismissively.

She took the heat off her past by asking, "How did you know we were monitoring the website?"

"I was concerned we wouldn't be able to coax the investment brokers to Vermont, so we spent weeks examining birth and death records. Then I created the account for Nora Star. Once Dunham believed the website entry was convincing enough to fool Wall Street types and Jordan, he filed to delay settling the estate. He assumed your firm or Jordan would find the website and Jordan's greed would win out and he'd agree to sell."

"Why did Nora Star, or should I call her Special Agent Eva Montanna, come to Starlight?" Maddie still couldn't believe how she'd been duped in so many ways.

"Dunham and his firm felt so positive about the progress, they believed by Nora simply showing up, Jordan would fold. My colleagues and boss at the FBI met to discuss things, and although we had nearly all we needed, we waited for them to travel to Vermont for a look-see."

"Aha. The suspects crossed state lines and subjected themselves to more federal charges," Maddie declared.

"Correct once again." Trevor rose slowly as if reluctant to conclude their time together. "You deserve tons of credit for saving Starlight, Maddie."

She gazed up at him. "Why do you say that?"

"You pressured the judge to make Nora available for deposition. Dunham, who was here with us, panicked."

"But he did bring Nora to town for a deposition." She stood, leaving her leather case on the floor.

"Yes, but Dunham wasn't convinced Eva's role-play of Nora would succeed. At the time, he had no clue she was an experienced undercover agent."

"And you and Eva didn't want to participate in a fraudulent court proceeding."

Trevor stepped toward her, closing the gap between them. "Maddie, both Eva and I take seriously our work for the U.S. justice system. We never would have permitted that. We decided to arrest everyone and disclose their criminal attempts to you."

Remorse burst through her and Maddie lunged at Trevor. She threw her arms around his neck.

"I'm sorry for the things I thought about you. You are amazing. I'm glad you arrested Beth Tandy. I was with Jordan when the realtor phoned and threatened him."

Her face flamed again and she freed Trevor. What had she done?

He held her by her shoulders. "Maddie, what a relief. I'm happy you feel this way. I'm glad this case will conclude because I want to know you better."

Trevor dropped his hands. He stood across from her, his face wreathed in smiles.

Though smiling at him in return, Maddie knew she had to shut this down. He had so much baggage that she didn't want to carry.

"I disliked you when we first met," she said. "I must admit, my feelings toward you have changed. Unfortunately, you may have outsmarted yourself."

"Now what have I done?" he asked, his eyes clouding.

"I understand you better, but your confiding in me won't change how I see you. It's like you have a split personality, part Trevor Kirk and part Trevor Wagoner. You played the undercover geologist so well, I remember his qualities more than yours."

Trevor pressed the palm of his open hand against his forehead. "Do you mean it? I have only myself to blame."

"That's the truth, Trevor," Maddie said softly. "I wish it could be different. Of course, I'll honor my agreement to tell no one what you've said, not even Jordan. I would like to tell my boss so he knows where we stand."

"Would you have dinner with me tonight?"

She declined. "Tonight I'm helping Jordan prepare for the Starlight festival. It's tomorrow night. Why don't you join us for the festivities?"

"Maddie, I just may do that. I don't intend to give up easily. I hope you grow to know and trust the real me, since I live in D.C. near you."

"You know where I live?" she asked, startled by how much he knew about her.

"No, Eva does. She did the research on you. I have no idea where you live."

"Let's keep it that way."

She thought of adding the words, "for now," and then changed her mind. Instead, she gathered her briefcase and jacket, and with a wave, she opened the door. Maddie walked down the hall, not looking back to see if Trevor was looking at her.

Chapter 30

The following day, Maddie felt worn out after Trevor's big reveal. She'd spent much of last night making Star Family Rosettes and Christmas cookies with Dexter, which helped take her mind off things. After breakfast, she asked Gretchen if she was free to go on a brief shopping trip.

"That works perfectly," Gretchen said, looking up from the computer screen. "My morning shift ends in twenty minutes."

Maddie ran upstairs for her purse and jacket, and before long, the two of them strolled along Starlight Avenue, buying goodies and treats at fun shops along the way. At Michele's Boutique, Maddie bought a sweater and illustrated book of Bible stories, having it wrapped especially for the ten-year-old Christmas child.

After hot cocoa, laughter, and a walk about the village, she and Gretchen returned to the lodge where a large box was waiting for Maddie to open.

"It's from my parents," Maddie squealed, running her finger over the mailing label. "I am so glad I purchased their gifts today."

Gretchen set down her shopping bag. "If you leave their wrapped packages for me, I'm happy to mail them for you. You run upstairs and open your gifts."

"You are the greatest," Maddie said, feeling like Christmas was finally coming for her.

In a flurry, she and Gretchen switched packages, with Maddie handing over her parent's Florida address. She practically ran upstairs to her room. The big box contained several smaller boxes and gift bags.

"Mom and Dad, I love you!" Maddie chimed as she scattered giftwrap and bows.

She pressed a fluffy robe and cashmere red scarf to her heart. Mom and Dad had each signed a devotional book with

Bible verses for her daily reading, and sent along lovely silver earrings.

Without waiting a minute more, she phoned them right away, but had to be content with saying, "Thank you, both! I love the star earrings, and everything! I hope to fly down for Christmas," on their voicemail.

Maddie spent the rest of the afternoon debriefing Jordan in his office. They sat around the conference table drinking coffee. She kept her bargain with Trevor, sharing with him facts already of public record. Jordan heaped praise upon his attorney for the successful outcome.

"I'm thankful for such a wonderful result for you, Jordan," she said, uneasy with his acclaim. "There are others you will thank one day perhaps. I spent much time praying and asking God to help us. He deserves our gratitude."

He nodded with solemn eyes. "I absolutely agree. You'll be happy to know an hour ago, I picked up Vanessa and Cole at the airport. They're resting in their room. Vanessa has glad tidings to share and I will allow her that pleasure."

"Can't I convince you to tell me the good news?" Maddie probed, immediately curious about what Vanessa might share.

"No deal." Without ceremony, he handed her an envelope, saying, "Open this later."

She turned the envelope over in her hands. "This is gorgeous, designed with silver snowflakes and stars. It is tempting me to open it now."

"It's all Vanessa's idea. There's a card inside, which I prefer you to read after the festival. Humor me, Maddie."

"I sense a new conspiracy is erupting in Starlight," she replied lightheartedly. "Is everything all set for tonight? Cole and I need to rehearse."

He checked his watch. "Oops. I was supposed to tell you. He's meeting you by the piano in thirty minutes."

Their handshake in parting exuded goodwill. Maddie considered this chapter of her life was closing. She retreated to her room and hurriedly began packing her bags for tomorrow's departure. All the while a question nagged at her.

Would Trevor be attending tonight's Christmas gathering? She'd thrown the invitation out on a whim during the powwow in his room yesterday. She hadn't seen or heard from him since.

"I could leave him a note," she mused aloud.

Maddie grabbed a pen and wrote on the lodge's writing pad, urging him to come to the village's main event. She ended it with a personal message, *You deserve to celebrate after all your hard work. Warmly and best wishes, Maddie*

The elevator took her down to the lobby, and when the doors swished open, she saw neither Trevor nor Cole, so she sailed over to Gretchen working the front desk.

"Ms. Stone, I can't believe it says you're checking out in the morning." Gretchen dropped her eyes to the computer screen. "Yes, that's what it says. You didn't mention it earlier when we went shopping."

Maddie clutched the folded note for Trevor in her hand. "I hoped the other D.C. cases didn't need my immediate attention. Thanks for showing me the bookstore and bath shop. Mom will adore the goat soap from your farm, and Dad will enjoy reading the historical account of Starlight."

Gretchen fingered her silver necklace with tiny stars. "Ms. Stone, thank you for buying me this beautiful gift. You shouldn't have."

"I'd love for you to call me Maddie before I leave. Anyway, you are welcome. You helped make my stay here so pleasant. You invited me to your home, and even shipped my parents' gifts."

"We will miss you. Do you have to leave so soon after tonight's festival?"

"My work here is done," Maddie said, feeling the weight of flying away from all the special people she had come to care for.

Gretchen's eyes grew large. "I didn't realize how important your work was."

"Oh?" Maddie fingered the fringe of the gray scarf looped around her neck.

"Ms. Stone, there's nothing more to hide." Gretchen fluttered a hand in the air. "Gramma Opal figured out long ago the resort and town were in danger of being sold. When I asked Sylvia, she insisted I tell no one, for Jordan's sake."

"How much have you known?" Maddie wanted to piece together this latest puzzle.

"I heard rumors, but it wasn't until Barnaby Ross from *The Ledger* barged in here yesterday and told me all the astonishing details."

"Ross does love making a scoop. I hope everyone else in Starlight is looking forward to the future."

Gretchen dropped her voice. "So, did you know all along, Ms. Stone?"

"Know about what?"

"I don't mean to stick my nose into your business. You were in the café yesterday talking with Trevor, the geologist."

"Yes?" Maddie was sick and tired of hearing rumors about Trevor.

"He looked like he was coming on to you and you didn't seem offended. Barnaby told me the truth, how Trevor isn't a geologist at all. He's an undercover secret agent for the government. How long have you known?"

Maddie flicked her free hand in the air. "Awhile. What else did Ross say about Trevor?"

"Oh my, how Trevor is a hero. He arrested all the criminals trying to steal the village."

Maddie studied Gretchen's innocent face. "Some might dispute your claim that Trevor wears a cape. After all, he caused anxiety by letting people believe Starlight was at risk to further his investigation."

"Oh no," Gretchen challenged. "He's a real champion. I was just doing an online search of his name. See what I found."

She pointed to her computer screen. "It says here, Trevor Wagoner was an Eagle Scout. He's a graduate of West Point and served as a commissioned officer with the Army Rangers in Iraq."

"Maybe he planted the information online," Maddie suggested.

"You can call him Superman, all right." Gretchen blushed and giggled. "Plus he's handsome and charming, and a secret agent carrying a gun and a badge. I can't wait to tell the other girls."

Maddie overstated her understanding by exclaiming, "You're so right. He is a hero to this town and everyone will want to thank him tonight at the festival."

"We do! I invited him a few minutes ago before you came down."

"Did he accept your invitation?"

"He said he may or may not come. It depends on how much work he finishes in the meantime."

"That's nice of you to include Trevor. One more thing," Maddie said, crushing the note in her hand. "Don't forget to tell your friends about your flight attendant sister and Trevor's blond girlfriend, who also must think he's a handsome hero."

Gretchen's lips drooped. "Oh, I forgot about her."

"You cautioned me so many times, I can't forget her," Maddie said sharply.

"Maybe she's out of the picture by now." Gretchen brushed off further concern. "Be sure to wear a jacket tonight. The barn is heated but temps are supposed to dip into the teens."

"This is my first festival in Starlight and I can't wait," had just escaped Maddie's lips when she heard the sounds of a guitar. "That's my cue."

Maddie rushed over to meet Cole by the piano. She flexed her fingers, asking him, "Ready?"

"I've practiced all week," he said, a light glinting in his eager eyes. "Think we'll sound okay together?"

"I have no doubt. You will be terrific."

Her fingers dancing across the ivories, it didn't take long for Maddie's inner turmoil over Trevor to recede. She created lovely music in harmony with Cole's strumming on his guitar. After they finished, light applause rippled through the lobby.

Maddie swept her arm toward Cole, and he dipped his head wearing a self-conscious grin. Vanessa stood by the Christmas tree looking proud. In this tender moment, Maddie knew God had arranged for this mother and son to visit Star Mountain in the first place.

Gretchen and Sylvia stood beside Jordan and Dexter clapping and smiling. Maddie smiled at them all, knowing come morning, she'd say good-bye to Starlight and its splendid people. Meanwhile, this was a night to be merry, and that was what Maddie would do, whether Trevor Wagoner showed up or not.

Chapter 31

The festive air enveloping the entire town of Starlight brought a thrill coursing through Maddie. She closed her laptop with a snap, having finished the paperwork necessary to close the Star estate, which she'd file in the morning before heading home. She glanced at the clock. Yikes, it was past time to get ready.

Mindful of Gretchen's advice to dress warm, Maddie donned jeans, a gray woolen sweater, matching puffy jacket, and boots. She caught a glimpse of herself in the mirror and was disappointed. Her bland outfit looked nothing like Christmas. She needed more color.

"Mom and Dad's scarf!"

Maddie dashed to a cardboard box and snatched out the pretty red scarf, which she tucked around her neck. For a change, she pulled her hair behind her ears to show off the star earrings. Maddie headed into the lobby and felt transformed in her spirit. There, beside the decorated tree with its mini-twinkling lights and gifts for the children, Gretchen had arranged a hand-carved scene with figurines of Mary and Joseph standing watch in a stable. Shepherds and the wise men all gathered around baby Jesus in the manger.

It was as if they were all saying, "Rejoice! Christmas will soon be here!"

Something else seemed to be missing. To Maddie, the empty space in the grandfather clock meant one thing. Jordan's stained-glass star, instead of being safely in its prominent place, was gone. She felt concerned until recalling that Jordan planned to feature his magnificent star at tonight's auction.

Not wanting to miss a minute of the festivities, Maddie dashed to her SUV and drove up to the Star family homestead. Parking was at a premium, and she squeezed in between a car parked crookedly and a TV truck parked at an angle. Hoping she wouldn't be sideswiped, she stepped out into the frosty December night.

A parade of stars, shimmering in the clear night sky, beamed down brightly. Maddie's breath swirled around her. Such resplendent surroundings seemed fitting for her final night in Starlight.

The lighted Star farmhouse stood a short distance away. So many unexpected twists had happened in her life since combing its attic with Jordan in a desperate search for his family heritage. Maddie began walking carefully across the snowy drive on the lookout for Jordan.

Happy sounds of jingling bells made her stop. A horse-drawn sleigh drew up alongside Maddie.

"Whoa, boy," Opal called to the horse decked out in red ribbons. She pulled on the reins, smiling at Maddie as a young couple climbed out of the second seat.

"Merry Christmas, dearie," she called to Maddie.

"Opal, you look as accomplished driving your sleigh as you do in your four-by-four truck."

"Oh, this isn't my sleigh. Meet Trooper. He's Jordan's horse and this is his sleigh. As I do each year, I've been shuttlin' revelers from town to the heated barn. Jordan fixed it up real nice."

Maddie stepped closer to Trooper and lightly touched his brown velvety nose. Trooper whinnied and tossed his head as if telling her hello.

"Trooper, at last we meet. Jordan promised to introduce me sometime, but that was before Vanessa arrived in town."

"You've got that right." Opal laughed with glee. "Speaking of Jordan's distraction, earlier I gave her and Cole a ride. This is my last run. Hop in and I'll drop you near the front door. Then I'll take Trooper to his barn for his oats."

Maddie climbed into the sleigh with Opal clicking her tongue and telling Trooper, "Walk on." They slid along and Maddie had visions of herself as a young girl on an early Christmas morning, her stocking hung on the fireplace and filled with candy and fruit. Her dad always put a shiny red apple and sweet orange in the toe. She giggled out loud at the wonderful memories.

Opal slowed Trooper to a standstill with another, "Whoa." She turned around, facing Maddie.

"I hear you back there enjoyin' yourself. That's how it should be in Starlight."

Maddie hopped out. "Thanks for being my friend, Opal. You encouraged me up on the mountain to keep a heavenly perspective. I'm also going to save this night in my heart and take it with me all the way back to D.C. as a precious gift."

"You are special, dearie. Sorry to hear you're leavin' us. See you inside."

Opal slapped Trooper's rump with the reins and he pulled off toward the barn with bells jingling.

SURELY JORDAN MUST BE INSIDE the restored barn and supervising tonight's festival. Maddie headed that way to find him. A TV crew trudged along with their camera, and that was thanks to Vanessa. She'd told Maddie she sought maximum exposure for the auction of Maynard's antique star. Jordan and Vanessa both wanted to raise as much money as possible for the scholarship program.

What a great team they make, Maddie thought as she walked along. A silver car pulling up seemed larger than life. She held her breath and drew closer. Was it Trevor? Sure enough, he was getting out. So he had accepted Gretchen's invite after all. Or maybe Maddie's, she couldn't be sure.

Her boiling emotions collided with cool logic. Before she could decide what to do, Opal sauntered up just then, giving Maddie a warm squeeze.

"Jordan's gettin' Trooper all set in his stall. Dearie, I'll miss your stirrin' things up around here."

"You're welcome to visit me anytime," Maddie said, fighting for composure. "I understand you rarely leave Vermont. Still, my home is your home."

"Wait until you see what Jordan's done for this year's festival. It tops every other one I've ever been to."

"You and the people of Starlight have much to celebrate," Maddie replied.

"You sound down in the mouth about your pendin' departure." Opal grabbed her hand. "There's one thing for it. A chocolate waffle has your name on it. Come on."

She pulled Maddie toward the barn so fast Maddie forgot to look for Trevor. The barn dazzled inside. Jordan's investment for tonight's Christmas festival was obvious. Large ceiling timbers had been painted white. Modern LED lighting flooded the tables that were set up for cheese tasting and eating rosettes and slices of apple pie.

Opal brought Maddie to the waffle station. "This cherry syrup is made from our trees for your toppin'. Try some."

"It all looks delicious," Maddie said with a song in her heart.

"Uh oh. Gretchen's talkin' to that fake geologist. I'm gonna see what they're up to." Opal dashed off toward Gretchen and Trevor.

Maddie whirled in the opposite direction, not caring to be caught watching Opal's "fake geologist." Fortunately, she spotted on an entryway table with a spotlight shining down on it, Maynard Star's priceless creation—the multifaceted star. Vanessa stood guard, beautifully decked out in a pleated red skirt and fitted floral jacket with embroidered white Edelweiss flowers stitched on the sleeves. Maddie hurried to her side.

"Vanessa, how wonderful to see you here," Maddie said, finding equilibrium at the sight of her co-worker and friend.

They traded hugs. Vanessa thanked Maddie for their first invitation to Starlight a few weeks back.

"Cole is so excited to return." She pointed to an open area with rows of chairs facing a stage. "He's helping arrange the seating. Jordan promised when this event is over, he's letting Cole drive the snowmobile."

Maddie raised her eyebrows. "Be careful. You don't want Cole being hurt if things between you and Jordan cool."

"No danger of that. Jordan and I had a serious discussion."

Maddie studied Vanessa's face, taking a quick glance at her left hand. "Is there an announcement to be made?"

"Not yet. You'll be the first to know," Vanessa trilled.

Maddie couldn't forget Jordan's promise to his grandfather to marry within five years. But he had told her that as a client. Holding his confidence in trust was sacrosanct to Maddie. Perhaps she could gently probe to see what Vanessa knew.

"You and I are friends, Vanessa. When you and Jordan discussed things seriously, I wonder how seriously."

Vanessa ran a hand down her sleeve. "Isn't this jacket beautiful? I bought it today at Michele's boutique."

"You look stunning, almost like a blushing bride." Maddie gave Vanessa a discerning look. "Are you avoiding my question?"

"We talked about our future. Jordan asked if I could love him. Maddie, he told me about his promise to Maynard, which I know he explained to you. Please don't worry. He loves me, Maddie. He knew it since we were all in the kitchen making rosettes."

Vanessa stopped talking long enough to grab Maddie's hands with fervor.

In return, Maddie said, "That's fabulous, Vanessa. What did you tell him?"

"That I love him too!"

Maddie patted her friend's hand. "When I walked in and saw you glowing with such happiness, I knew in my heart you and Jordan belong together. Soon, I think you will be exchanging wedding vows."

"I want you for my maid of honor," Vanessa gushed.

"I would love to. Now, I see Jordan trying to get your attention. The piano and I should make a final run-through."

Maddie's heart overflowed as she practiced the hymns, enjoyed a chocolate waffle, and helped Jordan finalize the auction to be held after the concert. Time flew by with Maddie steering clear of Trevor, though she kept him in her sights most of the time.

At Jordan's direction, she took her seat on the piano bench. Bows from the lighted Christmas tree on the stage behind her were displayed above her head as she softly and tenderly played the introduction to "Silent Night."

She spoke into the microphone, explaining to the audience, "Some of you may not know this favorite of Christmas songs was first written and sung in Austria. The Starlight teen singers feel privileged to perform it for you in this town, which has drawn much of its culture and influence from Austria. After all that's transpired in Starlight in recent days, this is truly a night of wonder."

Cole sat in an empty chair in front of the risers where the teens had assembled, all dressed in their Christmas best. He positioned his guitar and adjusted the microphone in front of him. Maddie nodded her head toward the singers and they burst into melodious song.

Her fingers lightly touched the keys, and her heart filled with the spirit of Christmas. She marveled at the joyous faces of Starlight residents. But for Trevor, things could have turned out so differently. Chef Dexter nodded, seated next to his mother Sylvia. Her eyes were closed, her head swaying slightly to the rhythm. Behind them sat Opal and Gretchen both wearing grand smiles.

Tension fled from Maddie's shoulders. She, too, rejoiced along with her newfound community in the birth of Christ. Peace and joy prevailed.

The final somber note from Cole's guitar hung in the air a moment before everyone burst into applause. Maddie signaled thumbs-up to Cole and the choir. Jordan took that as his prompt. He walked toward a microphone on stage, looking like he'd stepped from an Austrian clothing catalogue dressed in black jeans and a black and red wool sweater, white geometric snowflakes sprinkled across his shoulders.

Maddie had never seen him look more alive. She succumbed to the urge to check for Trevor, and saw him sitting next to Opal and Gretchen, the three of them engaged in a lively conversation. When Jordan tapped on the microphone, Maddie tore her eyes from Trevor to look forward.

Jordan stood on stage beside the sparkling Christmas tree, a spotlight illuminating him from above. It was a surreal moment for Maddie. Though she'd met every one of these folks less than a month ago, they were now her family.

"We've saved a special part of the evening for last," Jordan said after thanking everyone for continuing his grandfather's tradition. "During tonight's celebration, television viewers and friends have phoned in contributions for the Maynard Star Foundation. Grandfather started the foundation to bring underprivileged youth from the cities here to the mountain for winter skiing, summer camping, and mountain biking. Without these scholarships, many teens would never get to enjoy the beauty surrounding us each day."

Vanessa joined him onstage, carrying the cut glass Christmas star Maddie instantly recognized from the lobby display. Jordan lifted up a piece of paper.

"I'm pleased to announce this evening we've received a whopping total of $28,430 in pledges and contributions, a record for the foundation. This handcrafted star was created by Maynard Star nearly seventy-five years ago."

To intense clapping, Jordan held the star aloft. "Tonight, we will draw one contributor's name and this priceless star will grace his or her home."

He held out his hand to Cole who sat in the front row. "Cole, will you come up and draw the name, please?"

"Sure, Mr. Star."

The teen plunged up the steps as if delighted to be in the thick of things.

They're already acting like a family, Maddie thought, astounded by the extent to which Jordan was involving Cole and his mother. It wouldn't be long before Vanessa made a permanent change and left Maddie behind.

Cole dipped a hand into a basket, pulling out a folded slip of paper. He cleared his throat, and sounding quite grown-up announced, "The winner is Bill Barron, Washington D.C. Hey, isn't that super?"

More applause rippled through the barn.

Jordan whispered in his ear, and Cole reached for the microphone. "Mr. Star thanks you and asks me to say, we hope to see you next year. Merry Christmas, everyone, and God bless you all."

His sincere benediction caused Maddie to wonder if a wedding invitation would be in her mailbox tomorrow night when she arrived home. The lights brightened. Guests began leaving. Gretchen twirled her way over to Maddie, beaming a grin from ear to ear.

"What a spectacular event. It's the best ever, and all because you helped Jordan save the town."

"Have a wonderful Christmas." Maddie reached for Gretchen's hand. "You are blessed to live in such an amazing place."

Gretchen's eyes shifted to Maddie's left hand. "I hope because you both live in D.C., maybe you and Trevor can get together. After all, he's part of saving Starlight too."

A dark cloud passed over Maddie. She refused to let Gretchen's constant needling determine her future.

"Gretchen, you first warned me not to get involved with Trevor because he has a girlfriend in LA. While he says he's not involved, and now you think she's out of the picture, I don't find it so easy to change my mind," Maddie said, snapping her fingers.

"Won't you even try?"

"I saw you two talking tonight. Did he say something to you about me?" Maddie asked, battling her mounting frustration.

Gretchen's lips spread into a contagious smile. "He did say he was checking out tomorrow because you were. I may have mentioned to him how you looked terrific with your hair caught behind your head like that and he didn't disagree."

"Thanks for your compliment," was all Maddie could manage.

Her eyes were busy looking beyond Gretchen to see if Trevor might be watching her. He wasn't. She saw him over at the dessert table talking to Jordan.

Maddie had enough talk about him. "Gretchen, you mean well. But Trevor is from California where his lady friend is, and he admits he tells untruths. I don't need that kind of risky guy in my life."

"It was Trevor the geologist who lied and for a good cause," Gretchen protested. "Trevor the FBI agent is an Eagle Scout. I already told you. Gramma and I have been talking to him all night. You can trust him."

Jolly sounds of laughter interrupted their conversation. Maddie turned to see a group of young women descend upon Trevor and start taking selfies with him.

Maddie crinkled her nose. "See how the young women gush over him, Gretchen?"

Just then an attractive blonde put her arm around his neck and posed with a smiling Trevor.

"I don't see him discouraging any of them." Maddie tightened her scarf, preparing to leave.

"It does look like he might be interested in her," Gretchen said, a catch in her voice. "And she is another blonde."

Maddie tugged a lock of hair from behind her ear, and smirking at Gretchen, she said, "I rest my case."

She turned, but Gretchen stopped her. "Wait, Maddie. Why should Trevor be interested in her? He sent me over to see if you'd join us for a piece of pie."

"Not tonight." Maddie waved off the very notion. "I need to finish packing. Have a truly blessed Christmas with your family."

Gretchen wasn't done. She pulled on Maddie's sleeve. "Won't we ever see you again?"

Maddie heard the raw emotion in Gretchen's voice and relented. "Of course you will. There will be a trial in Rutland several months from now. I'll fly up for that."

"Good." Gretchen's shoulders heaved. "Will you see Trevor in D.C.?"

Maddie couldn't help smiling at her efforts to link her with Trevor. "Yes, he's the case agent and is in charge of witnesses, which includes me. He will have to testify too. Hopefully with these arrests, life will finally return to normal for Starlight."

"So you'll see Trevor again." Gretchen clapped her hands together.

Maddie's jaw tightened. She nodded in Trevor's direction, before heading for the exit. "Yes, and Gretchen, you be sure to enjoy your pie tonight."

She strode outside toward the SUV thankful one of her prayers had come true. Starlight was safe for the foreseeable future. After opening the car door, and sliding behind the wheel, Maddie thought she heard someone calling her name. The starting engine blocking out the sounds, she backed out of the parking spot.

From her camera screen on the dashboard, she saw it wasn't Gretchen. No, it was a man. Her eyes flew to the rearview mirror. It was Trevor striding toward her and waving.

Maddie pulled the selector into drive. Her mind told her in no uncertain terms, he'd missed his chance.

She gunned the engine. The wheels spun in the snow, and to her great consternation, she heard bits of gravel being propelled in his direction. It was too late to take back her gutsy move.

With cheeks flaming, Maddie sped to the lodge, and when she reached her room, she collapsed on the bed. Something crinkled beneath her head. She sat up and snapped on the lamp. It was the envelope Jordan handed her this morning. Tearing it open, she pulled out a handmade card with a photograph of snow-covered Star Mountain on the front. She read Jordan's handwritten note with rising emotion:

Maddie,

All of us in Starlight thank you from the depths of our hearts for what you've done for us. You have a special place here. Please know there is a room with your name on it anytime you are missing us.

As you know, we have taken up a scholarship collection for the Maynard Star Foundation, which will be announced tonight. In future years, the foundation will call this scholarship, The Madison Stone Scholarship, to bring young people from the city to Star Mountain. I have decided to tell you this now and not make it public yet. I know you don't go in for hoopla.

You may be able to guess there is one person who made a sizable donation in your honor. May God bless you mightily.

With forever thanks, Jordan Star

Tears of unbelief burned her eyes. And no, she couldn't guess the anonymous donor's identity. That was okay. Maddie splashed cold water on her face, and then turned on her laptop. She typed a heartfelt email to Jordan, thanking him for his generosity and also for keeping the scholarship fund in her name on the QT for now.

Jordan's note brought another change. After rebooking her flight, and reserving the last seat on tomorrow's afternoon flight from Bennington, Maddie phoned her folks.

When Maddie shared the good news, Mom squealed, "Yippee! Dad and I can't wait to hug you and share Christmas with you."

"I miss you both." Maddie wiped tears from her eyes. "The people here helped me see how much the three of us need each other."

"Your dad bought a stunt kite, so you and he can try it out on the beach. And how about taking a dolphin cruise in the Gulf? Does that sound like fun?"

"You are the greatest. I'm texting you my flight arrival in Tampa."

They said their teary good-byes. Now came the job of Maddie rearranging her two suitcases. Winter wear she tossed into one and in the other she folded in lighter clothes for Florida.

Happiness put a smile on her face and tickled her toes. Spending carefree days with her parents and running barefoot on the beach in the land of endless summer was just the restart she so desperately craved.

Chapter 32

Christmas Eve day dawned sunny and warm. Maddie dressed in a new pair of capris, flowery blouse, and sandals, feeling like a butterfly that had morphed from its tight cocoon. Tempting smells of coffee and bacon prompted her to find her parents in the kitchen of their rented condo.

"Hi, sweetie, have some coffee," her mom said. "After breakfast, we're heading to the beach. This evening is something special at church."

Maddie sat on a stool by the counter, sipping the hazelnut roast. "You remembered it's my favorite."

"Mine too," her dad piped.

"I can hardly believe two days ago I was knee deep in Vermont snow, then yesterday you took me to lounge on Clearwater's pure, white sandy beach. I am pampered and blessed."

Her dad hustled off to pack the car and her mom turned the burner down on the bacon. "Before your dad comes back in, tell me how you are doing. Have you gotten over your breakup with Stewart? What about the nice young FBI agent you met in Starlight?"

"Mom, Stewart is long gone from my heart," Maddie said forcefully, hoping her mom would drop the subject for good. "For everything else that happened in Vermont, maybe after Christmas I'll feel up to telling you about it."

"Fair enough," her mom said. "You deserve a happy Christmas. Now hand me the oven mitt. The egg casserole is ready to come out of the oven."

Maddie helped to serve up a delicious home-cooked breakfast. How she missed their family times. When the last dish was dried and put away, she joined her dad outside where he was looking up into a gorgeous blue sky.

She gazed upward along with him, asking, "What am I supposed to be seeing?"

"I'm watching the clouds," he said, his eyes fixed on the sky. "You can tell how fast they're moving in from the west. It's terrific kite-flying weather. Let's get a move on."

Maddie dashed in to fetch her mom, knowing in her heart this was a day to keep looking up and seeking God's intervention in her life.

MADDIE SIMPLY LOVED THE BEACH. After a full day running on the sand with her dad and keeping up with the soaring stunt kites, she'd taken a refreshing nap before an early dinner. After dinner, she and her folks mingled in the church's gatheria, a large open area decorated with greenery mixed in with red and white poinsettias. They were enjoying hot cider and cookies outside of the café.

Maddie knew she shouldn't, but she couldn't resist pulling her cell phone from her back pocket and checking the screen. Splashed across the front was a message from Harry Black. True to form, he kept it brief:

Well done, Ms. Stone. Merry Christmas.

For a few seconds, her mind replayed all the happenings in Starlight. A tiny corner of her heart ached to know how Jordan and Vanessa would spend Christmas with Cole. What about Gretchen and Opal? She pictured them out at their farm, drinking apple cider too, and opening their presents.

Her thoughts turned to Trevor. These Maddie pushed away.

Instead, turning to her mom, she asked, "Can we get someone to take our family picture by the giant Christmas tree?"

"I'll handle this." Her dad zoomed over to fetch a man from a nearby table.

He returned, introducing his friend, who in a starched white shirt and tie looked every bit the professional on this Christmas Eve.

"Bob, this is our daughter Maddie, visiting from D.C. Maddie, Bob Tubman will snap our picture."

"Okay, Al and Donna, you line up with Maddie in the middle," Bob ordered Maddie and her parents as if comfortable being in charge.

The group assembled in front of the tree, with Donna explaining to her daughter, "Honey, our friend Bob lived in D.C. when he was assigned there as an FBI agent."

Maddie mulled that over. She didn't suppose he knew Trevor, so she wouldn't ask. In their matching red Christmas tops, she stood in the middle, with their arms linked together as Bob snapped their picture.

Al took his camera back, telling Bob, "Our Maddie is the lawyer we told you about."

"Oh, right." Bob pressed out his lower lip. "Maddie, remind me if you work for the government."

"I'm with Barron and Rich, a smaller firm," Maddie said, wondering if he somehow knew her boss.

"Oh," her mom interrupted. "Honey, tell him about your new friend who's in the FBI. Maybe they know each other."

Maddie blushed. "Mom, the FBI is enormous. I doubt he does."

"Not so large for us agents," Bob interrupted. "Give me a try."

"Well, he's not a friend exactly. I met Trevor Wagoner on a case."

"Hah." Bob's face lit up like a Christmas tree. "I know him all right."

"You do?" Maddie's heart beat erratically at the thought. What might Bob say about him?

"Well, not personally, but know of him," Bob corrected. "Some agents' name are recognized throughout the FBI by their major mess-ups or their exemplary performance."

Maddie winced. More embarrassing news and her parents would get to hear all about it before she could filter it.

Storyteller Bob continued as though time were no issue. "Sometimes even a blind squirrel can find a nut and sometimes the law catches criminals due to their own stupidity."

He stopped, asking Maddie, "Is your office anywhere near Fourteenth and Eye Street Northwest?"

She answered with a smile. "Not far from there."

"Then you know how crowded restaurants and banks are during lunch hour. The story has it a masked bank robber chose to rob a bank during lunch hour when the crowds were swarming with FBI agents out for lunch. Can you imagine?"

"Was Trevor involved in solving the case?" Maddie asked, clutching her cell in her hand. She could sense her parents staring at her.

"Boy was he," Bob proclaimed. "And it's not what you're thinking."

Music started playing from the worship center, so Bob said, "I'll make it quick. Wagoner is standing in line at the bank. The robber pulls a knife on a teller. Trevor tackles him in one flying leap, and Trevor's stabbed in the process. He hangs on to the guy until the help arrives. Trevor is one of our legendary heroes, all right. And Maddie, when you see him, tell him I said so."

Donna's hands flew to her face. "Bob, I didn't realize. Your job is dangerous." She turned to Maddie. "Maybe you should give this Trevor a wide berth."

"Don't worry, Mom, I am."

"Nice to meet you, Maddie," Bob said. "Excuse me, the service is starting. I have to find my family."

Maddie caught her breath as she followed her parents into the dimly lit sanctuary. Lanterns with flickering candles lighted every aisle. Dad took them to the terrace level of the balcony, where she had a marvelous view of two musicians onstage, a cellist and a guitarist, who played lovely Christmas hymns. The pastor gave a stirring message on the baby Jesus being the greatest gift ever given.

"God gave Jesus as His gift to you," the pastor said, holding up a wrapped box. "Just as if I give you this gift on Christmas morn, until you open it and claim it, it's not really yours. Have you chosen to accept God's gift?"

Ushers hustled along the aisles, lighting tiny candles in clear plastic cups, lighting the first candle of the row. Each person lit their neighbor's candle and more lights burst forth until thousands of candles shone in reverence. To the sounds of cello and guitar, Maddie lifted her voice in unison with her parents and the congregation singing, "Silent night, holy night, all is calm, all is bright ..."

Her happy glow lasted all the way to the Tampa airport the next day on Christmas afternoon, where at her gate, Mom quenched her joy by asking, "Is your FBI agent picking you up at the airport?"

"No, I'm taking a cab home," Maddie said, her eyes tearing. "I love you both. Thank you for a wonderful and special Christmas."

She hugged them warmly, and they kissed her cheek. Maddie wiped her eyes and headed for security, regretting she'd ever mentioned Trevor to her folks. As she took her seat in row 27 toward the back of the plane, she spotted a man sitting in the aisle across from her. The way his hair curled on the back of his neck reminded her of Trevor. She leaned forward, her pulse rising. The lady beside him had long blond hair.

Could it be? Why would he be in Florida?

Maddie blinked. Then she heard the man speaking in French and realized they were most likely a vacationing couple from overseas. She rested her head against the seat, admitting that no matter how calm she'd acted when Bob regaled her about Trevor's act of bravery in the bank, strong feelings for him were flooding her heart anew.

The jet lifted off the runway. Maddie felt her stomach flip-flop and not because of the airplane ascending. She found herself wondering if she would hear from Trevor again. If she did, what would she do?

Chapter 33

It was nearly the end of March, which had begun with a roar, dumping a foot of snow in the nation's capital, and was ending like a playful spring lamb. The fine weather brought a whistle to Special Agent Trevor Wagoner as he stashed his weapon next to his baseball spikes inside an athletic bag. He locked his desk, pocketing the key.

After a long day of writing reports inside the office, he looked forward to breaking free and having fun after work. He rose from his desk, ready to leave the D.C. Task Force squad room, when Special Agent Eva Montanna stopped by.

"Trevor, it's great to hear you whistling again," Eva said. "I'm thinking you have a big weekend planned."

Trevor lifted his bag. "With this perfect weather, I'm playing softball tonight with my church ball team."

"Remind me of the position you play."

"Right fielder, left fielder, center fielder, wherever they need me," Trevor said with a snort. "I love these ball games. It's a chance to spend time with my buddies, who are usually busy with their wives and families."

Eva adjusted the purse strap on her shoulder. "I'd like to cheer you on sometime with my family. I can't tonight, though, because I'm hosting a pizza party for my oldest son's class."

Trevor walked with Eva toward the exit, swinging the door open to let her through, adding, "Tomorrow I'll be stuck here in the office, making last-minute trial preparations for Vermont. I fly up on Sunday."

"Oh, that's right." Eva stopped in her tracks. "You think you won't need me to testify until Wednesday?"

"That's my best guess now. You know things can change rapid-fire. Jury selection and opening statements will take up most of Monday. Some of our Colorado agents have flown in ahead of us. Plan on flying up on Tuesday."

Eva stood in the doorway arching her eyebrows. "Is Maddie Stone a scheduled witness?"

"She is," Trevor replied, shifting his weight.

Why did Eva have to get into this now? He didn't want to be late for the ball game. Besides, he noticed a keen light in her eyes as she studied him like she would a suspect.

"How are things going on that front?" she finally asked.

"You mean with Maddie?"

"I wasn't referring to the criminal case. I'm sure you'll get guilty verdicts."

Eva's smile back at him seemed genuine, and Trevor turned thoughtful. Things on the Maddie Stone front were a mess. What to tell Eva?

A sigh escaped his lips. "I don't know how to reach her. I've tried seeing her socially, but she'll have nothing to do with me. I call her with questions to prepare for trial and she's cordial. She even phones me with questions, but says she isn't open to dating."

"Her breakup with Stewart Dunham before you met was quite unpleasant," Eva interjected.

"How do you know?" Trevor mentally replayed his conversations with Maddie. "She didn't tell me that."

"Well duh! She told me. You're not giving up, are you? You'll see her in Vermont. Take her to dinner, talk things out."

"Your advice sounds similar to what my baseball coach at West Point always said."

Eva's face crinkled into a smile. "Another baseball analogy? I'm ready."

"When our team lost five in a row the first season, he really inspired us at the next practice by telling us, 'Imagine we are starting the season anew. This next game is our first game.'"

"Exactly! With a new name even," she declared, pumping her fist. "You're starting this season as Trevor Wagoner, and not Trevor Kirk."

"Hmm. You and coach think alike," he said.

Trevor started to close the task force door. Eva hustled through it first.

He checked the lock before telling her, "When I hinted at getting together, Maddie blew me off. Maybe she's involved with someone else. I don't want to be pushy. On the other hand, she did say she's been elevated to partner, so I can guess she's too busy for dating."

"Take it slow and be your charming self in Rutland."

"That's the problem," he replied, pressing the fob to open his rear hatch. "She insists she can never see me for the true me."

Eva winked at him. "I detected she has real feelings for you. And you can usually trust my instincts. Good luck on your game tonight."

"I hope your instincts are right this time, Eva." He tossed in his bag. "I never believed it would be this hard to get Maddie out of my mind."

MADDIE STONE WAS HAVING TROUBLES OF HER OWN. That same Friday evening, the strap of her leather satchel over her shoulder, she stepped out of the office elevator only to find Stewart Dunham pushing the up button.

"Madison, how fortunate. I came to see you," Stewart said, walking toward her. "Can I buy you a cup of coffee at the bakery next door?"

She bristled at his suggestion. "They close at six, which was ten minutes ago. Now if you'll excuse me."

"Not yet, please hear me out."

"We shouldn't be talking before your trial." Maddie walked right past him.

He reached for the strap of her briefcase to stop her from leaving.

"I will ring for security if you persist," Maddie snapped at him.

"Have it your way." He dropped his hand with narrowed eyes. "I wonder if you will testify for me at trial. You know, as a character witness. I did mean something to you once."

Maddie huffed in a breath, and exhaling, she let him have it. "Stewart, you know I'm scheduled to be a witness for the prosecution. My name is clearly on the list. You must have something else up your sleeve, but I refuse to ask. I don't want to know."

"I heard about Jordan Star setting up a scholarship for needy kids to go camping in the Vermont woods. I thought you'd be happy to know I donated to The Madison Stone Scholarship Fund."

That came out of nowhere. Maddie fought for composure and lifted up her chin. "The kids will be thankful. In my opinion, you have much to atone for."

"Do you forgive me?" he asked in a pleading voice.

Maddie forced herself to turn around. In his eyes, she saw a mixture of sorrow and hurt. "My faith tells me to, if you are sincere. I have no hard feelings about you personally. I will be praying for you."

"I guess that's all I can ask," he muttered.

"Yes, but you should consider praying for your future as well," Maddie said with conviction.

She wanted to say more yet decided she'd be risking too much given that in a few days she would take the stand at his trial. Maddie left the building with Stewart behind her. She imagined him following her all the way home as if testing her resolve. When she turned right toward the parking lot, he walked down the street to the left and disappeared around the corner.

Maddie fled to her car. What did Stewart mean by asking her to testify on his behalf? She had said she forgave him, so she stopped the simmering angst right in its tracks and willed herself to be calm.

The thing to do now was to notify her boss, so Maddie called Bill from her car. People talking and clinking sounds in her ear suggested he was in a restaurant. She quickly briefed him about Stewart's unusual request.

"He has some gall," Bill growled. "Phone the prosecutor on Monday and let him know. I suppose he's left the office by now on Friday night."

"I could try to reach the case agent," Maddie offered, her mind balking at having to tell Trevor about Stewart's suggestion, which bordered on the unethical.

"By all means, call him now. We can't risk your testimony being compromised."

Having said his peace, Bill hung up. It seemed his permission helped Maddie do what needed to be done. Trevor answered on the first ring.

"Maddie, it's great to hear from you," Trevor said, his inflection warm when he'd said her name. "Too bad I only have a minute to talk."

"Oh. You're probably out for dinner. I wanted you to know Stewart Dunham stopped me coming out of work tonight and asked me to testify for him at the trial."

"You turned him down, right?"

"Absolutely. We didn't discuss my testimony, except I reminded him that I'm a witness for the prosecution. Have a nice dinner, Trevor."

"Maddie, you have that wrong. The church baseball league starts in a few minutes, and I'm taking the field. You caught me grabbing gear out of my trunk."

She chuckled softly into the phone. "Sounds fun. I love baseball and used to play on a community league. I can just picture you slamming one over the fence. Anyway, I'm heading home to pack for Vermont."

"Maddie, thanks for calling. I'm glad you like baseball."

"I thought the prosecutor would want to know, so that's why I called you."

"I get it," he replied, his tone deflating like a tire losing air. "I hoped you wanted to talk with me because you are warming toward me. Let's try to connect before or after the trial. Gotta run. Bye."

On the crowded expressway, in the stop-and-go traffic, that sudden click by Trevor resounded in Maddie's mind, haunting her. Once home, she heated a leftover burrito in the microwave. The way he'd said he longed for her to warm to him coursed through her like a gentle spring rain.

IT WAS MONDAY AFTERNOON. Maddie sat at her desk pondering the wild roller-coaster ride her life had taken these last few months. She could write a novel if it wasn't so unbelievable.

Vanessa interrupted her musings by setting a stack of files on Maddie's desk. A lovely diamond ring glittered on her left hand.

"How does it feel to be engaged, Vanessa?" Maddie asked in earnest.

Vanessa was all smiles as she took a seat across from Maddie's desk. "Exciting and scary all at once. Jordan and I haven't set a date. It depends when my brother Charlie is rotated stateside."

"You don't have any idea when that might be?" Maddie asked, looking at all the files sprouting like mushrooms across her desk.

"Not yet." Vanessa shook her head slowly. "Bill is being super understanding and insists I can work for the firm in Vermont because so much is digital now. He plans on handling more cases up there, or so he claims."

Maddie flipped through a file absentmindedly. "You should consider his offer, Vanessa. I especially will miss your expert help and friendship around here."

"Since you've made partner, all you do is work."

"That comes with the territory."

"I hope you haven't given up on romance and marriage just because of Stewart."

The truth from Vanessa's barb hurt. Maddie closed the file with a snapping sound.

"I am making the right decision," she insisted. "Stewart took an oath to uphold justice. I believed in him and look where that got me. He turned out to be amoral. I failed to see the depth of his falsehoods."

"So you don't trust your own judgment, and you're giving up?" Vanessa leaned forward, her eyes gleaming. "I've seen the sparks you and Trevor have for each other. You're not suggesting he is anything like Stewart, I hope."

Maddie held up her hand to stop further discussion. "Trevor is a trained undercover agent. His job is to convince people he's whatever they want him to be. You've seen him at work."

Vanessa opened her mouth, but Maddie wasn't done.

"You saw him flirting and taking selfies with the young ladies at Starlight's festival. Somewhere in Washington or LA there's his contented blond girlfriend, who probably doesn't even know the real Trevor Wagoner."

"Did he tell you he's involved?"

"Everyone in Starlight knew he was," Maddie said through clenched teeth. "Do you know how silly I felt? There I am searching for the Star family imposter, thinking there's someone conniving to steal Jordan's inheritance. Then I discover that someone is a federal agent pretending to be Nora. And I don't find out until I'm sitting in court surrounded by dozens of reporters and TV cameras that Trevor is the imposter-in-chief."

"The Maddie Stone I know wouldn't be this upset if she didn't have feelings for Trevor." Vanessa crossed her arms and glared at Maddie.

"You may be right, but I won't let myself be fooled again."

"You may be interested to know Cole is planning to help Jordan with the mountain biking camp this summer," Vanessa said, thankfully switching the subject. "The entire town of Starlight is abuzz with our news."

Maddie pushed the files aside and picked up her cell phone. "I've had a gazillion calls from the intrepid reporter, Barnaby Ross. He wants an exclusive interview after the court ruled Jordan is the sole owner of Star Mountain, Starlight, and Edelweiss Lodge. Ross insists some landowners are disappointed because foreign investors won't buy their property for more than it's worth."

"But Maddie, others are happy life in the quaint village is unchanged. One more thing—what time is your flight to Vermont?"

"Tomorrow morning at seven. I'm heading out pretty soon."

"Have a super trip to Vermont. You will see Jordan and other old friends, like Trevor." Vanessa flashed a glowing smile as if privy to Maddie's hopes.

For her part, Maddie sat staring at her cell phone. "I never told you. Trevor phones me once a week. Not today, though."

"When he calls, do you stick to talking about the criminal case?"

"Pretty much."

Vanessa must have taken the hint the topic was off-limits because she turned to leave. "Oh, and just so you know, I spoke with Trevor at the festival after you sped off. He seemed frustrated you'd gone before he could talk with you."

Left alone in her office, Maddie leaned back in the swivel chair, conjuring up an image of seeing Trevor in her rearview mirror and her tires spitting gravel toward him. Her cheeks flamed.

Since then, every time he phoned, she mentally dressed in body armor to protect her heart. Even though their offices were less than two miles apart, she repeatedly refused to meet him for lunch, keenly aware of his love interest, thanks to Gretchen.

Maddie shoved the current file into the bottom drawer, locking it inside. There would be time to decide if she should fly to London to sort out possible international complications of her newest case. There, that decision had been simple enough.

Not so with her heart.

She could no longer lock up her feelings and pretend Trevor didn't matter. Tomorrow, she'd fly to Vermont where he was the case agent. How would Maddie handle being forced to look at him from the witness stand, sitting at the counsel table and gazing back at her with those lustrous eyes of his?

Chapter 34

Maddie strode inside the Crooked Rooster in downtown Rutland in her black boots. She tugged down the sleeve of her black jacket, which she'd worn over a gray-striped dress.

Annoyance bubbled up within her over the federal prosecutor choosing such a pricey restaurant to go over her testimony. She'd checked the menu online. Only a few dinner options cost less than forty dollars. Tonight of all nights, she wanted everything to go smoothly with no hiccups.

The restaurant was crowded, and she searched among the boisterous diners for a face she recognized. Way in the back, she saw him sitting with his back to the wall. Trevor happened to look up at her. Their eyes met for a moment of bliss. Maddie steeled her cascading emotions because she found him more dashing than ever in his black leather jacket and black shirt.

He was sitting next to AUSA Clayton Andrews at a square table for four, where a candle glimmered in the middle. Both Trevor and Clayton stood as Maddie arrived at the table. In an instant, she chose to sit across from Trevor's pleasant face.

Trevor introduced her to Clayton, who, bowtie and all, was prosecuting the long list of defendants including investment brokers, a geologist, realtors from Denver, and of course the notorious Stewart Dunham. Clayton handed Maddie a thick menu as they took their seats.

"Thank you," she said, placing the menu next to her by the empty place. "I already scoped out the menu so we can make the most of our time."

Clayton plunged right in. "We prosecutors like to meet our witnesses in advance. I want you, as the witness, to know what to expect."

"I completed an internship with the local district attorney's office in law school. I know the drill." Maddie's brown eyes sought Trevor's blue ones as she added in a taut voice, "In fact, they offered me a position as an assistant DA when I graduated, but I turned it down."

"You decided you don't have the temperament to be a prosecutor?" Trevor interjected.

Taken aback by his biting tone, Maddie tried softening hers. "No, that wasn't my issue. I found their salary didn't pay my student loans."

She waved the menu as though it was an exhibit. "Based on your choice of restaurants, Clayton, I'm convinced I should have applied to the U.S. Attorney's Office."

Her jesting must have lightened Trevor's mood because he laughed heartily.

"It's not too late." Clayton gestured with his palms up. "We always have openings. However, I suspect we couldn't match what you make now."

The server approached, taking Maddie's order first. "I'll have a deluxe burger with brioche bun, cooked medium. Please hold the onion."

The server wrote nothing down, telling her, "Fries come with that, ma'am."

"She'd like your sweet potato fries," Trevor answered for her. His friendly grin suggested he rather enjoyed knowing her tastes.

Maddie smiled back at him, her eyes again holding his. A thrill coursed through her when Trevor told the server, "I'll have the exact same thing."

His eyes twinkling at Maddie, Trevor added, "I'll wait on my drink order to see what the lady orders."

"Sprite with a lime." Maddie's smiled at Trevor never wavered.

Without missing a beat, Trevor told the server, "Diet Coke with a lime."

Maddie wasn't surprised when Clayton asked for baked halibut with wild rice and grilled asparagus, the priciest item on the menu.

"Oh, and hot black coffee," he said, removing a notepad from his jacket pocket.

The server said with a hint of a French accent, "Sir, you may order another side dish."

"Okay, for my side, bring me a side salad with ranch dressing on the side."

Maddie chuckled at his word puns. She stopped any laughter when Clayton turned to her and said, "Most of the defendants have pleaded guilty. We are left with four."

"I presume Stewart Dunham is one of the four?" Maddie asked, uneasy even mentioning his name.

"He is still on trial, yes." Clayton's free and easy tone suddenly became stern. "Trevor explained you once dated Dunham, which might become an issue. Most likely his defense attorney will try blindsiding you with it."

Maddie blushed to the roots of her hair. She lowered her gaze to avoid Trevor's disapproving eyes, and spread a folded napkin onto her lap, regretting the day she'd ever agreed to go out with Stewart.

"I don't like making you uncomfortable," Clayton declared. "It's essential we deal with the issue up front. I also understand he asked you to testify for him."

"Which I refused. If you ever met him in the courtroom as I did, you would believe him to be every bit as respectable as Trevor. It shows how we never know, do we?"

Maddie gazed at Trevor, reliving that instance when she'd learned he was someone other than who he'd claimed to be.

Trevor leaned forward, his brows drawn together. "I think you're saying you find it hard to believe someone you trusted has gone awry. Maddie, I assure you with all my being I am nothing like Stewart."

"Of course not." Clayton cleared his throat. "Now, Maddie, when you first testify I intend to ask about your knowledge of Stewart. That way we can frame it and minimize its effectiveness for the defense."

Maddie blinked her understanding, saying nothing more. Their drinks arrived and Maddie squeezed the chunk of lime into her soda. Some of its juice landed on Trevor's chin. He wiped it away with his napkin without looking at her.

"This case is unusual," Clayton said, putting down his coffee cup. "Stewart seems to have been the mastermind. He deceived your law firm and the court, in addition to other victims in Starlight. Did he have a revenge motive against you, Maddie?"

Maddie set her clasped hands on the table. "I debated the same question during the Star case and decided no. While my boss represented Maynard for years, I was only brought in after the Hunter law firm asked to delay the settlement. And it had been months since I even talked to Stewart. For the record, he ended our relationship, for which I am now eternally grateful."

"Fair enough," Clayton said. "Just testing what might be brought up. If he is convicted, my office will give evidence to the D.C. Bar's disciplinary committee. I intend to see him disbarred. How do you feel about that?"

"It's precisely what I would do in your situation."

Clayton gave an approving nod. "Trevor predicted you would agree."

"I'm glad the case agent thinks highly of me," Maddie said, giving Trevor a sideways glance. "Also for the record, Stewart's conduct stuns me. As I said, I thought I knew him."

"Seeing a lawyer going down an illegal path disturbs me too," Clayton replied, his eyes looking at her over the rim of his cup.

To Trevor's swift nod, Maddie felt compelled to add, "There's something else. Although I realized his firm initiated the probate action, I never dreamed Stewart was handling the case until he showed up in the Vermont courtroom. The Hunter firm has dozens of lawyers. It's hard for me to reconcile his deception."

"I'm sorry you're having to go through this and testify." Clayton sounded apologetic.

"I'm getting used to it. I was recently deceived by another man; fortunately I didn't know him as well."

"Oh?" Clayton asked, looking perplexed.

Trevor turned slightly and looped an arm over the back of his chair. "That dig is meant for me, if I'm not mistaken. But I'm hoping to make it up to her."

Clayton swung his head from Maddie to Trevor, and then again at Maddie as if he were refereeing a tennis match.

"I sensed something earlier between you two. Do I need to mediate here?"

Maddie laughed and so did Trevor. The tension seemed to evaporate.

"It's just that Trevor and I were dealing with each other when he was working undercover," Maddie explained. "I saw him as a threat to my client, and now I am trying to see him for who he really is."

"I can vouch for him." Clayton flexed his heavy brows. "Not only is he a good agent, he's terrific testifying before a jury. They see him as an 'all-American hero,' if you know what I mean."

Before Maddie could say, "Yes, he's as smooth as butter," the server delivered their food. As they ate their meals, conversation turned to pleasantries. Maddie answered Clayton's expected questions in between bites, and all the while, Trevor kept looking into her eyes with something like tenderness in his own.

Chapter 35

Maddie left the hotel the next morning dressed in her finest suit and new heels. After parking her rental, she walked along on the clear spring day, mustering the fortitude to testify against Stewart, no matter how painful it might be. Birds chirping in a nearby tree got her wondering when the hope of spring might burst forth in her life.

Well, it sure wouldn't be today.

She stepped around a slushy puddle, and when she looked up, there was the courthouse looming large and forbidding a block away. Though every fiber of her being said, "Hightail it back to the car and get on the first flight to D.C.," Maddie realized she'd made this too personal. She was no different from every other witness she'd examined in court. Only this time, it was her civic duty to tell the jurors what she had seen and heard.

A sudden cool breeze caught her hair, and brushing a lock from her eyes, Maddie spotted something blue in the nearby grass. She leaned down closer to have a look. Bright blue flowers, shaped like tiny stars, winked back at her.

Happy memories from her childhood stirred her heart. These darling little flowers were the same color as bluebonnets she'd skipped through once with her grandmother in the Texas hill country.

The flashback in time had been quick, yet Maddie believed these spring beauties were for her. Worry over her past fell away like disappearing snow. She set the briefcase strap over her shoulder and readied her mind to face the courtroom with strength and pluck.

Scheduled as the first witness of the day, Maddie walked into the U.S. District Court at nine thirty sharp, right on time. A man wearing glasses and a dark suit sat along the wooden bench in the hallway. Maddie took a seat next to him.

"Are you testifying?" he asked, clutching a file to his chest.

Maddie set her briefcase in between them. "I am."

"It's my first time ever being called as a witness. I'm a CPA. Why must we wait out in the hall like we're unruly students?"

"Didn't the prosecutor explain?" Maddie asked, stifling laughter. "He should have. We witnesses are sequestered and not allowed to hear other witnesses testify. So we stay out here until called."

"Ah ... I seem to remember," the accountant mumbled, rolling his eyes.

Maddie faced him with a smile. "If it makes you feel any better, I've never testified either. We'll do fine if we stick to the facts and tell the truth."

He said, "Thanks," and started rifling through his papers.

Maddie left him to complete his review. She was content to remember something quite pleasant from last night. Trevor had said a long good-bye at the restaurant, and even offered to drive her back to the hotel. She'd waved and eased into her rental car, seeing him once again in her rearview mirror. This time, Maddie was careful not to sling any dirt on him in this "mud" season in Vermont.

Time passed. Maddie found herself checking her phone every few minutes. Patience might be a virtue, but it certainly wasn't her strong suit. And the man's constant sighing beside her fueled her frustration. When ten o'clock arrived, and she still hadn't been called, she became concerned Stewart had failed to show up and the U.S. Marshals were out after him.

Then the courtroom door sprung open. Trevor hurried over wearing a radiant smile. "Sorry for the wait, Maddie. You're up."

"I wanted to explain last night—"

"There will be time for that. This judge doesn't like to be kept waiting."

Maddie slid her phone into the briefcase and followed Trevor into a courtroom jam-packed with spectators. In a row off to her right, Maddie spotted Jordan Star sitting with Opal, Gretchen, and others from Starlight. Barnaby Ross wrote furiously in his little notepad.

She walked hurriedly by, taking the witness stand with mixed feelings. As much as her eyes wanted to dart over at Stewart, Maddie made up her mind to not even gaze his way. It was his fault, and not hers, that he was on trial for criminal misdeeds.

Maddie took the oath to testify truthfully, and from then on, everything went as predicted. Prosecutor Andrews asked right away, as he said he would, and Maddie explained with no catch in her voice about her relationship with the Star estate and also with attorney Stewart Dunham, the opposing council in the probate case.

At length, her throat began to feel tight and dry. She figured the prosecutor had nearly finished his direct examination of her when Clayton lobbed another question.

"Ms. Stone, did the probate judge order you and Mr. Dunham to share information with each other if and when you identified any additional heirs to the Star estate?"

"Yes, he did," she answered, straightening her back in the witness chair.

"As a legal matter, why was that important for you and the court to know?"

Maddie snuck a glance at Trevor. He sat stoically behind the prosecutor's table.

She forced from her mind what he might be thinking and pondered Clayton's question before answering, "As the attorney for the Star estate, I would immediately depose the prospective heir to learn if he or she was a bona fide relative."

"Now Ms. Stone, if you had discovered such an heir, would you have so advised Mr. Stewart?"

"Yes. That would not only be the appropriate action, it's also what the court ordered."

"FBI Special Agent Trevor Wagoner testified earlier that Mr. Dunham asked the agent to create a fictitious entry on the Family Finder website in the name of Nora Star. Did there come a time when Mr. Dunham advised you that he'd identified an heir by the name of Nora Star?"

Maddie paused, looking at members of the jury, and then at the judge. "Yes, he did."

"Did you ask him to make Nora Star available for a deposition?"

"Yes."

"Did he produce Nora Star?"

"He claimed he was bringing her to town, but I never got to depose her. Mr. Stewart was arrested before the deposition."

"Objection," Stewart's lawyer shouted, jumping to her feet. "Her answer is prejudicial."

The prosecutor addressed the judge in respectful tones, saying, "Your Honor, Ms. Stone is simply stating the facts."

"I don't agree." The judge pounded his gavel. "The jury will ignore the last sentence of Attorney Stone's answer. Move along, Mr. Andrews."

"What did you advise your client about Nora Star?" Clayton asked.

Maddie looked at the judge. "Your Honor, I respectfully ask I not be required to answer the question. It violates the confidence between the attorney and her client."

"Yes, I am sorry," Clayton interrupted. "Let me rephrase my question. Did you form an opinion about whether Mr. Dunham would ever produce the heir?"

"I did." Maddie aimed her eyes at Stewart. "After I repeatedly requested Mr. Dunham produce Nora Star, and he didn't, I came to believe he'd created a fictitious heir in hopes Jordan Star would sell to Mr. Dunham's clients before another heir showed up, rather than have to share proceeds of the estate."

The prosecutor looked at the judge. "Your Honor, I have no further questions for this witness."

"Is there cross-examination for Ms. Stone?" The judge glared over at the three defense tables where attorneys were seated with the four defendants.

The only attorney to stand was Stewart's female attorney, whose blazing red hair Maddie couldn't fail to recognize. She was an extremely high-priced defender from D.C.

"Ms. Stone, isn't it true Maynard Star and later Jordan Star rejected many offers to sell their property?"

Maddie kept her eyes riveted on the lawyer with a laser-like focus. "Yes."

"Isn't it also true Jordan Star rejected an offer from the realtor codefendant of Mr. Dunham?"

"Yes, that is true."

Stewart's lawyer smiled toward the jury. "So then. The fact that Mr. Star refused is proof he wasn't deceived by any of the codefendants here today."

"Wrong," Maddie said before the prosecutor who had jumped to his feet could voice his objection. "He refused their offers because he listened to the good advice from his lawyer, who did detect their deception."

As jurors and spectators chuckled, the lawyer thumped down onto her seat, a clump of bright red hair falling into her eyes. "I have no further questions."

"The witness may be excused," the judge intoned.

Maddie grabbed her briefcase and left the witness stand in one swift move, passing by Trevor on her way out of the courtroom. She felt him walking behind her, no doubt coming to collect the nervous CPA. Maddie pushed the courthouse doors open with one overriding thought. She had run the gauntlet and survived.

AFTER PUSHING THROUGH the onslaught of TV crews and spectators who swarmed Rutland for the criminal trial, Maddie left the courthouse square quickly. She hoped to avoid being assailed by any reporters, especially the ubiquitous Barnaby Ross. In her car en route back to the Edelweiss Lodge, Maddie phoned the office.

Vanessa asked abruptly, "How did it go in court?"

"It's finally over." Maddie's deep sighed echoed off the car windows. "I looked at Stewart only once and practically ran out of court. Several defendants plead guilty already so they may testify against him."

"A good lesson for us to each walk down the narrow path," Vanessa said. "Where are you now?"

"Going to my room at the Edelweiss."

"How is Trevor?"

"I saw him for a moment when he called me into the courtroom."

"That's it? You haven't talked with him?"

Maddie deliberated and decided to confess. "We had dinner last night."

"Great! Maddie, what did he say?"

"It's not what you think. The prosecutor was there too, and we reviewed my testimony. Trevor smiled at me though."

"Maddie, don't miss this opening to set things right with him. I'll never forget his glum face after you left the festival. That guy cares for you."

"He's the farthest thing from my mind. Let Bill know I'm flying back in the morning and will begin to prep for the Acton trial starting next week."

"There you go again, nothing but work." Vanessa kept her voice low. "I already typed up your witness list and set of possible questions. Give yourself an extra day in Starlight to be sure. See you soon."

Maddie had enough of her prodding and said good-bye. She trained her eyes on the road to Starlight with an audio loop in her mind of her mom saying in their last phone conversation, "Honey, Dad and I are afraid you're teetering on burnout."

As Bill's newest law partner, Maddie knew she spent more time than necessary at the office. Life seemed so lopsided back in the city. Here in Starlight, she'd acquired more of a balance, getting to know and investing in people she cared about, like Gretchen, Gramma Opal, and even Jordan. She vowed to find more time to volunteer at her church and the food bank.

She sprung from her car in the Edelweiss parking lot. The afternoon sun sparkled on a beautiful lake. Maddie was amazed by the transformation. During the heart of winter, Maddie had walked near this same spot when it had been forbidding and thick with ice and snow. Spring thaw had shed the lake's frozen shell to reveal a shimmering body of water, which, as if a magnet, drew Maddie to its shores.

She hiked down to a pretty gazebo at the water's edge and watched enthralled as a mother mallard swam along followed by her fuzzy yellow ducklings.

"I love being here," Maddie cried, throwing her arms up in the air.

She felt free standing here by the water. Her testimony against Stewart was over. It was tremendous she could enjoy the riches of Starlight in such mild weather and observe nature in new ways. The respite didn't last long enough.

On the way to her room, Maddie stopped at the Stix and ordered a sandwich. Chef Dexter brought out her to-go order himself, telling her, "Ms. Maddie, you are a sight for sore eyes. Don't be a stranger."

"You can be sure I'll return for a certain wedding, when it happens," she said, smiling at the idea of not saying good-bye forever.

"Look inside the bag," Dexter urged. "I dropped in something special."

"You're the best."

She gave him a mock salute and trekked through the lobby, noticing Sylvia talking on the front desk phone. It was kind of Jordan to make changes and allow Gretchen to attend the trial. On her floor, she stepped from the elevator carrying her little bag and noticing the halls were quieter than at the height of the Christmas season.

Once in the room, the same one she'd stayed in during her previous stay, Maddie turned on the small coffee pot, dressed in comfy sweats, and dug into the bag. Atop the wrapped grilled chicken sandwich was a small red container. She opened it to find two rosettes, the house specialty she had introduced to Chef Dexter. He had given her a fun surprise.

She nibbled at her sandwich and salvaged part of her workday by e-filing court pleadings before flopping onto the bed. In time, a pillow found its way beneath her head. Maddie was unaware she'd dozed off until her phone rang, startling her. She groped to find her cell.

Trevor Wagoner's name flashed brightly on the lit screen.

"Hi there," she answered, trying to sound awake. All she could think of was she didn't want Trevor knowing she'd fallen asleep.

"Maddie, every defendant is guilty on all counts."

She paused to collect her bearings, realizing she was in Starlight at the Edelweiss Lodge and Trevor was calling with the jury's verdict.

"Maddie, did I lose you?" he said in her ear. "Did you hear me say all are guilty?"

At the note of triumph in Trevor's voice, Maddie told him, "Congratulations," and fluffing up the pillow behind her head, said, "You and your team worked hard for this."

"Yes, we did. And Maddie, don't forget, you're a part of our team. It was a long-fought battle, and I am thrilled you and I are on the same side. You sound kind of distant. Are you traveling or still in the area?"

"I'm at the Edelweiss. I wanted to stay until I knew the verdict. I fly home in the morning."

"Great," Trevor replied with fervor. "We, by we I mean Eva Montanna and I, are about to leave for Starlight. Jordan is keeping the Cinnamon Stix open late to celebrate. We're checking into the lodge for the night. Will you join us?"

"Ah ..."

Maddie doubted she was up to celebrating with Trevor. He did say "us," so others would be there. This wasn't like a date where she'd be alone with him.

"Is that a yes?" he asked.

"Okay, count me in."

"Game's on. I'll phone when Eva and I get there."

Maddie ended the call, letting the phone fall out of her fingers. Was she doing the right thing? Perhaps the wiser course would be for her to skip the party and board the plane tomorrow, forgetting all about Trevor Wagoner.

Nothing doing. She needed to go and at least say good-bye to her friends in Starlight after all the time she'd spent here, and because of how much they meant to her.

Chapter 36

Maddie was refreshed and energized by Trevor's call. She got busy changing clothes for the third time today, thankful she'd brought a silk blouse to pair with her nice slacks. All dressed and waiting for Trevor's second phone call of the day, she organized her suitcase in the meantime.

She was folding in her sweats when his call came. Because of celebratory sounds in the background, his voice sounded garbled. All she could make out was "In the Stix," so she said she'd be down in a few, and ended the call. Fluffing her hair in the mirror one last time, she snatched her coat and proceeded directly to the café.

The hooting and raucous laughter that reached her as she stepped on the mezzanine was evidence the trial was over. Maddie strolled through the mob of staff and townsfolk, her eyes searching for Trevor. Jordan Star first caught up with her.

"Maddie, I watched your testimony and you sure did your part. When the jury foreman pronounced the guilty verdicts, my mind finally relaxed. We in Starlight are safe, thanks to you."

She slid her hands into the pockets of her slacks. "It means so much knowing my time here counts for something important."

"Oh, a couple of things I want to talk about with you." Jordan drew her away from an animated conversation. "I realize how much you've come to mean to us here in Starlight. The Maynard Star Foundation will be moved from the local firm to yours. I am asking you to serve as the foundation's lawyer and on the board. We need your able assistance as we keep on helping kids."

Maddie was overwhelmed. "Jordan, what a pleasant surprise. I'm excited to get started."

"You'll be spending more time in Starlight, which we can talk more about later. Mark your calendar for next Christmas."

Jordan turned to leave when Maddie touched his sleeve. "You said there were a couple things you wanted to say to me."

"Oh yeah." He tapped his temple with a finger. "Vanessa wants you to be sure to talk with Trevor. I do too."

"Why is everyone pushing me toward him?" Maddie snipped, irritation rising.

"Because we think you are perfect for each other, plus he made a nice donation to the foundation."

"He did?" Maddie took a step back. "Stewart bragged how he'd done that."

Jordan laughed heartily. "Yeah, Stewart donated twenty dollars, but Trevor now, he wrote a check for a thousand bucks. Go see him. He's right there at the table by the window."

Gretchen grabbed Maddie in a bear hug before she could formulate a reply.

"Ms. Stone, you were a wonderful witness. You sure zinged that defense attorney. She wasn't the same."

"I'm happy you can all get on with your lives," was all Maddie said in response to Gretchen's gushing praise.

"It's a brand-new beginning, all right," Gretchen chimed in her singsong voice. "Reservations at the lodge are pouring in for summer mountain biking. Every room is filled for most dates all summer long. You probably heard Vanessa and Cole are moving to town. I can't wait for their wedding."

"They haven't set a date, but it's exciting for them both," Maddie replied, her eyes scanning the restaurant for Trevor.

Gretchen smiled and turned to a lady at her side. "Maddie, meet my sister, Iris. She's the flight attendant I told you about."

Of course. Iris. The eyewitness to Trevor traveling with his California girlfriend.

Iris snatched Maddie's right hand with gusto. "I've heard so much about you and your time in Starlight, I didn't want to miss one second of seeing those wily investors get their just desserts for trying to steal our town."

A deep voice croaked in Maddie's ear, "Hello there, dearie."

Maddie whirled around facing Opal. Gretchen's gramma pulled Maddie up close.

"Sorry you didn't pick Jordan, but dearie, I'm thankful you fixed him up with Vanessa. They're awful cute together. She's learnin' to be a mountain girl."

Maddie felt a strong urge to blast away from this bad-news bunch. She couldn't be happier for Vanessa. Still, the time would come when Maddie would train a new paralegal and say farewell to her friend.

"Iris, it's nice to meet you and to see you all again." Maddie gave a nod to Gretchen and Opal. "Please excuse me. People are waiting for me, and I'm really hungry."

She spotted Eva's swaying blond hair one table away and rushed to join her. Eva stood, and after giving Maddie a warm hug, said, "I saw your testimony today."

Maddie clutched her coat. "It was the first time I've testified as a witness, and it gives me new appreciation for what my clients experience. You must be pleased with the verdicts."

"We are, Maddie. It was a long run." Eva reclaimed her seat and coffee mug.

When she did, Maddie could see Trevor sitting at the same table. He jumped to his feet, immediately pulling out a chair for her.

"Sit here by me. I saved your seat," he said in the kind of tone that meant, "If you don't, you'll really disappoint me."

Maddie was in no mood for Trevor ordering her around, yet the seating arrangements left her with no other option. His prior deceit made her wary, though she had forgiven him. After all, he had been terrific at his undercover role. What Maddie could not overlook was his reported involvement with a California lady, despite his repeated denials.

What was real when it came to Trevor Kirk? Or rather, Trevor Wagoner?

Maddie turned her attention upon Eva, and sporting a grin, she chimed, "How nice to see you again, Nora Star."

Both ladies chuckled at her reference to Eva's earlier undercover role as Jordan's unknown cousin. Maddie imagined Trevor was probably laughing right along with her, but she didn't glance his way.

Instead, she asked Eva, "Were you on the stand very long?"

"Yes." A deep crease erupted on Eva's brow. "Trevor and I took the entire day yesterday. After you, Clayton put on the accountant. The defense called one witness. Stewart's mother testified about his caring for her since he was a youngster. The jury didn't buy it."

"I would have liked hearing about your assignment as Nora. I had court in D.C. yesterday morning," Maddie explained. She liked the federal agent. Under different circumstances, she and Eva could be friends.

"You would have been sequestered anyway," Trevor observed.

His penetrating look lingered on Maddie. She dropped her eyes to the dinner menu. She wanted to order before her stomach started rumbling and making a fuss.

Gretchen and her sister Iris burst upon the scene, approaching the table with a flurry.

"Sorry to interrupt, Ms. Stone, but I have to," Gretchen said, urgency in her clipped tone. She jabbed a finger toward Eva. "My sister Iris thinks she knows this lady. We wanted you to know."

"No, we have never met." Eva looked askance at Iris.

Maddie narrowed her eyes, and after introducing Iris and Eva, she explained, "Eva is a special agent from D.C. and Trevor's colleague."

Gretchen and Iris began to giggle and trade knowing looks.

"What's so funny?" Eva demanded, her hand on her hip.

"Remember, Ms. Stone, when I told you the girls in town were avoiding Trevor because of my warning?" Gretchen asked, her eyes flickering and her hands gesturing wildly.

"Yes, and don't forget my warning." Iris pushed ahead of her sister. "It's because when I was flying out of Washington National, I saw Trevor sitting next to a pretty blonde on their way to Los Angeles."

Iris paused long enough to point at Eva and announce, "That lady was this lady."

Maddie choked back an involuntary gasp. She couldn't believe what she was hearing. She struggled to keep tears from flooding her eyes.

Had Gretchen and Iris made a terrible mistake maligning Trevor?

Trevor bolted to his feet, arms folded. "That's wrong. I never did such a thing."

"Wait," Eva countered. "It could be. Iris, was this about six months ago?"

Iris's nod sent her shoulder-length hair trembling. "I think so."

"Remember, Trevor?" Eva flashed a broad smile. "You and I, along with Griff Topping, flew to LA for a three-day seminar on asset forfeitures."

Trevor gazed at Maddie with a knowing look in his eyes. "Eva, you are clever. That was the day Griff was so late we asked them to hold the flight."

"Who is Griff?" Maddie had to know, fighting for composure.

"I guess I've never mentioned him." Trevor's magnetic smile beamed across his face. "He's the other FBI agent on our task force. He wants to meet you, Maddie."

"Yes, he does," Eva assured.

Her swift agreement confirmed for Maddie the three agents had been discussing her.

"So let me get this straight." She gazed up at Trevor. "You're saying Eva is the pretty blonde I've asked you about several times?"

Trevor lifted his shoulders in an apologetic shrug. "I never thought about it possibly being Eva. I figured you resisted me because I'd told someone in Starlight I was involved in a relationship. We do that, you know, when we work undercover."

Eva turned to Iris, asking, "Did you really say I was pretty?"

"I did. You are very pretty."

Eva rose to her feet and gave Iris a high five. "I wish my husband Scott was here to hear you. Of course, he would agree with you. He has to, because I carry a gun."

Maddie felt weird just sitting with everyone else towering above her. The moment she stood, she felt Trevor tugging on her elbow.

"I need to talk with you outside," he whispered.

"Now?"

"Humor me for once," he said, striding on his long legs right for the lobby exit.

MADDIE THREW ON HER COAT and on unsure legs, she followed Trevor outside into the cool air. A hush surrounded them as they walked down to the gazebo, lit with strings of white lights and making shimmering reflections on the lake. He held her hand for an extraordinary moment as they climbed the few steps.

"This is a beauty of a night," he said, keeping his voice low. "I didn't want to say good-bye in there."

"I needed a breath of air too."

Maddie gaped up at the evening sky, feeling breathless under the sparkling expanse. She breathed in deeply, her eyes fixing on the brightest star glittering above her.

"Is that the North Star?" she asked Trevor, her frosty breath rising.

His eyes shifted upwards. "Would you look at all those stars? I believe you have nailed Polaris, the end of the Little Dipper's Handle, or so my grandfather taught me. And there's the Big Dipper. See the bowl and the handle? It's called an asterism, and is part of the constellation Ursa Major."

"You amaze me. How do you know so much about the night sky? Are you really a geologist?" Maddie wondered aloud.

"I do love science. Want to hear my story?"

Maddie tried hiding a shiver running through her. A little cold mattered not if she could learn more about the real Trevor. She gravitated toward him and listened.

"We lived on a hill in San Diego, not far from the Mount Palomar Observatory. Grandpa used to take me there to see their magnificent two-hundred-inch telescope. He also bought me a telescope when I turned twelve. We'd inspect the stars at night and he instilled in me a desire to serve my country. Grandpa was an FBI agent too."

"Your grandfather sounds special. You two must have been close."

Night air brushing against her cheeks stirred Maddie's spirit. The glimmering water beyond the gazebo enhanced her sudden confusion. Trevor was opening up like never before. Was he about to say good-bye, let's get on with our lives?

She refused to ask him, because she wasn't ready for his answer.

In the depths of her heart, Maddie faced the truth head-on. The last possible obstacle to a relationship with Trevor had been a terrible misunderstanding. Eva, his happily married co-worker, was the suspicious female in his life, and she was no threat.

Why had Iris perpetuated such a rumor? Maddie had no answer, yet she realized how easy it was to believe one thing when the opposite was true. She had done the same thing to Trevor herself.

She felt his presence, saw his breath swirling in the air between them. He took a step toward her. Maddie's mind whirled. What did he want to talk with her about, here outside, away from the others? She blinked, clasping her hands together as they stood on the gazebo a breath apart.

"I couldn't watch you testify, and I would have liked to," she said, exhaling softly. "Once I left the stand, my energy evaporated. I went to my room and fell asleep."

"After my cases wrap up, my adrenaline vanishes. But not tonight. Maddie, listen, let's quit the diversion."

Trevor wasn't done. He had something else on his mind.

"No more talk about this case or the law. You know I'm not involved in a relationship with some unknown California woman. Eva is my colleague."

"I think Gretchen is truly sorry for spreading gossip about you," Maddie said softly.

"Forget Gretchen. This is about you and me." He studied her face under the lights. "I'm in love with you. You're alive in my mind every day, and at night too. I don't sleep much. I find it hard returning to D.C., knowing you're there without me being with you."

He stepped right beside her. "Can't you find it in your heart to give me a chance?"

The sky above was exploding with spotlight stars. Maddie no longer felt chilled. Her breath came in short bursts. What she felt for Trevor crashed through her heart as powerful as thunder in a storm. He enfolded his hands around hers.

Was this really happening?

Maddie leaned into his hands, staring in his eyes.

"Trevor, you remember the gorgeous afternoon we spent skiing on Star Mountain?"

He looked down at her with something like shining stars in his eyes. "One of the best days I've ever had."

"That's when I began admiring you." Maddie felt so alive sharing her true feelings. "I so wanted you to be free. I so hoped you weren't a scheming geologist. Then when I was so afraid you'd been arrested, I knew how deeply I cared for you."

"You did?"

"I wouldn't admit it to myself. You played your undercover role so well it's taken me all this time to discover the real you. The clincher came when I saw you select a gift star from the tree for a child whose parent is in jail."

"How could I not? It's Christmas. Jesus would do that. I wanted to be responsive to God's prodding."

In that moment, Maddie felt God's approval swelling in her heart.

"Trevor," she whispered his name. "Now I know ... you are my hero. You are brave and good. Now I know ... I love you."

"I love you," he whispered, drawing his face near to hers.

Maddie touched the side of his face. He leaned down, and she stood on tiptoe. She kissed him. As Trevor held her tightly in his arms, Maddie's heart contracted with pure joy. She had come north, north by Starlight, to work on a legal case and put her past in the rearview mirror. And here she was tonight, back in Starlight and finding her future.

Maddie watched as Trevor struggled awkwardly to take something out of his pocket. At last, he pulled out a small silver foil box and gave it to her. Maddie began to blush. Could Trevor be so presumptuous, so soon?

"What is this?"

"A birthday present. Tomorrow right?"

"How did you know?"

"I have my sources. Go ahead, it's safe to open."

Maddie lifted the lid, a smile lighting her face, her heart. She touched a lacy silver star resembling a snowflake. Lifting it from the box, she saw it was on a delicate silver chain, with a small silver tab dangling on the side.

"It's beautiful. I've never seen anything like it."

"Read the inscription." Trevor took out his cell phone and shone its flashlight to help her see.

Maddie squinted. "Wow! It says, 'Where dreams find happy endings.' Trevor, this is absolutely lovely."

"It's what Gretchen told me the night I checked in at the front desk."

Maddie beamed. "She told me the same thing."

Holding the necklace in one hand, Maddie reached out for Trevor. With his arms circling around her, he leaned down and she kissed him from the depth of her emotions.

Trevor gave her another short kiss. "Happy birthday, Maddie."

"It's not until tomorrow," she objected. "I can't believe how hard Vanessa has been pushing us together."

Trevor shook his head. "No, not Vanessa."

"Who else could it be? Only she knows my birth date."

Trevor smiled again. "Remember when you wondered how I knew where you lived?"

"Is it true?" Maddie stomped her foot. "You did check me out."

"No. I told you it was Eva. She even knew your birth date. She's been pushing me, as Vanessa's been pushing you."

Trevor enveloped Maddie into his strong arms again. "And I'm so glad they did."

In his tender embrace, Maddie's spirit soared skyward. Her future looked brighter than the stars winking in the night sky above. God was guiding her to new unchartered paths. Maddie knew if she could run these paths with courage and with Trevor running alongside her, what a joyous adventure her life would be.

ABOUT THE AUTHORS

ExFeds, Diane and David Munson write High Velocity Suspense novels seasoned with a splash of romance, which reviewers compare to John Grisham and Dee Henderson. The Munsons call their novels "factional fiction" because they write books based on their exciting and dangerous careers.

Diane Munson has been an attorney for more than thirty years. She has served as a Federal Prosecutor in Washington, D.C., and with the Reagan Administration appointed by Attorney General Edwin Meese as Deputy Administrator/Acting Administrator of the Office of Juvenile Justice and Delinquency Prevention. She worked with the Justice Department, U.S. Congress, and White House on policy and legal issues. More recently she has been in a general law practice.

David Munson served as a Special Agent with the Naval Investigative Service (now NCIS), and U.S. Drug Enforcement Administration over a twenty-seven year career. As an undercover agent, he infiltrated international drug smuggling organizations, and traveled with drug dealers. He met their suppliers in foreign countries, helped fly their drugs to the U.S., feigning surprise when shipments were seized by law enforcement. Later his true identity was revealed when he testified against group members in court. While assigned to DEA headquarters in Washington, D.C., David served two years as a Congressional Fellow with the Senate Permanent Subcommittee on Investigations.

As Diane and David research and write, they thank the Lord for the blessings of faith and family. They are collaborating on their next novel and traveling the country speaking/appearing at various venues.
Check out their blog and their website below:

www.DianeAndDavidMunson.com

THE MUNSONS' STAND-ALONE THRILLERS MAY BE READ IN ANY ORDER.

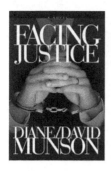

Facing Justice

Diane and David Munson draw on their true-life experiences in this suspense novel about Special Agent Eva Montanna, whose twin sister died at the Pentagon on 9/11. Eva dedicates her career to avenge her death while investigating Emile Jubayl, a member of Eva's church and CEO of Helpers International, who is accused of using his aid organization to funnel money to El Samoud, head of the Armed Revolutionary Cause, and successor to Al Qaeda. Family relationships are tested in this fast-paced, true-to-life legal thriller about the men and women who are racing to defuse the ticking time bomb of international terrorism.
ISBN-13: 978-0982535509
352 pages, trade paper
Christian Fiction / Mystery and Suspense
14.99

Confirming Justice

In Confirming Justice, the second thriller by ExFeds, Diane/David Munson (Ex-Federal Prosecutor/Ex-Federal undercover agent), all eyes are on Federal Judge Dwight Pendergast, secretly in line for nomination to the Supreme Court, who is presiding over a bribery case involving a cabinet secretary's son. When the key prosecution witness disappears, FBI agent Griff Topping risks his life to save the case while powerful enemies seek to entangle the judge in a web of corruption and deceit. Diane and David Munson masterfully create plot twists and fast-paced intrigue in this family friendly portrayal of what transpires behind the scenes at the center of power. The Munsons' thrillers are companion books, with characters reappearing in other novels, but each begins and ends a new story.
ISBN-13: 978-0982535516
352 pages, trade paper
Christian Fiction / Mystery and Suspense
14.99

The Camelot Conspiracy

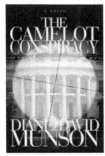

"The Camelot Conspiracy" rocks with a sinister plot even more menacing than the headlines. Former DC insiders Diane and David Munson feature a brash TV reporter, Kat Kowicki, who receives an ominous email that throws her into the high stakes conspiracy of John F. Kennedy's assassination. When Kat uncovers evidence Lee Harvey Oswald did not act alone, she turns for help to Federal Special Agents Eva Montanna and Griff Topping who uncover the chilling truth: A shadow government threatens to tear down the very foundation of the American justice system. The Munsons' thrillers are companion books, with characters reappearing in other novels, but each begins and ends a new story.
ISBN-13: 978-0982535523
352 pages, trade paper
Christian Fiction / Mystery and Suspense
14.99

Hero's Ransom

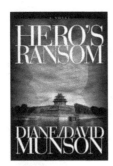

Could Chinese espionage disrupt your home town? CIA Agent Bo Rider (The Camelot Conspiracy) and Federal Agents Eva Montanna and Griff Topping (Facing Justice, Confirming Justice, The Camelot Conspiracy) return in Hero's Ransom, the Munsons' fourth family-friendly adventure. When archeologist Amber Worthing uncovers a two-thousand-year-old mummy and witnesses a secret rocket launch at a Chinese missile base, she is arrested in China for espionage. Her imprisonment sparks a custody battle between grandparents over her young son, Lucas. Caught between sinister world powers, Amber's faith is tested in ways she never dreamed possible. Danger escalates as Bo races to stop China's killer satellite from destroying America, and with Eva and Griff's help, to rescue Amber using a unexpected ransom.
ISBN-13: 978-0982535530
320 pages, trade paper
Christian Fiction / Mystery and Suspense
14.99

Redeeming Liberty

In this timely thriller by ExFeds Diane and David Munson (former Federal Prosecutor and Federal Agent), parole officer Dawn Ahern is shocked to witness her friend Liberty, the chosen bride of Wally (former "lost boy" from Sudan) being kidnapped by modern-day African slave traders. Dawn tackles overwhelming danger head-on in her quest to redeem Liberty. When she reaches out to FBI agent Griff Topping and CIA agent Bo Rider, her life is changed forever. Suspense soars as Bo launches a clandestine rescue effort for Liberty only to discover a deadly Iranian secret threatening the lives of millions of Americans and Israelis. Glimpse tomorrow's startling headlines in this captivating story of faith and freedom under fire. The Munsons' thrillers are companion books, with characters reappearing in other novels, but each begins and ends a new story.

ISBN-13: 978-0982535547
320 Pages, trade paper
Fiction / Mystery and Suspense
14.99

Joshua Covenant

CIA agent Bo Rider moves to Israel after years of clandestine spying around the world. He takes his family, wife Julia, and teens, Glenna and Gregg while serving in America's Embassy using his real name. While Glenna and Gregg face danger while exploring Israel's treasures, their father is shocked to uncover a menacing plot jeopardizing them all. A Bible scholar helps Bo in amazing ways. He discovers the truth about the Joshua Covenant and battles evil forces that challenge his true identity. Will Bo survive the greatest threat ever to his career, his family, and his life? Glimpse tomorrow's startling headlines as risks it all to stop an enemy spy.

ISBN-13: 978-0-983559009
336 Pages, trade paper
Christian Fiction / Mystery and Suspense
14.99

Night Flight

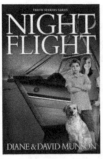

When CIA Agent Bo Rider adopts a retired law enforcement dog for his family, teenagers Glenna and Gregg are surprised to discover Blaze's special skills. They put the dog to work solving crimes, but a captured criminal seeks revenge forcing the kids to hide out at their grandparents' Florida home. In Skeleton Key powerful villains connive to stop the teens from discovering their criminal enterprise. As Glenna and Gregg face high stakes, they find courage to keep pursuing justice. In Night Flight, the Rider family learns the true meaning of loving your neighbor as yourself. This is the debut thriller for young adults and grand parents by these best-selling ExFeds who write factional fiction based on their careers.

ISBN-13: 978-0983559023
224 Pages, trade paper
Fiction / Mystery and Suspense
9.99

Stolen Legacy

Stolen Legacy, by Diane and David Munson, tells the daunting tale of Germany invading Holland, and the heroes who dare to resist by hiding Jews. Federal agent Eva Montanna stops protecting America long enough to visit her grandfather's farm and help write a memoir of his dangerous time under Nazi control. Eva is shocked to uncover a plot to harm Grandpa Marty. Memories are tested as secrets from Marty's time in the Dutch resistance and later service in the Monuments Men of the U.S. Army fuel this betrayal. The Munsons' eighth thriller unveils priceless relics and a stolen legacy, forever changing Eva's life and her faith.

ISBN-13: 978-0983559047
336 pages, trade paper
Christian Fiction / Mystery and Suspense
14.99

Embers of Courage

ICE Special Agent Eva Montanna discovers the world is ablaze with danger when militants capture her task force teammate, NCIS Special Agent Raj Pentu, during a CIA operation in Egypt. She risks her life to defeat tyrants oppressing Christians, and is plunged into a daring rescue mission. Eva's faith is tested like never before as mysterious ashes, her ancient family Bible, and fifteenth century religious persecution collide with modern-day courage under fire. This riveting novel, the ninth by ExFeds Diane and David Munson, is their third linking true historical events with their signature High Velocity Suspense.

ISBN-13: 978-0983559061
336 pages, trade paper
Christian Fiction / Mystery and Suspense
14.99

The Looming Storm

Tomorrow's headlines leap from the pages of The Looming Storm when Federal Agent Eva Montanna uncovers a menacing threat to harm Eva and her family. When daughter Kaley travels to Eastern Europe on a class trip, Eva's Christian faith is challenged, and their lives are altered in the blink of an eye. Tensions skyrocket as Eva and Griff Topping, her FBI partner, use every trick to infiltrate a band of Florida smugglers. The agents are shocked when their undercover charade reveals the criminals have sinister plans for America. Secrets are shredded in the Munson's tenth 'stand alone' thriller, as this spousal duo rips the veil from a labyrinth of covert criminal enterprises.

ISBN-13: 978-0-9835590-8-5
305 pages, trade paper
Christian Fiction/Mystery and Suspense
15.99

CPSIA information can be obtained
at www.ICGtesting.com
Printed in the USA
LVHW090203170119
604250LV00001B/6/P